Anne Marie McLaren

BELGRAVE SQUARE

SQUARE
A Novel of Society

Rachel Summerson

ST. MARTIN'S PRESS • NEW YORK

Library of Congress Cataloging in Publication Data

Summerson, Rachel.
  Belgrave Square.

  I. Title.
PR6069.U39B4   1981   823'.914   81-14516
ISBN 0-312-07427-1   AACR2

To Judith and Ruth
with love

Chapter One

'MONKEYS,' cried Mrs Peat, 'are you daring to suggest that we are *all* descended from monkeys?'

Flora opened her mouth to speak and then shut it again.

'I do not know where you found Mr Darwin's shocking book', continued Mrs Peat, drumming her fingers angrily on the marble-topped dressing table, 'but I was quite mortified to hear you actually arguing with Canon Grieve about it at dinner last night. You may believe *you* are descended from a monkey, Flora, and looking at your behaviour sometimes it would not surprise me, but the Canon is descended from one of the oldest families in the country! How could you insult him so! I declare I could have sunk through the floor.'

Flora shrugged. 'It was obvious he had not even read Mr Darwin's book.'

'That is beside the point!' snapped Mrs Peat. '*You* should know nothing about it. Ladies are not supposed to be clever. Just look at what happened to Helena Wooler and take warning, Flora! She thought that she would like to be emancipated and clever! She thought she knew better than her mother! Her young man called one day and found her reading *Jane Eyre* and do you know what? He was *so shocked* that he went straight home and *never popped the question*! You are twenty-seven, Flora, and how I am ever to marry you off, I do not know!'

Flora flushed painfully. She did not know either. All she knew was that whatever she did was wrong.

An impartial observer might have wondered what Flora had done to deserve such hostility. She was tall, but not too tall, and her figure was pleasing. She had a reasonable share of the feminine attributes considered alluring, that is to say, her skin was pale

7

and remained so even during the summer, her ankles were neatly turned and she had a trim waist. Her mouth was too wide and her nose rather too aquiline for beauty, but her face, when animated, had a great deal of charm, her best features being very large grey eyes and a plentiful crop of rich, brown hair.

Flora just did not make the best of herself, Mrs Peat would have said. She had a dowry of at least twenty thousand pounds, together with a sizeable share in Peat-Milford, her father's engineering business and a mother who made every sacrifice to see that her daughters were launched into the highest possible circles, but Flora was too selfish to appreciate how fortunate she was.

Mrs Peat, who herself had been a beauty in her youth, believed firmly in innocence and ignorance being the best attitudes for unmarried ladies. There were heroic worlds outside, of exploration and scientific enquiry, religious argument and political debate, but only faint echoes of these entered the drawing-room of their house in Belgrave Square: those heavy lace curtains and thick velvet drapes seemed to protect the ladies of the house from more than the injurious effects of sunlight.

Flora herself felt that there was something desperately wrong with her life, but she could not quite see what it was. She lived in an elegant house and she had as much pin money as she could spend. There were squalid, cholera-infested alleys only a mile or so away in Westminster and she knew she ought to be thankful that she had not been born into one of those hopelessly poverty-ridden families. She might have been, for her father had been brought up in just such a hovel in the north and it was only his industry that now enabled them all to be living in such solid and wealthy surroundings.

She must count her blessings. She was fortunate in being one of six healthy children. Ernest at thirty was the eldest, followed by Flora herself. Her next sister, Adeline, was her very closest friend, then came the pretty but malicious Blanche, and Tom, now away at Marlborough College. Last of all came Daisy, thirteen years old and the baby of the family: Flora loved her dearly.

But, just as Flora had given up all hope of life being different in any way, the Fates, with their usual unpredictability, decided

8

otherwise. During the summer of 1863 they started a chain of events with far-reaching consequences for Flora, most of which would have alarmed her considerably if she had had the remotest idea of what was in store for her.

It began, ordinarily enough, at the Royal Academy Summer Exhibition, when Flora first took seriously her mother's assertion that Dr Charles Woodcock, the son of their family physician, would soon propose to her sister Adeline. Mrs Peat took Flora, Adeline and Blanche to the Summer Exhibition more in order to be seen than to do any viewing themselves. This year she had an added reason, Dr Charles Woodcock would be there, and as he had a wealthy practice he would be a very suitable *parti* for her serious second daughter, Adeline.

'The most fortunate thing,' Mrs Peat was saying as she and Flora walked round the Sculpture Room. 'I do believe Adeline is with Charles.'

'Yes, I think they meant to look at some paintings in the North Room,' replied Flora, somewhat irritated by the idea that Charles with his pudgy, white hands, would be encouraged in his advances by the fastidious Adeline. She stopped in front of a bronze statue entitled 'Ino and Bacchus' and studied it carefully.

'Charles has made this little opportunity to be alone with her,' said Mrs Peat complacently. 'He wishes to be better acquainted.'

'Why is he always giving Blanche little squeezes in the garden, then?' asked Flora.

'You are talking like that common grandmother of yours again, Flora. I wish your father would settle her and that vulgar maid of hers up north somewhere, where she belongs, then perhaps I would not have to hear such coarseness from you. I never liked the idea of her living with us.'

'That is not fair,' said Flora, stung. 'Granny has never said a word to me about Blanche and Charles. I saw it myself. And if Charles is so nuts on Adeline, why does he not pop the question?'

'Charles will speak to Papa first, naturally. Mrs Woodcock has told me, in confidence, to expect a declaration very soon.'

It must be true then! Flora's first feeling was one of disgust: how could Adeline allow such a plump, lecherously inclined doctor near her? But she would not of course. The very idea was laughable. Adeline's disposition was reserved to the point of

9

being cold, and she had high ideals of service to God, and Flora knew that she would make no marriage from worldly motives.

She looked thoughtfully at the statue of Bacchus in front of her. (Bacchus at least had strong hands, unlike Charles' fleshy white ones.) He, too, was over-plump, with an unattractively protuberant stomach. Would Charles in the altogether look so puffy and self-satisfied?

'Flora!' said Mrs Peat in an angry whisper. 'I am ashamed of you! Stop looking at that . . . that . . . No lady even looks at such a statue! And for Heaven's sake do up the buttons on your gloves.'

At that very moment Adeline and Dr Charles Woodcock were standing in the North Room talking earnestly in a way that would have pleased Mrs Peat very much if she could have seen it.

Adeline Peat was now twenty-five. She was a thinner, more refined version of her sister, with the same rather aquiline nose, but her hair was a softer brown and her eyes a paler grey. Adeline always dressed with neatness and sobriety in dull colours, and today she was wearing a dove-grey silk afternoon dress with a high neck, covered by a slate-grey patelot with gimp cord trimming.

Adeline liked to feel that she had more genuine spirituality than most people. She would have preferred to live a quiet, useful life devoted to good works and service to God. She had her bible classes and her sewing circle, true, but Mrs Peat disapproved of these and insisted that Adeline give them up during the season, and Adeline, out of duty to her parents, obeyed. But she knew that one day God would call her to His service, and she held herself in readiness to answer that Call.

'This is the picture that I mentioned, Dr Woodcock,' she said, touching his sleeve lightly with one gloved hand and then withdrawing it quickly. She indicated a painting entitled 'The first introduction of Christianity among the Welsh'. 'The bishop spoke of it during his sermon last Sunday.'

'Jolly *good* picture,' said Charles solemnly, emphasizing every word because he could not think what else to say. He had wanted another peek at the statue of 'Leda' in the Sculpture Room, but felt obliged to steer Adeline swiftly past it.

'Yes, that is right,' said Adeline, her pale eyes shining with enthusiasm. 'It is truly *good*, do you not think? The bishop said it had the true spirit of piety.'

'Exactly so,' said Charles. He was rather pleased that Adeline liked the picture so much. It was what a lady should feel. It showed that he was right in picking Adeline rather than Blanche as his wife. A doctor needed a wife to give him standing and respectability. He would go and see Mr Peat tomorrow and ask for her hand and settle the whole thing. 'Do you know, Miss Adeline,' he said suddenly, 'they should have prints made of that picture. Properly distributed it would do more good among the poor than a dozen tracts.' Most of the poor buggers could not read anyway.

Here is a man of truly elevated moral tone, thought Adeline, with a rush of emotion. Could it be that God's path for her lay with Dr Woodcock? Oh, if only it might be so!

But Charles had had enough for one day of living on such a high moral plane and he was anxious to see some of the sporting pictures. So as soon as politeness admitted, he left Adeline talking to his mother and disappeared, promising to see them later.

Adeline returned to the Sculpture Room.

Alone, thought Mrs Peat crossly. Why could the girl not be just a little more conciliatory? It would take only a few smiles and a show of interest to get Charles to the point. She supposed she must be grateful that Adeline consented to talk to Charles at all, most men were dismissed by her as being too gross and worldly. Still, at least it prevented her from sewing those hideous petticoats for her Church Mission work or whatever it was. Why would he not make haste and take Adeline off her hands so that she might concentrate on her lovely Blanche? Just like a man! So selfish!

'Did you see anything you liked, in there?' asked Flora, as Adeline came up.

Adeline began telling her about the picture and what Charles had said. Flora looked at her with a growing unease. Charles Woodcock to talk of moral piety? Surely not! Why he was notorious at parties for always trying to entice some pretty, plump girl into a corner.

'What have you been looking at, Flora?' Adeline asked at last.

'Oh, I have been admiring "Ino and Bacchus",' said Flora.

Adeline looked disapprovingly at the statue in front of her. What a pity! The members of the Hanging Committee were all men of the highest integrity, she knew. But she did wish that they would choose more Christian subjects. It was not that there was anything wrong with Ino, who was decently if scantily draped (Adeline herself always dressed, as far as possible, under cover of her night-dress, even when alone), it was only that Ino would have looked so much *nicer* in flowing, Grecian draperies.

She ignored Bacchus.

At the other end of the Sculpture Room Blanche was standing talking to her sister-in-law, Geraldina.

Geraldina Peat was the only child of Gerald Milford, Mr Peat's business partner. She was rich, beautiful and capricious to a degree. As a child she had twisted Gerald round her little finger and she now did the same with a doting husband. Geraldina had a warm, creamy skin, a perfectly shaped rather full mouth and large dark eyes. Her hair was so black as to be almost blue and she wore it in a heavy chignon with thick, lustrous curls hanging down.

Some five years ago she had married Ernest Peat, Flora's elder brother, a match encouraged by both the Peat parents and Gerald Milford, none of whom liked the idea of Geraldina's fortune going to a stranger. From a financial point of view the match between Ernest and Geraldina had been an excellent one, but Mrs Peat, herself a vicar's daughter with some pretensions to gentility, regretted that Geraldina brought no 'tone' to the family. The Milfords had no connections worth mentioning. Besides, it was rumoured that Geraldina was 'fast'.

The rumour was true: for the last six months Geraldina had been engaged in an affair with her cousin, Captain Francis Grant. And why should she not, Geraldina asked herself. She had given boring, stodgy Ernest two sons, why should she not please herself?

Geraldina had come to the Summer Exhibition in the hopes of meeting Captain Grant. The fact that most of their meetings must be conducted in public only gave an added spice to the intrigue. She liked arranging an assignation with Frank practically under the noses of the stiffest of the Society matrons. To exchange a quick kiss behind a door when nobody was looking, with all the alarms of discovery, gave her great pleasure.

Geraldina and Blanche were standing in a fairly conspicuous position in the Sculpture Room, both of them for very similar reasons, although Geraldina had the excuse of looking out for Ernest which allowed her gaze to wander frequently over the crowds.

Blanche Peat at seventeen had the blue and golden looks of her mother. She had a straight little nose, a perfect rosebud mouth and her honey-coloured hair fell in artless ringlets down her back. She was consciously moving slightly as she stood talking to Geraldina, so that her blue dress belled to and fro seductively, revealing glimpses of red and white striped stockings. Blanche was not properly out yet, but her mother could not bear to leave her one presentable daughter in the schoolroom while her unsatisfactory elder sisters plodded through season after season without the smallest hope of success. Blanche had already had two years of beaux and parties and was beginning to long for headier excitements.

Geraldina tapped her foot impatiently. 'How long will Ernest be? Does he think I can wait all day?'

'I think he went to look at some hunting pictures with Charles,' replied Blanche. She too was looking around the room, but more discreetly, and under lowered lashes.

'If he likes to indulge in the chase, he should send Charles off after Adeline. God knows he is taking long enough about it.'

'Charles can try a bit of softy when he wishes to.'

'I know. He is always staring at me with those little piggy eyes of his, and giving me sly little squeezes.'

'I wonder if he is truly interested in Adeline,' began Blanche in a lowered voice. She had something to confide to Geraldina about Charles' behaviour. She glanced around to see if anybody was within earshot and saw Flora coming towards them. Why the devil could Flora not put her shawl on straight and tuck back her hair tidily under her snood, thought Blanche irritably. She felt embarrassed by everybody knowing that such a dowdy creature was her sister.

Blanche turned round swiftly to the statue behind her and began studying the inscription with spurious interest.

13

'Reduced model from a colossal bronze statue – The Queen with the Attributes of Peace,' it said on the plinth.

'The original is owned by the Prince of Wales,' said Geraldina, consulting her catalogue. 'I suppose so that his Mama may keep an eye on him.'

Blanche giggled.

'Awful, isn't it?' said Flora eagerly, coming up to them. She was trying ineffectually to tuck a stray piece of hair back under her hat. 'There is an even larger one of the Prince Consort over there. Have you seen it?'

Blanche watched Flora's efforts, then turned to Geraldina and shrugged.

'How are the children, Geraldina?' asked Flora, dimly aware that she was not wanted.

Why cannot she *go*, thought Blanche savagely. She felt degraded by Flora's awkwardness. At that moment Alice Banks came across the room, escorted by a young man: he was Hugh Dunster and she was engaged to him. 'Unofficially as yet,' said Alice, smiling shyly, 'but we hope to persuade my trustees before very long.'

The Peat ladies congratulated Hugh Dunster. Blanche now recognized him as the so-called wastrel younger son of one of her mother's acquaintances. She gave him a long, speculative look from under her lashes. How the devil had such a dull mouse as Alice Banks managed to hook such an Adonis? Hugh was quite strikingly good-looking, with the sort of careless charm Blanche found most attractive.

Hugh returned her look with interest. He did not believe in the gentlemanly approach, so he looked Blanche up and down quite openly.

'Do you think the pictures are up to standard this year, Mr Dunster?' enquired Blanche, raising her eyebrows at him.

'I do not care for them,' replied Hugh, 'that is why we were just leaving. Alice wished to see the bronze medallions and we have seen them, so now we are off.'

Blanche found his brusque rudeness very fascinating. Here was a man who knew his own mind, she thought. She glanced at Alice who was looking up at Hugh worshipfully. Alice's soft, shy look irritated her.

'I fear I do not care for the medallions,' she said. 'I find them a little dull myself.' Her glance flickered almost imperceptibly over Alice. 'I prefer a painting like the "Stag at Bay". There is something noble and tragic about such a magnificent animal being done to death when he should be wild and free!'

Hugh looked at her through suddenly narrowed eyes.

'And would you like to rescue the poor stag, Miss Blanche?'

'Such a magnificent animal should be able to rescue himself,' replied Blanche.

Alice looked from one to the other. Hugh patted her hand. 'Perhaps the stag is a willing victim, Miss Blanche,' he said teasingly. 'Come, Alice, we must go.' He bowed to the ladies and left with Alice on his arm. Alice looked back a little uncertainly and Flora smiled reassuringly at her.

'Well really, Blanche,' said Geraldina amused, 'you do not believe in the ladylike approach, do you?'

'Oh, I mean no harm,' said Blanche lightly, but her eyes followed Hugh to the door.

Fortunately Geraldina's attention was diverted by Ernest coming up, profuse with apologies and messages for Flora and Blanche to rejoin their mother.

'I do not expect to be kept waiting,' snapped Geraldina.

'Your cousin came up,' said Ernest placatingly. 'Sends his apologies. Sorry to miss you. Sends his love. He has to be back in the barracks, so he said.'

Geraldina glanced at Ernest suspiciously, then she shrugged. 'Frank? Oh, I daresay I shall see him another time.'

How like Frank to deliver a message to his mistress via her husband! With a sudden surge of spirits she took the arm Ernest offered her and allowed him to lead her from the gallery.

Charles Woodcock brought a message from his mother inviting Mrs Peat and her daughters home for tea after viewing the Exhibition. Mrs Peat accepted for herself, Adeline and Blanche. Flora elected to go home to Belgrave Square and Mrs Peat did not insist. Nobody could think poor Flora a satisfactory go-between: she was far more likely to discourage Charles by arguing with him and gentlemen did so dislike a blue-stocking woman.

Flora went home and had a cosy tea with Daisy up in the den.

Daisy Peat was a boisterous thirteen-year-old, with thick black hair that would never settle into proper ringlets. She was sturdily built and had a bounce and cheerfulness which Flora loved. No amount of strictures on ladylike behaviour had any effect on her liveliness. Recently Mrs Peat's bewailings of Daisy's tom-boyish behaviour had changed dramatically to praise for her good sense, for Daisy had become very good friends with Grace Lennox, a shy little girl at Miss Speedwell's Academy, but more important, a grand-daughter of the formidable Lady Kingsley.

'I say, Flora,' whispered Daisy conspiratorially, when they had both settled down to their seed biscuits and plum cake, 'did you hear that I am to have lessons with Grace Lennox at her house next term? I am leaving Miss Speedwell's horrid old Academy.'

'Are you sure?' asked Flora sceptically. It was extremely unlikely that Lady Kingsley had any intention of inviting the daughter of a *parvenu* family to share a governess with her grand-daughter.

'But I am,' insisted Daisy. 'Mama spoke to Lady Kingsley at the end of last term and Lady Kingsley said that she would look into it. Grace is my best friend, you know!'

'She was only being polite,' said Flora. 'Do not pin too many hopes upon it, Daisy. They move in quite different circles, you know.'

'But it would only mean my sharing lessons with Grace in her schoolroom at home. I cannot see what is so wrong with that?'

'Lady Kingsley has two grandsons, both extremely eligible and neither of them married. Little girls must be chaperoned to their lessons, possibly by their beautiful sisters.'

Daisy's eyes grew wide. 'Do you mean that Lady Kingsley is worried that they might wish to marry Blanche?' She looked astounded at these revelations of adult duplicity.

'Mama wishes a good marriage for Blanche. And why not? Blanche is very pretty. Mama will try and procure an introduction for Blanche through you. Lady Kingsley, on the other hand, being a prudent grandmama, will take avoiding action.'

'And what will happen, Flora?' Daisy regarded Flora as a fount of wisdom in worldly affairs.

'*If* Lady Kingsley agrees to your sharing lessons with Grace, then Mama will manage an introduction, you shall see.'

'You aren't a bit stuffy, Flora,' said Daisy suddenly. 'You tell me grown-up things. Nobody else would have told me all that.'

'Granny pointed it out,' said Flora smiling. 'But I should not have told you. Mama would think it most unladylike, I know.'

'No, Flora,' said Daisy sagely. 'It is only unladylike for you to *notice* it. It is perfectly all right for Mama to plot it.'

'But just as you do, I prefer to have these things clear in my mind,' replied Flora.

'Mama is always telling me not to spend too much time with Granny. She says she does not wish me to talk as she does. But that is not right, is it, Flora?'

'You must not be ashamed of Granny, Daisy. If it were not for her sacrifices none of us would be here today. She had to work in a mill for fourteen hours a day, and somehow she managed to save a little money so that Papa should have some schooling and a start in life. It was not an easy struggle, Daisy, and she is right to be proud of what she did. She does not wish to ape the fine lady. Why should she not talk in a North Country accent still?'

'I do hate to hear Mama laughing about her,' said Daisy soberly.

'I hate it too.'

The next morning Adeline sat quietly in the bedroom she shared with Flora. The maids had made the beds, cleaned the grate and removed Adeline's neat pile of dirty linen and Flora's untidy one. Adeline sat on the day-bed by the window. Next to her was her Missionary sewing basket and a small rosewood table with a variety of knick-knacks on it, pin cushions, a glove box covered with shells and a Berlin wool bookmark, all bought from one or other of the Church bazaars that Adeline patronized.

She wanted to think over the conversation she had had with Charles the previous day. Walking with Charles through the galleries she felt she knew something of what it would be like to walk with him through Life: how tactfully he guided her past the 'Leda' in the Sculpture Room, with a little cough of apology to indicate that he too found such exhibits of dubious taste. Flora said that he was stiff and pompous, but surely these were faults permissible in one whose profession was next in godliness to Holy Orders?

How understanding he was! He listened to her ideas on helping the Poor with such sympathy. Adeline explained her wish to do Visiting, but her mama forbade it because of the danger of cholera. She had to give way, but Charles understood how she felt.

'I think it is so important that the lower orders should know something of what true refinement is,' explained Adeline. 'I always feel that the girls who come into service are so fortunate. They at least have the opportunity to be part of a Christian family.'

'Quite, quite,' said Charles, his mind reverting to a pert little housemaid. Dismissed now, of course; she became somewhat uppish and had to go. 'I am sure you set a shining example, Miss Adeline. But the lower orders are quite degenerate. Even weekly family prayers are quite unknown in many poorer homes.'

'Do you do much of your work among the poor, Dr Woodcock?' Adeline tried to speak calmly, for his compliment embarrassed her.

'No, it is quite useless. They will not spend money on medicine. Besides, you know, the conditions they live in are so unsanitary, that sometimes I am concerned for my own health.'

'But you do at least try!' cried Adeline. 'The only thing that I can do is to sew for my Missionary basket.'

'Miss Adeline,' said Charles gravely, 'nobody who cares for you would wish you to risk your health in visiting the poor. I have seen some families with the children running around barefoot and wearing nothing but dirty shifts, and the women will even go hatless out of doors! A lady runs a grave risk of being severely shocked!'

Adeline felt her heart swell with emotion as she re-lived this conversation. Charles was not like the other young men; he had true religious feeling. He respected, nay admired, her special moral sensitivity. She was quite sure he was above flirting, he would never squeeze her hand in the detestable way that some men did, or attempt to steal kisses behind convenient pots of ferns. If Charles thought her worthy to be his wife, how gladly she would submit to him!

The bedroom door opened and Flora came in.

'What are you doing here, Adeline? I thought you were gone with Mama to pay a call on Isabel?'

Adeline shook her head. Isabel Rivers was Charles' sister. Adeline was fond of Isabel, but Charles might see a visit as unmaidenly forwardness. Charles must have no cause to think her lacking in delicacy.

'Really, Adeline! You cannot stop seeing Isabel because Charles is about to pop the question.'

'Flora!' cried Adeline, her mouth tightening. 'I admire and respect Dr Woodcock. Any woman must. But he has not yet spoken to Papa, so I cannot admit to any understanding between us. But I do feel he is a most noble man. He has been very sympathetic about my visiting and saying I should lead a fuller life. I feel he has Principle.'

'Do you love him?' asked Flora suddenly.

'It is my duty to marry,' Adeline answered evasively.

She turned away and, opening her work basket, took out a coarse cambric petticoat and began picking off the lace with a pair of sharp sewing scissors. Somebody in her sewing circle had put it on. So inappropriate. She would have to take it all off and put in a plain tuck instead.

Flora felt a wave of anger against her sister, but was instantly ashamed of it. She turned away to the window and parted the lace curtains to look down into the square. The houses had a solid grandeur about them, with their classical façades and pediments and elegant columns. They looked blind, too. In spite of the warm June sun, few of the windows were open and the light reflected back from the dull glass and lace or net curtains gave the houses a myopic look. There were a few nursemaids with their charges and their baby carriages in the square, which looked pleasantly cool with its grass and trees and fountain, but otherwise Belgrave Square was silent.

'There is some talk of Daisy taking lessons with Grace Lennox,' said Flora to change the subject. 'Some of the girls from the Academy had scarlatina and Lady Kingsley is removing Grace. But I do not know what will become of the idea.'

'It would be very good for Daisy.'

'I think,' said Flora mischievously, 'that Mama is thinking more of Blanche's prospects than of Daisy's education. Lady Kingsley has two very eligible grandsons, you know.'

'Do not blame Mama. It is the duty of daughters to get married.

I know that I have been a disappointment to her.'

'Oh, I do not blame her. Only I cannot like the idea of Daisy's being used to provide introductions for Blanche. Nor do I like the idea of Blanche flashing her charms at the Kingsleys. However, she will not go very far. Sir George always seems to be abroad and Algy Kingsley has a dolly-mop he keeps in Chelsea.'

'Flora!' Adeline felt her face grow hot with shame. 'How can you? Ladies never speak of such things! Or even think of them! We know nothing about such low creatures.'

'Of course we know. Do you not remember riding with Ernest in Rotten Row, and seeing that anonyma? The one who waggled her fingers at him, with that superb riding habit on and I asked him who she was?'

'He was very wrong,' cried Adeline passionately, 'both in knowing such a disgusting creature and in acknowledging her existence in front of his sisters.'

'I cannot agree. You know how often I say the wrong things. If Ernest had not told us about the women in Rotten Row and the houses in Chelsea and St John's Wood, I am sure I should have said something dreadful.'

'I hope Ernest has more refinement of mind now,' replied Adeline, pursing her lips. Men can be so coarse, she began thinking, but swiftly pushed it away.

There was a knock at the bedroom door.

'Come in,' called Adeline, sighing and folding away her sewing. It was Sarah, old Mrs Peat's maid and long-time companion. She peered round the door at Flora, her none-too-clean cap askew on her tight grey curls.

'She wants to see you.' Sarah never used any other way of speaking of Mrs Peat.

'You mean Mrs Peat,' corrected Adeline gently.

'She wants to see Miss Flora,' repeated Sarah. She knew she was annoying Adeline, but she didn't care much for this southern miss. That Adeline was due for a mucky fall one of these fine days.

'Tell her I am just coming, Sarah,' said Flora. She jumped up and whispered to Adeline, 'Granny may have some news about Charles. You know Papa always goes to see her before going to the office.'

Old Mrs Peat had her own two rooms on the first floor. She had a sitting-room and a bedroom, connected by a double door, and both rooms were full of the furniture, pictures and bric-à-brac she had brought with her from Darlington when her son first brought her south. Flora always felt it was like stepping into an entirely different world. Gone were the heavily upholstered arm-chairs with their rich brocades and hard little buttons, the shiny veneer of the rosewood and mahogany, the lush oil paintings of coy maidens or some dramatic scene from history. In their place was an old oak gate-legged table that Mrs Peat had had since she was first married; the chairs were oak too, with wooden or rush seats, made more comfortable with a variety of patchwork cushions. On the floor was a worn rag carpet, patched and re-patched with loving care. On the walls were framed prints, a certificate saying that William Peat had won the Sunday School Bible prize for reading, an early sampler of Flora's with 'The Lord is my Shepherd' sewn in very uneven letters at the bottom and various drawings, embroideries and photographs to remind her of her children—most, alas, now dead—and grandchildren.

Old Mrs Peat sat in a rocking-chair by the window. She wore a plain black dress with gigot sleeves, in a style that had been fashionable thirty years before, and a black silk apron. Around her shoulders was a plaid shawl, she had mittens on her hands and her feet were resting on a small beaded footstool. Her skin was almost paper white and lined and re-lined, especially across the forehead, but her grey eyes, so like Flora's, were still clear and bright.

Mrs Peat put down her knitting as Flora opened the door. 'Come in, lass, don't stand there hovering. I have some news for you.'

Flora embraced her gratefully, sniffing the familiar smell of lavender water and beeswax polish. She glanced, as she always did, at the lace-making bobbins and wooden shuttles on their shelf in the whatnot, and satisfied that nothing was changed, sat down opposite her grandmother.

'Charles?' she asked.

'He's going to see your Pa at the office this morning. A very proper letter Bill tells me, full of "the inestimable honour" and "unalterable feelings" from what I could make out. When I was a lass a man did his courting himself, he didn't write a business letter to the girl's father.'

'I do not think that Adeline would care for that,' said Flora quickly.

'No, I cannot see our Adeline allowing any kiss and cuddle. Mind you, I'd soon send any young man packing who hadn't the gumption to ask me first, whatever the proper thing is.'

'It is not very, well, loverlike, is it?' Flora touched the rag rug gently with her toe.

'Charles can do his bit of petting when he's a mind to. I've seen him down in the garden carrying on with Blanche. But I suppose Miss is too easy for him, the bold piece. A wife like Adeline will be respectable enough to bring him in some lady patients.'

Flora looked up uneasily.

'Adeline does not love him. She told me.' Flora looked across at her granny's worn, lined face, her own anxious and worried.

'You need to be generous to love.'

'You do not like her, do you?' said Flora sadly.

'I get very put out with all her airs and graces. Doesn't she shit like the rest of us?'

'Granny!'

'All this time she wastes sewing suitable garments for the deserving poor. She never asks them what they would like, I notice. It's always what *she* knows to be best for them. Oh yes, Miss Adeline always knows better than some poor woman struggling with a drunken husband and half a dozen children to make ends meet. Well, I was in that sort of position when my Henry died and I resented anybody's patronage, especially from some stuck-up miss who doesn't know what it's like having children crying for hunger and having nowt to give them. Deserving poor indeed! Is Adeline one of the deserving rich, I say?'

'But that is not Adeline's fault,' protested Flora, 'and she gives most of her pin money away.'

'Aye, to the Church's Missionary Society for Africa and the East.'

'But she does try,' pleaded Flora. 'I know she is priggish, but she is trying to do something with her life. Heaven knows, I have felt the awful dreary waste of mine. You must admit that she does have some opposition to overcome. Mama does not approve of all these bazaars in aid of Miss Nightingale's Nurses, you know. Adeline allows nothing to stand in the way of her conscience.'

'She certainly has her conscience buttoned up nicely,' said Mrs Peat tartly. 'I expect she has told herself that Charles is working for the Glory of God, or some such rubbish, when anybody with half an eye can see he's out for a nice, juicy practice. She's very like your mother in some ways, you know. Susan will never see anything she doesn't want to see.'

Flora rose and walked to the window and looked out. It overlooked the garden with its smooth lawn and cone beds and blue borders. It looked very neat and formal from where Flora was standing. The flower beds were kept in place by trim little box hedges and the cone beds went in careful gradations from the pansies and double daisies around the edge to the tall lupins and hollyhocks in the centre. Had Adeline so confined and pruned herself that she could no longer see things for what they were? As if she, too, was kept in place by neatly cut box hedges. How could that be so? Flora had always admired Adeline's ability to think out her own moral position, to stand up for what she believed to be right, even in the teeth of Mama's opposition.

But perhaps Adeline was right and there were qualities in Charles that she, Flora, had missed: his coming the spoon with Blanche was not very serious, after all. She must be careful not to misjudge him.

'Let me give you some advice, buttercup. Let Adeline marry Charles. Don't try to interfere. Adeline is doing the best she can for herself.'

'How can I sit and watch Adeline make a dreadful mistake and do nothing to prevent her? She will have Charles for the rest of her life!'

'Life has been very kind to Adeline for twenty-five years,' said Mrs Peat tartly. 'She has had more than her fair share.'

Dr Charles Woodcock, the object of the sisters' confidences and of Mrs Peat's matrimonial machinations, was sitting over the port late that evening in his brother-in-law's house. Charles was a portly young man, aged about thirty. He had very boyish features, with a fresh-faced complexion and pink, healthy cheeks, small blue eyes and a loud cheerful laugh. He had short, wavy, fair hair, parted in the middle and a moustache. In his youth he had been something of a dandy, but he now felt this inappropriate to his standing as a doctor. He usually wore a double-breasted frock coat of black superfine and peg-top tweed trousers, whose wide fitting at the waist and thigh admirably concealed a slight paunch. Occasionally, a relic of his youth as a swell, he wore a monocle.

Philip Rivers, who had married Charles' sister Isabel some five years previously, was a short, stocky man who liked to dress in the height of fashion. This he could afford to do as he was the manager and owner of a successful tailoring establishment – 'Mourning Clothes a Specialty' - recently transferred from the City to Oxford Street. He was wearing trousers of the best Scotch tweed in a loud mustard yellow and chestnut brown check, and the buttons on his coat were made of different exotic woods with large glittering rhinestones in the centre.

Charles and Philip were sitting in a pleasantly conspiratorial silence. Both gentlemen were feeling in an expansive mood. Once a week they patronized a discreet establishment in High Holborn. It was run by Madame Cora, a lady of uncertain age who prided herself on the fact that the police never touched her establishment. 'None of your funny stuff here,' she would say to each new client. 'None of your grotesques or chains and boots and such. Just nice, clean girls who can give a man some fun. They're good girls, my girls, and they know they're lucky to be here.'

For a very reasonable price clients could have a good supper with oyster and game pie and the company of several buxom girls. Charles' favourite had splendidly large, firm breasts, which she would stuff into Charles' mouth as he gobbled excitedly and buttocks like heavy, pink balloons.

Charles curled his fingers reminiscently round his glass of port and shifted back in his chair.

'So, our bit of nooky at Madame Cora's was your last fling as a bachelor, then?' said Philip.

'I'm seeing Peat tomorrow,' said Charles gloomily.

'A fine girl, your Adeline,' said Philip, sympathetically pouring the last of the port into Charles' glass. 'Isabel likes her, says she has true elegance of mind, or some such thing. Myself, I'd prefer Blanche. What a tasty little morsel. What deliciously plump shoulders, like a little chicken!'

'And what bubbies,' said Charles, licking his lips slightly, 'like juicy, round strawberries.' He glanced at Philip. A few weeks ago, in the seclusion of the Peats' garden, he had sampled the perfection of Miss Blanche's charms. She had allowed him to hold her waist while she leant over the goldfish pond to throw in some titbits and had she or had she not noticed when his fingers crept up over her bodice? He could still feel the swell of the material under his hand. He had begun to stroke her experimentally when she pulled away. He drained his glass and set it down firmly. The pleasant glow which had been with him all evening evaporated suddenly. He felt stone cold sober.

'All the same,' he said, 'it's not Blanche I'm asking to become Mrs Charles Woodcock, though I don't doubt she'd come running if I lifted my little finger. She's a little bit fast for me. Miss Adeline's the one. She is a lady; I can respect her. Besides, I don't doubt Peat will be generous.'

'What's she worth?' asked Philip. 'Of course, there are four daughters, but he's a very rich man.'

'Oh, about twenty thousand,' said Charles casually. But his voice held an eager ring in it and he straightened himself in his chair.

'Oh easily. But you've bought your practice, haven't you?'

'Yes, the Governor helped me. But I shall need a house now, and the extra expense of servants has to be found. I shall need at least five hundred a year to live with any reasonable degree of comfort.'

'But you'll have to settle something on Miss Adeline, won't you?'

'Of course, of course,' said Charles testily, 'but I regard it as an investment.'

Philip thought of Isabel, asleep, so he hoped, upstairs. How she went on at a fellow about duty and moral obligations! He had heard her talking to Adeline during afternoon tea about visiting some poor buggers somewhere near St Giles' and delivering tracts on leading a godly and sober life, when all the poor bastards wanted was to enjoy their beer and their women. Isabel, thank God, did not choose to know about his weekly trips into High Holborn. Whatever would Adeline think if she found out?

'If she'll have you,' he said.

For a moment Charles looked stupefied. His blue eyes bulged incredulously. 'If she'll have me?' he echoed. 'Of course she'll have me.'

Mrs Peat sat in her morning-room waiting for her husband's return from the City. She sat in a comfortable armchair by the fire, her feet on a beaded footstool and a small gilt fire-screen beside her to protect her face and hands from the heat. Her hands were busy with her embroidery, the needle darting in and out with exquisitely fine stitches and her mind was wreathed in pleasant day-dreams. Before the end of the year she would have a daughter married. Next year, she thought with a sudden surge of spirits, she would be able to devote herself entirely to her lovely Blanche. This season all her energies were directed towards encouraging Charles to pop the question. How like a man to wait until the end of June before proposing, when the season was almost over. A more thoughtful man would have proposed in the spring, then she might have given a proper engagement party for Adeline and Blanche could have been launched into Society at the same time.

If Adeline and Charles were so selfish as to take up the entire summer with their scruples and hesitations, then they must take the consequences. She would tell Mr Peat that Adeline must marry well before Christmas and leave her free to plan Blanche's season in the spring.

What parties she would be able to give, centred around her lovely Blanche. What receptions, what drums! She would soon overcome this stupid prejudice against trade. Already Blanche had captivated young Lord Pateley, what dukes or earls would be sure to follow? Her suppers would have every refinement that money could buy, and she would launch her beautiful daughter into the very highest circles. After all, she was the daughter of the Rev. Arthur Hebden, a gentleman's daughter, the cadet branch of a most respectable family. With Blanche she would return to her rightful social milieu.

Blanche was seated in a low balloon-back chair flicking through a back copy of *The Ladies Treasury*. She was dressed for dinner in a pale blue silk gown which showed off her pretty, plump arms and shoulders. Her hair fell in ringlets caught up at the back with a wreath of lilies of the valley. She was thinking about Hugh Dunster.

Of course he did not care for Alice Banks at all, anybody could see that, but he must marry a girl with money and he had agreed with what his dreadful mother suggested. He had such an intelligent mobile face, such wonderfully alive eyes, such strong hands. He was a very special person. Somebody like Alice, poor dull thing, would never see that of course, but then Alice would never bring out those special qualities in Hugh. Blanche felt herself to be particularly sensitive. Hugh was not happy, she could tell.

Well, if Hugh looked elsewhere then it would be entirely Alice's fault. If she could not keep her man then she had only herself to blame if a more desirable woman stepped in. Alice should have seen weeks ago that Hugh's real inclinations lay elsewhere. The trouble with that sort of woman was that they simply clung on, long after the relationship was dead. God knows what she hoped to gain. She was sorry for Alice, of course she was, but denying her feelings would not solve anything.

Adeline was sitting opposite Blanche with her Missionary basket by her side. She was sewing buttonholes with tiny, tight stitches. She was working very fast, her forehead puckered into a worried frown. Adeline was hoping that neither Mama nor Blanche would speak to her because she did not wish to discuss the news that Flora brought back from her talk with Granny that morning.

She also felt very guarded with Flora. Flora said nothing openly, but Adeline had the distinct impression that her sister did not approve of Charles Woodcock, and was disappointed, somehow, in her decision to accept his offer.

Flora did not appear to understand that Adeline was making a sacrifice in marrying Charles. Charles was worthy in every way of course, but the ordeal of allowing Charles access to her as a wife was something Flora did not appreciate. Adeline knew that the spiritual side of her was fully developed: she was unfailingly modest and pure in thought, word and deed. Of course, Charles would respect this in his wife. Nevertheless she was afraid.

Mrs Peat looked up from her sewing and frowned at Flora. She was curled up in the window seat, reading as usual, with one foot tucked up underneath her and quite oblivious to what was going on.

'Sit up, Flora,' said Mrs Peat sharply.

'Sorry, Mama,' but already Flora's shoulders were beginning to stoop over her book again.

'Flora,' said Mrs Peat again, this time as one prepared to make an issue of it. Flora looked up, still marking her place with her finger. 'Only look at yourself. Your dress crushed, a button coming off your boots and your sleeves covered with ink. Whatever have you been doing to get yourself into such a state?'

'Just romping with Daisy, Mama, and helping her to write to Tom. I am sorry.'

'You are far too old to be romping about at your age. Daisy can perfectly well write her own letters to Tom. Not that I see the slightest necessity for her to write to him anyway; he will be home in a couple of weeks, but that is neither here nor there. Go to your room, Flora, and take a long hard look at yourself in the glass, and do not return until you are dressed properly for dinner.'

Flora shut her book, rose and walked to the door.

'And,' continued Mrs Peat, 'you will oblige me by writing out one hundred times, "I have a slovenly disposition and must endeavour to do better".'

Blanche watched Flora's exit from the morning-room from under her lashes. Flora's squabbles with Mama were no concern of hers, except that it was mortifying to have a sister who was always a wallflower because nobody asked her to dance.

'Mama, have we any news of Daisy's sharing Grace Lennox's lessons? I notice you did not mention it to Lady Clevedon this morning.'

'No dear, nothing. The Kingsleys are in the country over the summer, of course. I am hoping that Lady Kingsley will call in September when she returns to Town. It was not a matter that I wished to discuss with Lady Clevedon while things were so unsettled.'

Blanche realized that this scheme for Daisy to share a governess with Grace was more her mother's fond hope than Lady Kingsley's expressed wish.

'Grace is so fond of Daisy, Mama. I am sure that Lady Kingsley sees the advantages of the scheme. Besides, Grace is so very shy that Lady Kingsley must be dreading her come-out.'

Blanche spoke a trifle consciously. Both the Kingsley grandsons were down on her mental matrimonial list. She was very, very interested in the possibilities of Hugh Dunster, but a girl needed more than one string to her bow. Algy Kingsley, the younger grandson, was extremely promising. He had inherited a substantial fortune from his godfather so he was perfectly suitable. She had never met Sir George Kingsley, but the title, as well as his wealth, deserved her serious consideration.

'Adeline,' said Mrs Peat suddenly, 'run upstairs and find my shawl, please. The Paisley. I think it will be in my dressing-room, but if not, ask Briggs.'

She waited until Adeline left, then turned to Blanche. 'I hope my dear, to concentrate entirely on you next season. By then Adeline will be off my hands.'

'Adeline!' gasped Blanche. The little duffer had actually hooked herself a husband! 'Who is it?'

'Charles Woodcock. He is seeing Papa today.'

Charles Woodcock! How dare he? That filthy cad! And she had allowed him to ... and he had popped the question to Adeline! Adeline! A dried-up churchy frump! Serve him right, thought Blanche furiously. Well, she for one would not accept Charles Woodcock if he offered on bended knee.

'How delightful,' she said at last.

Mrs Peat unfolded a letter from her pocket. 'He wrote to Papa, exactly as he ought. "Would you do me the inestimable honour of allowing me to ask for Miss Adeline's hand in marriage?" Adeline will accept, of course. I have quite decided on an autumn wedding. I shall need the winter to organize for your come-out in the spring, my darling, so a long engagement is out of the question.'

Blanche felt waves of shame and anger stain her cheeks. She felt so insulted that she hardly knew how to bear it. That afternoon by the goldfishes ... he had .... How dared he? What was he, after all? An over-fed doctor with an over-loud laugh.

Well, she didn't care! If he tried any of his liberties with Adeline he would soon learn his mistake. And serve him right.

She snapped shut *The Ladies Treasury* and left the room. She passed Adeline on the stairs coming down with the shawl and hissed maliciously in her ear, 'He's been doing the softy behind your back, so watch out!'

Adeline stared at her incredulously, but failed to understand.

When Mr Peat arrived home only his wife and Adeline were in the morning-room. He sank down into a chair and Mrs Peat rang the bell for some tea. Mr Peat was a tall, well-made man with thinning grey hair and somewhat lined features. He was now in his late fifties but even in his well-made town suit he still retained the aura of a strong working man, in the breadth of his shoulders and in his purposeful, rather heavy walk.

'Sorry I'm late, Susan. There was some hold-up in the Strand. A damned-fool barrow boy tried to cut across a cab. Oranges all over the place and ladies shrieking like engine whistles. Nobody hurt though.'

'William,' said Mrs Peat firmly, 'never mind about the cab. Tell us how you fared today.' The look in her eye was rigid.

Mr Peat interpreted its significance correctly and turned to his daughter. Adeline sat quite still, her hands folded tightly in her lap. Mr Peat cleared his throat.

'Dr Charles Woodcock called on me today, Adeline. He came to ask for your hand in marriage. I asked him to take an informal dinner with us tonight. He will wish to hear your answer from your own lips.'

Adeline did not move, although all colour was driven from her cheeks. 'I shall do my duty, of course,' she said tonelessly. 'I shall accept him.'

Mr Peat looked at her uneasily. Susan had assured him that the girl was waiting on hot cinders for Woodcock to pop the question. Didn't care for the fellow much himself: he used too many words to very little purpose.

'My dear, dear Adeline!' Mrs Peat jumped up and embraced her daughter effusively. 'At last, one of my daughters can be happy! I have talked to dear Charles and I can tell you how much he admires and respects you.' At last Fortune was on her side.

Adeline had succeeded quite as well as could be expected. A doctor was nothing much, but at least he was not a tradesman like Philip Rivers.

The door opened and the butler entered.

'You called, Madam?'

'You may serve tea, Ketton. And there will be one more for dinner tonight. We expect Dr Charles Woodcock. That is all.'

Ketton glanced at Adeline. 'Very good, Madam.' He closed the door behind him with less than his usual dignity in his eagerness to tell them downstairs of this interesting development.

Later that evening Adeline and Mr Peat were waiting in the study. Mr Peat was unaccountably nervous; he had not liked Charles Woodcock particularly, finding him an irritating mixture of mediocrity and pomposity. But he would suit Adeline. He would have been more at ease if he had seen some signs of emotion in his daughter, but Adeline was sitting calmly in the leather armchair, her hands folded in her lap, her face quite expressionless.

'You are not nervous, my dear?' he said kindly, to hide the sudden burst of irritation he felt against her. 'You have no need to be, you know. I shall not leave you alone together. All that you need to do is accept his offer.'

He did not suppose that she had even allowed Charles to steal a kiss or two.

'I am perfectly all right, thank you, Papa.' Adeline wondered why her hands felt like ice, although it was a warm day. She felt a moment's impulse to fall to her knees and beg her father to take away this horrible thing that was happening to her. But as swiftly as the impulse rose, she buried it. She would do her duty to her family and her duty to God.

How on earth did he sire such an iceberg, he wondered, not for the first time. Susan was lively enough when he married her, in spite of that vicarage upbringing. Where the devil had Adeline's primness come from? He hoped Susan had seen fit to tell Adeline something of the duties of married life. However, it was not for him to interfere in her upbringing of her daughters.

Adeline was staring resolutely out of the window. Mr Peat guessed that the Leighton and Etty nymphs on the walls offended

31

her sensibilities. Well, he would dower her handsomely and she could lead her own life.

There was a knock at the front door and steps across the hall.

'This way, if you please, sir,' he heard Ketton saying. 'Mr Peat asked me to show you in here.'

The door opened and Charles entered.

'Splendid, splendid,' said Mr Peat, wondering why he felt so awkward when confronted by his prospective son-in-law, though he had supported an introduction to the Prince of Wales with equanimity. 'I have told Adeline of the great honour you have done her. Here she is to answer you for herself.'

Charles' face had turned a dull beetroot red, but he swallowed and came forward. 'I hope Adeline will not deny me?' he said, but with the air of one who knows he will be accepted.

Adeline rose and moved towards him. She felt her heart swelling. Apart from her father and brothers, no man had ever called her by her Christian name before. He truly cared about her! 'I will be yours,' she said, holding out her hand.

Charles bent over it and thanked her.

Mr Peat looked from one to the other in exasperation. Neither of them seemed to know what to do next.

'You may kiss your bride, Charles,' he said at last. Adeline received Charles' kiss on her forehead as if it was holy.

Chapter Two

Mrs Peat rented a villa in Ramsgate every summer so that she might recover from the season and her children enjoy the benefit of the sea air. This year, however, the party was depleted. Only Flora, Tom – now back from Marlborough College – and Daisy went down, chaperoned by old Nanny.

Flora was thankful to get away from London. She loved the moment when they were all standing on the station platform with the strapped and corded trunks, the fishing rods and the shrimping nets in a pile beside them: the clatter of doors being opened and shut, the whoosh of the steam, the shrill whistle of the guard and the clackety-clack of the train as they slowly gathered speed and pulled out of London. Even before they cleared the station Flora tossed her gloves and cloak up on to the luggage rack and relaxed happily in a corner to play Happy Families with Daisy.

Blanche was quite content to remain in London. She never enjoyed Ramsgate very much, such shoppy kind of people went there. How Flora could go shrimping in the rock pools with the horde of vagabonds with whom she made friends, Blanche did not know. It was all very well for Tom to make friends with shopkeepers' children, but Flora should have more discrimination. Blanche quite enjoyed Ramsgate last year, when her old schoolfriend Griselda Clevedon stayed for several weeks. The two girls would saunter along the beach to where the men were bathing and peep at them from underneath their parasols, giggling uncontrollably at the sight of their naked pink bodies. But this year Griselda was going to Scotland. Blanche preferred to remain in London, where at least she might have the chance of becoming acquainted with the Kingsleys.

So Adeline and Blanche stayed in London with Mrs Peat to buy

Adeline's trousseau and household linen and to supervise all the arrangements for the wedding in October. Adeline begged for Flora's company, but Mrs Peat would not hear of it. Flora, she said, was looking peaky and must go to Ramsgate for some nice, fresh air and take some healthy walks along the cliffs. In fact, Mrs Peat felt that she deserved a rest from her eldest daughter. In any case, she hardly knew velvet from moiré. Mrs Peat intended to indulge in an orgy of shopping and Flora would only be a damper.

Mrs Peat had a happy task before her. Should she buy Adeline's trousseau from Mrs Addley Bourne of Piccadilly? Or should she patronize Christian and Rathbone who had made Princess Alexandra's trousseau? Adeline, of course, would hardly notice what she wore. Perhaps Mrs Addley Bourne's twenty-pound trousseau would be perfectly adequate. On the other hand, Adeline was the first of the Peat daughters to be married. The guests must know that everything was the best that money could buy.

She would buy Adeline's handkerchiefs from Mrs Addley Bourne, she decided finally and they sold some excellent French weave corsets. But she would buy Adeline's chemises, night-dresses and other underwear from Christian and Rathbone: it would look so much better.

Adeline hated it. 'It is all worldly show,' she wrote to Flora. 'Every extra tuck and ribbon Mama insists on adding feels like a burden on my soul. Dear Flora, I wish you were here with me. We have always seen eye to eye on these vanities and it would be such a comfort to see you. Do write to me soon.'

Flora wrote at once, and warmly, but she felt oppressed by the tone of Adeline's letter nevertheless. Of course, she agreed with Adeline, all these things were only worldly vanities, but on the other hand, they were only night-dresses and petticoats her sister was complaining of. Was there truly so much danger to the soul in buying some pretty underwear on her marriage? She walked soberly along the Promenade to post her letter to Adeline and then took off her shoes and stockings and ran back along the sand to where Daisy and Tom were building a sand castle.

The social columns of *The Times* announced that Lady Kingsley, accompanied by her grandson, Sir George Kingsley and her granddaughter Miss Lennox, were returned to the Metropolis. Mrs Peat might not call on Lady Kingsley first, that would be unthinkable, instead she wrote a firm letter to Daisy, directing her to write to Grace and say that she would soon be returning to London and would love Grace to come to tea. Mrs Peat then sat back and waited.

Her main object was to secure an entrée to the house through Daisy who had become extremely friendly with Grace Lennox, Lady Kingsley's granddaughter. Mrs Peat knew from the teachers at Miss Speedwell's Academy that Grace was the cause of much concern to Lady Kingsley on account of her almost pathological shyness. Orphaned at birth, she had been brought up in the seclusion of the country with only her grandmother for company. Until Lady Kingsley had decided to educate her at a suitable school in London, rather than privately at home, Grace had known hardly anybody her own age. She spent the first two terms at the Academy either sitting silently in the back desk or weeping in the cloakroom. But for some reason she became very attached to Daisy, perhaps because they were opposite in temperament, Daisy being boisterous and cheerful where Grace was quiet and shy.

Grace had blossomed under Daisy's protection and Lady Kingsley allowed Grace to invite Daisy home to tea. All seemed settled when an epidemic of scarlatina hit the school and in a panic Lady Kingsley removed Grace. The question now remained: what to do about Grace's schooling without forfeiting her new-found confidence? It was Grace herself who suggested that Daisy be invited to share a governess with her and Mrs Peat felt it was a social opportunity not to be missed.

Lady Kingsley was an old woman of enormous force of character. It was rumoured among the members of the Cabinet that she was the only woman capable of brow-beating Lord Palmerston. Certainly her judgements were held to be sacrosanct in the Polite World. She had no opinion of the modern age: she refused to allow gas lighting at Linchmere, Sir George's country home, and she had forced the London to Brighton railway line to take a huge loop to avoid cutting through a small portion of the estate. The infuriated railway contractor of the time had to submit a new bill to Parliament, and when he eventually obtained permission for his line he found himself paying for a row of swift-growing poplars along the railway embankment as Lady Kingsley did not wish to see the distant locomotives, although they were fully half a mile away.

Lady Kingsley was the granddaughter of an Irish earl of supreme indolence, whose only interests were his horses and his family tree. This was a surprising document which traced her ancestry back to several royal lines (those of lesser degree being discreetly omitted). She found it not at all incongruous that the lines which started from such diverse sources as Duke William of Normandy, Llewellyn the Great and the High Kings of Ireland should meet in herself.

The Kingsleys came from decidedly less exalted stock, but Lady Kingsley was able to ignore this: they provided the land and the wealth. The first Kingsley to be made a baronet was Sir Paul Kingsley. He had managed to hold onto his estate during the upheavals of the Civil War by the simple expedient of switching his allegiance to Parliament at the right moment. He had even increased his estates at the expense of his less fortunate Royalist neighbours. During the last years of the Protectorate he had sent the exiled King several useful pieces of information and was rewarded with a baronetcy, an honour which Charles bestowed all the more graciously because it cost him nothing.

Her son and daughter having died, Lady Kingsley had only three surviving descendants: her two grandsons, Sir George and Algernon Kingsley and her granddaughter, Grace Lennox.

Lady Kingsley had the Regency indifference to her grandsons' discreet liaisons, although she expected both of them to settle down and marry well in the not too distant future.

Sir George, the eighth baronet, was now in his early thirties and he had inherited the title while still a schoolboy. He was tall and dark, with high, jutting cheekbones and a beak of a nose. The boniness of his face was accentuated by the lines around his mouth and eyes, eyes of such a dark brown that the irises seemed to merge into his pupils. For the rest, he dressed elegantly but soberly. He wore a Norfolk suit in the country and a frock coat when in Town. His moustache was not waxed nor his side whiskers unnaturally bushy. Sir George prided himself on being a perfect English gentleman.

He was a man who knew his worth. He was polite and kind to his tenants, and was scrupulous in seeing that his bailiff attended to any complaints. He was attentive to his grandmother and to his little cousin Grace, and he had amicable though not close relationships with a number of cousins and friends. He could pass the time of day with many fellow members of Brooks's and could visit one of the lighter haunts of pleasure with Tommy Clevedon or various other cronies from Eton days.

His year was organized with monotonous regularity. He usually spent the autumn in London with Lady Kingsley so that she might do the little season without becoming too exhausted. If the attempts of his hostesses to marry him off became too blatant he would go down to Linchmere for a week or two. After Christmas he went abroad, usually timing it so that he would miss the horrors of the season. He would spend the summer at Linchmere fishing and shooting and in the autumn the whole process would start again.

Apart from his fondness for foreign travel, Sir George had one taste that his grandmother considered highly unsuitable to his station. This was his interest in science, and the friends he made from it. He was on visiting terms with the Huxleys and the Darwins, families of no social distinction, as his grandmother pointed out. He was interested in the debate on the source of the Nile and even knew the reprehensible Burton.

His brother, Algy, lived almost entirely in London: in theory in rooms in Albany, but in practice in a pretty house that he had bought for his mistress overlooking the Thames in Chelsea. Lady Kingsley knew of the existence of Anny, but made little of it. A young man must sow his wild oats somewhere and the charms of an Anny would keep him out of the clutches of such females as Mrs Peat, anxious for the future of her daughters. Doubtless Algy would settle down in time; he would pension off Anny – it would be expensive but he could afford it – and he would choose a suitable wife with the approval of his grandmother. She had steered Algy away from a most unfortunate attachment to a vicar's daughter down at Linchmere and had no doubt of her ability to do so again if need be.

Lady Kingsley had decided over the summer that Grace should be allowed to share a governess with Daisy Peat. The old blue bedroom could be fitted up perfectly well for a schoolroom with the dressing-room beyond as a bedroom for the governess. Accordingly she set out with Sir George one afternoon to pay the longed-for call on Mrs Peat.

Mrs Peat was at home. They were announced. Introductions were made and Mrs Peat rang the bell for some refreshments. Lady Kingsley was first struck by the glaring vulgarity of the gold-embossed wallpaper and pointed out to her grandson in a whisper as they went upstairs the ostentation of having in the hall a large stuffed bear carrying a silver salver to take the visiting cards, but all these comfortable thoughts faded rapidly when she saw Blanche. Lady Kingsley saw at once that in Blanche Mrs Peat had the ammunition capable of carrying out her social ambitions. She glared at Blanche, addressed one brief remark to her and then ignored her. If her grandson proved to be seriously affected by the charms of this pretty piece then she would have nothing whatsoever to do with Mrs Peat's scheme for Daisy to share a governess with Grace. Blanche had the sense to look perfectly unconscious and continued quietly with the embroidery she had by her.

Lady Kingsley was slightly mollified and allowed herself to congratulate Adeline on her engagement and to sit down beside Mrs Peat to discuss her plans for Grace.

Sir George, after a few moments conversation with Adeline, turned to Blanche.

'Have you been in London all the summer, Miss Blanche?'

Blanche put her embroidery down slowly and lifted her head to look straight at him. Her eyes were of so vivid a blue that Sir George was quite startled and could only stare.

'This summer, yes,' said Blanche, speaking in a soft husky voice. She smiled at him and then added, with a half-pouting look at her sister, 'Dearest Adeline is to be married in the autumn, you know, and I am helping her buy her trousseau. But usually, of course, we are at the seaside.'

'Why of course?' asked George, smiling at her and hoping she would smile back, because he had never seen such entrancing dimples.

'Well, nobody stays in London after the season, do they?' said Blanche seriously.

'Or should we say, only nobodies stay in London?'

Blanche laughed and glanced speculatively at Sir George from under her lashes. She leant back slightly in her chair and began to play with the ringlet that had fallen over one cheek, twisting it round and round her finger.

What a superb figure, thought George appreciatively, and she knew it. That artlessly seductive pose was quite deliberate. Of course she was on the catch, and why not? Would not most men give a gold ring to have such a delectable morsel in their beds? Blanche's colour rose at his scrutiny but she did not move and continued to twist the ringlet. This pretty little piece was a man-eater, George decided.

'Are you to be a beautiful bridesmaid then, Miss Blanche? And your sisters too?'

'We are all to be bridesmaids,' replied Blanche, with a little grimace that asked for his masculine indulgence for such feminine vanities, 'although Adeline and I are the only ones in London. Flora and Daisy are in Ramsgate. Flora does not care much for shopping, she is bookish. She even likes history and science! Mama fears that she is a blue-stocking. You may believe me when I tell you that I had to intervene when she was discovered arguing with Canon Grieve about Darwin. It was only my representations, I assure you, that saved poor Flora from bread and water for a week.' She laughed prettily. 'No, I fear that my tastes are more frivolous, for I positively adore shopping!'

'I am sure it is a pleasure to serve you,' said George and watched the conscious blush rise.

Gracious, he works fast, thought Blanche breathlessly. She was not sure that she liked such innuendoes, especially on a first introduction. She felt out of her depth and she could not be certain whether he really liked her or whether he was merely amusing himself.

Mrs Peat was highly delighted at the turn things were taking. She took care not to look in Blanche's direction, but she could hear Sir George's deep tones and Blanche's lovely laugh. If he should fall in love with Blanche it would be quite like a fairy-tale!

'Dear Lady Kingsley, your governess sounds exactly what Daisy needs. She can be sadly boisterous at school. I feel she needs more individual attention and discipline. I have often deplored the laxness at Miss Speedwell's Academy.'

She made no mention of Grace's problems, Lady Kingsley would not thank her for raising them.

'Insufferable,' said Sir George, as their carriage drove away down Wilton Crescent. 'Grandmama, do you really wish to give that woman the entrée to the house?'

'Daisy sharing lessons with Grace in the schoolroom is not going to give Mrs Peat the entrée, or should I say *carte Blanche*, to the house!'

George laughed.

'Besides,' she continued, 'I doubt if Mrs Peat will bother me. She knows that Algy does not live here, you are going abroad at Christmas, what else can she want?'

'But do you wish to be associated with such a family?'

'My main concern is for Grace. I should have preferred it if she had chosen to be friends with somebody more of our own order, but quite frankly, I am extremely thankful to see her talking to anybody. I cannot cavil at her choice at this stage. Daisy Peat has given Grace the confidence in herself she sorely needs. I blame myself, of course, for keeping Grace with me in the country for so long, where there are no suitable children within twenty miles.'

'Nonsense, Grandmama. Cousin Jane brings John and Maria to stay every summer.'

'And Grace spends every summer locked in her bedroom or hiding in the woods.'

'She is very shy, of course,' said George.

'She is always charmingly behaved with me when I take her on calls. Several of my old friends at Linchmere are devoted to her. But it is not the same as being able to converse with children your own age. Since Grace has known Daisy I have seen a great improvement. The Colefax boys came to tea just before we left London at the end of June and I was so thankful to see how much better she was.'

'Let us leave Grace aside for one moment,' said George. 'You cannot be blind, Grandmama. Mrs Peat has other motives than a desire to be of use to Grace, or even to give Daisy pleasure. If she has not ear-marked either me or Algy for Miss Blanche I should be very surprised!'

'Doubtless. But William Peat is a very wealthy man: my shares in Peat-Milford are very profitable. Neither you nor Algy are likely to be taken in by Miss Blanche. I think it is a fair return if I give a boost to Mrs Peat's social aspirations in return for what Daisy is doing for Grace.'

'I suppose you will allow that they are very *parvenu*?'

'Certainly.'

'Oh well, you know best,' said Sir George, dismissing it from his mind. 'I think I shall visit Algy, Grandmama, if you have nothing further you wish me to do?'

Long did Mrs Peat re-live her triumph after Lady Kingsley and Sir George left, with Blanche as a quieter, but no less jubilant echo. Every look, every gesture that fed their wishes was analysed. Mrs Peat outlined her scheme for Blanche to chaperone Daisy to her lessons.

'I am not underestimating the opposition we will meet with from Lady Kingsley, Blanche. However she has her own set of rooms on the first floor and rarely sets foot in the ground floor saloons. If Sir George does not mention your presence and he will not, then you have nothing to fear. You will be shown into one of the downstairs saloons and if Sir George does not seek you there, I shall be very much surprised.'

Adeline looked disgusted and made an excuse to leave them. She went swiftly upstairs and shut herself in her room, now unnaturally tidy since Flora was away. She and Charles, thank God, had higher values. She would be marrying a man who appreciated her true worth – she felt a sudden shiver of disgust as she remembered Sir George's warm brown eyes resting on Blanche's face and moving slowly down her neck and the curves of her figure. Thank goodness Charles respected her. Adeline longed for her wedding to be over. She wished she might wake up to find she had been married already for some time. She would sit quietly with Charles in their new drawing-room in Upper Cavendish Street and discuss Charles' patients. If she took up a Sunday School class, they would talk over her various protegées. With Charles' help she could place some of the girls in suitable Christian households – he would be sure to know some among his clients. Their interests would turn on higher things.

Perhaps she might visit some of the poorer families among Charles' patients – even persuade him to have a special evening surgery for them. She had heard Charles' arguments on the importance of cleanliness in treating cholera. Ventilation and sobriety of living, said Charles, could halve the incidence of the disease. Modern medical science had shown the importance of salt in such cases. It was a known fact, said Charles, that cholera was most prevalent among the lower classes where immorality was at its highest.

To help and encourage Charles, thought Adeline, would be to help humanity and work for the glory of God. She would follow up Charles' pioneering work and visit the afflicted families. The mother would offer her a chair in a small but spotless room and show her the new baby (Adeline had the haziest idea of the home conditions of the poor) and they would come to trust her. Eventually – he would write a brilliant paper for *The Lancet* – Charles' merits would be recognized. . . .

Mrs Peat, in a mood of unusual affection for her second daughter, decided to give a dinner party for Adeline and Charles to celebrate their engagement. It would not be a truly family affair, of course, as Flora was still down in Ramsgate, but she would invite Ernest and Geraldina, Charles' parents and Isabel and Philip Rivers and make an evening of it. They would dine early and then go to the theatre.

'Is Mr Milford coming?' asked Blanche.

'Not to dinner, darling, but he and Captain Grant will meet us at the theatre.'

Mrs Peat kept a firm eye on Gerald Milford, her husband's business partner and invited him whenever Geraldina came. He was now a widower in his middle fifties and although astute in money matters, seemed unable to regulate his private life with any success. Since Geraldina married, Gerald was too often to be found getting outrageously drunk in the Casino de Venise and having to be brought home by his long-suffering coachman.

Francis Grant, Gerald's handsome but impecunious nephew, was another matter – Mrs Peat would have avoided inviting him if it had been at all possible. But Captain Grant was dining with Gerald and Mrs Peat felt obliged to extend the invitation.

Mrs Peat distrusted Captain Grant. She had heard the rumours that the relationship between him and Geraldina was rather warmer than cousinly affection would warrant. One of her friends had whispered to her that now Geraldina had given Ernest two sons did she consider that she was at liberty to please herself? Mrs Peat had snubbed her severely. 'Ernest thinks nothing too good for Geraldina,' she said frostily, 'and I am sure Geraldina realizes her good fortune in being married to so devoted a husband.'

Privately she was not so sure. How far did Geraldina take her cousinly affection for the handsome Captain Grant? And what would happen if somebody dropped those malicious rumours in Ernest's ear?

Algy Kingsley lay back on the leather-buttoned Chesterfield, his slippered feet resting on a small footstool and one arm around Anny who was sitting beside him. Anny held a pair of opera glasses to her eyes and she was trying to see into the houseboat moored on the opposite bank of the river. The sofa faced some French windows, now open to the warm summer air making the chintz curtains billow in the breeze, and outside, in front of the houseboat that so intrigued Anny, two swans floated by lazily.

'Let the poor beggars enjoy their holiday in peace,' said Algy.

'Ah, there now, what did I tell you,' Anny handed him the glasses. 'He *is* wearing a wig.'

'By Jove! You're right. He is as bald as a coot.'

The conversation continued in a desultory way, by turns intimate, tender and at times petering out into a companionable silence. In both looks and temperament, Algy Kingsley could not have been a greater contrast to his brother. He was very good-looking: his hair was fair, his eyes were blue and his features so perfectly moulded that more than one young lady had likened him rapturously to Apollo. He had the looks, charm and the wealth to gain him the entrée to any social circle he might wish to enter, or win him any woman he might wish to possess. But Algy's inclinations were quiet and domestic. He had no wish to make husbands jealous or to carry on intrigues with bored married ladies, or even to pursue the pleasant dissipations offered to young men of rank and fortune by the anonymas of the modern Babylon.

He had always known that he wanted a quiet, domestic life, perhaps because he had never known either of his parents – his mother dying shortly after he was born and his father being killed on the hunting field when he was just two. When he was twenty-one, Algy had fallen in love with the daughter of the vicar of Linchmere. But Sarah Dinsdale had no money, Algy himself had only a younger son's expectations, her family was barely passable and both Sir George and Lady Kingsley had united in opposition. Lady Kingsley had pressurized the bishop into offering Mr Dinsdale a canonry in some remote cathedral, and more reprehensibly Sir George had informed Sarah that such unequal matches could never be happy and that Lady Kingsley would oppose it to her dying day. In tears, Sarah had given in and within three months of Algy making his wishes known the Dinsdales had moved, Sarah was lost to him and the entire episode appeared to have been forgotten by every other participant except Algy. A year later Sarah was dead. Consumption, Canon Dinsdale wrote in his letter informing Algy of the event. Very unhealthy stock, commented Lady Kingsley, and what had happened was all for the best. Algy had said nothing, but he had thought that at least he could have given her a year of happiness. He resolved never again to put himself in such a vulnerable position.

A few years after this event Algy inherited a fortune from his godfather, so his financial independence was secured. He met Anny and took her to live with him in Chelsea and seemed perfectly content with the arrangement, much to Lady Kingsley's fury. To detach him from an unsuitable girl at twenty-one seemed prudent, to find him still unwed at twenty-six was more worrying. Occasionally, in the watches of the night, Lady Kingsley wished she had not been so precipitate.

Anny was just twenty: she had a wistful face with soft brown eyes and hair and a pointed chin. Her skin had a pale transparency as if she could never make up for the half-starved years of drudgery that lay behind her. Anny had worked as a sales girl in a milliner's in Burlington Arcade earning eighteen shillings a week. Even so, there was never anything left as she had to buy her own black silk dress for work and she lived out. She had met Algy late one evening just as she was leaving work. It was sales time and Anny had been on her feet for fifteen hours, except for a twenty-minute lunch break. It was eleven o'clock and beginning to sleet as Anny was allowed finally to leave. As she left the Arcade the cold and her tiredness and hunger hit her all at once and she would have fallen if it had not been for Algy who caught her, hailed a cab and put her and himself into it. The next morning he removed her to more suitable lodgings and informed her irate employer that she would not be returning to work.

He had never regretted his impulsive action. He found Anny suited him down to the ground. She had the kind of delicate prettiness that he liked, in looks she was demure, in temperament loving. Algy had been the first man she had gone with and as by nature she was faithful, she had never so much as looked at another man.

Sir George had chosen this day to visit his brother, mainly because it was his grandmother's At Home day and he wished to avoid the tedium of receiving calls, especially the return call from Mrs Peat and her daughters.

'Well, George,' said Algy as his brother was announced, 'how was the beautiful Blanche?'

Sir George shook Algy's hand and bent to kiss Anny's cheek. 'I did not stay to see. I came to see you and Anny instead.'

'We are honoured. But will they not be very disappointed?'

'I daresay,' shrugged George. 'If vulgar girls throw themselves at you, what can they expect? I detest women who are so obviously on the market. You are lucky, Algy. You have Anny, and that puts you out of circulation, so to speak.'

'You are abroad much of the time. That puts you out of reach.'

'Quite. But why should I have to go to Afghanistan to escape predatory women?'

George had no intention of allowing any woman in his life. They upset everything with their emotional demands: they wished to be in Town for the season, just when he wanted to travel abroad, most of them could never conduct a rational argument, and those who could were either arty types with their flowing Pre-Raphaelite robes and intense faces, or else absolute frights, probably educated at the so-called Ladies' College at Cheltenham. If he needed a woman, there were plenty to be had in the houses of accommodation or in such pleasure houses as Kate Hamilton's just off Leicester Square.

'But don't you ever want to settle down, George?' asked Algy, moving his hand slightly so as to play with Anny's curls.

'No,' said George shortly.

'But in India you had a more permanent arrangement, did you not?'

'Oh well, that was different. The first thing you are warned against was picking up women in the bazaars. My godfather sent me half a dozen pretty girls and I chose the prettiest.'

'George!' cried Anny shocked. 'You mean he picked them out for you, like a horse fair?'

'I found it quite a good system,' said George callously. 'You have a pretty girl to come home to. She is free from disease and has been taught European ways, can make a cup of tea and so on. Besides, if you are known to be living with a native girl, the match-making mamas avoid you.'

'I think it is absolutely disgusting,' said Anny hotly. 'Poor thing, I suppose that she has no choice at all in the matter? And did you oblige your replacement in the same way?'

'Yes, and you are wrong. She has a choice. It's me or starving back in the village she came from. But Kamela was all right, she stayed on with my replacement, so I knew that she was provided for.'

Poor girl, thought Anny indignantly, handed about like musical parcels.

'Look at Anny! She is quite shocked,' teased Algy, kissing her cheek. But Anny was still feeling the manifest unfairness of the casual male dominance of life and would not turn towards him.

'In any case,' continued George, suddenly dropping his voice and looking straight at Anny with very deep brown eyes, 'she was extremely well taught in the arts of, er, bringing-on a man. It was quite an education to be with her.'

He was smiling at her. Anny looked at him, flushed and looked away, both stirred in spite of herself and resentful. George was a very attractive man and he found her desirable. Anny was very conscious of it. A fact they were both well aware of, but neither mentioned.

'But you ought to settle down,' put in Algy. 'Damn it, George, think of the name.'

'You sound just like Grandmama.'

46

'You are the head of the family. The seventh baronet.'

'Eighth,' said George.

'Well, eighth, then, and it is your duty.'

'Why not you?'

'I am very happy where I am, thank you. And you,' said Algy unanswerably, 'are the elder.'

It gave Algy a curious pleasure to see George in a less advantageous position than himself. He respected George, he even liked him, but he resented his power as the elder son, able to claim the total inheritance, lands, title, everything, and he had never quite forgiven George's interference over Sarah Dinsdale. Algy knew that George wanted Anny, that he envied Algy for having her, but he also knew that his brother would never act so dishonourably as to try to steal her from him. The fact that he could see that Anny was attracted by George and that George knew this, only gave the situation an added piquancy for Algy. George would never love Anny as he did, probably was not capable of it, but he did desire her, and it was pleasant to know that just occasionally Sir George Kingsley, Bart, did not have everything his own way.

Geraldina Peat sat in her dressing-room and sulked at her reflection in the glass. She was not comforted by her warm, creamy skin or the smooth knot of blue-black hair that curled so prettily in the nape of her neck. She held a ruby drop ear-ring in one hand and a garnet and pearl ear-ring in the other and she was turning her head from side to side trying to decide which to wear. Her husband had entered her dressing-room a few moments earlier as her maid was finally hooking her into the bodice of her wine-coloured evening dress and paid her a number of extravagant compliments. 'Ah, my dear, you look like a queen,' he had said with that respectful admiration in his voice that so annoyed her. 'Like some divine goddess, does she not, Marie?'

Geraldina pulled her shawl of Spanish lace across her shoulders and savagely stuck a brooch pin in it. The lace tore. Damn him, damn Ernest for being such a prosy, slow *bore*. She threw the shawl on to the ground and tugged at the bell-pull.

'Marie! Where have you been you stupid girl? Fetch me my black cashmere shawl, this one has torn.'

Ernest came in again, respectfully eager in his dress coat with its narrow velvet collar. 'Are you nearly ready, my dear? It is about time we were off.'

'No, I am not!' snapped Geraldina. 'I look a wreck. No, it is no use. Marie must do my hair again.'

'You look very attractive,' said Ernest placatingly, glancing down at his pocket watch.

But Geraldina was ripping the pins out of her hair and seemed not to hear him.

'I do not know why I am bothering,' she said pettishly. 'Just because that dowd Adeline has found herself a man at last. About time too, I bet your mother thought that she was never going to get her off her hands.'

'Adeline will only be getting married once. Mama is particularly anxious that Charles should meet all the family.'

'You mean that Adeline must be disposed of at all costs,' replied Geraldina ungraciously. She was probably the only woman left in Town who had not had her *derrière* pinched by that fat windbags, Charles Woodcock. 'I suppose that I may look forward to three more family dinners for stolid young men of no interest whatsoever, although God knows who would offer for Flora. Do not pull so hard, you silly bitch.'

'Charles is all right,' said Ernest awkwardly.

'A doctor! As for Philip Rivers – a jumped-up shopkeeper and his terribly genteel wife.' She looked at her reflection in the glass. 'Oh well, that will have to do. I shall not be back until about two, Marie, so you may occupy yourself with repairing the torn lace on my Spanish shawl. That will take your mind off your followers.'

'Followers are forbidden, Madame.'

'You think I have not a very good idea of what goes on downstairs? I pay you twenty-five pounds a year, Marie. For that kind of money I expect your full attention.'

The carriage rumbled down towards Belgrave Square. The only bright spot in an otherwise totally unsupportable evening, thought Geraldina, was that she would be seeing Frank Grant. At least he never called her a divine goddess! When Frank praised her it was always with a wealth of explicit and erotic detail: it amused him that she could be so aroused by his talk. Even thinking about it made Geraldina sigh and lean back in the dim light of the carriage, relieved that Ernest could not see her face.

Ernest was so terribly respectful and dull! She thought he had rather more to him when they were first engaged. He used to dress very well, and first excited her interest in a black velvet morning coat with black and white check tweed trousers, and a beautifully embroidered waistcoat. He affected a slightly languid drawl in those days and Geraldina, in her innocence, mistook it for evidence of a sophisticated and mature man. He seemed that summer, a summer full of Ernest playing cricket, to be the kind of man she wanted. Five years ago it was Frank she saw as the spotty, lanky overgrown schoolboy, the one she despised for his callow youth. Now she realized that she was mistaken in both of them: for Ernest ladies were respectable and modest, for Frank ladies were women, to be treated as both desirable and desiring. How could she have been so wrong?

The carriage stopped and Geraldina, with a sigh, allowed herself to be escorted into the house. It was much as she expected, the food was indifferent, the room not properly warm. The only advantage was that nobody lingered over dinner as they were due at St James's Theatre. Opposite her at the dining-table sat Isabel Rivers, properly but hideously dressed in purple mourning for some great-aunt. She was looking terribly correct and was slightly flustered by Geraldina's presence.

Geraldina derived a great deal of amusement from watching Blanche plant tiny arrows in Adeline's flesh. She suspected some firkytoodling on Charles' part to make Blanche quite so malicious. In any event, it served Adeline right for being such a prude. There she sat, with eyes downcast, trying to ignore Blanche's jibes. She wore a dove-grey silk dress, with only the plainest of tucks and ribbons and the low neckline filled in with a lace chemisette. Well, whatever could you do with a girl who behaved like a heroine in some religious tract? If Adeline wished to be a martyr, then in Geraldina's opinion, she was going the right way about it, marrying Charles Woodcock. What a name! Still, it probably suited him.

'Now, Charles,' said Blanche gaily, 'where is the honeymoon going to be? Adeline, you know, only blushes. I can get no information from her.' Adeline cast her a look of burning reproach. Blanche took no notice. 'Adeline would like a remote cottage where you can both be lost to the world. She hinted so only the other day.'

'Blanche, that is not true,' Adeline managed to say, between stiffened lips.

'Oh, Charles,' said Blanche reproachfully, 'have you been a naughty man? Now Adeline does not wish to be all alone with you.'

'You must not tease your sister, darling,' said Mrs Peat, but she was smiling.

Adeline forced herself to speak. 'Charles' godmother is kindly lending us her country house on the Thames.'

'Near Maidenhead, no doubt,' murmured Geraldina.

'Near Windsor,' said Charles, frowning.

'Windsor!' echoed Blanche brightly. 'You must visit the mausoleum and pay your respects to the Prince Consort. He did so much for sanitation, I believe.' She paused. 'So suitable.'

Charles' face turned a dull red.

'Pray enlighten me,' said Mr Peat sternly from the head of the table. 'In what way does Prince Albert's mausoleum seem suitable for your sister's honeymoon?'

Blanche opened her eyes very wide. 'I meant so suitable for a doctor, Papa.'

The carriages were ordered and the party gathered on the steps as doors were opened and steps let down. Geraldina was happy to stand for a few minutes in the warm summer air. The light had not faded yet and the golden glow of the summer evening shone through the plane trees and the fountains in the gardens of the square. It was a relief to be outside after the oppressive tensions of the dining-room.

Geraldina took Blanche's arm firmly and hurried her towards their clarence. 'Hurry up, Ernest. Get in, or we shall have to take Charles. Blanche, you are a first-class bitch.'

She pulled her willing sister-in-law into the carriage with her, Ernest followed them and signalled to the coachman to drive on. The clarence moved forward. Geraldina pulled down the sash and leaned out. 'There they all are, so polite and deferring to each other. The question is, who is going to have to put up with that bore, Charles?'

'Adeline,' said Blanche with a giggle, 'for life.'

'You were very naughty,' said Geraldina. 'What has the virtuous Adeline done to deserve it? Or was it Charles?'

'You know, I get a tiny bit tired of Adeline,' said Blanche sweetly. 'She is exactly the sort of dowdy prude that the men seem to want. God knows why.'

'So that is it,' said Geraldina. Ernest sat in the corner and stared out of the window. 'I wondered if Charles had been trying the naughty with you.'

Blanche shrugged her pretty shoulders non-committally. 'Oh, Charles is such a bore,' she said.

Geraldina allowed the subject to drop.

The carriage drew up outside St James's Theatre with its classical portico supported on slender, fluted columns which jutted out over the pavement and protected the patrons of the theatre from the inclemency of the weather. The doorman came up and assisted Geraldina to alight. Several theatre flunkeys leapt forward to take her cloak and to relieve Ernest of his coat, hat and cane. Blanche followed more slowly, admiring the panache with which Geraldina swept into the vestibule, hardly bothering to turn her head to see if the flunkey caught the cloak she tossed him.

Gerald Milford and Francis Grant were waiting for them. Gerald kissed his daughter, his puffy eyes shining with pride as he looked at her. He greeted Blanche with a kiss and a squeeze.

'What have you done with Ernest, eh?'

'I expect the Peats' carriage has arrived,' said Geraldina with complete unconcern. 'We came on ahead.'

Captain Grant was standing silently by the wall. He moved forward to greet them. He was tall and slim, with a crop of rich brown hair that curled over his ears, and heavily hooded eyes of a clear blue. He held out his hands to Geraldina as he came forward and when she had put hers into them he raised them to his lips, first one and then the other, watching her all the time under those heavy eyelids.

'My lovely cousin,' he said, smiling down at her in a way that made Blanche's heart suddenly contract with envy. 'Ah, here comes the worthy Ernest.' He released Geraldina's hands as Ernest arrived with the rest of the party and moved to greet them.

The party made their way to their boxes. Blanche found herself seated between Geraldina and her mother at the front of the box, behind them were Francis Grant, Gerald Milford and Ernest. The play was *Lady Audley's Secret*, and Blanche had heard that it was very modern. Adeline would not like that.

Adeline was sitting in the next box trying not to look at the ceiling. Recently it had been re-painted with a riot of nymphs on clouds and supported by gilded caryatids – 'emblematical of music' said the programme note. She could see several of the gentlemen in the boxes opposite looking at the ceiling and whispering to each other. The programme might go on about the 'artist's considerable classical merits' but Adeline knew better. It was a blatant invitation to all sorts of luxury and vice. When she was married, Adeline decided, she would not patronize the theatre: most of the plays were too unwholesome. Even the Bard had several most indecent passages in spite of the uplifting moral efforts of Dr Bowdler. She turned to Charles. He too was looking at the ceiling and through his opera glasses too. Then Charles was a doctor, and of course doctors had excellent medical reasons for looking closely at limbs. But even so. . . .

She touched him briefly on the arm. Charles turned at once towards her.

'Euterpe,' she said.

'Eh?'

'The Muse of flutes and music.'

'Ah, exactly so, my dear. How clever you are.'

'I hope you do not think . . .' began Adeline hesitantly. 'I hope you do not think that it was my idea to come to see this play, Charles. I have heard that it is terribly modern. I would not wish you to think me lacking in womanly delicacy.' She looked down in extreme embarrassment, her face flushed.

Charles was rather looking forward to seeing *Lady Audley's Secret* which shocked many reviewers with its frank portrayal of a scheming woman. He felt slightly irritated by Adeline's scruples and wondered uneasily if she expected him to be quite such a puritan once they were married. But he pushed the thought away almost at once. Naturally his wife would have feelings which would place her high on a pedestal above the baser impulses of man.

'I share your scruples entirely, my dear,' he said earnestly, and resumed his covert survey of the nymphs on the ceiling.

In the other box Captain Grant was leaning familiarly over Geraldina's shoulder and whispering in her ear. Blanche, sitting next to Geraldina, pretended to be absorbed in reading her programme and listened. Geraldina unfurled her ivory and lace fan and gently waved it to and fro to hide her face.

'Dina! Why St James's Theatre?'

'I thought you wished to see the play. You have quite a penchant for married ladies who behave badly.'

'It is such a public place.'

'So?'

'People are talking, Dina, you must know that.'

'Oh dear, am I ruining your reputation? But you need not have come.'

'Damn it, your father pays my allowance. I could do nothing else.' He leant forward and under cover of her fan kissed her shoulder. 'And you know perfectly well that I could not keep away.'

'Perhaps. Shh! The curtain is going up.'

'But when may I see you alone?'

'Sunday at eleven. I shall have a headache and be unable to go to church.'

'But I cannot come round. Your servants suspect already.'

'The garden door then. I shall be in the summer house.'

Blanche suppressed a gasp of excitement. They were lovers! She was sure of it. Lucky, lucky Geraldina! She could see Francis' hands, strong and brown, out of the corner of her eye. Now they were stroking Geraldina's neck, up to the nape and then caressingly down to her shoulder. Blanche could feel a flutter of sympathetic desire in the pit of her stomach. If only she could be in Geraldina's place with stupid, stuffy Alice Banks beside her not knowing what was going on and Hugh Dunster sitting behind, his fingers touching her neck and shoulders when nobody was looking!

Did she really wish to marry Hugh? Was she in love with him enough to forget the social benefits of marrying one of the Kingsleys for instance, or even young Lord Pateley? They were the 'feather in the cappers' and Hugh had no money and the reputation of being a wastrel. Oh Hugh! Just to be with him made her flesh crawl with excitement. With Hugh she knew what it was to be alive!

She must think seriously: Lord Pateley for instance. He was a feather in the cap only by virtue of his title and estates, in himself he was nothing. Blanche found him very young and slow, he could hardly ask her to dance without stammering and blushing and the mildest flirtation threw him into confusion. However he had land and a title and Blanche wanted both.

She turned her mind to Sir George Kingsley. He was rich and he had a title, but there were several disadvantages. It was true he admired her and did the agreeable on the one occasion that they had met, but Blanche was not too sure that she liked him. He was old, being on the shady side of thirty, moreover he was out of the country for long periods of time. He travelled extensively round Italy and the Levant. Blanche could picture herself with the cream of Italian society: tea on the terrazza, or cruising round the Bay of Naples, shading her flawless English complexion – so much admired on the Continent – with a saucy parasol, but somehow she could not see Sir George there. He was far more likely, she thought bitterly, to be crawling on his stomach through some marsh with Garibaldi. A man who had spent the better part of a year going on a mule through Anatolia, wherever that was, was no fit mate for Blanche Peat.

On the other hand, he had spent a year out in the Punjab and had returned with the most fabulous jewellery, if Grace Lennox was to be believed.

Gerald Milford watched the unfolding of the plot on stage in a mood of mounting exasperation. Women's nonsense this sort of play was. Lady Audley had apparently been married before, but deserted her husband and allowed him to believe that she was dead. Here she was, now bigamously Lady Audley and suddenly confronted by her first husband, George Talboys. Gerald disliked the melodramatic acting of Mr Talboys and was not surprised Lady Audley attempted to do the fellow in and stuff his body down a well. He must be a mug too, if he accepted his wife's death from the evidence of a newspaper. Where, in heaven's name, was his lawyer? What about the register of burial? The plot was quite preposterous by any standards, any man could pick a hole in it in a couple of minutes.

However, Lady Audley had a splendid bosom, heaving as it was just now with emotion. Her hands were clutching at her neck as if at any moment she was going to rip open her bodice in her rage and two full white breasts would spring out. Gerald cleared his throat and glanced at Ernest. Ah, Ernest appreciated it as well. He was glad to see that his son-in-law had some red blood in him. Just lately he had begun to wonder if Geraldina was quite as satisfied as she pretended. He glanced at his daughter.

The box was dark, but not too dark for Gerald to see Francis' hand gently caressing his daughter's body. All at once a hundred small details made sense to Gerald. His daughter's little cover-ups, her surprising wish to visit an old governess, her sudden headaches which left her at home while Ernest went out, her indulgent contempt of Ernest.

If Ernest was not such a milk sop this would never have happened. What the devil did he mean by making her so bored that she was willing to risk public scandal and disgrace for a few moments' adulterous pleasure?

What the hell was he to do? Beat his erring daughter? Have his favourite nephew posted abroad? He was an old man now. He had just got his life nicely organized, the business, his clubs, his mistress; he did not wish a great domestic upheaval. Gerald began to feel very ill-used.

Mrs Peat, sitting at the opposite end of the box had seen nothing. Nevertheless Ernest's sulks were enough to make her feel extremely uneasy. She had never liked Geraldina, who did not have the modesty and decorum proper to Ernest's wife. What Geraldina needed was a firm, strict mother who would not hesitate to discipline her as she deserved. Such flirtatious ways – and she hoped that was all it would prove to be – between her daughter-in-law and Captain Grant should be beaten out of her. Captain Grant was a thoroughly unprincipled scoundrel and deserved to be cashiered.

On stage the drama was unfolding. The hero was striding up and down, fists clenched and occasionally beating his forehead in agony as he related to his friend the story of his wife's early death.

'It crushed me for a time; but I was obliged to fulfil my duties [here he looked noble] or sacrifice my appointment. But during all that time, Bob, the scorching sun of India was nothing to the fire that was raging here – here – here!'

He pressed his hands to his forehead and his companion groaned sympathetically.

Mrs Peat brought her thoughts back to the stage with a jerk. India! Why did she not think of that before? Have Captain Grant transferred abroad. It could be done with very little fuss; a few strings pulled and the machinery would begin to grind. By the time the Captain had quelled a few tribes on the North-West Frontier and sweated out a summer or so on the Plains, she trusted he would be a sadder and wiser man. Now, how might it be done?

Adeline went to the theatre expecting to be shocked. She even spent several days wondering how far she might take her protest. Should she walk out of the theatre, for example? She was in a state of prepared moral sensitivity from the moment she entered the theatre. Throughout the play her outrage grew: Lady Audley was an immoral woman, no Christian lady should be asked to witness such an exhibition of filth and degradation. But her eyes never once left the stage.

Remorse at her dastardly deeds had turned Lady Audley mad and as she fell to the ground a thrill of horror rushed through Adeline. Lady Audley pulled the pins out of her hair and it floated wildly round her head. Her white neck was twisting to and fro and her eyes were rolling in a frenzy. Adeline felt a sudden leap of recognition at the wildness of her gestures, her arms writhing above her head and her face contorted. It was her abandon and loss of control that so disturbed Adeline, she felt that somewhere in herself lay such madness if she did not rigidly keep it in check.

Lady Audley stared at the husband she thought she had murdered and laughed wildly. Charles stared too, his blue eyes swelling slightly as she fell to the ground, her writhings revealing the shapely curves of her legs encased in white silk stockings with the hint of pink garters above the knee.

Charles leant over towards Adeline as thunderous applause broke out and the curtain fell. She was sitting rigidly back in her chair, her face working and her hands clenched.

'Most interesting,' he observed. 'From a clinical point of view, you know, my dear. She caught the antics of frenzy particularly well, I thought.'

'Was not her madness a little sudden?' asked Adeline, trying to pull herself together. 'Could it really strike a sane person without warning?'

'Such cases have been known indeed,' said Charles, shaking his head. 'But the seeds of madness have always been found much earlier. In Lady Audley's case, the seeds of her own guilt. And George Talboys said, you remember, when he married her, that she was a passionate woman. I don't doubt that that had something to do with her sad condition.'

Adeline rose a little shakily from her chair. 'Yes, yes, of course,' she said thankfully. 'It could only happen to a woman who forgot her true womanliness.'

Shortly after the theatre excursion the Ramsgate party arrived back in London, complete with dried seaweed, shells to be varnished and mounted in a frame and Tom's interesting pieces of driftwood (soon to be confiscated by Nanny). Tom returned to Marlborough College and Daisy, accompanied by Blanche, went for her first day's lessons with Grace Lennox.

The whole family stood at the door to see Daisy and Blanche off, and Mrs Peat gave far more advice to Blanche on her behaviour and the expectations of future triumphs than she gave to Daisy. Daisy was wearing a neat cotton dress, let down from last year with the old hemline disguised by some velvet ribbon. Blanche was wearing a new dress, a summer silk of Buchanan tartan. Her hair was swept up in a chignon (three times Briggs had to do it until Blanche declared herself satisfied), secured by floating follow-me-lads ribbons.

Blanche had decided that she would follow Geraldina's example. She would secure a husband like Sir George and then she would indulge in an affair with a Hugh Dunster. She thought about it for several days and did not see why she should settle for less.

They arrived at the Kingsley house in Berkeley Square. The butler opened the door to them. Blanche smiled demurely and murmured something about escorting her sister. Penton's experienced eye took in Blanche's pretensions at once: she was after Sir George, if he was not much mistaken. Penton had served the Kingsleys for forty years and he felt the family honour as acutely as even Lady Kingsley could wish. He was not going to let this piece of jam have her way.

'Miss Grace is awaiting you in the schoolroom, Miss Daisy,' he said. 'If you will follow me I will show you up.' He turned to Blanche. 'You too, Miss.'

Suddenly the inevitability of Mrs Peat's plan did not seem quite so certain. 'Oh, anywhere will do for me,' said Blanche, with an assumption of ease, glancing surreptitiously at the half-open library door where she could hear somebody moving about. 'I do not wish to disturb the children's lessons.'

'I think you will find the schoolroom quite comfortable, Miss,' said Penton firmly. 'I will have some refreshments sent up.' Such was his authority that to her fury Blanche found herself following him.

Penton trod downstairs, his mission achieved. He found Sir George in the hall.

'Congratulations, Penton. You did it very well.'

'Sir?' said his butler blankly.

'Nevertheless,' continued Sir George, 'if Miss Blanche comes again you had better show her into the Pink Saloon. It will fulfil the same purpose, only rather more politely.'

'Certainly, sir,' said Penton, permitting himself a slight smile. He withdrew to relate his success downstairs. Sir George went back to his library.

Chapter Three

BLANCHE returned home in a state of ill-concealed fury. She stormed upstairs to her mother's dressing-room and slammed the door behind her. That odious Lady Kingsley had given orders that she should stay with Daisy in the schoolroom, she was sure of it. Nobody took the slightest distinguishing notice of her, the butler brought her the same refreshments as he brought that dowd of a governess. There was nothing to read except some fusty old school-books *and* she could hear Sir George in his library and he did not even come out to say good morning. Blanche found her voice was trembling with indignation and rage. Mrs Peat endeavoured to soothe her.

'Very well, Mama,' said Blanche at last. 'I shall try not to be upset, but I am not going again. Let Flora.'

Mrs Peat was reluctant to let go of her dreams. However as Flora could sit equally well in the schoolroom in Berkeley Square as at home, it could make no difference to her. Besides, the *ton* were drifting back to Town and Mrs Peat wanted to pay a few calls to collect her friends' congratulations on Adeline's engagement. Flora's presence always reminded her unpleasantly of her failure in that direction. It would be much better if Flora chaperoned Daisy.

Flora took Daisy to Berkeley Square the next morning. Penton stopped her as she was about to follow Daisy upstairs and escorted her into the Pink Saloon. She kissed Daisy at the bottom of the stairs and followed Penton with mixed feelings. What if Sir George had meant to approach Blanche after all? Perhaps yesterday's rudeness was only a ruse to blind his grandmother to his intentions. Whatever would he think to find her here instead of Blanche? Whatever would Blanche think if she got to hear of it?

Flora was so overwhelmed by her thoughts that she nervously refused the refreshments Penton offered and sank down into the nearest chair and stared somewhat blindly in front of her. What an embarrassing position she was in; it was as if she was here under false pretences. She picked up a copy of *The Englishwoman's Domestic Magazine* and began flicking through its pages when the door opened and Sir George Kingsley entered. Flora jumped up and knocked the magazine onto the floor in her embarrassment.

'I'm Miss Peat. I am only waiting for Daisy,' she stammered, suddenly conscious of a creased skirt. 'I am sorry, am I in your room?' She looked agitatedly around. 'But your butler did show me in here.'

'It is quite all right,' said George reassuringly, and came in. 'I am Sir George Kingsley.' They shook hands. 'Are you being looked after? Why has Penton not brought you anything to drink?' He reached out for the bell pull.

'No, no, I do not wish anything,' said Flora, feeling terribly flustered. Whereas before she had felt it an imposition to accept some wine and cakes, now she felt she had committed a social solecism in not doing so.

George had come in with the intention of snubbing Blanche quite comprehensively, but being balked of his prey he found himself treating Flora with an over-conscious politeness. Flora felt his condescension and was both intimidated and annoyed by it.

'Now, let me see, Miss Peat,' George continued with affable superiority, 'are you not the one who likes books?'

'Yes, I suppose I am,' said Flora sullenly. She disliked his tone of voice, as if he thought she read only Ouida or the sentimental romances in the magazines.

'Your sister, Miss Blanche, mentioned it,' George continued. 'She said that you were quite a blue-stocking.'

'I have not had the education to be a blue-stocking,' said Flora frostily. 'But, yes, I do enjoy reading.'

'Would you care to choose some books from the library,' asked George in a kinder tone. 'There is not much choice here.'

'Yes, I would. Thank you very much.'

'Come and have a look then.' He held the door open for her and Flora followed him across the marble hall and into the library.

There were shelves from floor to ceiling on three walls of the

60

library, even around the top of the door and up to either side of the fireplace. The fourth wall was a large bow window with a cushioned window seat overlooking the lawn. In the space between the windowframe and the corner of the wall was a vertical row of pictures. There were a couple of hunting pictures, a family tree, some Japanese prints and an assortment of tiles in vivid blues and greens, brought back by Sir George from Arabia.

In front of the bay window was a large mahogany desk covered with papers. The room had a large Turkey carpet on the floor and several leather-covered armchairs and a large Chesterfield, designed with comfort rather than elegance in mind. In front of the fireplace was a large brass fender with a leather seat, above it was a portrait of Sir George and his brother and on the mantel-piece an assortment of curios.

'Oh, what a lovely room!' cried Flora, gazing round and touching the leather bindings gently. She wandered along slowly, looking at the books, every now and then touching the heavy embossed leather with the stamped Kingsley crest in gold on the back. 'Oh, I wish we had a proper library at home. At least, Papa has some books in his study and I have mine upstairs, but this is a proper room for books.'

He liked books! He even had the works of Charles Darwin. He could not be such a stuck-up prig as she had at first thought him.

George found himself warming towards her. She was quite a nice, unaffected girl after all, and she could not help being gawky and badly dressed. At least she was not on the catch, like that odious sister of hers.

'What would you like then? I imagine I have most things.'

'I should like to read Burton's *First Footsteps in East Africa* please, if you have it.'

George looked at her in alarm. 'Why do you wish to read that? It is a man's book, surely?'

'Is it?' asked Flora. 'Why? I did wish to buy it, but Papa would not allow me. You see, he knows Mr Arundell who says that Burton is a dreadful scoundrel. Although I must say it seems a little hard to call your son-in-law a scoundrel.'

George allowed himself to smile and handed her the book. After all, there was no harm in the girl, even if she did have some curious tastes.

'Here you are, then. Only keep it out of Papa's way, would you? But he is wrong about Burton, you know. He is a most interesting man.'

'You know him!'

'Yes, that is to say, I met him out in Aden in '54. He is probably the most remarkable man I have ever met, a brilliant linguist, with a powerful, original mind. But he is not a happy man. His ideas are too shocking for our timid bureaucracy. I have always thought that he should have been an Elizabethan.'

'Papa says Mr Speke is much more of a gentleman.'

'If you like muscular Christians.'

'And you do not?'

George shrugged. 'Not sanctimonious prigs. I believe Speke has treated Burton very badly over the Nile business. I doubt whether he has heard the last of it. There has been some talk of a public debate, perhaps with Livingstone to chair it.'

'Well, if there is, I shall be there,' said Flora smiling, 'and I shall probably carry a placard supporting Burton!'

Flora was meaning only to amuse, but George had this sudden vision of her as one of those dreadful women like Josephine Butler, protesting about things they ought to know nothing of. She had a total lack of womanly modesty.

'I hope you enjoy your book, Miss Peat,' he said dismissively, and turned back to his desk.

He wanted her out of his room. Why should he waste his valuable time talking to some dowdy girl? He had work to do. He had yet to decide whether he needed any more fishing line before he went down to Linchmere. She was not a lady, no lady would ever come in and demand to read Richard Burton. Whatever had Grandmama been thinking of to allow these tradespeople into the house? It was all very well for her to say that the Peats would not bother them, she was not the one who had to deal with them.

Flora, flushed and mortified, swiftly left the library. She hated him! He was self-satisfied and stuck-up and above his company. How could he humiliate her so, turning her out so abruptly? She had done nothing to deserve it.

Should she not have mentioned Burton? But if so, why did he continue the conversation? Or was he angry at finding her there and not Blanche? But he must have known that it was not her fault. Oh, why did she ever agree to come?

When Flora returned home she found that she was evading all the questions. She told herself that she did not wish to parade her humiliations in front of her mother and Blanche. In any case, she was now several chapters into *First Footsteps in East Africa* and wanted to finish it.

'I suppose the high and mighty Sir George Kingsley was there, working in his fusty old library?' remarked Blanche, stabbing at the meat on her plate.

'I believe he was in the library,' said Flora vaguely, 'but I understand that he will be going down to Linchmere soon, is that not right, Daisy?'

'Then we shall keep to our present arrangement,' said Mrs Peat, glancing at Blanche's stony face. 'So please do not complain, Flora. It is a little enough thing to do for me, after all.'

'Very well, Mama,' said Flora, and the subject was allowed to drop.

Having embarked on a course of subterfuge, Flora found it impossible to confess to Adeline that she had evaded the truth. She had meant to pour out her indignation at Sir George's behaviour in Adeline's ear – she knew Adeline would be sympathetic and concerned for the slight on her sister. But whatever would her sister say about her borrowing a book Papa had forbidden her to read, let alone discussing Richard Burton with a man? Would Adeline not say, and rightly, that his morality must be dubious? But of course it did not matter how openminded Sir George was about some things, now that she knew he was so detestable.

She said nothing.

That afternoon Adeline began to pack up all her things and Flora went with her up to their bedroom to help. Two new haircord trunks stood in the corner of the bedroom. One of them was nearly filled with Adeline's new linen and underwear, all wrapped neatly in layers of tissue paper. The other trunk Adeline was packing with all the books, ornaments and knick-knacks she had acquired over the years. There was a growing pile of old toys and dolls on the floor, waiting to be taken to the Children's Hospital.

Few of Flora's toys had survived childhood, but Adeline's were all neat and mended. Her dolls still had their hair on, their clothes were fresh and neat, and no bonnets, parasols or ribbons were missing. Half a dozen dolls sat in a neat row at the bottom of the bed. Their wax faces with slightly parted lips, faintly rouged cheeks and glass eyes stared sadly in front of them.

'But Adeline,' protested Flora, sinking down on the bed and picking up a doll with fair curls and blue glass eyes. 'Look, here's Princess Rosina, how can you bear to give her away? Ah, Rosina, what a lot of adventures you had. Look, here is the chip where she fell out of the nursery window trying to be Rapunzel. And there is Rabbit.' Flora picked up from the toy pile a rabbit, with one cloth ear not quite matching the other and droopy black wool whiskers, and hugged it. 'You are cruel, Adeline. How can you bear to?'

'Put them down, Flora,' said Adeline, turning away.

'But Adeline, you will have children soon. Do you not wish your daughters to have Rosina and your other toys?'

'Do not be so disgusting, Flora,' said Adeline icily. 'You have the most unwomanly, common mind, sometimes.'

'I think that is most unfair,' cried Flora, stung and hurt. 'When you and Charles marry, you will have children, everybody knows that.'

Adeline turned with a set, grim face and strode over to Flora. She seized the rabbit and doll from Flora and hurled them onto the pile of toys on the floor. Then she seized the other dolls on the bed and threw them down too, threw them with little savage cries deep in her throat.

'Go away, Flora, go away, do you hear me? You are talking about disgusting things, horrible things. I do not wish to talk about it, or think about it. I wish to rid myself of everything and start again.' She drew in several quick breaths and Flora could see the pulse in her neck fluttering. 'I shall be making a solemn sacrifice, Flora. I shall be serving God through Charles. Nothing must get in the way, do you hear?'

'Adeline, Adeline,' cried Flora alarmed. 'You do not know what you are saying! Please, please think very carefully. You cannot sacrifice yourself like this! You are blinding yourself. Charles is a very ordinary doctor with an eye to getting on in the world. He is not very sensitive, not very clever, and he is the kind of man who . . .'

'Stop!' cried Adeline, putting her hands over her ears. 'I have said yes and I shall marry him. You are wrong, Flora. God has shown me His will and I must follow it.' She took several deep gulps of air and walked in a distracted way across the room, pulling aside the heavy lace curtains for a minute and letting the sun flood into the room and then dropping them again.

'Take Rosina and Rabbit, if you wish, Flora, and anything else you may care for. But leave me alone. Never, never bring this up again, Flora. I am perfectly happy and I am doing God's will. I am absolutely certain in my own mind.' Her eyes, usually so mild, were bright and challenging.

'Very well, Adeline,' said Flora sadly, 'but if you ever need me . . .'

Adeline opened her mouth as if to say something and then shut it again, and turning her back on Flora, continued silently with her packing. Flora picked up Rosina and Rabbit and left the room. Adeline did not turn.

Sir George did not go down to Linchmere, so Flora found herself seeing him most mornings. She either met him in the hall and they exchanged a few polite words or he came into the Pink Saloon to enquire after her. At first Flora found his politeness most unnerving, she stammered and blushed and dreaded hearing his footsteps coming across the hall, but gradually George's 'Good mornings' lost their formality and became more friendly. He would stay for a few minutes and chat about the book that Flora was reading. He had an intelligent and trenchant wit and Flora found his observations both stimulating and amusing.

She began to feel more at home there. Daisy took her up to the schoolroom and introduced her to Miss Martin, Grace's governess. She met Lady Kingsley, who seemed quite unalarming, although extremely sharp and needle-witted. Lady Kingsley saw no harm in Flora and even praised her manners to George. 'A bit of a plain Jane, of course, but nice manners. I hope you are kind to her, George?'

'I do not see much of her,' said George indifferently, 'but when I do, I smile and am polite.'

'Good. Of course William Peat is just nobody at all, and it would not do to become too familiar.'

George said nothing, but whether in a mood of defiance, or whether he had decided to do it anyway, he asked Flora if she would like to come into the library the following morning.

'Penton,' he called, 'Miss Peat is in the library with me. Bring the wine in here, would you please?'

It was the second time Flora had been in the library and this time she felt freer to look around. She looked at the curios and asked him about his travels. George found her intelligent and interesting and was impressed in spite of himself.

'Where did this come from?' asked Flora. 'It looks like a capital.'

'It is. It comes from Palmyra. I picked it up a couple of years ago.'

'Ah yes, Zenobia.'

'You are very well read, Miss Peat.'

'I know only what I have read in Gibbon,' replied Flora apologetically. 'I have travelled nowhere, done nothing. Do not begrudge me the little knowledge I pick up.'

'You are perfectly entitled to be as clever as you please,' said George coldly.

Flora stopped feeling apologetic and began instead to feel cross. She walked across to George's desk and stopped in front of the family tree and looked at it. It was written in very neat italic script with a border of beautifully coloured coats of arms. The Kingsley family itself went back in a direct line to Sir Paul Kingsley and there was a small inscription under his name saying why he was honoured by Charles II and where his lands came from. The remainder appeared to be Lady Kingsley's family tree, for it was her ancestors who sprawled over the rest of the paper. Nearer the bottom of the paper the family contented themselves with earls and honourables but at the top of the page were the unlikely names of William the Conqueror, Llewellyn the Great and one of the High Kings of Ireland. Flora looked at it carefully. Why it was preposterous! No rational man could take such a tangle of fairy-tales seriously, especially one who had the works of Darwin in his library.

'It is highly selective,' she said at last.

'Whatever do you mean?' George came over, prepared to be amused.

'It goes back eight centuries, if this William, Duke of Normandy, is accurate.'

'Yes, it does,' said George with pride. 'I believe we can trace our family back to William the Conqueror.'

'That is thirty generations,' said Flora sceptically. 'About nine hundred ancestors if you go back as far as that. You have precisely six here on the top line. I daresay even I could go back as far as William the Conqueror if I was as selective as that.'

'We are directly linked with the Plantagenets through the Beaufort line,' said Sir George angrily. His lips had tightened and he was staring at Flora with an expression not far removed from fury.

'But most of them are not even Kingsleys,' protested Flora. 'And who was McMurrough, King of Leinster anyway?'

How dared she! A jumped-up tradesman's daughter and she dared to criticize him! George's fury was all the greater because Flora had hit unwittingly on the weak points in George's pride in his breeding. Most of it came through his grandmother and not through the Kingsleys at all and he himself did not know who McMurrough, King of Leinster was. He had always contemplated his family tree with the eyes of welling emotion and pride; Flora now forced him to look at it with the eyes of reason.

'You are going too far, Miss Peat. I am proud to be descended from so many illustrious lines. I hope and trust that I shall continue in a tradition of honourable service to my country as my ancestors have done. Your father, I am sure, is a very worthy man but there is a certain dignity and pride that comes only from breeding.'

'There is nothing very honourable about Sir Paul Kingsley,' retorted Flora. 'He received his title from Charles II and royal thanks for giving information, and he acquired an estate of sequestered lands from Cromwell for "services rendered". God knows what happened to the wretched family whose lands he took. They were less "honourable" I suppose.'

George felt an urge to take her by the neck and shake and shake her until she hung limp and broken. Instead he took a step closer to her and said, in a voice whose fury even Flora could not mistake, 'I suppose you think that your wretched family, who come from the dregs of society, are to be counted on equal terms with mine!'

Flora spun round to face him. 'Yes, I do. But I am making no claims for my family and no apologies either. It is you who are making false pretensions for yours!' Flora found herself trembling so violently that she had to put her hand on the desk to steady herself. She felt a sudden rush of tears to her eyes and with a half-murmured excuse swiftly left the room.

She went into the Pink Saloon, shut the door, sank down on the nearest chair and burst into overwrought tears. He was pompous and overbearing, he did not like to be criticized and he was a stuck-up, self-satisfied boor. Flora's rage flowed angrily through her tears for several minutes when a thought struck her cold. Supposing he stopped Daisy's lessons? Supposing he found her so objectionable that he told Lady Kingsley? However had she been led to treat him so rudely? If he thought too much of himself that was a fault shared by many men. Who was she to disillusion him? It was none of her business who his ancestors were. Why had she not let it ride?

She got up, dried her eyes and began pacing the room, deep in thought. She paced for many minutes, her hands clasped behind her back, a frown on her face. Finally, she took a deep breath and went to the door. She walked across the marble hall and knocked on the door of the library.

'Come in,' called a curt voice.

'I have come to apologize,' said Flora, still very pale and her eyes suspiciously red.

George did not look up from his desk.

'I had no right to pass remarks about your family. And I did not mean to insult you. Please believe me. I am truly very sorry.'

George rose from his chair and came towards her.

'Have you been crying?' he asked, reluctantly. Flora turned her face away. George felt acutely uncomfortable. 'Let us forget the whole incident,' he said quickly, striving for a safe, neutral tone.

'That is what I would like,' whispered Flora.

But the topic lay between them, unresolved.

68

Sir George convinced himself that it was all Flora's fault. She herself had admitted as much by coming to apologize to him. He would be magnanimous, as befitted a gentleman, and allow no word of the matter to pass his lips: he would treat her with scrupulous politeness. He even went so far as to choose some books he thought she might like and put them in the Pink Saloon. He greeted her every day with a cool 'Good morning' and spent some minutes enquiring punctiliously after her family.

He was not destined to pursue this course of action for many days for, returning from Berkeley Square on Friday, Flora found the house in an uproar. Old Mrs Peat had had a minor stroke.

'How typical,' said Flora's mother crossly. 'Just when I am up to my ears in preparations for Adeline's wedding. You must help nurse her, Flora. I am sure I cannot spare the time and she will not have a trained nurse.'

'But what about Daisy's lessons?'

'Nanny must take her. I cannot spare Lottie, because I need her to mark Adeline's linen. How selfish old people can be.'

'Of course I shall look after her. I shall go up straight away.'

Old Mrs Peat was lying in bed, propped up by pillows. Her face looked grey and drawn and her vitality seemed to have drained away. There was some red medicine in a bottle beside her bedside table but, apart from that, it did not look as if anything had been done for her. The grate was not cleared, nor the bed tidied. Flora peeped into the sitting-room. Sarah was lying on the sofa, fully dressed but with her shoes kicked off and lying where she had left them. She was asleep and snoring. She had probably been up with Mrs Peat all night. Flora wondered with a pang of anxiety for how long such attacks had been going on carefully concealed from the rest of the family. She tugged at the bell-pull and then sat down by Mrs Peat and took her hand.

'Oh, you are awake, I hope I did not wake you up. You do look poorly, Granny. But I have come to look after you.'

A maid came in and Flora quietly directed her to tidy up and clear the grate. Flora then buttoned up Mrs Peat's night-dress, changed her night-cap and found her a shawl.

'Thank you, pet. That is much better.'

'How are you feeling, Granny? Would you like to sleep? Shall I leave you?'

'No, I'm all right now, pet. I've had these little turns before, Flora. They're nothing to worry about.'

'We shall see what the doctor says. Now, you are not to worry, Granny. I am staying at home to look after you until you are better.'

Flora spoke cheerfully, but she was worried by the suddenness and ease with which her apparently indestructible grandmother could slip from an earthy vitality to this frail exhaustion. She mentioned her anxieties to Dr Thomas Woodcock, Charles' father, on his visit. Dr Woodcock looked at Flora over his glasses for a moment or two.

'Now, now, Flora,' he said kindly, patting her hand, 'she will be all right. Fortunately the attack was a minor one, and with care and attention you may have her with you for some years yet. She needs plenty of rest and to keep calm.'

'But she told me that as a child, working in the mills, she suffered from breathlessness and dizzy turns,' said Flora anxiously.

'Quite so.' Dr Woodcock thought such things were best forgotten. 'I believe that was caused by damp inadequate housing and poor diet. It may have nothing to do with the case, Flora. During the years your father has been able to look after her, she has had good health, which leads me to be optimistic about her chances now.'

'You must tell me exactly what to do. You know that Mama is busy with Adeline's wedding. Sarah and I are nursing her.'

'You must keep her on a very low diet, a little gruel or arrowroot only. I mention this, Flora, because well-meaning but ignorant people can severely retard recovery by giving patients fruit or other wholly unsuitable food. I shall come every day and apply blisters and mustard poultices. I have bled her, which should help. And the bowels should be opened as freely as possible – I have left you a bottle of castor oil and calomel.'

He looked at Flora with slight unease. He disliked discussing such details with a lady, but Flora was a sensible girl. In any case, his first duty was to his patient. What a pity she would not accept a trained nurse.

'There is no cause for concern,' he said kindly. 'Now mind, Flora, that you have some sleep. I shall call again tomorrow.'

Flora nursed Mrs Peat for two weeks, there was no relapse

and she made steady progress towards recovery. Several times, as they were quietly talking, Flora tried to tell her grandmother about the quarrel she had had with Sir George Kingsley and how she had not mentioned it to her mother, allowing her to go on thinking that she sat with Daisy up in the schoolroom, but somehow the words never came. She told herself in the end that her Granny would not wish to be worried by tales of her granddaughter being insulted. It was not at all important, Flora decided. What was important was that Granny should get well again. Nothing else mattered but that.

At the end of two weeks Mrs Peat made enough progress to sit in her chair and look out into the garden. She no longer needed Flora or Sarah constantly by her side.

Adeline's wedding was now a mere ten days away, and Flora returned to the Kingsleys to chaperone Daisy once more.

The Kingsley house was quiet when Flora and Daisy arrived the following day. Penton seemed surprised to see Flora, but he greeted her arrival with a quiet smile and took the liberty of asking after her grandmother. He escorted her into the Pink Saloon and promised her some refreshments. The room looked bare and cold and Flora wondered where Nanny had waited. She took off her jacket, but she felt chilly and put it on again. She walked carefully around the room, looking with pleasure at the now familiar ornaments and pictures and going to the window to see the garden. Outside the autumn chrysanthemums and dahlias were glowing brightly orange and white and yellow and there was a gardener on the lawn sweeping up the first of the fallen leaves. Flora turned back to the room, found *Jane Eyre* in one of the alcoves and, with the pleasantly guilty knowledge that it was one of the books Mama had expressly forbidden her to read, sat down with it.

Penton came in with some wine and biscuits. She heard him talking to somebody in the hall and a few moments later Sir George came in.

'Good morning, Miss Peat. I trust that your grandmother is better?'

'Yes, thank you, Sir George.'

'I am happy to see you again. Your nanny terrified me.'

'Oh dear, whatever did she do?' Flora looked at him a little doubtfully but he was smiling.

'She glowered at me every time I came in and clicked her knitting needles. I do not think that she actually spoke, but I had the distinct impression that she would have liked to order me upstairs to wash my hands.'

Flora laughed. 'Oh, she is dreadful, she always was. But it is not you she was glowering at, it was Grace's governess.'

'What is the matter with Miss Martin, for Heaven's sake?'

'She is French.'

'Half-French,' corrected George.

'That makes no difference to Nanny,' replied Flora. 'She thinks Miss Martin is either a revolutionary or has libertine propensities.'

'Good God!' said George blankly, unable to imagine Miss Martin, who was meek, rather skinny, and on the shady side of forty, in either role.

'And,' added Flora darkly, seeing that George was prepared to be amused, 'she said that she suspected Miss Martin read "French" books!'

George gave a shout of laughter. 'Capital! I must admit she sat there a bit like a tricoteuse herself.' He stopped and looked at Flora. 'Why are you still wearing your jacket? Are you cold?'

'No, no. I am quite warm, thank you.'

'Nonsense, Miss Peat. You are cold. I'll order a fire for you.' Flora opened her mouth to protest. 'Do not try to be polite, Miss Peat. It is freezing in here.' He pulled the bell.

He is obviously in a good mood this morning, thought Flora. I must be careful not to annoy him again.

Penton appeared and George gave his orders for a fire to be lit. He then shook hands with Flora, smiled on her quite tolerantly, and returned to his library.

A few days before the wedding Mrs Peat sat in her dressing-room and watched her maid put the finishing touches to her hair.

'Thank you, Briggs. That looks very nice. Now would you bring the satin chair over here, please. No, not too close.' She arranged the chair and cushion with careful informality. 'Yes, I think that will do. Would you tell Miss Adeline that I want a word with her? And I do not wish to be disturbed, Briggs.'

A few moments later, a pale and subdued Adeline scratched at the door. 'What is it, Mama?'

'Sit down, my dear.' Mrs Peat fiddled with the gold-topped scent bottles on her dressing-table. 'Now Adeline, you are to be married in a few days' time. I think it only right that you should not enter into the married state in complete ignorance.'

Adeline said nothing.

'The relationship between a man and his wife is not the same after marriage as it is before,' began Mrs Peat, hesitantly. 'A man may expect certain things of his wife after marriage that would be completely out of place before it. Do you understand me, Adeline?'

'Yes, Mama,' replied Adeline in a stifled voice.

'When that moment comes, Adeline, I expect you to submit, however distasteful it may seem. My dear mother told me always to remember that you must never allow your husband to suspect that you are not perfectly acquiescent. I found it very good advice. Charles has the right to expect his wife to be pure and refined in the performance of her marital duties. Anything else belongs to a lower order of Society. I hope I have made myself clear. Do you wish to ask me any questions?'

'No, thank you, Mama.'

'Very well, my dear,' said Mrs Peat with relief. 'I think that is all. You will be wanting to get on with your thank you letters, I expect.'

Adeline rose and left the room.

Adeline woke up very early on the morning of her wedding day and slipped out of bed quietly so as not to disturb Flora. She went over to the day-bed and sat down to read the Gospel and Epistle for the week. She read slowly and carefully, then marked her place with a bookmark and put the prayer book carefully in her trunk to go with the rest of her things to her new home in Upper Cavendish Street.

She tried to think of the day ahead, of her promises and vows and the solemnity of the step she was taking, but all she felt was that she was cold and rather sick. She seemed to be quite numb inside. All the anxieties and worries were gone, leaving her totally distant and calm. Perhaps it was God's way, she thought, of helping her through the ordeal. He had calmed her emotions and raised her to a more distant plane so that she could cope more easily with her new role of wife. She offered up a silent prayer of thanks and then went to her jewellery box and took out a small parcel that had arrived the day before. Inside was a pair of diamond ear-rings with a letter from Charles.

My own wife,

This is a small token of my affection for you, to commemorate our marriage. They belonged to my grandmother, who was, my father says, a most noble woman and an inspiration to her husband and all who knew her. I have every confidence, my dear Adeline, that you will be the repository of all my noblest hopes and ambitions. I remain affectionately yours,

Charles Woodcock

Adeline tried to re-live the elation she had felt on first receiving the letter, but it had vanished. In its place was a dull dread and terror of what was to come; an ignorance which even Mama's helpful words had done nothing to dispel. For a moment Adeline thought of waking Flora and confiding in her, telling her that it was all a dreadful mistake, that she could not go through with it. But it was too late for all that. She had made her choice with her eyes open and must abide by it.

The day began. Maids came in, laughing and excited, to do her hair and help her into her petticoats and corsets. She was brought her tea and breakfast in bed, but could eat nothing. Sly remarks were passed on her lack of appetite. Her hair was dressed in a dignified chignon with careful curls pinned at the sides to help secure the veil. Her dress, heavy and ivory-coloured, was slipped over her head and fastened at the back with little loops.

Adeline sat quite still through all this, hardly noticing the chatter and excitement behind her. She looked at herself in the glass. A pale face looked back at her, shrouded in white, with heavy blossoms of lilies and white rosebuds in her hair.

'You look beautiful, Adeline,' Flora was saying. 'A little pale perhaps, but most queenly and dignified, does she not, Briggs?'

'Perhaps a touch of rouge, Miss?' suggested Briggs, who was

privately appalled at the wax-like figure in front of her.

'No, no,' said Adeline, shuddering.

'Well, well, your veil will be down until after the wedding, anyway,' said Briggs, 'and I daresay your husband will put roses in your cheeks before long!'

'That will do, Briggs,' said Adeline calmly.

Adeline moved through the wedding service as if in a dream. She tried to concentrate but past images kept slipping into her mind: herself and Flora sitting together in the den waiting for the news of Daisy's birth; herself cuddling her doll; the day she twisted her ankle and the doctor giving her a boiled sweet which she hated, but kept in the pouch of her cheek so as not to hurt his feelings.

She made her responses in a flat, almost toneless voice, hardly aware of what she was saying or why. Charles standing beside her seemed a blurred image, his ring on her finger heavy like a lead weight. Part of her wondered what she was doing there. She did not look at her mother, who was sitting in the front row, delicately dabbing at her cheeks with a lace handkerchief. Once she caught Flora's eye, but looked away. Flora's look of love and pity was more than she could bear. 'This is the most solemn moment of my whole life,' she kept saying to herself.

Charles was staring steadfastly at the stained-glass window. He was hungry. He had been on a spree with Philip Rivers the night before, had returned home late and as a consequence he overslept. He had had to gulp down his kidneys on toast in a way that he knew would give him indigestion later. Then he had lost the ring and he and Philip had a frantic search for it and finally discovered that it had been tossed into the dirty-linen basket along with his shirt.

The service ended. Adeline waited for Charles to raise her veil. He did so, and the sudden clearing of her vision made her blink. Charles' face bent down and Adeline offered him her cheek.

'Thank God that is over,' he said, squeezing her arm. 'I did not have much breakfast, you know, and I am starving.'

'I shall try to be a good wife to you,' whispered Adeline, desperately looking for some reassurance in his face.

'Well, the first thing you can do, my dear, is to feed the Inner Man. After we have signed the Register, of course.'

The search in Adeline's eyes faded. She smiled carefully.

'Of course, Charles.' She put her hand on his arm and moved towards the vestry.

It all went off very well, thought Mrs Peat, after the reception was over. All that was left of the wedding breakfast were piles of dirty plates and glasses and Adeline's wedding presents. They had been duly displayed and admired and must now be packed up and sent off to Upper Cavendish Street.

It had been the most elegant affair, two hundred guests to a buffet lunch in the two drawing-rooms. She had managed to have a discreet word with the Editor of the Court Circular and kept his glass filled with the best champagne. If there were not a few tributes to the elegant Mrs William Peat and her ravishing younger daughter, she would be very much surprised.

Blanche, too, had reason to be satisfied with the wedding breakfast. She had had a most satisfactory talk with Hugh Dunster. She knew now that he liked her, more than liked her if only he would allow himself to admit it.

'How is dear Alice?' Blanche asked, smiling at Hugh and carefully pulling out the puffs on the pink silk of her sleeves and blowing an imaginary speck of dust off her shoulder.

'Very well,' said Hugh shortly. 'She's on some boating trip with a party of friends. Sounds rather noisy and messy to me.' Hugh, in fact, was sulking as he had not been invited. The hostess of the boating trip did not approve of Alice's interest in such a wastrel.

'I am very glad that you could spare the time to come here,' said Blanche softly. 'You know, Hugh, I think you and I are alike in being rather discriminating in our choice of friends. I do not care for a noisy crowd of people. I prefer to know one or two people intimately.'

Hugh turned and looked at her. 'Who do you choose for your intimate friends, I wonder?'

'I choose exactly whom I like,' replied Blanche. 'I act purely on instinct and I make up my mind about people very, very quickly.'

Hugh glanced round at the guests and then leant closer to Blanche. 'What would you say if I asked you to be my friend?'

'Why don't you ask me, and see,' replied Blanche very softly.

On the other side of the room Charles was standing with a group of bachelor friends who were toasting him in champagne. There was a lot of male laughter and then a hush as a sly voice whispered some innuendo or salacious joke, followed by a roar of approval.

'That's right, Charles,' cried out one wag, 'give her a shot of your physic.'

Adeline, at the top of the room talking to Cousin Helen, smiled nervously and tried to concentrate on what Cousin Helen was saying. Soon afterwards, accompanied by Flora, she went upstairs to change before leaving for her honeymoon. The next time I come here, she thought, I shall be a wife. And she shuddered.

The guests slowly departed and Flora was left to wander around the drawing-room among the half-eaten oyster patties, feeling somewhat forlorn. She had not been able to eat much during the wedding breakfast, but now she felt hungry. She found a clean plate and began helping herself to some lobster salad and veal and ham pie. Around her the maids were beginning to clear up. The room looked shabby now and the presents tawdry. The floor was covered in crumbs, bits of salad and splashes of drink. The side table, which was loaded with Adeline's presents, dominated by the superb silver cutlery, bowls and serving dishes 'from the bride's parents', took on the appearance of having been hired for the occasion.

Flora thought of Adeline, now in the closed carriage that was carrying her and Charles to Paddington station and the Windsor train. She had been so cold, so reserved, as if keeping off anyone who might address a kind word to her. Flora could not reach her. Even Adeline's last words to her were disquieting. 'I have made a great and holy sacrifice,' she said. 'My life is henceforth dedicated to Charles.'

'Dear God, let it be all right,' Flora prayed frantically, fearing she knew not what. Let Charles be kind and Adeline have the happiness she deserves.

Charles and Adeline spent their wedding night in Windsor. Charles had behaved with exemplary politeness and escorted

Adeline to the foot of the stairs half an hour before he came up to bed, so that she might get undressed and ready for bed without the embarrassment of having him by while she struggled with stays. Adeline undressed, brushed her hair, said her prayers and climbed into bed.

Charles came up, fortified, did she but know it, by several glasses of port. He undressed – Adeline turned her face to the wall – turned down the wick and blew out the lamp. He climbed into bed and turned to her.

'Now, my dear, let us get down to business.' Charles meant to sound friendly, even jocular, and he was prepared to be understanding of her qualms. Adeline did not move. Encouraged by this acquiescence, Charles pulled up her night-dress. Adeline gasped and tried to push it down again.

'No, no, Charles, what are you doing?'

Now Charles' hands were under her night-dress and moved up to her breasts, squeezing and pumping them. Not bad bubbies, my God, thought Charles with satisfaction.

Adeline was almost rigid with shock. 'No, no, please,' she begged, her voice shaking. 'Oh, don't, please don't.' She tried to push his hands away.

'But we are married,' said Charles impatiently.

Adeline tried to turn over onto her front. 'No, no, please.' She found she could say nothing else. 'No, no, please don't, please don't.' The shock drove everything else out of her head. Oh, God, this cannot be happening to me. 'No, no, please don't.'

Charles put one arm heavily across her to keep her still and bent over to suck her nipples. With his other hand he stuffed her breast into his mouth. Adeline tried to struggle but could not. She could feel something hard pushing against her leg but could not think what it might be. She started to kick.

Charles removed his hand from her breast and put it between her legs. Adeline snapped her legs shut. She began to heave her body about violently, trying to get him off, to get rid of this heavy body by her side. She was becoming hysterical and starting to cry.

With a sudden jerk she caught Charles in the throat. He choked and loosened his grip and with a bound Adeline was out of bed, tearing off a blanket to cover herself. She ran to a corner of the room and crouched there, panting and sobbing.

'Do not come near me. It was all a mistake, please let it be a mistake. I do not want to marry you. Charles, you must believe me.' Her voice was shaking and the sobs tearing in her throat.

Charles got out of bed, his face flushed with anger: anger against Mrs Peat for not instructing her daughter in her duties and against Adeline for rejecting his advances. But he felt waves of excitement too. Adeline's twisting, writhing body and her pitiful cries had roused him to such a pitch of lust that he could hardly control himself. He could feel his penis hard and hot against his stomach. He wanted to twist her legs apart and ram himself into her and feel the hot seed coming out of him in spurts.

Adeline had never seen a naked man before and the sight of his erection, huge, red and angry-looking terrified her. It was disgusting, horrible, something animal and brutish, like the man himself. She glanced at his face. It was contorted with rage so that he looked like a total stranger to her.

Charles grabbed both her shoulders and pulled her to her feet. He tore off the blanket and then, as she raised her hands to cover her nakedness, slapped her twice across the face. He took hold of her arm roughly and dragged her back to bed.

'You're my wife, don't you understand?' he shouted.

'No, no, never,' cried Adeline. 'It's disgusting, I never thought. Oh Charles, don't make me, please don't . . .'

Charles took no notice. He threw her down on the bed, pinned her down with his hands and forced her legs apart with his knees. He pushed into Adeline with all his strength, felt something give and came almost at once. Adeline gave a scream of pain, followed by a long shuddering moan, which died away in whimpering sobs.

Charles rolled off her and pretended to fall asleep. Adeline lay crying for a long time, biting her pillow to muffle her sobs. She hugged herself with her arms and rocked backwards and forwards. She felt the trickle of something between her legs and looking down saw a spreading patch of blood. She looked at it in horror, her sobs arrested. At first she thought that Charles had actually stabbed her in his anger and then that somehow he had caused her to haemorrhage and that she would slowly die. Well, it did not matter, she thought wearily, nothing mattered any more. She felt utterly drained and dead, as if something was broken inside her.

The pain between her legs subsided to a dull ache. Adeline lay with her eyes shut, feeling the blood seeping down with a kind of resigned languor. Soon it would be over. She would sink slowly into unconsciousness and that would be the end. Then bit by bit fear began to trickle back into her. She was not prepared for death. Might it not be a kind of suicide? Should she not do something? Call a doctor or at least ask for help?

'Charles,' she whispered at last.

Charles grunted sleepily.

'Charles, I am sorry to disturb you. But I seem to be bleeding.'

'There's a towel by the window,' said Charles sleepily and turned over.

Adeline got out of bed shakily, wincing as she walked and the torn edges rubbed together. She found the towel and crept back to bed, stuffing it between her legs.

She lay for a long time staring at the ceiling. It was dawn before she fell asleep.

Chapter Four

Flora felt ashamed of herself and guilty too. With Adeline gone she realized suddenly how oppressive the atmosphere was around her sister. Flora had not considered before the extent to which Adeline dampened down and repressed any ordinary flow of spirits and affections. It did not take effect until a week or so after the wedding, when all at once she found herself ringing the bell for the maid and ordering the room to be altered around, the desk brought forward, the pier-glass placed so that the light from the window struck it, and the armchair brought nearer the fire. She then went through her winter wardrobe and discarded the suitable grey and brown merinos she had worn the previous year. She threw her brown Talma mantle onto the bed, it suddenly seemed dowdy. It was too short for one thing, she could not imagine how she had not noticed it before. She would buy herself a smart sealskin jacket for the winter.

Sir George came into the Pink Saloon one morning and asked Flora about the wedding. He had read about it in *The Times* and it sounded most elegant – privately he thought it sounded ostentatious to a degree, but he was being polite to his guest and taking an interest in her concerns.

'It went off very well, thank you,' said Flora, 'but there were too many people there for comfort. At least, I do not care for that kind of squeeze myself. However, everybody else enjoyed it, I think.'

George gathered that the display of wealth was not entirely to her taste and he smiled at her approvingly.

'Well, what are you reading now, Miss Peat? Ah, I see it is *Jane Eyre*. Are you enjoying it?'

Flora confided that Mama had forbidden her to read it, but that yes, she was enjoying it immensely. 'I do not know what Mama thinks is so dreadful about it,' she finished, 'but I have not yet reached the end, so perhaps there is some truly scandalous revelation to come.'

'I believe many people find it shocking that Jane declares her feelings for Mr Rochester before he has declared his intentions towards her.'

'But Rochester is not shocked,' observed Flora. 'I suppose ladies may be allowed to have feelings, even if they are not sanctioned by masculine authorization?'

'Indubitably, Miss Peat.' George disapproved somewhat of this open championship of Jane's position. If Flora had found the book shocking, as he had suspected she might, with her dowdiness and social gaucherie, he would have been amused and tolerant and perhaps attempted to coax her out of it. As it was, he found himself thinking with disfavour that there was a lack of feminine modesty about her reactions.

'You think me indelicate,' said Flora, looking at him anxiously, 'but I am sure that I would never, never dare declare my affections with the freedom that Jane shows.'

George laughed: Flora's admission disarmed him and he felt his annoyance melt away. 'Well, I am pleased that you like it and it has provoked an interesting discussion between us. Do you wish me to do you a book list?'

'Oh, would you? Miss Speedwell, when I was at school, used to do book lists for us, but they were always boring works of a highly moral nature.'

'Do I take it you wish me to give you a list of highly immoral books?'

'Do you have any?' Flora blurted out before she could stop herself.

George laughed. Flora blushed crimson and turned her head away. 'Really, Miss Peat! I suppose that if I admit it you will be demanding to read them!'

'I am sorry, I should not have said that. It comes from talking to Granny, she always encouraged me to talk freely. But I know I should not have mentioned such things.'

George's smiled faded. He did not mind her reference to books of a highly libidinous nature such as most gentlemen had in their libraries, usually with a spurious Latin title on the cover. What he objected to was that she talked to him as she did to her grandmother. Everybody knew that old Mrs Peat was born in a slum and talked with an accent you could cut with a knife. He felt Flora was taking advantage of his kindness in talking to her at all and introducing into a conversation a relative who ought to be left behind in the North where she came from, or at least quietly forgotten. George felt that there was an assumption of equality in Flora's mind between himself and, God forbid, her grandmother.

It would be a kindness to tell her. 'Miss Peat, I do not advise you to imitate the conversation of your Granny, as you call her. Such a connection can do you no good.'

Flora stared at him.

'You have had the advantage of being brought up as a lady, but unfortunately for your social position, you have relatives from the lower, if not the lowest, orders of society. You would do well to lose them as quickly as possible. And certainly do not come to this house talking about them.'

'Are you suggesting that I should disown Granny?'

'Not disown, precisely, although your father might have been better advised to leave her in the North. But keep discreetly quiet, certainly.'

Flora jumped up and walked to the window, striving to control the rising anger at the implications of his words. Then she turned back to where Sir George was standing on the hearth rug.

'How dare you!' she shouted, in a voice so angry that it shook. 'How dare you insult me like that? Yes, it is an insult to think I would disown Granny, or anybody else I loved, just to fit in with your barbaric notions of what Society would think! Well, a Society that thinks it is right for a woman to disown her grandmother because of an accident of birth, is rotten. Rotten to the core, do you hear? And I want nothing to do with it. I love Granny, she has been very good to me. I am glad she is living with us because now it means that we can be good to her in her old age.

'She slaved in a flax-mill for fourteen hours a day, and brought home ten shillings a week if she was lucky. She reared her children to be decent and God-fearing and saved enough to send my father to school. We owe everything we are to her courage and self-denial and faith in my father. I am proud of her and not for anybody will I disown her!'

'If it were not for Grace's sake I should have you thrown out of the house,' shouted George. 'I told my grandmother she would regret it. I cannot think why she allowed people of your sort in the house in the first place!'

'Perhaps because she has a little more understanding of what it takes to be human than you have. Do you seriously think that I would disown my Granny? All you think of is whether somebody has a bogus family tree and whether or not they are in Debrett. Well, I am not in Debrett, and what is more, I do not care!'

'You would be better off in my kitchen,' shouted George furiously. 'Do you realize to whom you are talking?'

'I am not talking to a true gentleman, at any rate! What makes you think you have any right to dictate my behaviour? Or that your own views are so acceptable? Gentleman indeed! You are an insufferable stuck-up cad!'

George turned on his heel and walked out, slamming the door behind him, so that the pictures shook.

'And good riddance!' shouted Flora. How dared he talk to her in that way? She paced angrily up and down the room. Granny was worth a dozen of him. The French were right, all you could do with people like that was decapitate them. He pretended to be so nice too, lending her books and chatting to her, when underneath he was a condescending prig! Flora thought of several things she wished she had said. And another thing, she said to herself, he does not have to look at me always as if I were a dowdy nobody, he is not exactly an Apollo. He has a beak of a nose and his face is far too lean and craggy. The sooner he came a cropper the better she would be pleased.

George walked irresolutely up and down his library, more than half inclined to take her by the scruff of the neck and pitch her out of the front door. He had told her where she belonged and it certainly was not in his house! She was only the jumped-up daughter of a tradesman after all, and had to be taught her place. Well, it was a lesson to him, and one he would not forget easily! This is what happened when the classes mixed, the next thing would be revolution! It simply did not work. How dared she assume they were equals?

He paced up and down the floor. He would tell his grandmother she must get rid of them. Throw them out. He would enjoy composing a letter to that odious Mrs Peat. He walked to the door full of righteous indignation and then hesitated. He walked back to his desk, stopped in front of the family tree and looked at it. He paused. However did he come to lose his temper in that way? If she had the vulgarity to express herself with such coarseness, how the deuce had he allowed *himself* to sink so low? George began to feel ashamed of himself: he had behaved quite unlike any man of breeding.

All right, he told himself, perhaps he should not have lost his temper, but why on earth could she not keep quiet about her disgraceful relations? Was he expected to welcome in his house a girl whose grandmother had worked in a mill?

Then suddenly the enormity of his conduct struck him. Of course Miss Peat must stand up for her grandmother. Would it not be cause for the gravest censure if she denied any feelings or knowledge about her grandmother at all? Miss Peat had done nothing but stand by truth and decent feeling and he, in his arrogance, had blamed her for it.

She was right. He was a cad. His behaviour was inexcusable. He had told her that he did not want her in the house. However could he have done such a thing?

He stood irresolutely for a few minutes wondering what to do. Suddenly he decided. He took the family tree off the wall and walked to the door. Penton was hovering in the hall.

'Here, Penton, take this. Put it in the attic. I do not wish to see it again.'

'Very good, Sir George. Are you going out, sir? Shall I order the carriage?'

'No thank you,' said George curtly.

'He just walked straight past me,' Penton told the housekeeper later, 'and took a *common hackney*!'

To Flora's relief, Adeline's honeymoon seemed to be satisfactory. She had received several letters from her sister. They were bright, cheerful letters, telling of boating trips on the river, visits to

Windsor Castle and the Great Park. Charles had told her his ideas for the treatment of cholera and he was planning to write an article about it. She said nothing that could have alerted Flora in any way.

Flora was therefore totally unprepared for the thin, tense figure of her sister when she visited her shortly after Adeline's return to London. It was not that Adeline looked unwell, but there was a tension that had not been there before and a withdrawn look on her face.

'Adeline, dearest,' cried Flora, kissing her sister effusively to cover her shock, 'you are looking very well, I must say.'

'Am I?' said Adeline curiously. She felt that she wore a crimson brand of shame visible for all to see. She wondered if Flora noticed and was both relieved and resentful that her sister should be so unobservant.

'You look the same person, perhaps a little tired,' said Flora uneasily. 'Why do you ask?'

'Oh, that is only the settling in,' said Adeline lightly, 'come and take some tea, Flora.' If she only knew what it was like, thought Adeline, busying herself with cushions and tables for tea. She saw Charles' glistening heaving body in front of her eyes, like some inflated porpoise. He was like some pig with its trotters in a trough, grunting and wallowing, until he rolled off and sank into a heavy sleep. It amazed her that during the day Charles should be kind and courteous, when at night he turned into such a brute.

'Well now,' Adeline continued brightly when tea was poured out, 'what have you been doing with yourself, Flora?'

'Nothing of note. Granny of course has been a worry to us all, but she is better now I think. But I told you that in my letters. What else? Daisy and I travelled on the new underground, and we both got rather dirty, but it was very exciting. And I took her to see how the Victoria embankment is progressing.'

'Has there not been some trouble about it?'

'Something to do with the railways, I believe. All we could see was a quantity of scaffolding and piles of mud and stone. So we came home.'

'And things are going well at the Kingsleys?'

'Yes, thank you.'

'So,' said Adeline brightly, 'things certainly have changed for us both in the last year. I have a new life to become accustomed to and you have had much thrown on your shoulders with nursing Granny, dear Flora.'

'Of course, Granny has been a worry to us all,' repeated Flora, casting a covert glance at the clock on the mantelpiece. She could not tell how, but a touch of impatience had crept into her mind. She stayed only long enough to greet her brother-in-law coming back from his surgery and then she went home.

'I thought your sister looked very well, my dear,' said Charles, standing with his back to the fire and lifting his coat tails to warm himself.

Adeline averted her gaze and rang the bell for some fresh tea.

'Flora is beginning to take some trouble with her appearance now,' she replied.

'Perhaps she has learnt her lesson from you, my love.'

'Whatever do you mean?'

'I mean that she sees now what a lady can do with a little trouble. I am no Apollo, but I flatter myself that I am quite a *bon parti* as you ladies say. I should certainly not choose one of those blue-stocking tabbies.'

'Perhaps Flora has not yet learned to ponder on the delights marriage has to offer,' said Adeline, with an edge of sarcasm.

Charles cast an approving glance at himself in the glass over the mantelpiece. 'Oh well, who knows, Flora may yet find some man to marry her. For what time have you called dinner, my dear?'

Since Adeline's wedding Mrs Peat spent most of her days closeted with Blanche in her boudoir with plans for her come-out in the spring. She was planning a large coming-out dance in June and was hoping that Lady Clevedon would present Blanche when she presented Griselda. She was happily occupied in writing out lists: of guests to be invited to Blanche's dance; of clothes Blanche would need; and, more discreetly in pencil, of eligible young men, some with question marks attached to their names, when their source of income needed her careful investigation.

'Now you must not think that I wish you to be tied up in matrimony by the end of your first season,' said Mrs Peat to Blanche. 'I wish you to enjoy yourself thoroughly and look about you a little. Of course my papa was in Holy Orders and did not approve of anything but the mildest hop, so I never had the opportunity to. . . . In fact, if I had not met your Papa, I do not know how I should have managed. Two of my sisters never married, and my sister Mary married only after Papa died. I do not know why, he did not seem to wish his daughters to marry.'

Blanche had never met her two unmarried Hebden aunts and had only seen Aunt Mary once some years ago, so she was not much interested in their trials.

'Why are all the eligible men so dull and the detrimentals so dashing, Mama?' Blanche peered over her mother's shoulder at the list of young men. 'It is almost as if there were some law about it.'

'Whatever can you mean, Blanche?' cried Mrs Peat uneasily.

'Look at Francis Grant. He is one of the most spiffing men I have ever set eyes on. And yet, what is he worth? Four hundred pounds a year? But it does not seem to matter, does it?'

And Hugh Dunster too, she thought to herself. Last time she met him he hinted that all was not well between him and Alice Banks. Not that it surprised Blanche at all, she never thought Alice good enough for Hugh. Alice did not deserve a man like Hugh, she simply could not appreciate him! What a truly special person he was. How strong and alive his hair was, so thick and wavy. Blanche longed to run her hands through it and grasp hold of it to hold his face close to hers. Of course Hugh's engagement to Alice was not announced yet. It was only a matter of convenience, Hugh had hinted as much. There was hope yet! If only he would say something – not leave her in this agonizing limbo!

'Blanche!' said Mrs Peat sharply. 'I hope you are not indulging in hopes of securing Captain Grant's affections?'

'Captain Grant?' laughed Blanche. 'Good Heavens, no! Of course, he is pleasant for a little flirtation, but I would never allow myself to be carried away.'

'I knew you would be sensible, my love,' said Mrs Peat with relief. 'You would hate to live in a poky house, darling, with only a few servants. I have such hopes of you, too. With your beauty – which you get from my side of the family – you should be able to fulfil all my wildest dreams for your success. Do not, I beg of you, throw it all away for some penniless nondescript, however charming he may be. I warn you, Blanche, Papa would not give you a penny and you have no money of your own, you know.'

'Yes, yes, Mama, do not go on so,' said Blanche, resentfully.

There was a noise outside the window. Mrs Peat started up from her chair. 'Whatever is that?' Blanche rushed to the window and looked out. 'It is a barrel organ, Mama. I wonder how it got into the Square? The watchman must have been asleep.'

The man with the barrel organ was standing directly under their window. He had a dark swarthy face, with a mop of curly black hair. A shapeless felt hat was pushed down onto his head, and a red and white handkerchief was tied loosely round his neck. The barrel organ was a large box hung round his neck with a handle at the side. It was decorated with a floral design with panels of people dancing in the centre. On the top of the barrel organ sat a monkey, dressed in a greatcoat and wearing on its head a tricorne, from which stuck a large feather. As the man turned the handle and the strain from *Il Trovatore* began to grind out, the monkey began swaying and dancing on the top of the box, until finally, as the music got faster and louder, the monkey was twisting and twirling with dizzying speed, its coat tails flying and its tail flicking from side to side. It looked quite possessed, pursuing its strange gyrations on top of the box and Blanche leant out, fascinated.

'We cannot have that noise outside a gentleman's house,' said Mrs Peat. 'Come in at once, Blanche, and pull the bell. Tell Ketton to move him on.'

'It is all right, Mama. One of the maids has gone out.'

A housemaid came out of the front door and hurried down the steps in a flurry of indignant starched, pink check.

''ere,' she said to the organ grinder, ''ere you, a penny to be orf. This is a gentleman's 'ouse. We don't want no barrel organ's 'ere.'

The organ grinder glanced up at the house.

'I charge a tanner 'ere,' he said firmly, turning the handle more vigorously.

'Tuppence,' said the housemaid. 'And 'urry up. I 'aven't got all day.'

''ow about a bit of threepence upright?' leered the organ grinder.

'The very idea!' exclaimed the maid, retreating hastily. 'I'm a respectable woman. Now, be off with you, before I calls the constable.'

On impulse Blanche ran back into the room and took sixpence out of her purse. She threw it out to the organ grinder. The six-penny piece glittered and shone as it spun through the air and it landed on the ground in a small flurry of dust. The man picked it up, spat on it for luck and blew a kiss to Blanche. The monkey took off its hat and bowed and then lifting its coat tails turned round and exhibited its backside. Blanche shut the window quickly and came back to sit by her mother, unfurling her fan as she did so and fanning herself briskly.

Flora had half-expected to be called to account for her quarrel with Sir George, but the days passed and there were no reper-cussions. Sir George was visiting Linchmere, Penton told her, and although apparently he had talked to Lady Kingsley about the length of his stay there, he appeared to have mentioned nothing about their quarrel. Flora met Lady Kingsley once on the stairs and received a very polite 'Good morning', and a kind enquiry after her grandmother. Flora even dropped a hint to Daisy about the quarrel, but although Daisy looked serious, she said that nothing had been said in the schoolroom.

Flora found herself unaccountably disappointed. There was a sort of exhilaration in her anger. She had repeated over and over in her mind all the things she wished to say to Sir George – his unwarrantable superciliousness, his caddishness, the way he thought himself above an apology. It was annoying to be unable to deliver them. She wished to see him, but only in order to tell him that she never wanted to set eyes on him again.

Sir George was living through one of the most uncomfortable weeks of his life. Almost immediately after his quarrel with Flora he had left for Linchmere. He would rid himself of those upstart Peats, he told himself. It remained only to find an opportunity. But it could wait a week or so. His grandmother looked a little off-colour, he would wait until she was better. In any case, Miss Peat could stew in her own juice for a while – it would reduce her conceited opinion of herself.

But the peace of the autumn countryside did not quieten

George's conscience over his behaviour. Flora had been in the right. No matter how George tried to convince himself that Flora lacked breeding and was totally unfit to be treated on equal terms with any gentleman, he knew that the fault had been his and not hers. He realized suddenly, striding along the churned-up furrows of earth one frosty morning, that he held two contradictory assumptions. One was that people of breeding respected their families and were courteous to their relations, and the other was that anyone climbing the social ladder should shake off their undesirable forebears as soon as possible. But there was no avoiding it: the two views were mutually incompatible.

Whether he liked it or not, he owed Miss Peat a sincere apology. He told himself that although she might have enough proper feeling to stand by her 'granny', breeding would out. She would harbour an implacable resentment and it would become impossible for him to continue their morning talks. George told himself he did not much care.

Nevertheless that evening he packed his bags and the next day he returned to London.

Flora made up her mind that she was not expecting to see Sir George again. He would be away until the Christmas holidays and after that he would be abroad. In any case, she did not want to see him, she had nothing whatsoever to say to him.

The following morning she met him unexpectedly in the hall. She had been so sure he was too cowardly to face her. She turned white, then red, and walked stiffly to the Pink Saloon, bowing distantly to him as she passed. She closed the door and sank trembling in the nearest chair. Oh Heavens, whatever was he going to say?

Then she heard footsteps, a firm, masculine tread. Let him go away! Anything but an angry shaming scene which would disgrace her and poor Daisy.

The door opened and George entered. There was an awkward silence while Flora stared down at her hands and waited for the outburst, the angry dismissal. It did not come.

'I owe you an apology, Miss Peat. I hope you will be generous and accept it.'

Flora looked up and stared at him in astonishment. George noticed with surprise that her eyes were a luminous grey and fringed with very black lashes. Her hair, too, was a rich chestnut brown and her skin clear and pale. George found himself wondering why he had never noticed before that particular combination of hair and eyes and skin.

'I said things to you which no gentleman should have said,' went on George. 'I have been unable to think of anything else. I feel that I have behaved very badly towards you.'

'It was what you said rather than how you said it that upset me,' cried Flora.

'Miss Peat,' said George with sudden energy, 'I do not know how I was led to say what I did. I am ashamed of myself now. I understand that I insulted you and I beg you to forgive me.'

Flora stared at him. He is very pale under that tan, she thought confusedly. He truly does look concerned and worried. What a lean, bony face he has. A multitude of disjointed thoughts were rushing through her mind, but none of them with enough coherence for her to form a sentence. She remained silent.

'Will you not even shake hands with me, Miss Peat?'

Flora held her hand out quickly. 'Please say no more about it, Sir George,' she said hastily, 'the incident is forgotten.'

'You are very kind,' said George quietly, and after a short pause he left her. Flora stared at the door for a long while after he had gone.

Daisy came down from the Kingsleys' schoolroom the next day with a letter in her hand. It was addressed to Miss Peat and Miss Daisy Peat and it contained an invitation in Sir George's writing to a small Christmas party Lady Kingsley was giving for Grace. Three o'clock, it read, for tea and games. Mrs Peat was delighted.

'You said you had never met him,' said Blanche accusingly when she heard about it. 'You sly, horrid thing.'

'Flora is only being asked as a chaperone,' said Mrs Peat, reaching out to tease a strand of Blanche's hair into a ringlet by curling it around her finger. 'You do not really wish to go to a party where there are young children to look after and keep an eye on, darling.'

Flora felt deflated. Somehow, she had been sure that this was Sir George's way of offering an olive branch, of saying he thought her a suitable person to acknowledge. But Mama was probably right. She was expecting too much.

'I am delighted that you can both come to the party,' said Sir George a few days later when he met Flora and Daisy in the hall one morning.

'I will do my best to look after the children,' said Flora ungraciously, although she tried not to sound resentful.

'But I do not wish you to look after the children,' said George, in surprise. 'I am hoping that you will give me a little adult conversation, and I would like to introduce you to my brother Algy who is coming. I think he might amuse you.'

He can be generous and he is not such a cad after all, thought Flora triumphantly.

'Thank you for inviting us,' she said a little shyly. 'Daisy and I are both looking forward to it.'

'Mama,' said Flora suddenly that evening, 'I would like the carriage sometime, please. I need some new clothes.' Mrs Peat and Blanche raised their heads and looked at her in astonishment.

'And what is the matter with your present wardrobe,' enquired Mrs Peat with a sudden spurt of anger, though Heaven knew she had been trying in vain for years to make Flora interested in her clothes.

'I do not like it.'

'You have never even worn that nice magenta silk I bought you.'

'It is not my colour, Mama. You and Blanche can wear those bright colours. I only look sallow.'

'I suppose I must be grateful to see you take any interest in your clothes,' said Mrs Peat ungraciously at last. 'You may have the carriage on Thursday afternoon.'

'Why this sudden interest?' asked Blanche curiously. It could never be a man. Perhaps it was Flora's last, desperate effort to get herself off the shelf now Adeline was gone. She'll never make it – well, perhaps with a widower.

'I just need some clothes,' said Flora, coldly.

'I don't care I am sure,' retorted Blanche and went back to her magazine.

Mrs Peat sat up. She looked at Flora appraisingly, as if she was a piece of merchandise that had been left so long on the shelves that it was now coming back into fashion. Of course Flora was twenty-seven and almost a blue-stocking and next season, naturally, was to be devoted entirely to Blanche. But if Flora was beginning to take an interest in her appearance, she might just manage to push her off the shelf. Now, who was there that would be a suitable match for Flora? What about Maurice Dunster? Normally she would not even consider the Dunsters, with Hugh being such a wastrel, but Maurice was the elder son, and he at least was careful and thrifty. He may have helped to pay for Hugh's extravagances, but could Flora expect to do any better than Maurice? She would put her mind to it.

The first thing to be done was to improve Flora's appearance. 'You must do your hair differently, Flora,' said Mrs Peat at last. 'I never thought it suited you bundled just any how in a snood. You must do it more like you did for the wedding.'

'Oh, I do not wish to be bothered with things like that,' said Flora, impatiently.

'Lottie can just as well do your hair when she has finished with Blanche,' said Mrs Peat. 'She does not have Adeline to worry about now.'

'Oh God, no!' cried Flora. 'I am not having all that fuss with rag papers every night.'

Blanche looked up, her interest caught.

'I do not suppose that you will need rag papers,' she said. 'Your hair is rather like mine, slightly wavy. Lottie could probably do it with the hot tongs, could she not, Mama?'

'I expect so. Now, Flora, I do not wish any more argument. Lottie will come to you when she has done Blanche's hair. It is high time you took some trouble with yourself, anyway.'

'I wish I had never mentioned it,' said Flora crossly.

Flora was surprised at the informality of the Christmas arrangements in the Kingsley household. Somehow she had expected it to be as formal as it was at home. In Belgrave Square, Ketton and the maids put up all the decorations. Usually Flora hardly noticed them.

The Kingsley household was quite different. Sir George had ordered several fir trees to be sent up from Linchmere as well as huge bunches of holly and several hampers full of ivy and mistletoe. Flora and Daisy arrived one morning to find large cane hampers overflowing with greenery in the hall, and the smell of pine needles everywhere.

'We are not doing any lessons today,' shouted Grace, her cheeks pink with excitement. 'Instead we are going to decorate. You will help us will you not Flora?'

'Miss Peat, please, Grace,' said Sir George, sternly.

'No, no, let her call me Flora,' said Flora, smiling at Grace's downcast face. 'I call all my sisters' friends by their Christian names, and Daisy and I cannot help it if we are at opposite ends of a large family.'

Grace had looked like crying for a moment, but now she smiled at Flora. George felt grateful to her; in his anxiety to give Flora her social dues, he had forgotten Grace's absurd sensitivity.

'Well, that is settled,' said George briskly. 'Now then come along everybody. We need a long rope to go around the hall. Miss Peat, would you care to help me with that? There are some long strands of ivy in that box over there. You twist it together to make festoons and add some holly for decoration. Grace and Daisy, here is the frame for the kissing bough. That should keep you two quiet for a while.'

Penton came in with a ladder and placed holly behind all the pictures, with cottonwool balls dotted among it for snow. The rest of the party sat on the stairs and made the decorations. Sir George told them stories of Christmas at Linchmere when he was a boy, of ice skating on the pond and sleigh rides and Algy breaking his collar bone. Flora discovered an unsuspected talent for making holly and ivy wreaths. The morning had never passed so quickly. Finally, Miss Martin came down and said that milk and biscuits were waiting upstairs.

'Up you go then,' said George, rising. 'Penton, Miss Peat and I will have some wine in the library.'

'I enjoyed that,' said Flora as she got up, scattering leaves and pine needles as she did so.

'Do you not do the same at home, then?' asked George as he led the way to the library.

'No. The servants do it. But it is so much nicer to do it yourself.'

Sir George opened the library door for Flora. Inside were

several large trunks, gun cases, shooting bags and piles of books on the floor.

'I fear it is somewhat messy today,' said George.

'It looks as if you are going away for at least a year,' said Flora.

'Only until Easter. Come in, Miss Peat. Give me the benefit of your advice while we are waiting for Penton.'

'What about?'

'Tell me what books to take.'

'I do not think my advice would be of much value. Every year, when we go to Ramsgate, I take all four volumes of Macaulay's *History of England*. I always have the idea that I shall be able to settle down to some serious study. But every year I get stuck at about page fifty.'

'Oh, I do not wish to embark on anything very strenuous. I was looking for something quite light.'

Flora wandered casually round the bookshelves. Then she stopped. There was a very noticeable bare space on the wall where the Kingsley family tree had been. Sir George watched her.

'You are quite right, Miss Peat. The thing was probably worthless. I have had it removed to the attics.'

Flora felt the colour rushing to her cheeks. She could think of nothing whatsoever to say. She was conscious at once of their quarrels, the aftermaths and the most acute embarrassment. She sat down quickly beside a pile of books on the floor and hastily picked one up, trying to hide her face. It was Greek.

'Euripides,' she spelt out slowly. 'Medea.'

'You read Greek?'

'No, no. My brother Tom taught me the alphabet, that is all.'

'I thought you had added Greek to your other accomplishments.'

'But I do not have any accomplishments.'

'Nonsense, all young ladies have accomplishments. What about the piano or embroidery, or making wax flowers or something?'

Flora shook her head.

'Dear me,' said Sir George. 'Shell-work then, or bead-work?'

Flora wished that he would stop. She was unable to decide whether he was serious or joking. 'No,' she said shortly.

'Well then, you will just have to rely on intelligence and a well-informed mind, won't you?'

Flora looked up startled. His brown eyes were quite steady and he was smiling. Her own eyes widened for a moment and then she turned her head away. She did wish he did not feel obliged to offer her these vapid compliments. He seemed to delight in making her feel uncomfortable. 'Like a blue-stocking,' she said ungraciously. 'You confirm Mama's worst fears for me, you know.'

'I do not think I am very interested in what your Mama thinks,' said Sir George dryly, and turned the subject.

Gauche, awkward, ill-bred, she could not accept even the lightest compliment. Perhaps Algy would have better luck with her, he was the lady's man, after all.

Despite this setback Flora was looking forward to the Kingsleys' tea-party. She and Daisy went shopping to choose a Christmas present for Grace, and Flora's new dress arrived. It was a dark blue silk with Pagoda sleeves and multiple flounces around the hem. It was trimmed with bands of dark blue velvet and ivory lace and had little carved ivory buttons down the bodice. Lottie arranged Flora's hair becomingly in a chignon secured with a blue silk ribbon and some white silk roses. Flora looked at herself with confidence in the glass. At least Mama would not be there to comment adversely on her lack of social popularity.

Daisy arrived in Flora's bedroom looking sweet in a white silk dress with a tartan sash, and clutching in one hand Grace's present wrapped in pink tissue paper. They went to show themselves off to old Mrs Peat.

'Ah, two lovely lasses. Well, enjoy yourselves, my pets.'

'You'll take the shine out of them all, Miss Flora, now you've prettified yourself a bit,' said Sarah, standing with arms akimbo and nodding her head sagely.

Flora laughed and said, 'I do not suppose that there will be anybody there to practise on, but thank you.'

Mrs Peat noticed with approval that Flora's eyes searched for the looking-glass on the wall and that she smiled momentarily at her reflection.

When Flora and Daisy were shown up to the schoolroom only John and Maria Springfield, Grace's cousins, had arrived. John, a tough ten-year-old with black springy hair, was kicking moodily at the table legs. He was dressed in a knickerbocker suit and he was twisting his head around as if the starched white collar was too tight for him. Maria was sitting stiffly upright in a chair, staring hopefully at the array of cakes and jellies on the table. Grace was nowhere to be seen.

Flora and Daisy crossed over to where Lady Kingsley was sitting with Sir George by the fireplace. Sir George rose as Flora came forward and Flora bowed politely to him. She then paid her respects to Lady Kingsley.

Lady Kingsley said petulantly, 'I told you so. Grace has vanished and Miss Martin cannot find her.'

Flora bent over Daisy and whispered, 'See if you can find Grace. I expect she is feeling very shy. Perhaps you could get her to show Maria her dolls' house?'

Daisy looked apprehensively at Lady Kingsley and tugged at Flora's sleeve. 'I expect she's behind the screen. Shall I go and get her? Will it be all right?'

'Yes, go on.'

'Grace!' shouted Daisy, suddenly and loudly so that Lady Kingsley started in her chair. 'Grace, it's me, Daisy! Where are you?'

A muffled voice came from one corner of the room. Daisy ran across and pounced behind the screen with a triumphant squeak. 'You silly girl,' she scolded. 'Why don't you show your cousin Maria your dolls' house?' She dragged Grace out into the room. 'You'd like to see it, wouldn't you, Maria?'

Maria rose and came over. 'Mine's got real chimneys,' she confided. 'We tried to push a doll up once for a sweep, but he got stuck.'

'Mine's got stairs you can pull out and there's another room behind,' said Grace shyly.

'Well, come on then,' said Daisy, pulling at her.

'There you are, George,' said Lady Kingsley. 'What did I tell you? As soon as Daisy came she would be all right. Is that not so, Miss Peat?'

'I fear that Daisy's company manners leave something to be desired,' said Flora, apologetically.

'They are far better than Grace's manners in disappearing altogether,' replied Lady Kingsley, tartly.

More guests arrived: Lady Colefax with three of her children, Robert and Charles and little Rose. Rose took up her position by John and stared at him worshipfully. 'I've got some bon-bons,' she said, 'Would you like one?'

John scowled at her and resumed kicking at the chair.

'Never mind, Rose,' said a voice behind them. 'In another ten years the positions will be quite reversed!'

'Algy, old man, it is good to see you,' George went forward to welcome his brother. Algy shook hands with him and then greeted his grandmother and the other guests.

'Come along, George. Introduce me to your pretty friend.'

From the moment Algy Kingsley walked into the room Flora could not take her eyes off him. She had never seen a man so good-looking. He was tall, slim and elegant and he had classically perfect features, with the bluest of blue eyes and curly fair hair. He had an affectionate, easy manner that Flora found totally captivating. He shook his brother's hand and clapped him on the shoulder, and greeted Grace and Lady Kingsley exuberantly with hugs and kisses. Flora felt that he was a man who loved his family and was loved by them in return.

George performed the introduction most unwillingly. It was not Algy's interest in Flora that annoyed him – Algy always went directly for the prettiest girl in the room and Flora was the only one available, Lady Colefax being too old and Daisy too young – it was Flora's interest in Algy. George had long ago allowed her to be intelligent – he had described her to his brother not two days ago as a *jolie laide* – and here she was, looking suddenly very much younger and absolutely pretty! It was as if someone he always thought of as his private 'find' was daring to make herself publicly available. She was gazing at Algy as if she had never seen a man before, thought George savagely.

'Go away, George,' said Algy, smiling warmly down at Flora. 'You have done your duty and can now go and look after your other guests. I shall be very happy here.'

'My brother is a worthless flirt, Miss Peat,' said George with an attempt at humour. 'You can believe one word in ten.'

Flora hardly heard him. She was gazing at Algy. She was both exhilaratingly conscious of him standing near her and intensely aware that he was looking at her. The way his glance rested on her neck and shoulders. He liked her!

'So you are George's friend, Miss Peat. I have been looking forward to meeting you.'

'Am I?' said Flora smiling. (Could anybody's eyes really be so blue?) 'I mean, we always quarrel.'

'That's very brave of you. I should never dare quarrel with George.'

'Oh, I do try not to,' said Flora smiling, 'but sometimes he quarrels with me, so of course, I must defend myself.'

Did she, by Jove, thought Algy, looking at Flora with approval. What the devil did George mean by talking about her as if she was a cross between Miss Buss and some dowdy maiden aunt?

'You must keep it up, Miss Peat. I am sure it does him a lot of good.'

The whole afternoon held a magic glow for Flora. The candles on the Christmas tree sent flickering lights dancing over the room, while the warm light from the oil lamps with their pink silk shades gave the faces of the guests a softened look, smoothing out the harsh swarthiness of George's features and Lady Kingsley's crow's feet and wrinkles. Flora was content to sit and watch the children's games, the little girls with their white dresses and sashes flying, the boys in their Eton suits or Norfolk jackets whooping and shouting, cheeks like apples. They all bounded and flew about in Musical Chairs, or gave muffled squeaks of excitement in Hunt the Slipper. At the centre of it all was Algy, with his wonderful blue eyes and heartbreakingly lovely smile, who quite took her breath away.

Lady Kingsley called her over to introduce her to Lady Colefax, and such was Flora's new-found assurance that she was able to make the two ladies laugh with a couple of schoolroom anecdotes that Daisy had related to her.

Lady Colefax watched Flora with interest. She had heard the rumours that Mrs Peat had wormed her way into the Kingsley household with the intention of marrying off that brassy daughter of hers, but she was pleased to see that the rumour was without foundation. When Flora had moved away and was occupied in turning the pages for Miss Martin at the piano, Lady Colefax did a gentle probe.

'So that is the eldest daughter?'

'I believe so.'

'I have only met Miss Blanche, and, of course,' she lowered her voice, 'one cannot be in Town long without encountering Susan Peat.'

'To do Mrs Peat justice, she has not taken advantage of Daisy coming here,' replied Lady Kingsley – neither George nor Penton had seen fit to tell her of Blanche's rout. 'I must confess, my dear Harriet, I was a little alarmed lest Miss Blanche should give herself the entrée to the house. But it is usually Miss Peat who chaperones Daisy, and I have found her quite ladylike and unassuming.'

'I am so pleased it is working out well,' replied Lady Colefax. 'Children, especially girls, can be such a worry. And dear Grace seems to be enjoying herself.'

'I am very happy with the arrangement. The credit for Grace's improvement must certainly go to Daisy Peat. And Miss Peat is very good at managing the children.'

Flora and Algy now joined the children in a game of Grandmother's Footsteps and Flora was the Grandmother. She was acutely aware that Algy was among those creeping up behind her and as he came closer he might spring forward and grab her! The thought made her feel quite breathless as she spun round to catch them moving and she could not tell whether to feel relieved or disappointed when she caught him moving and he was out. Finally, amid shrieks of laughter Maria caught her, flinging her arms around her with a breathless 'Oh, Miss Peat, I've won!'

Flora hugged the compact, warm, little body to her and over the dark curls saw Algy looking at her. Their eyes met and Algy smiled. A delicious pang shot through Flora. She hugged Maria more tightly and buried her flushed cheeks in Maria's mop of curls.

'Come along everybody,' called George briskly. 'It is time to get the presents off the Christmas tree. Algy, could you find the ladder? Miss Martin, I shall hand them down to you.'

Flora released Maria and joined the crowd round the tree. She moved to Daisy's side and whispered that she must not forget her thank yous. Maids were coming in with cloaks and coats now and Flora could hear the distant doorbell as carriages called for the guests.

'Robert, John, Rose,' called out Miss Martin. 'Grace, Maria,

Charles.' George took the last couple off the tree and climbed down the ladder. 'Daisy, Miss Peat,' called Miss Martin.

'But I am not a child,' said Flora involuntarily, wondering whether it would be proper for her to receive a present and suddenly conscious of Mama's strictures on the subject.

'It is all right, Miss Peat.' It was George who came forward. 'Grace and Miss Martin did some shopping one afternoon. Grace wanted to give you something, do not spoil it for her.'

Grace exchanged glances with Daisy. It was Cousin George who suggested that Flora should be included on the list. So Grace had dutifully bought Flora a little china trinket box with moss roses on the lid, and written a note saying 'To Flora, with all affectionate wishes for the Christmas Season, Grace Lennox.' Grace was far too shy to contradict her cousin, so she accepted Flora's thanks and kisses, and determined to mention it to Daisy after the Christmas holidays.

Algy came up as Flora was waiting with Daisy for their carriage to be announced and took hold of her hand.

'I escort Grandmama around a certain amount while George is away,' he said. 'Doing the Stilton you know, dances, parties and so on. I am looking forward to knowing you better, Miss Peat, and I hope you will dance with me.'

'I should love to,' stammered Flora, looking with a kind of wonder at her hand in his.

Algy raised it to his lips. 'There is no mistletoe up here, unfortunately, Miss Peat,' he said, 'so this will have to do.'

'Can you not be anywhere without flirting, Algy?' said George disapprovingly, watching the glow in Flora's face.

'If you have such pretty friends, what can you expect?' retorted Algy. He bowed to Flora, patted Daisy on the head and ran downstairs.

Penton now announced the Peats' carriage. Flora took one last look back into the lighted room. She felt reluctant to go, to move a step into the shadows of the stairs and cut out finally that warmth and light. She wanted to hold back the moment, to find something of it that she could take with her. But Sir George was preparing to escort them down the stairs and out to their carriage.

'I see my brother has been amusing you,' said George, walking down the stairs beside Flora.

'Yes,' replied Flora happily. Then she added suddenly, 'Oh, look, Daisy! Look at the decorations we made. How the holly berries glow in the lamplight. Isn't it beautiful?' She felt suddenly that she loved this house and everything in it. The whole place seemed touched with a magic that she had not recognized before. She turned to George and put her hand on his arm. 'Thank you very much, Sir George, for inviting us. I have enjoyed myself very much. You had a nice time too, did you not, Daisy?'

'Mm,' said Daisy, clutching her going-home present in one hot hand.

George bowed formally and moved away. 'I'll show Miss Peat and Miss Daisy out, Penton. I fear that I shall not see you again before I go, Miss Peat. So I shall wish you a Happy Christmas now. And my best wishes for the New Year.'

'Of course,' said Flora, coming to earth slightly and holding out her hand. 'I hope you have a pleasant journey. I expect I shall see you when you return.'

'I hope so. I shall be back in England by April.'

'Oh well, not too long then,' said Flora brightly. They shook hands and Flora and Daisy climbed into the carriage.

Fog was beginning to swirl around the square. The trees in the centre were already almost obscured, leaving only faint ghost-like impressions of themselves, spidery grey outlines of trunks and branches. A floating mist blew round the street lamps and the carriage lights, dulling the yellow glow, and almost extinguishing those on the far side of the square, so that all that could be seen was a faint dull gleam, glimmering intermittently as the bands of fog passed in front of them.

George watched the carriage as it turned and was swallowed up in the mist, the horses' hooves muffled by the fog. It was not until the last clip-clop on the cobblestones died away that he turned slowly and went back into the house.

Chapter Five

CHRISTMAS in the Peat household was usually a family affair, but this year the family was depleted. When Mr Peat bowed his head to say grace over the Christmas turkey only his wife, his mother and four of his six children were there to share it. Ernest and Geraldina were spending Christmas with Gerald Milford and Adeline was with the Woodcocks. When Ernest married they had not noticed the change – he was bringing a wife into the family, and then Charlie and Harry were born which carried the Peats forward for another generation. When Adeline married she left the family. She was a Woodcock now, and her children would be Woodcocks.

Flora sat at the table, dutifully passing bread sauce and listening to Tom's account of how Bevis Minor, for a dare, had climbed onto the roof at Marlborough College and nailed the skull and crossbones to the flag-staff and how he, Tom, had kept *cave*. Her thoughts, however, were far away. Algy's face and smile haunted her. She day-dreamed about him most of the time. Those marvellous blue eyes and that wonderful way his mouth curved when he smiled! Whenever she thought about it her heart practically stopped beating! She re-lived again and again that moment when he took hold of her hand and kissed it. She longed to see him again, to hear him, to touch him. She felt a glow of happiness that he should be alive and in the same world as herself.

'Flora!' said Mrs Peat sharply. 'Your father is waiting for the salt!'

Mrs Peat rarely wasted much time thinking about her eldest daughter, but after she heard Flora's laugh ring out for the second time in one day, she sent for her to come to her dressing-room. She gave Flora a short, pungent lecture on the quiet refinement to be observed by young ladies, and ended by holding up Adeline as a model, pointing out how a dutiful daughter, with no more than Flora's looks, managed to earn herself a very respectable husband.

'I would rather die than be married to Charles,' said Flora passionately.

'Do not talk such nonsense,' said Mrs Peat sharply.

'What I have seen of Adeline's marriage does not lead me to view the state with the expectation either of pleasure or satis-faction.'

'One does not marry for one's own selfish pleasure, Flora,' said Mrs Peat. 'One marries to do one's duty to one's family.'

'Does this apply to Blanche as well,' retorted Flora, amazed at her own boldness. 'Or is she allowed to marry for pleasure and satisfaction?'

'How dare you talk to your mother in that fashion?'

'Take Adeline,' continued Flora, unheeding. 'She is still a bride and just look at her! She is so thin and tense that she almost vibrates every time you talk to her. She sits in that dark, gloomy house of hers and does nothing. She is pale and drawn, she has huge rings under her eyes and when Charles comes home, he does not even notice!'

'Charles is absolutely devoted to Adeline. But it is you I wished to talk about, Flora. I do not care for this new forwardness of yours: there is something rather vulgar in such a display of mere animal spirits. I mention it now because I have accepted an invitation for you and Blanche to go to Ellie St Alleyn's dance. Unfortunately I shall not be there and Adeline will be chaperoning you. Now I do not want to hear any of your usual nonsense about not going, Flora. However am I to get you off my hands, if you never meet anybody?'

The St Alleyns were connections of the Kingsleys – Algy might be there! Flora's heart sang.

'Oh, how lovely!' cried Flora, 'I should love to go!'

'The St Alleyns' dance tonight,' Blanche confided to her diary, 'and H. is to be there! I am sure he loves me, if only he would let himself. He did tell me I was somebody very special, and, of course A.B. knows nothing of this! Anyway, it is the first time

I have been to a dance since it all began, and I'll see how he behaves to A.B. I hinted to him that that sort of girl was very worthy, no doubt, but very boring for such a lively man – he said nothing, I think he didn't quite like to agree with me, but I know he did secretly. Well, we shall see.'

There were other sources of satisfaction for Blanche at the St Alleyns' dance. The sticks of her fan were filled with names before she was in the room ten minutes. Even Lord Pateley, so agonizingly shy, managed to stammer out a request for the two dances after supper. Tommy Clevedon, Maurice Dunster and James Anning all asked her to dance, as well as Hugh, who made his way to her side as soon as he saw her.

Just now she was sitting with Griselda Clevedon, eating fruit salad while their beaux went to fetch them some drinks.

'I saw you dancing with Maurice Dunster, Blanche,' said Griselda. 'Now do you not agree with me that he is very dull?'

'Oh, he's as slow as a wet week,' whispered Blanche. 'He spends the whole dance wanting to introduce you to his mother!'

'And who wishes to talk to Mrs Dunster? Especially at a dance!'

They both giggled and Griselda, bending lower over her fruit salad, said, 'Now, Hugh Dunster is quite different.'

Blanche looked at her sharply. Whatever did she mean? Surely she had not given anything away? 'Oh, do not waste your time on Hugh, Griselda,' she said after a moment. 'He is a real detrimental. Only Maurice's help keeps him out of trouble.'

'He may be a detrimental,' replied Griselda, 'but he can certainly do the naughty when he wishes.'

'Whatever do you mean?'

'You know he has this engagement with Alice Banks? It would be official, too, if Alice's trustees would allow it. Well, you must know he was caught with Alice coming the spoon behind a pot of ferns. He was being quite a dirty thing and Alice, it seems, was enjoying it. Anyway, who should come along but Mrs Banks – you know how strict she is with Alice. There was quite a kick up about it. Of course Alice was delighted because she is nutty about the fellow and she was longing to get away from home, and Hugh had a stroke of luck too – Alice's dowry is at least fifteen thousand.'

'I am sure Alice would never go behind a pot of ferns,' said Blanche, put out and annoyed. 'You must have got it wrong, Griselda.'

'Some of us mousey ones can be quite as naughty as you, Miss,' replied Griselda with an affectionate little squeeze. 'But you are such a beautiful girl, the tabbies suspect you first!'

Flora went to the St Alleyns' dance in a tingle of anticipation. Would he be there or would he not? She entered the ballroom and one five-second sweeping glance of the room assured her that he was. She had developed the ability, common to those in love, to spot the object of her affections across a crowded room with only half of the back of his head showing. Would he notice her? Would he remember his promise and dance with her? She sat down reluctantly beside Adeline and asked dutifully how she was.

Adeline was looking rather pale, but she said she was well. 'Charles will not be coming,' she told Flora. 'He has some notes to write up. He says that his dancing days are over.'

Flora thought it odd that a bride of not yet three months should be deserted in this way, but she said nothing. She tried to keep her mind on what Adeline was saying and not look around the room. Several people came up to Adeline to pay their respects, while Flora found that the sticks of her fan were quite full of names for the dancing. Even if Algy did not come up, at least she would not have the humiliation of being a wallflower.

Suddenly there he was, slim and elegant in his evening dress.

Flora introduced him to Adeline, muttering something about 'Meeting Mr Kingsley at Grace's party,' and hoped that it would go unremarked.

'I know it is not the done thing to engage oneself to dance beforehand, Mrs Woodcock,' said Algy, after chatting amiably to both ladies for a while, 'but let us say that Miss Peat and I have a previous agreement. Come, Miss Peat, my dance I think.'

Adeline watched with pursed lips as Algy led Flora onto the floor. Mama had told her, 'For Heaven's sake, Adeline, try to see that Flora dances with some young men!' But did she mean dance with a man who was well known to keep a mistress and was plainly a libertine! Of course that sort of man appealed to the lower instincts of some women, but her sister was too pure-minded to be taken in by his flattery, surely? She watched Flora's flushed cheeks with concern. Of Mr Kingsley's behaviour she would say nothing: it was well-known that men had coarser feelings than ladies. But she feared that he would not be chatting to Flora with that glint in his eye if he had not received some encouragement to do so.

Flora felt exhilarated, entirely happy, and at peace with the world. She was dancing in the arms of the man with whom she had fallen in love and the ballroom, to her enchanted eyes, seemed glowing and dazzling, full of life and laughter.

'I was not expecting to see you here, Mr Kingsley,' said Flora happily but completely untruthfully. 'You have the reputation of avoiding such entertainments.'

'I came solely to dance with you, Miss Peat,' replied Algy, smiling down at her. 'Can you doubt it?'

'I . . . I don't believe you,' said Flora, slightly shaken. 'In any event, is not Ellie your cousin?'

'But it is true! George asked me particularly to be nice to you while he was away. And, of course, while he is gone, I feel I must squire Grandmama around.'

'Sir George asked you to . . .' How dared he! Anger made her stop still in the middle of the floor and stare at Algy. 'What right has he got . . .! Oh, how like him! Ordering everybody's life around.' Flora drew a deep breath. 'Sometimes, Mr Kingsley, I could cheerfully kill your brother. And you may tell him, with my compliments, that I do not need his patronizing!'

'But, Miss Peat,' protested Algy, amused, 'George meant it kindly.'

'Of course he meant it kindly,' snapped Flora. 'He says the most insulting things with the highest possible motives! Only this time I cannot answer back.'

'And you would like to?' Algy looked at Flora with a new interest.

'Wouldn't I just! No! No, of course not! As far as I am concerned the longer he stays in Italy the better.'

'I am sorry if I upset you, Miss Peat,' said Algy, soothingly. 'Come let us go into the hall for a breather. And I really do not need my brother's instructions, you know, to induce me to dance with a pretty girl.'

The hall of the St Alleyn house was cool and dim after the heat and lights of the ballroom. There were cold marble slabs on the floor and green flower arrangements in the corners. Behind one of these ferneries Blanche and Hugh were standing concealed. They were standing very close together and almost motionless.

'But Blanche,' whispered Hugh, his fingers gently caressing the nape of her neck, 'I do not wish to hurt Alice.'

'Of course not, Hugh,' Blanche whispered back sweetly. 'I would not dream of taking anything that was rightfully hers.'

'Whatever am I to do?'

Blanche allowed a pause. 'You must do exactly as you wish, Hugh. Only don't forget, I have feelings as well.'

'Oh, God, Blanche, it is *you* I want! I have never felt like this before.'

Blanche thought she would die with sheer happiness. She turned in the dim light and pulled his head down to hers, frantically, passionately kissing his cheek, his chin until she could reach his mouth. She could feel the beating of his heart under his jacket, a fast, unsteady beat, and her own heart echoing it. She held him closer so that he could feel the swell of her breasts. Hugh's hand moved gently down from her neck until he could cup one breast. The nipple hardened against his finger. Blanche sighed. She wanted him. Why should she be ashamed?

Whether Algy's intentions were amorous, or merely friendly, in taking her out of the hot and crowded ballroom into the cool of the hall, Flora never discovered. For as they came down the stairs which led into the hall Flora happened to glance over the bannisters behind a group of ornamental ferns. There was Blanche! Her sister! Encouraging the intimacies of a man everybody knew was a cad! A man who was practically engaged, certainly engaged in honour, to Alice Banks!

Flora gave a gasp of shock – all the greater because of her own envy of Blanche's position. Algy stopped and took in the situation immediately.

'Oh Heavens,' stammered Flora. 'Whatever shall I do?' Her own hopes and wishes now looked irredeemably sordid. She was behaving exactly like Blanche! Or at least she would like to!

What must he think of her? 'Let us go back, at once!' Flora clutched at Algy's arm. 'Please!'

'No,' said Algy decidedly. 'You cannot go back to the ballroom in this state. Let us sit quietly on this step and have a talk. Now listen to me.' He took her hand comfortingly in his. 'Nobody in their senses, Miss Peat, is going to equate you with your sister.'

'You mean that it is common knowledge?' gasped Flora.

Algy shrugged. 'Some women are only interested in a man if he belongs to another woman. Your sister is that sort of article. Hugh Dunster is an experienced man of the world – he should understand that well enough. Be sensible, Miss Peat. If it becomes serious and your parents get wind of it, your sister will be packed off to cool down with some old aunt in the country. The Dunsters may encourage the match, but I doubt if they will get very far. The worst is that Miss Banks may be made very unhappy for a few months, but she is probably better off without him anyway.'

Flora was silent for a few minutes. 'I suppose you are right,' she sighed. 'But people do not respect Blanche very much, do they?'

'Ah, Mrs Grundy!' said Algy lightly, getting to his feet and assisting Flora to rise. 'I think we should all concern ourselves a little more with how we treat our fellow creatures and less with what Mrs Grundy may think.'

'Do you think I am being very silly?' asked Flora and she could not help the coquettish note in her voice.

'No. Only inexperienced.'

'Oh!' Flora felt the colour rushing to her cheeks. Had she given her feelings away? It was one thing to fall in love with Algy, to dream about him night and day, but quite another to have him suspect it for a moment.

'I promised George that I would keep an eye on you,' went on Algy, 'and I cannot allow you to worry yourself ill over your sister's carryings-on.'

'Sir George again!' snapped Flora, feeling that even at a distance of several thousand miles he managed to throw cold water over those precious, rose-coloured moments with Algy.

Flora did not return home until three o'clock. The Peat carriage collected her and Blanche at about half past two and the two girls drove back, each gazing out of their respective windows in silence. Blanche sighed every now and then, as if re-living some ecstatic dream; Flora snuggled her hands deeper into her muff and smiled at her reflection in the window.

Flora woke early the following morning. There were sounds opposite from her granny's room. Sarah was up and about, probably making Granny's breakfast. It must be about seven o'clock. If she went across now, she might get a cup of tea.

'Hello, my pet.' Old Mrs Peat greeted Flora with a smile. 'You're up early!'

'I could not sleep. Too much excitement, I expect.'

'Bring another cup, Sarah. Sit down, buttercup. How was your dance?'

Scenes of the dance began to flood back into Flora's mind. 'Lovely thank you, Granny. Ellie was looking very pretty. Adeline seemed a little tired I thought.' Flora paused and fiddled with her cup. 'Blanche was awful, Granny.'

'Why? What was she doing?'

'Firkytoodling with Hugh Dunster! What is so dreadful is that he is practically engaged to Alice Banks! We . . . we saw them in the hall, they were hidden behind some ferns, but even so, anybody might have seen them, doubtless many did.'

'It's a poor dance where you cannot steal a quick kiss,' observed Mrs Peat.

'Mr Kingsley . . . the man I was with . . . said that it would come to nothing. I think he thought I was making too much of it. Maybe I am, and he was very kind and told me not to worry, but Granny I *know* Blanche! She has always gone to any lengths to get what she wants and perhaps Hugh being a wastrel and a detrimental and Alice being nutty on him only gives spice to her hunting!'

'Miaow!' said Mrs Peat tartly. 'Puss is jealous.'

'I am not being catty, Granny, truly I am not. I know people are prepared to be indulgent if the young man is your sweetheart. I remember when Ida Clevedon got engaged, nobody minded a bit of spooning on the sly. But Blanche disappears with such cads!'

'Now don't take on so, Flora! I shall have a quiet word with Bill. He knows I often hear things up here that he doesn't. I daresay Sarah's gossip from the servants will bring me your news anyway.'

'Surely it has not reached the servants!' cried Flora in alarm.

'My dear,' said Mrs Peat, looking at Flora a little severely, 'the entire dance last night was run by servants. Who took your coats, brought you drinks, played the music and drove you home? They all have ears like the rest of us, even though you think them invisible. Use your head Flora! There were, what? a hundred guests at your little hop and at least a dozen servants running round them.'

'But servants are not supposed to gossip about their betters.'

'If you were a housemaid earning fifteen pounds a year, Flora, your only chance of bettering yourself might easily depend on your knowledge of current gossip. Rumours of a wedding and the chance of being a lady's maid or a housekeeper could nearly double your income.'

'I never thought of that,' said Flora, soberly.

The pretty house that Algy Kingsley had bought for Anny in Chelsea was run very efficiently with a housemaid, a cook and a groom-cum-gardener. Anny herself was not above helping with the housework or the cookery, and indeed had been known to tell Algy not to come on a particularly wet washday as the laundry was too heavy for Lizzie to manage without her help.

When Anny first lived with Algy she thought that he only wanted a wanton, as they said, who could crack nuts between her tail. She swiftly realized that he wanted a home and a pretty and beddable woman to come back to and to take out without worrying about offending a lady's sensibilities. She only once allowed herself be shocked, near the beginning of their acquaintance, when they were strolling in Cremorne Gardens. Algy was lightheartedly surveying the charms of the anonymas there, and he pointed one out to Anny with his cane. 'Now there's a good fuckish piece of jam.' Anny drew her breath in sharply, but before she could say anything, Algy brought his cane down on her buttocks with a sharp swish. 'Now don't you play the prude, Anny,' was all he said, but he never had to repeat the warning. Anny yelped and then laughed. 'All right,' she said, twirling her parasol in imitation of Algy's cane. 'Am I allowed to point out a real bang-up swell?'

'No, by Jove, you are not,' shouted Algy, grabbing her parasol. 'If ever I find you with any other fellow in your eye, you will not sit down for a week, that's all!'

Anny laughed and capitulated. For Algy had come like manna from Heaven when she was unhappy and worried. He loved her and gave her everything. If sometimes, when she was alone, the old nightmares came back, at least when she was with him they vanished like phantoms before the dawn. This god-like creature was welcome to claim all her attention if it should please him to do so.

Anny knew she must lose Algy some day: he would wish to marry and have a family of his own. No doubt, she thought resentfully, she would be very rich and beautiful, and of course Lady Kingsley would encourage the match.

Anny dreaded it when George was away, for then Algy felt it his duty to go more into Society, and against the angelics and their match-making Mamas, Anny had no protection. Sooner or later Algy would succumb. Just now Anny had the strong impression that Algy had gone to the St Alleyns' dance with at least a partial intention of squiring some girl. 'Let him not like her, please God', she prayed. 'I know he'll have to leave me sometime, but not just yet. Please don't let him leave me just yet.'

For some reason Flora felt very reluctant to visit Adeline after the St Alleyns' dance. She knew she ought to go, Adeline would be expecting to enjoy their usual sisterly gossip. Besides, Adeline was looking far from well and expressed such a pathetic desire for Flora to come to see her soon that Flora felt very guilty that she had allowed several days to pass after the dance without making any effort to go.

Blanche meanwhile, informed Mrs Peat rather spitefully that Flora had danced with Algy Kingsley. 'And of course, she did not think to introduce him to me, the mean cat.' Flora replied hastily that she had met Mr Kingsley at Grace's party, and that he was simply being kind to her. She contrived to give the impression that Lady Kingsley had more or less forced him to be polite and that she felt she barely knew him, certainly not enough to warrant introducing him to her sister.

Blanche shrugged and Mrs Peat allowed the subject to drop,

but Flora had the uneasy feeling that Adeline would not let her off so easily. Flora felt that she could not bear to have Adeline poking about in her secret life, certainly not a secret which she herself hardly understood. How could she have fallen in love with Algy so suddenly? She barely knew him. She knew he had a dolly-mop in keeping. But that made not the slightest difference. She knew that it had no future, that he thought of her merely as an acquaintance, but all these sensible warnings were swept away in a rush of quite indiscriminating emotion.

Then one evening Mrs Peat returned from paying calls with momentous news, and Flora could no longer avoid visiting her sister.

'Now, girls, I have some wonderful news for us all. Dear, dear Adeline is expecting an Interesting Event in the autumn!'

Poor Adeline felt somewhat differently. Charles told her nothing of what to expect. It was not until she was sick for several mornings running that she diffidently consulted Charles. Could it be Cook's food? Perhaps the pork at the weekend was not quite fresh? Did Charles think she should turn Cook off?

Charles laughed at her ignorance, but he did not attempt to enlighten it. She was going to give him a child in the autumn was all that he would say. Adeline tried to put aside her embarrassment and beg him to tell her more. All Charles would say was that she was not to worry and he would look after her.

Adeline was left with hideous nightmares of her body splitting open in the night and shooting out a baby like a seed from a broom pod. Adeline had subscribed previously to the 'God is sending a little soul into the world' school of thought, and prided herself on the purity and innocence of her mind. Now, reluctantly she was beginning to perceive its limitations.

Perhaps Isabel would be able to help her. It seemed so dreadful to be married to a doctor and not to know. Adeline began to feel bitterly ashamed, both of herself for her ignorance and of Charles for not enlightening her. However, there was an unexpected bonus: Charles' marital duties now included abstinence. Her weekly ordeal was postponed. He had the bed in the spare bedroom made up so as not to disturb her if he came in late. The relief of not having him in bed beside her was great indeed.

When Flora visited her Adeline was able to forget the whole

disagreeable topic, for Flora was showing a most unladylike vivacity and was dressed in a walking dress of green merino with the skirts hitched up to reveal the flounces of a scarlet petticoat! Adeline could actually see Flora's ankles! Or at least she would have seen them if Flora had not been wearing black buttoned boots. And the dress was of so very fashionable a cut, quite unsuitable to the quiet restraint she had always admired in her sister.

Adeline brushed aside Flora's offered congratulations on the Approaching Event and went straight to the crux of the matter.

'How do you come to be acquainted with Mr Kingsley, Flora?'

Flora's first reaction was panic and a desire to deny all knowledge of the gentleman. But there was something in Adeline's attitude of moral indignation and prepared righteousness that made her change her mind. Flora might hide her feelings, but she saw no reason why she should feel ashamed of knowing Algy.

'I met him at Grace's party. He is nice, is he not?'

Adeline sat up straighter in her chair, her mouth tight. 'He has no business to be in Society. He is a libertine.'

'A very good-looking one,' put in Flora saucily.

Adeline held up her hands to cover her ears. 'Flora! Whatever has come over you? Have we not often discussed the problem of Wild Oats? A man who does such things should be cast out of Society as a woman is. I distinctly remember you agreeing with me.'

'Yes, I remember it too. I think now I was wrong. We should all be more charitable.'

'There is time enough to be more charitable when he gives up that disgusting creature and behaves in a more Christian manner!'

'I daresay he is very attached to her,' said Flora, irritated. Adeline always did have that mean, pinched-up look when she was trying to be Christian, she thought resentfully. Sometimes I think that I really dislike her.

'In a coarse way, perhaps.' Adeline pressed her handkerchief to her lips. Was it possible that Flora, too, was deserting her? She had the sudden awful feeling that cracks were appearing all over and that any minute the whole fabric of her life would fall apart. Adeline took up her baby knitting with shaking fingers.

Flora's irritation evaporated. She crossed over and sat down beside Adeline. 'There, there, I am sorry if I upset you. Now,

115

dearest, tell me all about the baby and what you and Charles have been doing with yourselves? Mama mentioned something about your meeting some grand doctor. Now who was it?'

'A Dr Embsay. Have you heard of him? He has invited us to dinner.'

'The one who has something to do with that new hospital?'

'St Thomas's, yes.'

'You are moving in exalted circles. He has become quite influential, has he not?'

'His family is something to do with the Embsay Iron Foundry. Apparently he has been most generous to the hospital.'

'It will make a lot of difference to Charles, having his acquaintance?'

Adeline hesitated. 'You will not repeat this, I know, but Charles says that there are rumours that some of Dr Embsay's methods have not been quite scrupulous. Something to do with the building contracts, I believe. But nothing has been substantiated.'

'So it is a mixed blessing?'

Adeline nodded. 'I feel myself that we should be a little more careful before being on dinner-party terms with him, but Charles disagrees with me.'

Adeline had tried to drop a word of warning in Charles' ear. It would not be Right for them to know a man of blemished character; had dear Charles considered the moral implications? 'Eating a man's dinner does not mean we have to approve of his behaviour,' said Charles testily, irritated by Adeline's assumption of moral superiority. 'Besides, I hear he has a capital cook, even if his other actions may stick in our gullets!' he continued, with an attempt at humour. 'Anyway, I have accepted the invitation, Adeline, and we are going.'

Adeline mentioned nothing of this to her sister, but the conversation about Dr Embsay made her uncomfortable all the same and she was relieved when her sister took her leave.

On returning from his honeymoon, Dr Charles Woodcock swiftly decided that his marital obligations did not include fidelity. He told himself that ladies did not like it anyway and that Adeline would look the other way. Of course, she would receive all the respect and affection due to his wife, but he was sure she would far rather be relieved of his attentions, especially now that the baby was on the way.

In fact, far from spending the evening studying while Adeline was chaperoning her sisters at the St Alleyns' dance, Charles had spent a highly convivial evening with his brother-in-law. Isabel had gone to spend the evening with her mama. Philip Rivers was entertaining Charles in the smoking-room, which was filled with cigar smoke and a smell of brandy. Charles was sprawling in an armchair, his jacket and waistcoat buttons undone and his feet on a small table. Both gentlemen were a little bit on the go.

'Women,' pronounced Charles ponderously and a trifle slurred, 'are not like us!'

Philip nodded his head gravely.

'We need to have a good rogering at least once a week.'

'At least.' Philip poured out some more brandy.

'Or even twice,' said Charles.

Philip gave a hiccup. 'Twicer is nicer,' he agreed.

'Mind you, speaking as a doctor, twice a week can debilitate the system and cause bodily weakness through spending too much.'

'Quite so,' said Philip.

'Speaking as a man,' added Charles, 'that's rubbish.' He paused for thought. 'Ladies are different.'

'The Ladies!' echoed Philip, raising his glass.

'Ladies would rather not have it at all. Their sensibilities are extremely delicate.'

'Ladies,' added Philip with finality, 'do not like fucking.'

'They do not.'

Both gentlemen sat and pondered on this state of affairs. They seemed to be sinking into a state of maudlin self-pity. Charles poured himself some more brandy and sat sipping it moodily.

'Nancy likes fucking,' said Philip suddenly.

'So does Fanny,' said Charles, sitting up. 'And who's that new one at Madame's?'

'Kate. Now she has thighs like vices. What muscle control!'

'And what a pretty little bum, so smackable!'

'I'm a bosom man myself.'

'Nobody can accuse me of not liking bosoms,' said Charles

117

belligerently. 'It's those pendulous ones with the strawberry tits.'

'I don't care for those,' said Philip. 'They always remind me of horses' nosebags. I like those bouncy round ones.'

'Ah, give me a pretty article with a firm bum and nimble hips and I'm suited.'

Philip stood up. 'What's the time?'

'Ten-ish,' replied Charles, buttoning himself up.

Philip rang the bell. 'Call us a hackney, will you please,' he said. 'Dr Woodcock and I are just going out.'

The Christmas holidays were drawing to a close. Tom was already packed up to return to Marlborough. His hair-cord trunk was waiting down in the hall to be taken to the station and Tom could be heard up in the old schoolroom lamenting the inadequacy of his tuck box and the awful punishments ahead of him if he couldn't find his Latin grammar. Daisy was due to go back to the Kingsleys on the following Monday. She was longing to see Grace again.

'It is nothing but Blanche, Blanche, Blanche,' she confided to Flora. 'How many beaux she has, who is coming to her dance, who will present her at Court. I tell you, I am longing to go back to Miss Martin, even if it is boring old Racine all the time!'

Flora could not help but agree with Daisy. In any case, Algy might put in an appearance in Berkeley Square from time to time, now that Sir George was away. Otherwise, apart from Lady Clevedon's Twelfth Night dance, she would have very little opportunity of seeing Algy – and that thought was unbearable.

Lady Clevedon's Twelfth Night dance proved to be a turning-point for several members of the Peat family.

Geraldina, who was taken to the dance in the Milford carriage, sustained a very unpleasant half-hour with her father. Gerald Milford, his usual laziness over his daughter's affairs triumphing, had done very little about Francis Grant. The episode at the St James's Theatre angered him, but Mrs Peat's subsequent interference made him so furious that he promptly declined to take any further action in the matter. It was entirely her fault, he told her, his face thrust forward on an angry red neck, if she gave birth to such a milk-sop. Ernest should be able to keep his wife satisfied and if he could not then he should not have married Geraldina!

Mrs Peat retreated, flustered and shocked. But a few months later Ernest came to his father-in-law, spluttering like a turkey-cock and muttering some rigmarole about divorce and adultery, so Gerald was forced to take some action. The night of the Clevedons' dance, he peremptorily ordered Ernest to go in his own carriage, for he wanted a private word with Geraldina.

'Now, Geraldina,' said Gerald, as soon as they were in the carriage. 'What have you been about? I have had Ernest worrying at me about divorce, and Bill Peat tells me that people are beginning to talk.'

'Divorce! Ernest? He would not dare!'

'By himself, no. However he might with the backing of his parents. You do realize what that would mean, do you not? You may be an heiress, Geraldina, but you would no longer be accepted in Society. Dammit, girl, I thought that by getting you married off early and giving you plenty of the actual, you would be kept out of this sort of thing!'

'All Ernest wants is an angel in the house,' said Geraldina scornfully. 'He does not know what to do with a woman. You should have chosen a proper man for me if you were so keen to have me tied up in marriage!'

'A husband has the right to expect his wife to be faithful,' began Gerald, asserting his male authority.

'Rubbish! Why the blazes should I not have a fling if I feel like it!' shouted Geraldina. 'You have been carrying on with that Mrs Hunter all these years, do you think I don't know? What do you want me to do with such a gaby as Ernest? Take up embroidery?'

'You should at least have been more discreet.'

'Very well, I will be more discreet. Only I cannot give up Frank.'

'You will have to, my dear. His colonel is posting him to Secunderabad!'

'This is your doing!' cried Geraldina, white with passion.

'Yes, it is. I am not risking any scandals in my family.'

'Then I shall follow him.'

'You will not,' shouted Gerald, banging the seat so that the carriage springs twanged. 'Have you no sense? If you do, you can say good-bye to returning here. You will never see your children again, Ernest will see to that. You will hardly be accepted in India, a very stuffy society out there, just a few white women, all with close ties to home. Your invitations would soon cease once they understood who you were. What would you do then? Live by yourself with a few Indian servants? Join the kept women, going from one officer to the next?'

Damn Father, damn the Peats, damn Ernest! thought Geraldina furiously. Imposing their petty rules on her! They had the Milford money safely tied up, what more did they want? She sank back in her seat and closed her eyes. The future, which had seemed so full of excitement and promise, suddenly narrowed to the stuffy social round she thought she was escaping. She lived almost entirely through the excitement of her stolen love affair with Frank. What was there left for her now?

Gerald patted his daughter's hand. 'Come, come, my dear. It is not as bad as all that. Let Francis go. He has his career to think of too, you know. If, in a few years, when all this has died down, there should be another fellow in your eye, well, Society will turn the other way, provided you are discreet. Good gracious, it is being done all the time. What do you think this new Marl-borough House set is doing? But you were not abiding by the rules, Geraldina.'

Brazen it out! That is what she must do, thought Geraldina furiously. Go to this stupid dance and show them that she was the sweet, devoted wife. Dare them to cast the slur of scandal at her! Cling to Ernest like a limpet, hang affectionately on his arm, protest her ignorance, admire his strength, his superior knowledge! Butter up his masculine pomposity with layer upon layer of flattery. He would take it, lap it up and beg for more! The whole stupid, self-satisfied male sex would take it, more fools them! Well, if that was the way Ernest wished it to be, he should have it. Only let him beware! For next time she would make no such mistake!

The morning of the Clevedons' dance found Flora and Adeline shopping in Regent Street. The afternoon was the really fashion-able time for shopping, but Flora and Adeline preferred it when the shops were not too crowded. Flora hoped to buy Adeline a new, warm shawl to keep her sister warm during her pregnancy, especially as Adeline seemed to spend most of her time sitting lethargically on the day-bed and complaining of the January cold. They tried Farmer and Rogers' Great Shawl and Cloak Emporium, but the pretty Indian, Chinese and French shawls there seemed too light and summery. Now they were on their way to visit the London Scotch Warehouse where Flora thought they might find a Shetland shawl for Adeline.

They wandered slowly down Regent Street, stopping every now and then to look in the shop windows, followed at a discreet distance by Adeline's maid, when Adeline stopped to look at some baby linens.

Flora was not much interested, happy to look around her at the bustling crowds, when her heart gave a great thud. For there, over the road, quite unmistakably, was Algy Kingsley with a very pretty fair-haired girl on his arm. The girl was pointing at something in the window and Algy was looking down at her with such an expression of tender concern on his face, that Flora felt quite sick with jealousy.

'But she is pretty!' she thought incredulously. 'She is fair, and elegant and *real*. Algy *loves* her!'

The misery swelled up in her throat and she felt an intense desire to burst into tears. How could she have been so stupid, so self-deluding as to imagine he might ever become attached to her? It was all a dream and she had told herself that it was real. He had never given her any reason to suppose he cared for her more than as a sister.

Adeline's voice made her turn back and when she was able to look again, Algy and his companion had gone.

When Flora finally found herself alone in her room, supposedly resting before the dance, she flung herself face down on her bed and burst into tears. She found she was weeping as a kind of luxury, weeping for herself, not for the loss of Algy, but for her own lost hopes and wishes. She was crying because she was nearly twenty-eight and the only man she had ever loved was, and always had been, attached to somebody else. She had squandered all her emotions on a figment of her over-heated imagination and not on somebody real.

She had only herself to blame! She knew very well that Algy kept a mistress, but she deliberately let herself be blinded, thinking in her arrogance that somehow Anny did not really count. She had not even allowed her a name, but she knew it well enough. Anny. Algy and Anny, that was what it really was.

She had always been so scornful of Blanche's heady excitements. But was she any better? Blanche, at least, was able to fall in love with men who wanted her – here Flora burst into tears again – she may choose cads, but at least she gets her kisses!

Mrs Peat was sitting in the drawing-room, waiting for the carriage that would take them to the Clevedons' dance to be brought round. She smoothed her dress down with satisfaction and looked complacently across to where Blanche was sitting. Nothing, in the last few months, had curbed her rising joy in the fact that this season she would be bringing out her prettiest and best-loved daughter. In Blanche's triumphs her own successes over thirty years before would come alive again. Her daughter would not labour under the disadvantages of a stern vicarage upbringing and very little money. Susan Hebden had had to make do with the occasional Christmas romp and the dubious excitements of eyeing the young curate during Morning Service. Blanche would have all the opportunities she could possibly desire. Her choice of young men would be so much wider. There was Lord Pateley, who was plainly besotted, and Tommy Clevedon would be a viscount one day. . . .

The door opened and her husband entered.

'Susan, come down to my study a minute if you please. I wish to have a word with you.'

'But the carriage will be here any moment, William.'

'It can wait.'

Mrs Peat sighed and accompanied him downstairs.

'Now, William, what is it?' Then, with a sudden rush of anxiety, 'Nothing to do with the business I trust?'

'No. No. It is about Blanche.'

'Blanche! Are you telling me that young Pateley has offered?' cried Mrs Peat, turning towards him excitedly.

'No,' said Mr Peat shortly. 'Nobody is going to offer for Blanche at all if she carries on the way she has been doing. I have never interfered with your upbringing of our daughters, Susan, but now I think I must. Blanche has acquired the reputation of being a very fast young lady. Do you know what they are calling her in the clubs? The Venus Fly-trap.'

'Oh, men in clubs always talk like that, I am well aware. But you are being most unfair, William. I have always done my very best for all our daughters. Adeline, I think you will agree, has been most successful – a devoted husband, a baby on the way, what more could a girl wish for? As for Flora, what can one do with her? At least she has decided to make herself slightly more presentable. I think you are being most unkind to dear Blanche. She cannot help being a very pretty girl and if a young man wishes to take her into the conservatory, can you blame him?'

'Susan,' said Mr Peat sharply, 'you are not attending. Society does not blame the young man who tries a bit of firkytoodling on the sly. It *does* blame the girl who allows him to go too far.'

'Blanche would never do such a thing!'

'She certainly has that reputation.'

'Whoever has been telling you this silly nonsense?'

'Mrs Peat, either you control your daughter or I tell you plainly that I will not advance one farthing towards her coming-out. We have quite enough problems on our plates with Geraldina's headstrong behaviour. Do you wish the whole Peat family to be ostracized? And what of Flora's chances, and Daisy's? Do you realize Lady Kingsley may refuse to have Daisy in the house because of the unsavoury reputation of her sister?'

'I know who it is,' cried Mrs Peat, who had not been listening to a word of this. 'It is that sanctimonious prig, Charles. Good gracious, Mr Peat, Blanche is a very pretty girl. What do you expect her to do? Join a nunnery?'

'There is a difference between a quick kiss and the sort of firkytoodling Blanche has been allowing. One of these days one of the johnnies she goes with will mean business and then she will be in trouble. If you are looking for a good marriage for your daughter Mrs Peat, then you should warn her not to sell herself so cheaply.'

'Well, I shall tell Blanche that she must not go out of my sight,' said Mrs Peat resentfully, 'and she will blame me for it, poor darling. I shall have to tell her, "Your Papa is determined you shall be left on the shelf" and I am sure I do not know what I have done to deserve all this.'

The dance was to be a small one: just to while away the tedious-ness of the winter, Lady Clevedon said. She had not particularly wanted to invite the Peats – the rumours surrounding Mrs Ernest Peat were so very unsavoury and now Miss Blanche was beginning to be talked about. But as Griselda was such a friend of Blanche's and Ida had been at school with Flora and Adeline it would look too particular to omit them from her invitation list. Lady Clevedon was very strict where her daughters were concerned, but even she did not wish to be the first to ostracize the Peats. Moreover, it would be most unfair on Flora and Adeline, neither of whom had done anything to deserve such a snub. But it was Daisy Peat who quite unwittingly swung the day. Lady Clevedon went to pay a call on Lady Colefax and heard in the course of conversation that Lady Kingsley had taken Daisy Peat and, to a certain extent, Flora, under her wing. They were pronounced 'nice, well-behaved girls' and Lady Clevedon had no wish to offend the Kingsleys. Nevertheless the cards were sent with some reluctance.

Lady Clevedon greeted Mrs Peat politely but coolly and was relieved to see that Blanche was content for once to sit quietly beside her mother. She did not know that throughout the carriage journey Blanche had been subjected to a complaining monologue of the ingratitude of daughters, the unreasonableness of Papa and the dangers of appearing fast. Blanche was silent and subdued from resentment, but underneath her mind was working furiously. Very well, if that is what people were saying, she would be demure and retiring this once. It was going to be a very flat, horrid party anyway, Lady Clevedon was so beastly strict and she knew from Griselda that the Dunsters were not coming. She would be the very picture of insipid propriety, but that did not mean that she was going to give up what she wanted. She would just have to be more careful, that was all. Or more daring.

Geraldina came in on Ernest's arm. She was looking magnificent in a cherry-coloured heavy glacé silk with the sparkle of diamonds around her throat and in her hair, setting off the creaminess of her skin and the shining black of her curls. As soon as she appeared a crowd of men gathered round her, Tommy Clevedon among them, as his mother saw with distaste. But Geraldina was behaving with ostentatious wifely submission and she did not so much as glance at the gentlemen around her.

Ernest prepared to move away to allow her admirers access, but Geraldina's hand tightened on his arm. Ernest ran a finger inside a suddenly tightened collar and stayed where he was. Geraldina was standing, talking to Ernest, when Mrs Padgett came up. Mrs Padgett had once been a very affectionate friend of Gerald Milford's – a friendship that Geraldina had successfully thwarted some years ago.

'Geraldina, dear,' she trilled, inclining her head graciously. 'Your husband has just been telling me that you have decided to go to Paris with him next month. I am surprised, I must confess, that you wish to go on what is surely just a business trip! I always had the impression that you found more attractions at home, particularly,' she lowered her voice and continued archly, 'when your husband is away. Or am I wrong?'

Ernest shuffled uneasily and cleared his throat.

'My dear Mrs Padgett,' said Geraldina sweetly, 'if one's husband offers to take one to Paris, no woman in her senses would refuse. I am looking forward to seeing the Empress Eugenie and all the gaieties of Paris. I expect it will be quite like a second honeymoon, will it not, darling?' She smiled winningly at Ernest.

Mrs Padgett's eyes snapped angrily. 'I am sure you will find Paris to your liking. I hear the ladies of the *demi-monde* are quite the stars of Society over there. You will feel quite at home.'

There was a moment of dangerous silence, then Geraldina laughed.

'Certainly they are among the leaders of fashion,' she replied. 'Your own delightful gown, Mrs Padgett, is an Agnes Sorel robe, named after a king's mistress. So you, too, are in the forefront of French fashion!'

Mrs Padgett drew in her breath with an audible hiss. Then she picked up her skirts as if to remove them from Geraldina's contaminating presence and swept away.

Ernest stood smiling awkwardly. Once or twice he opened his mouth to speak, but was quelled by the malicious glare in Mrs Padgett's eyes. He did not know what to think. It was almost as if Mrs Padgett was trying to insult his wife. It was true he suspected that Geraldina was going with that good-for-nothing cousin of hers, but Gerald Milford assured him that he was mistaken, and whispered in his ear that that Grant fellow was soon to be posted off to India. Well, he was willing to admit he might be wrong. Of course it was only cousinly affection: ladies did not have the coarser passions of men, he knew that, and he always tried to be most considerate of Geraldina that way and not make too many demands on her.

Several gentlemen now approached Geraldina and begged the honour of a dance. Smilingly Geraldina refused them all.

'I am staying with Ernest tonight,' she said, patting his arm with one gloved hand. He smiled uneasily.

'It's a beastly shame,' cried Tommy Clevedon. 'Peat, let me dance with your wife, there's a good fellow.'

'Geraldina must please herself,' said Ernest.

'No, go away, Tommy. I mean to dance only with Ernest.'

Blanche was still sitting among the chaperones as the dances began. She saw with resentment that she was being avoided. True, there were still several names on the stick of her fan, but Tommy Clevedon at least only asked her out of politeness when Flora was obliged to refuse him. God knows what he saw in Flora, except that she was a friend of Ida's, and probably Ida begged him to see that Flora was not quite a wallflower.

Blanche glanced speculatively round the room and saw Lady Clevedon watching her. Spiteful old cat! How Ida and Griselda stood being such models of propriety she could not think. But it would do her no good if she was ostracized. Ah, there was Alfred Pateley! Blanche gave him a shy and fluttering smile and then lowered her eyes in maidenly confusion. Would he come over, or would he not?

Well, she did not care. The whole stuffy lot could go to hell! Hugh Dunster might be a detrimental, but he could certainly come up with something more exciting than this inspid lot. The trouble was Hugh felt himself under an obligation of honour to Alice Banks. How could she make him feel under a greater obligation to her? Of course, they were right for each other. Hugh thought so too. But she wanted him to act on that. What would push him to make that final leap?

Flora watched Algy across the room with mixed feelings. The feeling of deep affection was still there; she regarded anything he was or might do with a kind of loving indulgence. But the wild, heart-thumping excitement had gone. Algy would always be rather special to her, perhaps more special because it had all been so secret, but as a loved brother, not as anything more.

When Katie Anning came over, quite starry-eyed over Algy's charms, Flora found that she could respond quite naturally and even joke about it.

'Flora! How lovely to see you, my sweet, and what a beautiful gown! We have just arrived. We brought Mr Kingsley with us Is he not too spiffy for words? I am quite smit.'

'An Adonis!' said Flora lightly, laughing at Katie's exaggerated sigh. 'Unfortunately, unless we murder his *chère amie* there is no hope for either of us!'

'Well, you seem to be very cool about him, I must say,' complained Katie. 'And he said such nice things about you, too, in the carriage.'

Flora looked up quickly.

'So we are not so cool after all,' said Katie with satisfaction, watching the tell-tale flush on Flora's cheek.

'All right,' said Flora crossly. 'I, too, have had my bones turned to water by Algy Kingsley. He has been very kind to me, indeed all the Kingsleys have. He stopped me making a fool of myself when I saw Blanche canoodling at the St Alleyns' dance. But he can be nothing more special to either of us, Katie, you know that.'

'You are more sensible than I am,' said Katie, with a sigh. 'But I cannot be jealous of you, dear Flora. So I will tell you that he told me you were very charming and even his dour brother was very struck by you.'

For some reason, the reference to George seemed to affect Flora more powerfully. 'What!' she cried. 'But we were always quarrelling!'

'Quarrelling? But he has the sweetest temper.'

'No, no, I meant his brother,' said Flora, blushing painfully at the mistake. '*He* was always quarrelling with me. I wonder what Algy meant? But perhaps he did not mean it as a compliment.'

'If Algy Kingsley called *me* charming, I should think it a very great compliment,' said Katie indignantly.

Flora was not listening. She realized suddenly, somewhat to her surprise, that she was going to miss Sir George. The house in

Berkeley Square was going to seem sadly flat without Sir George's astringent conversation.

Young Lord Pateley munched his oyster patty reflectively. What a stunner! How sweet and innocent she – Blanche – was, white and pure as a lily! She had promised him the first two dances after supper. He watched her now, helping her mother to some strawberry Chantilly, her flowered dress swaying slightly as she bent over her mother's chair and fetched her shawl. He allowed his gaze to fall on her smooth cheek and the rounded contours of her neck and shoulders. He swallowed. She was like a goddess, so delicately fair.

There! She had caught his glance and given him a shy little half-smile before her lashes fluttered down and she looked away.

'Hello, Pateley.' It was Algy's voice behind him. He gulped and turned round.

'You are admiring Miss Blanche, I see,' said Algy rather unkindly, 'as must we all.'

'Quite a slap-up filly, eh?' stammered Lord Pateley, trying to appear knowledgeable and unconcerned – a sophisticated connoisseur of female beauty.

'She certainly has a rag on every bush,' replied Algy.

'You do not say so!' gasped Lord Pateley, his fresh young face painfully flushed.

'Miss Blanche is getting quite a reputation for being a little too easy. Do you know what they call her in the clubs? The Venus Fly-trap.'

'You should not say such things to ruin an innocent girl's reputation,' said Lord Pateley hotly, and with extreme embarrassment.

'If we were still at Eton,' said Algy pleasantly, 'I would give you a kick up the backside to knock some sense into you. Here in Lady Clevedon's charming drawing-room I can only point out under cover of the oyster patties – thank you – that Miss Blanche is rapidly becoming one of Society's pitfalls.'

'The Peats are the most respected family, and very well blunted. She is not looking for a gold-mine.'

'If you pop the question to Miss Blanche,' said Algy bluntly, 'in a couple of years you will find yourself sharing her with any johnny who cares to take a slice.'

'You cannot be serious,' cried Lord Pateley, much agitated.

'You are besotted,' said Algy, with disgust. 'Well, do not do anything rash.'

What nonsense, thought Lord Pateley. Why, was not the youngest Peat girl having lessons with Grace Lennox? The thought crossed his mind that Algy might be after Blanche himself, but he dismissed it. It was common knowledge that Algy kept a shop girl in Chelsea. Lord Pateley began to feel uneasy: Algy had been the leader of Oppidans at Eton. He had been Algy's fag. It was not possible that Algy should be misleading him deliberately. He looked at Blanche again. She was talking to James Anning and pouting prettily at something he said. Now she was leaning back in her chair, her breasts thrust slightly forward. Lord Pateley looked at James' goggling eyes and felt himself prickle with embarrassment.

He rose to his feet and began to button up his gloves. With a sore and puzzled heart he walked over to claim his dances.

Chapter Six

THE Christmas holidays were over and Twelfth Night was past and gone. In Belgrave Square the Christmas tree was thrown out and the paper chains and bells put away for another year. The smell of pine needles and hot candle wax faded slowly from the drawing-room and was replaced by the more usual fumes of gas and paraffin. Tom, under protest, went back to Marlborough College, fortified by a guinea from Papa and an extra half-guinea slipped to him by Flora as he was getting onto the train. The following week Daisy resumed her lessons at the Kingsleys.

Even before Penton opened the door Flora and Daisy could hear Grace's excited voice and the scamper of her feet as she ran downstairs.

'Christmas has been so dull, you can't think,' she cried to Daisy, hardly giving Daisy time to hand her cloak to Penton. 'Grandmama has not been well this last week and Cousin Algy hardly ever came over. I have seen practically nobody all holidays.' Her shyness was quite overcome in a gush of words and she ended by impulsively flinging her arms round Daisy and hugging her and then hugging Flora for good measure. After a few minutes Miss Martin's voice was heard calling and Daisy and Grace went upstairs.

To Flora's surprise Penton escorted her into the library.

'Sir George's orders, Miss,' he said respectfully, as Flora started to protest. 'He hopes you will use the library while he is away. A fire has been made up for you, Miss, and I'll bring some refreshments up for you in a few minutes.'

How kind of him, thought Flora, looking round the familiar book-lined room with pleasure. She wandered round, as she had done that first day, and looked at the curios and the prints. There were the Arabic tiles in that beautiful deep, vivid blue. There was the broken piece of capital from Palmyra, there the space on the wall where the family tree had been. Everything seemed to have George's astringent personality stamped on it and was a reminder of some conversation or quarrel, usually quarrel, Flora reflected with a grimace.

Penton brought in some wine and cakes and Flora sank down in one of the comfortable leather armchairs with the tray beside her. She looked up at the portrait of George and Algy above the mantelpiece. Algy was leaning negligently against a tree, his fair hair glinting under a shooting-cap. He held a gun under one arm and a pointer was lying obediently at his feet.

Flora looked at Algy a little ruefully. He was so very good-looking: his features were so perfectly chiselled and his eyes so very blue. She had allowed herself to be very spoony about him on the strength of a few evenings' flirtation. He had never allowed her to think it might be anything more. And truthfully, had she ever wished it to be anything more? He was kind and tolerant and she appreciated those qualities, but they had nothing else in common. She had heard that he enjoyed racing, which bored her stiff. Otherwise he appeared to like a life of quiet domesticity. Flora felt she had had enough quiet domesticity to last a lifetime.

After thinking along these lines for several minutes, Flora realized she could not have been very much in love with Algy Kingsley. She looked steadily at Algy's portrait, trying to define the attraction, and then transferred her gaze to his brother. Sir George was seated on a bay horse, his rather swarthy features staring out sternly over the heads of any onlookers. Behind him was an elegant Georgian house, neatly set amid rolling lawns with woods rising behind. Underneath the picture was inscribed, 'Sir George Kingsley, Bart, of Linchmere, with his brother Algernon, 1861.'

Even as Flora looked at him, she felt her hackles rise. He was not at all good-looking. He was far too dark for one thing, almost un-English in fact. His eyes were too deep set, their very dark brown being too piercing for comfort. His features were too sharp. He was wearing an olive-green velvet hunting-jacket with white Bedford cord breeches and black shiny boots. He was sitting, thought Flora indignantly, as if he owned the place and thought the world beneath him.

At least she would be spared his insufferable arrogance for a few months. Flora remembered she had promised to read *Wuthering Heights* by Ellis Bell. She went to the bookcase and found it. As she took it out a piece of paper fluttered down. She picked it up. It was very short and in Sir George's handwriting. It was headed 'Books for Flora' and underneath were some dozen titles. 'Books for Flora'. It was the heading that caught her startled attention. Yet he never called her anything but Miss Peat. Flora found herself staring at the innocuous piece of paper as if it held some hitherto unknown menace or promise that she could not puzzle out. The books he listed were ordinary enough: they were all works of fiction and most of them Flora had already discussed with Sir George.

Flora found her hand shaking. She felt breathless with . . . with the insult! Yes, that was it. It was an insult to assume such familiarity between them. Doubtless he called his housemaids by their first names too. The most dignified thing to do was to ignore it. She quickly replaced both the piece of paper and the book on the shelf.

It was silly of her to be so embarrassed and upset. She would read something improving, Mr Carlyle's *Past and Present*, for instance. But in spite of the benefits of Mr Carlyle's moral, if sombre, views, Flora's thoughts kept returning to the note. 'Books for Flora.' What had he meant by it?

A mild January turned into a cold, foggy February, with driving sleet and rain, which the London smoke soon turned to yellow slush. Then it froze. The wretched cab horses could be seen slipping and sliding on the cobbles and hordes of ragged boys, with feet blue with cold, sprang out of God-knew-where and offered to sweep the pavements and crossings for a penny. Many of them looked half-starved and shaking with fever, and one particularly cold morning Flora gave away all the change in her purse within barely half an hour. Some of the braver urchins, those at least with socks and shoes, could be seen skating on the Serpentine.

Old Mrs Peat was far from well. In her sitting-room a fire

burned perpetually in the grate and the room was well curtained against draughts. Mr Peat bought his mother a foot muff and Sarah smothered her in shawls and rugs, but she could not keep warm. Her face became pinched and pale and her skin looked dull and greyish.

Flora spent much of her time with her granny now. Somehow it seemed as if there might not be much time left. Flora told herself that when spring finally came she would get better and be her usual tart and lively self, but underneath was the fear that there might not be another spring for her to see.

Flora told old Mrs Peat about Algy Kingsley.

'I suppose I should have done all this falling in love at eighteen,' Flora finished rather sadly, sitting on a low footstool, her hands clasped around her knees and gazing into the fire. 'Then such infatuation would not have seemed so silly. I mean, I could have indulged in kisses and cuddles during Postman's Knock or Sardines, or something of the kind and it would all have seemed more natural somehow!'

'Better now than never, pet. And you did have the sense to choose a man who would not take advantage of you. Whether Blanche has done the same, I rather doubt.'

'I think Papa must have spoken to Mama about Blanche. Something was said before the Clevedons' dance, I am sure.'

'I spoke to Bill about it.'

'So that was it. Mama was furious.'

'You, too, have come under her scrutiny, you know.'

'Me!' cried Flora. 'I have not been canoodling on the sly!'

'She thinks you have come on a lot lately and is turning over various suitable matches in her mind.'

Flora laughed shortly. 'She is wasting her time.'

'Now don't you go getting it into your head that because one young man doesn't care enough to pop the question, there won't be others.'

'I . . . I hope so,' said Flora hesitantly. Her usual stock reply was that she was quite resigned to being the spinster in the family, coupled with some joke about becoming an eccentric aunt. But it was not even half true any more. She did not wish to spend the rest of her life living on the edges of other people's families: she wanted a life and a family of her own.

'I thought I was left on the shelf until I met Henry, your grandfather,' Mrs Peat said with a reminiscent smile. 'Of course it was over fifty years ago now and things was different then. He was a blacksmith in West Auckland – a good job he had, what with all the farm horses and the pit ponies to be shod. He had a good bit of work from the mines, welding and repairing and that. He was a good craftsman was your grandad. Always cared about what he was doing, you see. He did it proper.'

As she spoke her worn face seemed to light up and Flora felt she could see traces of the young girl who had won her Henry fifty years before. Her accent became more marked and her gnarled hands, now in lacy mittens, fluttered coyly as she described how they would walk out together of an evening.

'He knew about things did your grandad. He had an enquiring mind. Other people said he had a grasshopper mind, but I didn't think so. I remember him once going down a mine with one of the face workers because he wanted to see what it was like down there. Folks thought he was mad, but it was one of the things I loved about him. He always wanted to know, you see.'

'I wish I had known him,' said Flora.

'You're a bit like him, pet. Sometimes I catch an expression on your face and I think, there! that's Henry.' She sat silent for a moment gazing into the fire and Flora sat quietly on the footstool beside her. 'Fetch me the Bible box, Flora,' said Mrs Peat suddenly. Flora jumped up and did so.

Mrs Peat opened it and took out a small, battered book, with a black leather cover. 'Here Flora, I'd like you to have this. It's his journal. Well, it's more of a notebook really. Just observations on this and that. Perhaps you won't find it very interesting, and of course our lives were very old-fashioned and quiet. But it's written just the way he talked. I often wish he'd lived long enough for us to have our photographs taken. There used to be travelling portrait painters, who would do quite nice little pastels for people. A lot of folks had them done when they married. But somehow we never bothered, or when he came round there was a lot of work on at the forge and we was too busy. And then he was ill and we had no money and the bairns to look after and feed somehow.'

Flora took it carefully and opened the cover. 'Henry Peat,' it said in spidery brown writing, 'born 1776.' Flora felt she was regaining something very precious – a link with the past that had been allowed for too long to lie dusty and forgotten. They were all so eager to establish their credentials in their new social milieu. If their relations were not acceptable then they forgot them and quickly acquired friends who were. It was not only the Peats who did this. It was being done all around them. It was even encouraged explicitly by someone like Sir George Kingsley, who himself had no need to hide his ancestors. Bury your grandparents and great-grandparents, even your parents if need be! Pretend they never existed! If you want to stay at the top there must be no whisper of the ungenteel struggle of the way up. Send your sons to Public School! Marry your daughters into the gentry! Teach them to despise the very energy and enterprise that got them there!

Sarah came in with Mrs Peat's cordial and Flora rose.

'Thank you for this, Granny,' she said. 'I shall treasure it.'

Flora did not know it, but that was the last conversation she was to have with her granny. She visited Mrs Peat briefly the following afternoon, but she seemed very restless and disinclined to talk. Flora did not wish to tire her. Instead she took Daisy shopping and changed her library books at Mudies. She allowed Daisy to take out *The Heir of Redclyffe* on her ticket. Mama could have no objection to Charlotte Mary Yonge. She told Daisy that she would enjoy a good weep. 'Although I always found Guy and Amy somewhat too good to be true,' she finished. 'I am sure I would have behaved like poor, erring Laura. But I will not say any more. Read it for yourself.'

Flora thought of finding her granny some light magazine to read. What she would really enjoy was the racy *Reynold's Miscellany* but Flora did not have quite the effrontery to go and buy one. All that the book shops sold were *The Ladies' Cabinet of Fashion* and *Sylvia's Home Journal*, which carried such articles as 'How to wear a shawl'. Granny should be spared such idiocies.

That night Flora was woken by her mother. There were moans and footsteps and someone banging the front door and then a frantic knocking on her bedroom door.

'Flora, wake up. Your grandmother is ill.' Flora sat up with a jerk. 'She has had a stroke and Sarah is altogether useless.'

Flora leapt out of bed and flung on her dressing-gown. Somehow she had known it would be like this. She pushed her feet into her slippers and ran across to Granny's room. Mrs Peat was lying in bed, snoring loudly. Her face was grey and beads of sweat stood out on her forehead. There was one hastily lit candle on the dressing-table and a glass of water and sal volatile, testimony to Sarah's attempts to rouse her mistress. Sarah herself was wailing in her chair, her apron flung over her head, rocking backwards and forwards with heavy movements that made the chair groan rhythmically.

Mrs Peat stood nervously by the door and looked at Flora. 'That stupid old woman can do nothing but moan.'

Flora glanced at Sarah. 'Leave her. Where's Papa?'

'He went to fetch Dr Woodcock. He said it was quicker than waking the servants. But it would not take Ketton more than twenty minutes to get dressed, I daresay, and he might have gone for Dr Woodcock, and William need not have left me here to deal with a sick, old woman. She is his mother after all. Besides it is so unsuitable for him to be rushing off for the doctor, just as if he were a servant.'

'He will be at least half an hour, probably longer,' interrupted Flora. 'We must bleed her.'

'If only Sarah would stop moaning and do something!'

'Fetch me Papa's razors, Mama. Dr Woodcock said last time it was of the first importance she was bled.'

'You will never bleed her, Flora.' Mrs Peat looked helplessly around. 'Wait until Dr Woodcock arrives.'

'By then it may be too late. Hurry, Mama.'

Mrs Peat left, still half-inclined to argue the point. Flora felt the panic rising in her throat. Quick, she must remember. What was it Dr Woodcock had said? She shook Sarah, but was greeted only by a renewed burst of hysterical weeping. Oh God, thought Flora, am I the only person who can *do* anything? 'Sarah! Sarah! You must help!' Why does Mama not hurry up! Oooh! Sarah's wails rose louder. In a sudden fury Flora boxed her ears. She dragged Sarah roughly by the arm and almost flung her out of the room. 'Just get out!' she screamed. 'I am at my wits end and all you can do is moan. Get out and do your moaning elsewhere.'

Blanche came out of her room and stood hovering in the passage.

'Can't you stop making such a noise? I was just getting into a deep sleep.'

'Granny's ill.'

'Whoever is making that row?'

'Sarah. Remove her, Blanche. Take her up to Nanny or something.'

'But the woman's hysterical,' Blanche stepped nervously back. 'Why do you not fetch Mama?'

'Why do *you* not do something?' yelled Flora. She slammed the door in Blanche's face and went back to old Mrs Peat. The vein in the arm, that was it. She must tie something tightly around the upper arm and then she must cut the vein. Flora was just winding a shawl round her Granny's arm when her mother returned, gingerly carrying a cut-throat razor.

'There is no need for you to shout at Blanche in that way, Flora,' began Mrs Peat in a complaining tone, averting her gaze from the snoring figure on the bed.

'Light some candles, Mama,' said Flora impatiently.

'Where are they?'

'On the mantelpiece. Oh hurry!'

'I cannot bear to see blood. If anything happens to your grandmother it will be your fault, Flora. I shall tell William you did it against my express wishes. Dr Woodcock will know best what is to be done. Flora! My carpet will be ruined!'

'Fetch me that bowl then.'

'But what shall I do with the flowers?'

Flora took the bowl and threw the contents on the floor. She put the bowl carefully on the carpet and took the razor.

The vein had come up just as it had when Dr Woodcock prepared to let blood. Flora was pleased to see that her hand was quite steady. When the first gobbets of dark blood began to flow, Flora felt a moment's queasiness. It began to run down Mrs Peat's arm and drip off the ends of her fingers. Flora picked up the bowl and held it steadily. Her mother had sunk down into the chair vacated by Sarah and was shivering helplessly.

Flora released about a pint of blood and bound the arm up carefully. Old Mrs Peat stopped snoring. To Flora's anxious eyes she looked a shade or two less grey. The erratic pulse seemed to flutter more strongly. Flora wiped the sweat off Mrs Peat's face with a damp towel and sat quietly beside her.

'I think she looks better, Mama.'

'Oh, why does William not hurry?' Mrs Peat cried.

Minutes passed and Flora sat on in the darkened room feeling quite drained and exhausted. She tried to think what else she should be doing, but all that came into her head was senna tea mixture and she could not remember what Dr Woodcock had said about it. Should the patient be kept warm or should the blood not be overheated? Should she try to bring Granny round with brandy, or was alcohol dangerous?

At last there were sounds of a carriage, the scrape of feet on the doorstep and the welcome sound of the front door opening and voices in the hall.

'William! What a relief!' Mrs Peat burst into tears.

Dr Woodcock came swiftly up the stairs and crossed straight over to the bedside. Flora began to tell him in a low undertone what she had done, and under his direction brought the oil lamp, lit candles and fetched bowls of water and towels. Mr Peat waited only to hand over the carriage to a sleepy and resentful coachman and then he, too, came up the stairs. He stopped at the bedroom door and looked around in stupefaction. The oil lamp illuminated a dark huddle in the bed and a wet red stain on the floor. Dr Woodcock had accidently knocked over the bowl with the razor in it and blood was running out and soaking into the carpet.

'Whoever is responsible for this?' he demanded.

'Flora would bleed your mother,' cried Mrs Peat. 'I told her to wait.'

'She did very well,' put in Dr Woodcock, looking up momentarily from his examination. 'Miss Nightingale herself could not have done it better.'

'I cannot bear blood, William. Or I am sure I would have done it myself.'

Mr Peat looked across at Flora. She was pouring some water from the jug on the wash-stand into the wash bowl and beginning to mop up the blood on the carpet and to clear away the sodden heap of flowers on the floor.

'Go to bed, Flora,' he said harshly, 'there is nothing more for you to do here. You can go up to the attics and wake a couple of the housemaids. It is their job to do this tidying up. You had better go to bed too, Susan. A sickroom is no place for a lady.'

He saw them out and turned back to Dr Woodcock.

'Will she live?'

'Her heart condition is poor.' Dr Woodcock closed his bag. 'I suspect she has tried to keep this secret for some time. But at her age it probably makes very little difference, so do not blame yourself. Flora's prompt action may enable her to rally round, but do not place too much hope on her recovery.'

'I see. Thank you for telling me.'

'I am no advocate for hiding the truth, Peat. I shall do my best for your mother, but I fear she is reaching the end. I do not imagine she will suffer much distress. I have given her something to help her relax and I shall send a trained nurse round in the morning. This time I think it is essential.'

'There is nothing else I can do?'

'Nothing.'

'I shall pray for her.'

'Then you are doing all you can. We can only trust our Maker.'

It was nearly four o'clock by the time Flora returned to her room and she found she could not sleep. Thoughts kept buzzing round and round in her head. Should she have done anything earlier? She had noticed that Granny was a little more withdrawn than usual. She should have been more sympathetic to Sarah. Had these turns happened often before without Flora noticing, like the rest of them? Only she *should* have noticed, she was the one who was closest to her granny. The room was freezing: the fire had gone out long ago and the bed was cold. A whistling draught was coming in at one of the windows and even when Flora tried to bar the shutters, they shook with the wind outside. Finally she swallowed some laudanum and climbed into bed. She could hear the murmur of voices coming from Granny's room and then footsteps as Dr Woodcock left. Then the sounds slowly faded away and she fell into a heavy, troubled sleep.

She was woken only by the housemaid coming in to clean the grate. 'I'm ever so sorry, Miss. I thought you was down at breakfast.'

'What is the time?'

'About half past nine, Miss. But Madam has only just gone down. Everything's at sixes and sevens this morning.'

Mrs Peat was alone in the breakfast-room when Flora entered.

'I am sorry I am late, Mama. I took some laudanum last night and overslept.'

'Blanche has had to take Daisy to her lessons this morning,' began Mrs Peat in a complaining tone.

'How is Granny?'

'We shall not know until Dr Woodcock comes this morning. But your Papa says there is little hope. Well, as soon as your grandmother goes I shall get rid of Sarah and that is flat. Dr Woodcock was here until half past four dealing with that silly old woman, and who has to pay for it? We have! I never liked her, never. Common and so sullen. I shall be glad to see the back of her.'

Flora stared at her mother across the table. Mrs Peat glanced up and began hastily, 'Now Flora. Your grandmother has had a long life. She would not wish to stay to be a nuisance. It is a great comfort to me to know that we did everything possible to make her last years happy. Her own room, her own maid, every attention. In my opinion she would have been happier among her own kind up North somewhere, but William would have it so. What a pity it has all happened just when I am up to my ears in plans for Blanche's dance.'

She wished Flora would not stare at her so. The girl was looking positively odd.

'Is anybody with Granny now?' asked Flora in the same flattened voice.

'No need for anybody to nurse her. Dr Woodcock has sent round a trained nurse and I am bound to say she has things as she wants them and no interference. And it means six months of deep mourning, and by then the season will be over. First she managed to upset Adeline's wedding and now this.' She did wish Flora would not look at her in that peculiar way. 'I am not accusing her of deliberate selfishness, of course,' Mrs Peat finished.

'I think you are the most selfish person I've ever met,' burst out Flora suddenly. 'All you can think of is whether Granny will upset your precious plans. Never mind that she is dying! That does not mean a thing to you, does it? It is the inconvenience of it! And I suppose you only wanted her up North because then if she died you would not have to take too much notice! Blanche's season could still go ahead, so long as Granny did not upset your plans by dying *inconveniently* before the season started. You are not only selfish! You are monstrous!' Flora got up and pushed back her chair so violently that it fell onto the floor. She threw her napkin down on the table and ran out of the room.

Flora refused point blank to leave the house while her grandmother was ill and Blanche, to her fury, had to escort Daisy to her lessons every day. She sat glumly in the library and stared at the portrait of Sir George in dislike. Horrid, selfish man! He could at least have left orders that whoever accompanied Daisy had one of the pretty saloons to sit in, with a magazine or two, instead of this fusty bookroom. It was like being back in the schoolroom at home, with Tom's butterfly collection and those awful fossils Flora brought back from Dorset one year. It would serve him right if he was shot by brigands while out in Italy: at least Algy Kingsley would make a more interesting baronet! Blanche felt she might then be prepared to sacrifice her mornings in this boring house. As it was, there was nothing for her to do. And now it looked as if her season was going to be postponed.

Mrs Peat was quite as cross. She avoided her mother-in-law as much as possible. In any case, old Mrs Peat was quite unconscious and would not appreciate a visit from her daughter-in-law. She expressed her displeasure with Flora by ignoring her and by being disagreeable to Sarah. She could not bear to see such a streak of misery moping around the house, she said one morning, to nobody in particular but well within Flora's hearing and Sarah was transferred to the top landing and put in Nanny's charge.

'She's just a useless old body, Ma'am,' said Nanny. 'She won't even help me with the darning. She just sits there and moans. Sometimes I think she wouldn't eat unless I almost forced her.'

'Well, you must do the best you can, Nanny. As soon as all this is over, out she goes and so I have told Mr Peat. But for the moment she must be kept out of the way.'

February continued cold and wet: yellow fogs drifted up from the river and seemed to hang around Belgrave Square, never quite dispersing, even after a few days' sun and an easterly wind which blew the fog away from most of the higher ground. Old Mrs Peat became slowly weaker. Dr Woodcock ordered her to be tube fed with beef tea, but there was no improvement. Privately he thought it was useless and from the hints dropped by Mrs Peat he guessed that his patient's death would come as a welcome release. He allowed Flora to relieve the nurse for short periods: she was a sensible girl. If his son had chosen Flora instead of the pious Adeline he would have been better pleased. He was worried about his daughter-in-law. Her pregnancy was not making her ill, but she was plainly not happy. Dr Woodcock even dropped a hint to Flora of his concern and suggested that Adeline might confide her problems more easily to a sister. He refrained from adding 'than to her husband', but Flora understood him well enough and promised to find time to do what she could.

'Flora is very sensible,' he told Mr Peat after one visit. 'She can call Nurse if there is the slightest need. You may be proud of her, Peat. There are not many young ladies who can bleed someone as coolly as she did.'

'She should have been a boy; I have often thought so. Did I ever tell you I used to take her into the office with me sometimes when we lived in Islington? I remember one occasion very clearly. Flora was about thirteen at the time. We were doing some work for Stephenson – it was for the Menai Bridge – and he was at my office for some discussions. I left him for a few moments with Flora and when I returned she was sitting with him at my desk and he was explaining to her the principles on which he was designing the tube sections for the bridge. He told me afterwards she had an astonishing grasp of basic engineering principles. I remember it well.'

Dr Woodcock rubbed his nose reflectively. 'Ah well, it always works that way,' he said easily. 'It is always the boys who have the curly hair.'

'Sometimes I think she would be of more use to me than Ernest, who is good enough with the clients but does not appear to know iron from steel. It is out of the question, of course. Susan would never hear of it. She says that she has enough problems trying to get Flora off her hands as it is.'

'My wife would agree with you,' said Dr Woodcock, walking slowly downstairs. 'She says girls are ten times more trouble than boys. The trouble we had with Isabel, lounging about the house, not knowing what she wanted to do with herself and making everybody uncomfortable. I can tell you I was relieved to get her safely buckled to Philip Rivers, even though I think she might have done better for herself. But there you are, that is women all over. You earn enough money to keep them in ease and luxury and all they do is complain.'

'Susan is thinking of Maurice Dunster for Flora.'

'Dunster, eh? A very earnest young man. I should not worry about Flora if I were you, Peat, she is one of those girls who takes her time and cannot be rushed. You leave her alone and she will be popping up with a young man before you have time to turn around.'

Mr Peat saw Dr Woodcock to his carriage and then shut the door.

Flora lived through that last week in a curious state of heightened sensitivity. It was as if every moment held a special significance because it would not be repeated. There would be loss and grief ahead, but just now she must store up every memory and hold fast these last, few, precious days. She felt she understood every restless movement her grandmother made: whether she wanted her forehead cooling, a drink of water or her pillows puffing up. Flora found a deep pleasure in being able to do these simple things: she alone could understand her grandmother's needs and give her ease.

Then one Sunday morning Mrs Peat regained consciousness. Her eyes opened and Flora saw, with a wild beating of her heart, that Mrs Peat recognized her. Hope sprang up in her: Granny would recover, she would be all right!

'It's me, Flora,' she whispered, bending down towards the worn face on the pillow. 'Can you hear me, Granny?'

Mrs Peat's thin hand plucked at the sheet, 'Flora,' she said, in a tired voice.

Flora felt her throat choked with tears – tears of relief and thankfulness. She made to get up to ring the bell but Mrs Peat's fingers feebly clutched her.

'I am only going to call Papa.'

'Wait . . . something.'

Flora bent over her, stroking the hand she held. All the while tears poured down her face and fell gently onto the sheet. But Mrs Peat did not speak, her eyes shut again. She seemed to be drifting off.

'I am here, Granny', said Flora quietly. 'What is it you want to say?'

'You'll be all right, pet.'

'Yes, yes, Granny. You are not to worry about me. Think about getting better. That is all I want.'

Suddenly Mrs Peat's eyes opened wide as if seeing something that Flora could not see. She made as if to sit up. Flora's heart began pounding with a mixture of fear and awe. She glanced nervously at where Mrs Peat was staring but could see nothing. She jumped up hastily and rang the bell: a wild jangled peal that brought Mr Peat running from his dressing-room. Simultaneously the nurse came swiftly in from the housekeeper's room.

Mr Peat went at once to the bed. Flora found she could not move. She stood by the wall next to the bell pull and leaned her head against it. Her heart was so full that she could not speak a word. She could hear her father talking, a low, soothing voice, and there were a few whispered words from Granny. Then there was a sudden burst of activity, a harsh croaking from the bed and all was over.

The nurse came forward and started to clean the body; somebody opened the curtains and light flooded the room. Suddenly everything that Flora had by her in readiness, the medicines, the tumblers of water, the extra pillows, all became useless. In a moment, the careful preparations of days became superfluous. Already the living were taking over from the dead.

'Mr Peat,' said the nurse firmly, 'take Miss Peat downstairs and give her some brandy.'

'Come, Flora.' Her father's hand was guiding her arm. She allowed herself to be led away. She said nothing: time had already moved her down half the stairs and ten minutes into the future and she could not hold it back.

They went down to Mr Peat's study and he poured out two brandies. 'Drink, Flora.'

She stared at him, uncomprehending.

'It's brandy, Flora. Drink it.'

She took the glass, drained it, and burst into tears.

Mrs Peat was satisfied that she was doing everything possible to be a help and a support to her husband. It was she who remembered to send black gloves and cards to all their friends and acquaintances and who saw that the correct notices were put in *The Times*. The funeral would take place on Thursday and Mrs Peat longed for it to be over. She could barely repress a shudder every time she went past old Mrs Peat's rooms where the body was lying, ready for burial. Mr Peat spent most of his time there, and he and Flora sat watch between them.

Mrs Peat was torn between irritation at the immoderate grief her husband was showing and resentment that Blanche's season would have to be postponed. However, there was always the pleasure of ordering mourning clothes from Jay's Mourning Warehouse. If it were only for herself, she thought, she would not mind: a handsome black silk or black crêpe was not to be despised. Mrs Peat knew she looked well in black. But Blanche must be in full mourning for three months and by then the season would be half over. Blanche and Daisy might wear white mourning, thank goodness – there was something so depressing about black for young people. Blanche in white silk with black embroidery would look most striking. Her blonde colouring would in no way be diminished by it. Mrs Peat gently patted her own fair hair.

In the meantime she could contemplate the mutes, top hats swathed in black and holding staves draped in black crêpe, outside the front door, and the door knocker tied with more black crêpe. She set about ordering a suitable tablet for St Paul's Church, and she could not help thinking that it was so much better to have her mother-in-law, metaphorically speaking at any rate, nailed on a marble tablet to the wall of the nave, where she need only be contemplated on Sundays and where the awful vulgarity of her accent and her common ways would be forever obscured by the stonemason's eulogy.

The ladies of the house did not go to the funeral. Instead, they stood by the drawing-room window and watched the procession. The long cortège, with the hearse drawn by four black horses with sable plumes, followed by the carriages of the mourners, the mutes and the feathermen, bearing trays of black ostrich feathers, moved slowly down the road towards St Paul's Church in Wilton Crescent.

Adeline, looking paler than ever in her black crêpe, spoke of the solemnity of the occasion: the outward trappings of grief gave a proper display to the inner sensibilities. Flora was not so sure. She looked with distaste at the mutes, their faces suitably grief-stricken, holding black silk handkerchiefs to their faces. It seemed to her a gross travesty of grief that they, who never knew her granny, should be weeping so copiously. She knew that they were there to display the family's grief, but Flora, who had spent many nights crying over her loss, felt that bereavement should be privately mourned, not publicly displayed.

The funeral procession moved out of sight, followed by the carriages carrying Mr Peat, his sons, his son-in-law, and other guests who wished to pay their respects.

Back in the drawing-room, Mrs Peat was graciously receiving compliments on the elegance and dignity of the procession.

'So worthy of the respect Mr Peat would wish to show to his dear mother,' said Mrs Thomas Woodcock with her thin smile, her eyes ranging over the lavish crêpe on her hostess' dress. 'I always say it is an occasion when expense must not be spared.' She paused hopefully.

Mrs Peat did not disappoint her. 'Mr Peat wished everything to be of the best,' she said with pride. 'I believe the bill will come to nearly four hundred pounds. And that does not include the mourning clothes.'

'It shows a very proper feeling in William,' put in Cousin Helen from the other side of the room. 'I have seen the notice in *The Times*!'

Daisy tugged at Flora's sleeve. 'It seems an awful lot of money,' she whispered.

'It is,' replied Flora. 'Granny once told me that many families think themselves lucky to bring home a pound a week.'

'I do not think she would have enjoyed all this very much, do you?'

'No. But everybody else is,' said Flora dryly.

All Mrs Peat's calculations returned to the same unpalatable point: there was no possibility of Blanche coming out that year. Blanche would not be out of deep mourning until the end of May and Mrs Peat herself would be in deep mourning until the end of August. If only she had brought her out properly the previous year, then at least she might have held a musical soirée with perfect propriety. Even if Blanche was unable to dance, she could at least have some sort of social life. But to bring a daughter out while in deep mourning was impossible.

There was absolutely no help for it. Blanche must wait another season and she would have to concentrate on Flora. This did not seem quite such the hopeless task it had been in previous years. William was right, Adeline's marriage had given Flora just the push she needed. She was even growing quite pretty, in spite of her twenty-eight years. Of course, she would never rival Blanche, but she had a trim figure and a good complexion and was certainly quite passable. She dressed better too and had a greater air of self-confidence. Mrs Peat had been complimented by both Mrs Anning and Mrs Dunster on the improvement in Flora.

Mrs Peat summoned up the credentials of Maurice Dunster – she had even mentioned it once or twice to her husband. He was the right age. His income was reasonable – certainly enough for Flora – and he was exactly the sort of serious young man Flora would like. That he had never shown much interest in the ladies she dismissed as irrelevant: he had just not met the right one.

Mr Dunster's business was steady but not spectacular and their younger son, Hugh, was proving expensive. No parent in their senses would turn down the prospect of a match which carried with it a dowry the size of Flora's. She disliked Mary Dunster, but she was prepared to make a push to settle her daughter. Mrs Peat felt very virtuous: the things one does for one's children. And except for dearest Blanche, they are quite unappreciative. She resolved to drop a hint in Mrs Dunster's ear.

Mr Peat missed his mother very much. She was his permanent link with the past, to the poverty and want of his earlier days, and the more recent memories of when they first came to London and lived in Islington. While his mother was alive he was able to ignore the fact that he and his wife had long since drifted apart and that their points of contact were sadly reduced to the children and the flourishing state of Peat-Milford. Even in discussing their offspring the contact was minimal, for Mr Peat agreed that his wife should have sole charge of the upbringing of their daughters and Mrs Peat was only concerned that Peat-Milford should continue to provide the funds to enable her to live as she felt a lady should.

Why the devil had they ever left Islington, he wondered? They had lived in a modest way, but comfortably. They employed only five servants, but there they were a family. Mr Peat often invited the clerks who worked for him to small evening parties, with perhaps a little parlour music and a buffet supper. Ernest, Flora and Adeline were old enough to take part in these mild festivities, and it was always Flora who fared best with the bright but gauche young men he employed.

He had an easier relationship then with the men who worked for him. It was 'Mr Peat' or even 'Mr Bill' from some of the older hands, and he often came down and took his midday snack with the men. Now he had his mahogany-lined office and a directors' private dining-room to eat in and his men called him 'Sir'.

In the early days he found it useful as well as sociable to see his clerks or young managers in a more informal setting. He was always willing to promote a young man who was clever and hard-working. To see how such a candidate behaved while playing spillikins with his young daughters was often more instructive than a formal interview in his office.

Susan had pleaded with him to move, he recalled. When the family business improved she insisted on entering a different sort of society. There were tears and a barrage of argument. Flora was growing too bookish: it was doing her no good to hob-nob only with clerks and junior managers. If Mr Peat wished the best for his daughters he should give them the opportunity to move in a more exclusive society. In Mrs Peat's view, if her daughters mixed with clerks, then sooner or later they would marry clerks. Surely he wished them to do better?

She had worn him down and he had agreed. Susan had charge of his daughters: he would not interfere in what she thought best for them. But he simply had not considered how the move would break up their home life. There were to be no more cosy evenings with old work mates popping in, no more snipe-shooting excursions with Ernest out on the Hackney marshes in the long summer evenings, no more Saturday afternoon strolls to watch cricket on the Green.

The move coincided with a sudden upsurge in business. For several years Mr Peat was kept extremely busy and when at last he found time to relax again with his family the situation was changed. There were no more cosy supper parties. They were too vulgar, Mrs Peat informed him. She fancied the clerks would feel out of place in Belgrave Square. Mr Peat looked round at the knick-knacks and elegancies in the drawing-room and did not insist.

He was wrong. It was his responsibility to think more seriously about the move to Belgrave Square. Opportunities for marriage were the main arguments put forward by his wife, but he did not think that the results had justified her. Flora, at least, might have been happier with one of his young managers, he was sure. He remembered young Talford taking quite a fancy to her when she was only fourteen and he would have welcomed the match. Talford had fully justified his faith in him and was now doing very well in the engineering department. Of course, it was too late now. Talford had been married for some years and was the father of a young family.

Susan had pointed to her success with Adeline, but Mr Peat did not care much for Charles and thought that there, too, Adeline might have been more content with a less self-important man. Perhaps if they had remained in Islington she might have grown out of this tiresome piety that only served to make everybody around her thoroughly uncomfortable. And at least in Islington he could have kept an eye on the young whipper-snappers Blanche seemed to care for.

The feeling of resentment against his wife and guilt at his own behaviour lay at the back of his mind all day. When he returned home from the office that evening his wife quite unwittingly added fuel to it. Mrs Peat had a grievance that had been rankling ever since the older Mrs Peat's death.

'Sarah cannot be got a seat on the railway train until Monday,' Mrs Peat complained at dinner. 'I had hoped to be rid of her long before this.'

'I told Sarah she might stay until the lawyers arranged about her annuity,' said Mr Peat firmly.

'I am glad Granny left her something,' said Flora. 'Poor Sarah, she was not much use in an emergency, but she was devoted to Granny.'

'She certainly made sure that she was indispensable,' said Mrs Peat sourly.

'That is not fair, Susan.' Mr Peat felt a wave of quite savage dislike for his wife, but he endeavoured to speak calmly. 'Sarah did much for Mother and it was only right that she should be left something for her trouble. If Mother had not done so, I should certainly have seen that she was provided for.'

'She had such a vulgar mind,' said Mrs Peat, dipping her fingers in the finger bowl and energetically wiping them. She meant her mother-in-law, but did not dare say so.

'Talking of Sarah, that reminds me,' put in Mr Peat. 'I should like Flora to move into Mother's old rooms. She could have her own sitting-room and more space for her things.'

'Flora to have your mother's rooms!' cried Mrs Peat outraged. 'Do you wish to *encourage* her to become a recluse? I have enough trouble winkling her out of her bedroom as it is. What about Blanche's claims, pray?'

'I should not dream of placing Blanche's claims above her eldest sister's,' replied Mr Peat. 'Blanche may move into Flora's room, if she wishes. I daresay Daisy will be glad to have a room to herself now that she is growing up.'

Mrs Peat cast Flora a look of acute dislike. She had a sudden premonition that Flora was going to become like old Mrs Peat, up there in the same rooms, thinking thoughts and holding opinions that Mrs Peat knew to be unsuitable for any lady. But if William would encourage her. . . .

Charles came round one evening after the funeral. He was concerned about Adeline, he told Mrs Peat. She seemed nervous and depressed. Could Flora be persuaded to come and stay for a few weeks to cheer her up? In fact, Charles felt both resentful and guilty about Adeline. He told himself that it was all right for him to visit an accommodation house with Philip: Adeline did not know, and in any case she would prefer to be relieved of his attentions. Besides, if she was reluctant to play her marital part then she had only herself to blame if her husband looked elsewhere. But his conscience would not be quiet over the matter. He kept pushing away the ugly remembrances of their wedding night – that was Mrs Peat's fault for not instructing her daughter better – anyway it was natural for a lady to be a trifle upset at such a time. He certainly had no cause for complaint now. Adeline accepted his advances completely and lay quietly until he was finished.

Mrs Peat was delighted with Charles' invitation. She disliked seeing Flora, hand on cheek, staring out of the window. It made her feel acutely uncomfortable. She, as wife of the chief mourner, should feel the most grief. It was a constant reproach to her to see Flora in that role and gaining her husband's sympathy. It would be good for Flora to visit her favourite sister.

Mr Peat was not so keen. 'Do not let Adeline depress you,' he said to Flora the evening before she went. 'I know the way she can cast a gloom over everything and make you feel you ought not to be enjoying life. You have enough to bear already. Adeline chose to marry Charles. If she does not like it then I see no reason why you should have to pay for it.'

'To tell the truth, Papa, I do not think it matters very much where I am at the moment. I can see that I worry Mama, so perhaps it is just as well that I go. Anyway, it will be good for me to rouse myself to be polite to Adeline's friends.'

'It will take your mind off things, at any rate. Write to me if it becomes too much and I'll bring you home.' He patted her cheek. 'I shall miss you, you know, Flora.'

Flora found that she was looking forward to the visit with mild pleasure. There was nothing at home for her now. The mornings at the Kingsleys, arguing and talking with Sir George, now seemed very far away. In any case, Sir George had spoiled her pleasure in it by his stupid book list – he had probably written it for a joke in any case. She must look forward to meeting Charles' and Adeline's medical friends, at least they would be new people.

The reality was very different. Far from paying calls and receiving visits, Adeline saw nobody. She spent most of her time lying on the day-bed. Occasionally she took up her knitting for the baby, or did some sewing for her Missionary basket.

Usually she just lay there, a book unopened at her side.

Fortunately Flora brought the inevitable Macaulay with her, and such was the boredom and dreariness of the days, that she found she was half way through the second volume before she knew where she was. She became quite knowledgeable about such obscure people as Edgar Atheling and Richard Strongbow (who married the daughter of Dermot, King of Leinster – no doubt another ancestor of Sir George's!). She found herself mentally challenging him about it, but then remembered she was cross with him and in any case he was in Italy.

But there was her duty to be done. With a sigh Flora turned her attention back to her sister.

'Adeline,' she said firmly, after several mornings passed in almost total silence, 'it cannot be good for you to lie on that sofa all day.'

'Charles says that I must not overdo things,' replied Adeline, sighing and glancing wearily at the clock on the heavily ornate marble mantelpiece.

'Overdo it! You have been doing nothing. Why do you not pay some calls? Ask some friends to tea?'

'Who can I ask? Apart from Isabel there is nobody. Charles' colleagues' wives are only interested in criticizing my servants and pricing my furniture. They have no interest in higher things. I told one of them that I made little things in aid of the Church Missionary Society and all she said was "How very odd".'

Flora looked at the mantelpiece. It was almost empty of invitations. Now she came to think of it, the basket left for the visiting cards was almost empty as well. Adeline was seeing nobody, and she supposed that that selfish Charles had not even noticed. What was happening to Adeline? She was not even bothering to see such old school friends as Ida Clevedon or Katie Anning.

'But this is ridiculous, Adeline. No wonder you are feeling low.'

'I do not suppose I shall be here much longer to trouble anyone.'

Flora sat down at the davenport and wrote a note and sealed it with one of Adeline's pretty blue wafers – almost unused too, she noted with disapproval. Then she rang the bell. Whiley appeared.

'Will you see that this note is delivered to Mrs Peat at once, please? I shall be taking Mrs Woodcock out to luncheon today, and we shall want the carriage at half-past eleven with a warm rug.'

'Very good, Miss.'

'Oh yes, and send Mrs Woodcock's abigail up please.'

'Certainly, Miss.' Whiley looked at Flora with approval. He was used to a situation with a bit of life. This house was like a morgue; there were no guests, no visitors, and the mistress sat on her backside moping all day. He, personally, didn't blame the doctor for having a bit on the side, which everybody knew he was.

'Now, Adeline,' continued Flora, 'you are going to give a small dinner-party for me some time next week. Find me some nice medical friends who are interesting. Whatever would Mama say if she learnt I was not meeting any young men! So while you are changing to go out, you may be thinking about it.'

If Flora felt some sympathy towards her sister, this did not extend to Charles. Frequently Flora would have liked to punch in his face and take the self-satisfied smile off his fat features. Unfortunately, so unladylike a reaction was forbidden. How dare he allow his wife to fall into such a state of depression, and he a doctor! Flora did not know whether Adeline had any good reason for thinking she was going to die, or whether it was one of those fears pregnant ladies were always subject to. Distasteful though it might be, she would have to tackle Charles. She did not relish the idea. She knew Charles disliked her. He had snubbed her several times when she attempted to break the frigidly polite silences in the drawing-room after dinner and ask him some question about his work. It was a subject above her understanding, he would say. Or, it was not fit for a lady's ears. There seemed to be an awful lot of the world, according to Charles, that was unsuitable for ladies.

Mrs Peat was not too pleased at Flora's unceremonious descent on the house for lunch, but she too was concerned when she heard about Adeline from Flora. Of course, she did nothing so ungenteel as to mention the pregnancy in detail, but she endeavoured to tell Adeline how important it was to keep her mind busy and take a little, gentle exercise. Adeline returned to Upper

Cavendish Street looking somewhat more hopeful and Charles was even able to congratulate himself in inviting Flora. Adeline needed another woman with whom to chatter. He approved Adeline's diffident enquiry about a small dinner-party and even suggested several guests who might be suitable.

He seemed to be in a good mood Flora thought, at least, in quite as good a mood as she was likely to find him. The moment was propitious for her talk with him. Adeline had conveniently excused herself early and retired to bed and Flora was left alone with Charles in the drawing-room.

'I am glad to see you alone, Charles,' said Flora.

Charles looked alarmed. 'I would be only too delighted to stay and talk to you,' he said, 'but I have to go and write up some notes in a minute.'

'It concerns Adeline.'

'Adeline! What's the matter with her? What's she been telling you? Some fancy, no doubt.'

Flora saw that Charles was going to be difficult. 'It is a subject of some delicacy,' she began.

'I do not understand why Adeline should confide in you,' said Charles testily. 'I am her husband. If she has any worries, she should talk to me.'

Did Adeline suspect his nights out with Philip? It would be like her to play the prude about it. Charles felt it was typical of female deviousness to choose this roundabout way of upbraiding him. He could place no dependence on Flora's refinement – a true lady should be ignorant of such things. It would be Isabel, of course, who found out and carried tales to Adeline. Philip assured him of Isabel's ignorance, but Charles felt he knew his sister better. Isabel had always been unscrupulous in her methods of obtaining information. Charles often wondered if she went through Philip's pockets and Heaven knew Philip was careless in the notes he kept from Nancy or Kate.

'What is this tittle-tattle, then?' asked Charles, looking at Flora with dislike.

'Adeline thinks she is going to die with this baby,' said Flora bluntly.

'Oh! is that all,' said Charles in relief. Then seeing Flora's startled face, he added hastily, 'but she is perfectly healthy. Ladies in delicate conditions always have these odd fancies, no reliance is to be placed on them.'

'Possibly,' said Flora dryly. 'However, you have not told Adeline that, so she fears the worst. Charles, Adeline is in complete ignorance, do you not understand? She does not know what to expect and I am not competent to tell her. But you are.'

'Adeline has a very refined mind,' said Charles repressively. 'I do not wish to say anything that will bring a blush to her cheek.'

'Good God, Charles,' cried Flora exasperated. 'It is your baby!'

'I prize my wife's purity above everything,' said Charles, his eyes starting angrily. 'If it makes you easy I shall tell my father to come and talk to Adeline one morning.'

'I am not concerned with myself, but with my sister.'

'You will excuse me if I say, Miss Flora, that for a lady, and my wife's sister, I find your language rather too free for what I am prepared to tolerate in this house.'

Flora was about to retort that as it was Charles who had got Adeline into bed, he could at least explain the consequences to her, but she swallowed it. 'I apologize,' she said stiffly after a moment. 'You must put it down to my concern for my sister.'

She turned quickly and left the room.

Dr Woodcock came to visit Adeline a day or so later, after a very off-hand note from Charles and a much more comprehensive talk with Flora. He was absolutely furious with his son, and Flora had to restrain him from going in to Adeline until his rage had calmed down.

'It is a perfectly natural process,' he said crossly to Flora. 'Whatever can Charles be about allowing his wife to think that the baby is going to pop out one night through her belly-button? Sometimes I have no patience with these modern namby-pamby ideas. I shall give him a severe talking to, Flora, that you may depend on. Now take me in to your sister, my dear.'

Adeline was excruciatingly embarrassed by her father-in-law's visit. 'Charles need not have asked you,' she kept saying. 'I am perfectly all right.' But gradually his calm and quiet sympathy soothed her and she found herself confiding in him far more than she would have believed possible. Dr Woodcock heard her out in silence, only asking a few questions now and then, and patting her hand sympathetically. Then he told her in a few plain words what she could expect, how she would know the baby was on its way and what would happen. He ended by tapping her tummy gently with one stubby finger – an action which shocked Adeline, but which she recognized to be affectionate.

'Now, my dear Adeline, I want you to stop mollycoddling yourself and take plenty of exercise.'

'Oh thank you, thank you,' whispered Adeline, tears starting in her eyes.

Dr Woodcock rose and collected his bag. 'Now be a sensible girl and let Flora take you out. Go and look at the new Embankment, not that there is much to see just now.' He took out his pocket watch. 'Now I must go, my dear. Send Charles round to see me, will you? He deserves a good scold for allowing you to believe such nonsense.'

'No, no,' cried Adeline. 'I would rather not. Indeed, I would rather not.'

'Very well, my dear.'

Dr Woodcock left her. How the deuce did his son ever get her with child if they both lived on this rarified plane? Well, it was not his business, thank goodness, to interfere in people's marriages. Adeline seemed healthy enough, anyway. All the same, he would try dropping a hint in Charles' ear at a suitable moment.

With Flora's bullying and Dr Woodcock's sanction, Adeline's life now began to assume a more varied pattern. They now went out most afternoons and paid calls. Adeline let it be known that on Thursday afternoons Mrs Charles Woodcock was 'At Home'. They went to tea with Isabel Rivers and Flora was glad to go up to the nursery for a romp with the children and leave Adeline and Isabel to enjoy a comfortable talk. Flora was quite happy to make a little house with Amy and Johnny Rivers under the nursery table, despite the disapproving looks from Nurse, who did not like her charges' routine disturbed. But Flora, who found she was missing Daisy and her lively conversation, felt she needed to relax and enjoy herself.

Flora took Adeline for morning drives in the carriage. The weather was still unsettled, but on warm days they would stop the carriage in St James's Park and take a short walk. The crocuses were out and even a few primroses: Flora wondered how the crocuses were doing in the garden at home. The exercise, even if it only involved feeding the ducks, brought a new colour to Adeline's cheeks and Flora was able to congratulate herself on helping her sister.

In spite of all these mild diversions, Flora was bored. She had been staying with her sister for nearly ten days now. She did not see how she could possibly endure another three or four weeks. The torpor Adeline lived in, Charles' inability to regard ladies as anything other than a cross between Little Dorrit and the Idiot Boy, almost reduced Flora to screaming point every evening. She found herself longing to be home – even her dull routine there held charms for her now. She thought wistfully of the comforts and ease of Sir George's library, where she could tuck her feet up under her on the old leather sofa and enjoy a good book. She would write to her father, he did say she might, and he would find a good excuse to bring her home. She would still keep an eye on Adeline, of course, but at least she would not have to stay with her.

Having decided this, Flora felt better. She had made the right decision and even when she woke up and saw that a short spell of fine days had given way to drizzle and a cold wind, it did not dampen her spirits.

'Never mind,' she said to Adeline, who was bemoaning the change in the weather. 'Why not pay calls just the same? I daresay people will be very pleased to see somebody on such a horrid day.'

Adeline agreed and they set out, but even the fur-lined rug in the carriage could not prevent the draughts from whistling around their feet. Adeline took out her list and consulted it.

'We did the Annings yesterday, so I can cross them off. I suppose we had better do Mrs Dunster.'

'Mrs Dunster!' echoed Flora. 'Why on earth do you wish to call on her?'

'Mama said she was enquiring after me,' said Adeline, slightly consciously. 'It would be only right to visit her.'

In fact, Mrs Peat told Adeline very firmly that she must visit Mrs Dunster. 'I have decided that Maurice Dunster is most suitable for Flora,' she added. Adeline had to agree. Maurice was a most estimable young man, most solicitous to his mother, a steady worker in his father's business and with serious principles, for Adeline knew that he gave most generously to charity. A little voice told her that Flora would be furious to have her life thus disposed of without her knowledge, but Adeline was able to ignore it. Parents knew what was best for their children. Besides she was sure that Flora would esteem Maurice when she knew him better.

Mrs Peat had spent much time and energy in dropping hints to Mrs Dunster on Flora's poise and intelligence. Was Maurice not serious in his tastes? It would be nice for Flora to meet somebody who shared her interests.

Mrs Dunster's reaction was daunting. Mrs Peat did not know it, but Mrs Dunster's one strong emotion was her doting fondness for her elder son. Maurice was too busy. He did not care much for Society. She was afraid he was cut out to be a bachelor.

Unperturbed, Mrs Peat concluded that Mrs Dunster needed to meet Flora again. Without exactly deviating from the truth she magnified Mrs Dunster's polite enquiry after Adeline's health. Adeline really must pay a call. Flora was staying with her sister, what could be more natural than for Flora to accompany her?

Flora and Adeline found themselves coldly received in Mrs Dunster's drawing-room. They were offered no refreshments, and plainly Mrs Dunster was only looking for a formal twenty-minute call. She congratulated Adeline on the approaching Event, but it was obvious to Flora that her mother's report of Mrs Dunster's interest was largely invented. Her purpose remained as yet obscure.

Flora decided she could not like Mrs Dunster. She was quite content to sit back and allow Adeline to do the honours. She disliked Mrs Dunster's rigidly curled hair and tight smile. She thought the lengths gone to to hide even the piano legs, as indelicate, beneath chintz frills, ridiculous. The house was uncomfortable, formal and stuffy, she decided, exactly like their hostess. She was beginning to wonder how soon they could go, when Mrs Dunster addressed her.

'Well, Miss Peat. How do you feel with your younger sister already married? I suppose you are "on the catch" yourself?'

Flora stared at her: there was no mistaking the rancour in Mrs

Dunster's voice. What the devil did she mean by being so gratuitously rude? Flora was just opening her mouth to say something far from polite, when Adeline swiftly forestalled her.

'I do not know where you get your information from, Mrs Dunster. But I can assure you Flora is not "on the catch" as you say.' Adeline's indignation was all the greater because she was upset at having allowed herself to consent to her mother's machinations and had not foreseen what a disagreeable position it might place Flora in.

'I have no expectations of getting married,' said Flora coldly, her temper now in check. 'There must always be one daughter to remain at home, you know.'

'I am sure your mother does not wish to lose you yet,' replied Mrs Dunster more temperately, permitting herself a thin smile. However much she resented Mrs Peat's hints, Flora was worth at least twenty thousand pounds.

There was a short pause. Flora was determined not to say another word to this rude, insinuating woman. Adeline rose swiftly to her feet. They positively must leave, she told Mrs Dunster, but before they went, she must beg to be allowed to see Mrs Dunster's fine glasshouse. Mrs Dunster became more cordial and the rest of the visit passed in a polite exchange of platitudes.

'Whatever was that about?' asked Flora, as they drove away.

'I do not know,' said Adeline shortly.

Flora wondered if Adeline had heard any of the rumours surrounding Blanche and Hugh. Of course, it would be a great coup for the Dunsters if they could pull off a match with Alice Banks. Hugh Dunster may have every bit of his reputed charm, but his mother's sour face was not calculated to bring round the trustees. Flora was not sure how much Adeline had heard about Hugh, so she confined herself to a general hint.

'Certainly Hugh's propensities must cause any mother distress,' said Adeline repressively.

'It cannot be Maurice,' went on Flora, deciding it would be wiser to leave the subject of Hugh alone. 'I doubt whether he has ever caused his mother a moment's anxiety in his life. Quite the Goody Two-shoes.'

'You should not talk in that way,' said Adeline, feeling very uncomfortable. Should she tell Flora? But Mama had expressly forbidden it. In any case, Maurice was in no way to blame for his mother's peculiar behaviour and Flora might yet find that she liked him. No, it was better to leave well alone. 'Anyway,' she continued, 'any mother would be delighted to have a son as devoted as Maurice.'

'Oh well,' Flora dismissed it from her mind. 'At least we can say we have been.' She sneezed suddenly. 'I think I have caught a cold, Adeline. I do hope I shall not give it to you.'

'Oh, you poor thing,' cried Adeline. She tucked some of her fur-lined rug over Flora's knees. 'You must have your supper upstairs tonight and Charles will give you some of his lozenges.'

Flora revelled in the unaccustomed luxury of not having to listen to Charles' pomposities in the dining-room. Almost for the first time since coming to stay with her sister, she could be alone. Charles duly gave her the promised lozenges and a truly disgusting draught consisting of a mixture of linseed and liquorice with rum added. 'Infallible for colds,' Charles informed her, 'and mind, Miss Flora, I want it all drunk up. I shall send Adeline up later to make sure you have done so.' Flora suspected that Charles had given her this foul-smelling mixture deliberately and her guess was strengthened when she overheard him telling Whiley on the stairs what she was to have for supper.

However, she was pleasantly surprised when Whiley brought up her supper tray. Charles had ordered a small bowl of gruel for her, followed by two boiled mutton cutlets with Brussels sprouts and a little tapioca pudding. Whiley had ignored the gruel and tapioca and substituted Brown Windsor soup and plum tart. Miss Peat did not want to mess up her insides with gruel, he said to Cook. Such stuff was fit only for invalids. Let Mrs Woodcock have gruel if she wished, he was sure Miss Peat would prefer something more tasty.

Whiley's championship encouraged Flora to confide in him about the tumbler of linseed and liquorice mixture Charles had left her and the lozenges.

'Have no fear, Miss,' said Whiley, with a conspiratorial smile. 'I will dispose of them and bring you back the empty tumbler.'

Adeline might go on about servants knowing their place, but it was obvious to Flora that Whiley did not miss a thing.

Charles and Adeline were in the drawing-room, waiting for Whiley to announce dinner. Charles was feeling very pleased with himself: he had managed to hook a most eligible patient, old Lord Colbourne, once the finest example of a Regency rake and now a martyr to gout. Dr Embsay had been kind enough to recommend him to Lord Colbourne and Charles was going to give the old fellow every possible attention. And he paid on the nail, too, Dr Embsay assured him. God, it was worth every penny of his wife's dowry to live in such an expensive part of town: the dividends were enormous.

Charles was quite glad Flora was out of the way tonight, for he had some important news to impart to Adeline and he did not wish Flora's caustic tongue pouring scorn on it.

'Well, my love,' he said jocularly. 'So poor old Flora has caught a chill, eh? You ladies will be fashionable rather than warm. I trust *you* took no unnecessary risks?'

'We both wrapped up very well. But the carriage is draughty, Charles, you yourself remarked on it.'

Charles looked at Adeline with satisfaction. Her hair looked thick and shiny and a few wisps had escaped from their usually tight confinement and clung against her neck. Charles found himself wondering whether now she was three months' pregnant he might resume marital relations for a while; for a couple of months anyway. She was looking very inviting, by Jove. Her stomach was still almost flat, but her bosom had increased, straining her dress slightly.

'You are looking very pink and pretty, my dear.'

'I am feeling much better, thank you,' replied Adeline, smiling.

'Good, good,' said Charles, licking his lips slightly.

Adeline glanced nervously at him. 'Of course I do feel a little queasy from time to time,' she said hastily.

There was the sound of the gong from the hall downstairs and Whiley came in to announce that 'dinner was served'. Charles offered Adeline his arm and together they descended the stairs to the dining-room. Charles took his place at the head of the table, and Adeline went to the foot, some eight feet away. She bent her head and murmured Grace and allowed Whiley to help her sit down.

Whiley handed round the Brown Windsor soup and assured

Charles, without so much as a flicker, that Miss Peat had a basin of gruel, as instructed, up in her room.

That'll teach her to be so damned superior, thought Charles with satisfaction, as he slurped his way noisily through the soup, helping himself liberally to half a dozen spoonfuls of croutons.

'Oh, by the way, my love,' Charles continued as Whiley left the room. 'I have been thinking about the baby's godparents. Dr Embsay has kindly agreed to stand godfather.'

'You asked Dr Embsay!' Adeline cried, the colour draining out of her face. 'I thought you said he was an unprincipled scoundrel?'

'I do not care for some of his methods myself,' replied Charles judicially. 'But he is becoming very influential at St Thomas's and he is the sole surviving heir to the Embsay Ironworks.'

'Wealth will not wipe out the stain of a man dishonoured!'

'Whatever are you talking about?'

'Do you really wish a man whose principles are, to say the least, dubious, to become the godfather of our child?' cried Adeline, pressing her hands over her stomach as if to shield her baby.

'You are becoming hysterical, my love,' said Charles. 'It is an opportunity to give our child some influential patrons in life. Besides,' he added sulkily, 'I have asked him now.'

'You might at least have had the courtesy to consult me.'

'I am consulting you,' said Charles impatiently.

'Very well,' said Adeline coldly. 'You have consulted me and I have said no. So now we must think of somebody else.'

'We are not going to have anybody else because I have asked Dr Embsay,' cried Charles, thumping his fist on the table. 'I am your husband, Adeline and while I make every allowance for your condition, I expect to be obeyed.'

Adeline swallowed and was silent.

Chapter Seven

Burlington Arcade was one of the most sophisticated and fashionable shopping areas in London. This delightful Regency arcade, with its bow-fronted windows and uniformed beadle, sold every luxury imaginable. There were jewellers and perfumiers, glovers and milliners. In fact, as Sir George once trenchantly observed, 'There is not a shop in the arcade that sells anything we could not do without.'

Did you want a silver-mounted whip for your spaniel, embroidered garters or a sword knot? Then you went shopping in Burlington Arcade. It was the height of exclusiveness, for you had to be rich to afford the expensive trifles and fashionable to be admitted by the beadles. It also provided the perfect alibi.

For next door to Urling's Lace Warehouse at No. 24, and not too far from the elegant Shawl Emporium (by Royal Appointment to Queen Victoria), was the astute Madame Parsons, Milliner, specializing in guinea bonnets, at Nos. 26–28. Above Madame Parsons' fashionable shop was an accommodation house, where ladies and gentlemen of the *ton* could meet discreetly for an hour or two in one of the bedrooms provided.

A lady, unremarkable amid the throng of fashionable shoppers, descended from her hired hackney and walked slowly up the arcade, pausing occasionally to window shop. She drew no attention to herself in her Balmoral mantle of light brown mohair and black felt hat with its short veil. She hesitated again outside the milliner's shop and glanced up at the inscription in flowing gold letters above the bow window. *Madame Parsons*, it read, *26–28 Burlington Arcade. Guinea Bonnets.* She ignored the shop door and went swiftly and noiselessly into the side door.

The uniformed beadle who was watching the lady's progress

from the hired hackney exchanged a knowing wink with the jeweller's door-keeper, with whom he was passing the time of day.

Inside No. 26 was a small passageway leading to some stairs. It was varnished a dark brown and reflected very little light. The only light, in fact, came from the fanlight above the door, and the lady stood for a moment accustoming her eyes to the dimness. There was a small office at the foot of the stairs and inside it, very neat and pretty, sat a young girl. She came forward as the lady approached and a muffled conversation took place, which ended with the girl giving a room number and directions and the lady taking her hand out of her muff and pushing some silver across the table.

The lady went swiftly upstairs. She paused briefly to look at some mildly erotic prints on the wall of the passageway, Fragonards and Watteaus, but the sound of footsteps coming down from the top floor made her hurry on again. She reached room eight and entered.

A gentleman sat dejectedly by the window, his jacket slung carelessly over a chair, and his boots off. He sprang up as the door opened.

'Dina!'

Geraldina pushed up her veil impatiently and looked around. 'I have never been in one of these places before,' she said with interest, 'and I shop for gloves and fans only a few doors away.' She looked saucily at him. 'Have you been here often, Frank?'

'Madame Parsons is quite well known in the trade,' he said, grinning in spite of himself.

'Does she really sell guinea bonnets as it says in the window?'

'I expect so. This is just a sideline, although a profitable one.'

Geraldina threw her hat on the table and her coat on the chair. Then with complete unconcern she began to undo the buttons on her bodice. Francis watched her with fascination. She might have been in her own bedroom with her maid to pick her things up, as she walked around dropping stays and petticoats on the floor. She stopped in front of two pictures that hung on the wall and straightened one a fraction. It was a print in a pretty gilt frame entitled 'The Night Before'. It showed a young girl in eighteenth-century disarray with large calves, breasts like balls and a profusion of drapery. She was disporting herself on the knee of a buck with wig and ruffles and elegant knee-breeches. Her struggles, thought Geraldina ruefully, were designed to show the maximum amount of the lady's charms and the minimum amount of his. The second picture was 'The Morning After'. The lady and gentleman were getting dressed the following morning. He was sitting on the far side of the bed and she was facing the viewer with pouting lips and a bubble coming out of them saying, 'Alack! What shall I do for I have lost my pretty bauble?' A similar bubble from the gentleman proclaimed, 'A pox on't! 'Twas already tarnished.' A serving maid was putting her hand into the gentleman's coat pocket and taking his purse.

There was a large looking-glass opposite the bed with an extravagantly rococo gilt frame, complete with a riot of cupids, cornucopias and a couple of coy nymphs sitting on the corners. 'I suppose this is so that you can do the naughty and watch yourself at the same time,' said Geraldina, bending over so that her drawers tightened over her buttocks. She glanced at Francis coquettishly in the glass but he was not looking at her. He sat astride the chair, his arms along the back of it, his head down.

'What is it, Frank?' she asked a trifle impatiently.

'I leave this country, probably for ever, in three days' time, and all you can do is admire yourself in the glass. I love you Dina and I thought you loved me. But over the last few months you have made no real effort to see me. I feel as if I am your pet lap-dog, allowed a few tit-bits to keep him going. I have even had to beg to see you in the Park for a few minutes. You do not really care do you, Dina? It was all just a game to you, and I, poor fool, was too much in love with you to see it.'

'But darling, I am devastated. I truly am, Frank. You must believe me. But we always knew it must end sometime.'

'You have no heart, Dina. You only want to enjoy it while you can.'

'And why not? Is it not better that we have happy memories to part with than useless tears? You have to go, Frank, and there is nothing we can do about it. So why don't we enjoy ourselves while we may?'

'You have never really loved me!'

'I do not know how you can say that! I have put my reputation in jeopardy for you, do you call that nothing? What more could I have done?'

'I cannot help feeling that you take as much pleasure out of deceiving that pompous husband of yours as you do out of meeting me.'

'Well, I do,' said Geraldina candidly, 'because he is a prig and a virtuous bore.' She knelt beside him and slipped her hand inside his shirt to touch the bare skin. 'But I find you very exciting,' she whispered. 'I have only to look at you, Frank, and you turn my bones to water. So come on.'

With eager fingers she began undoing the buttons on his trousers.

Some time later they both lay on the bed. Francis' eyes were closed and Geraldina was lazily tracing her name with her finger on his skin. His skin was fair, much fairer than hers and she liked to see the curling fair hair on his chest gradually tapering away to a small line down to his navel. He had a very exciting body, she decided, looking slowly down the length of it, with strong shoulders and narrow hips. Ernest never undressed completely, but always wore his nightshirt. He preferred to carry out his marital obligations in the dark and under several blankets. Geraldina liked to see what she was getting.

'I wonder how many men are deceiving their wives at this very moment,' she said dreamily.

Francis frowned and opened his eyes. 'Why do you ask?'

'I like to feel I am redressing the balance.'

He grunted. 'I hope I am worth it.'

'Absolutely tip top. A bit of nooky with you is worth ten times what I am offered at home.'

Her mind drifted back to one hot afternoon two years ago when she was sitting in the summer house and Frank came to see her. It was very quiet that afternoon, she remembered. Nanny had taken Charlie and Harry out to the Park – usually Charlie played in the garden and Harry had his afternoon nap in the baby carriage in the shade under the lime tree – but today it was silent. All she could hear was the low humming of the bees in the lavender bed and the lazy call of a wood pigeon in the square somewhere.

Geraldina had discarded her stays and was wearing only a thin

166

silk chemise underneath her flowered muslin dress. Frank sat down beside her and gave her his usual cousinly embrace, but it did not take him more than a couple of seconds to realize that the guard of whalebone was missing. Within another couple of seconds the embrace on both sides turned into something very much more ardent. It seemed to Geraldina quite without premeditation, she did not think of what she ought to do, no thoughts of Ernest or the children crossed her mind. Nobody had ever touched her body in that way before, or kissed her with such exploratory sweetness.

Frank was a very tender and experienced lover, Geraldina decided, both on that occasion and on every subsequent one. But he was going away and no amount of heartache was going to change that. Geraldina told herself that she was not going to repine over what could not be mended. She would turn her thoughts to reforming Ernest: Geraldina rather liked the idea of seducing one's own husband. Failing that, she would look discreetly elsewhere.

Frank had no such hopes for the future to sustain him. He was well aware that the machinations which resulted in his being posted to Secunderabad were started by Gerald Milford, or possibly by an interfering Mrs Peat. He was losing the one woman he cared for. Why was it invariably the third party in these unfortunate triangles who lost out? Geraldina at least had the security of her husband and home to fall back on, he had nothing. Frank at that moment felt utterly bereft. There was nothing more for him to do now, nothing else he could say to change the future one iota. In fact, not only was he back where he started, but he had actually lost everything he had learned to care for. Wearily he got up and began dressing.

'Don't,' cried Geraldina. 'I thought we had only just started.'

'I must. I have to be back in the barracks by three.'

Geraldina sat up impatiently. 'It is quite absurd that your colonel can have you posted abroad because of a love affair. I am sure he does the same. Why do you not sell out?'

'Because, my darling, I have to live,' replied Frank, smiling sadly at the unreasonableness of the female sex. 'The barracks provides me with three square meals a day and enough money to drink with. If I left, what would I have to live on?'

'Your wits!' cried Geraldina. 'Father was no better off than you when he started and look at him now.'

'Yes, look at him! Reeling in and out of brothels and having to be escorted home by his coachman.'

'How dare you! How dare you talk about my father in that way?' He did not seem to care that it was their last time together! He was just knuckling under! 'At least Father has made something of his life! He has more guts in his little finger than you will ever have. How far do you think your captaincy is going to take you? You only get paid a pittance! You can never afford to do what you want and I am beginning to think that you prefer it so.'

'So that's it, is it? I always suspected it. For you a man's cock is how much money he has! That is why you married Ernest. He may not be able to ring the changes in bed, but he can certainly ring the cash tills!'

'You mucked-out little creeper!' shouted Geraldina. 'You have done well enough out of Milford money. But for that you'd be eking out a miserable existence on a clerk's pay. Father was right: cocking is all you are good for.'

'Thank you,' retorted Francis, picking up his jacket from the floor. 'You have played around with me for long enough. Sometimes, you know, I have felt like your pet lap-dog, only there to serve your pleasure. But I am going to do the playing for a change. In case nobody has told you before, Geraldina, you are the most stuck-up, selfish little bitch I have ever met. It is going to give a lot of people a lot of pleasure to see you take a tumble in the mud.'

'Whatever are you going to do?' cried Geraldina, suddenly alarmed.

'I am going to tell Ernest what you have been up to. Everything. I shall give it to him right where it hurts – in his case in his wallet. That is what he has dangling between his legs that you wanted, it is not? Moneybags! Who knows, I might even give him a few ideas to liven up his bedroom performance.'

'You would not dare!'

'You shall see.'

'Frank, you wouldn't, you couldn't,' she faltered.

'So we're now prepared to try a bit of softy, are we?'

'You would ruin me. Do I mean so little to you?'

'Ruin you? Nonsense. You must live on your wits, my dear.'

Geraldina burst into tears. 'How can you be so cruel,' she cried. 'You just do not understand what I go through for you. First I had to fob off Nanny who came with some long-winded tale about nursery misdemeanours. Then Watchet kept insisting that he would order the carriage for me and get Marie and I know my excuses sounded lame to him, I'm sure they did to me.'

'And that was part of the fun of it, was it not? Your entire household knows very well what is going on, and you love it. It is only that poor dupe Ernest who is left in ignorance. Well, not for long.' Frank put on his shirt and began buttoning it up.

'Oh Frank, please, please,' begged Geraldina, tears streaming down her face. 'Call me any hard names you please, darling. I know I am selfish, but I do love you! I do. Oh Frank, please be kind to me!'

'It is not so easy now, is it?' said Frank scornfully. 'Now it is your reputation that is at stake. You are perfectly prepared for me to lose my commission and live on my wits. But it is a different kettle of fish if you have to do it.' He came over and gripped her by the shoulders so tightly that Geraldina cried out with the pain. He began shaking her to and fro, like a terrier with a rat. 'You are selfish, Dina, only out for what you can get. You do not love me, admit it. It was just the lure of the forbidden.'

He tried to push her away but Geraldina clung to him, careless of the bruises he inflicted, conscious not of his threats of telling Ernest all, but of a wild and growing desire. She tried to remind herself of the danger she was in, but all she could think of was the mounting excitement. Never had she felt so humiliated and shocked and never had she wanted him more.

She began clawing at his shirt buttons, frantically kissing his body, then his neck and reaching for his face. 'Oh Frank! Oh, Frank! Please . . . please . . .'. She stopped and looked timidly up at him, her face swollen with tears.

'Frank,' she whispered, 'do as you please. If you wish to tell Ernest, tell him. I am entirely yours. Only I wish you to know that I love you and I want you.'

Francis looked at her for a moment, the anger still set in his face, then he jerked her into his arms and began kissing her savagely, as if everywhere he kissed he wanted to leave a bruise, to mark her for his. His last coherent thought as he pushed her back on the bed and crushed her beneath him was the bitter-sweet one that at last, at the very moment he must give her up, he had won the response from her he always wanted.

But this only served to make the love-making more poignant. And when it was over they were only able to lie in each other's arms, spent and exhausted, with scarcely the strength to murmur each other's names.

There was a long silence. When they finally did speak, it was on impersonal topics.

'I shall be late, I expect,' said Francis, reaching for his watch.

Geraldina sat up. 'You go first, Frank. I shall come later.'

'You had better let me help you with your stays before I go.' He began picking up her discarded clothes from the floor.

Geraldina left Madame Parsons and wandered up the Arcade and out into Cork Street. She felt curiously flat and disjointed as if somehow things were no longer quite real for her. She hardly knew what she was doing or where she was going. She walked aimlessly down New Bond Street and eventually found herself crossing Piccadilly and sitting on a bench in Green Park. It was by no means warm, but Geraldina hardly noticed. All she wanted was somewhere to hide until she could decide sensibly what she must do. Part of her recognized very clearly that she was in the sort of state where she might do something very foolish.

Wild thoughts of telling Ernest and begging him to release her passed through her mind. She toyed with the idea of going to her father's office and imploring him to find a way for her and Frank to be together. But she had just enough hold on reality to reject it. That way lay disaster.

She could not go home and face the inquisitive glances of her servants. Finally, not knowing what else to do, she summoned a hackney and drove to Belgrave Square. She had vague thoughts of seeing Blanche. Blanche was the most sympathetic of her sisters-in-law, and Geraldina felt reasonably sure of her discretion. In any case, she must have somebody to talk to and there was really nobody else.

As the hackney pulled up outside the Peats' house, Geraldina adjusted her veil and clutched her cloak more firmly round her. She paid the cabman and knocked at the door. Ketton looked at her curiously as she entered.

'I do not think that any of the young ladies are At Home, Madam.' he announced. 'But I will enquire.'

Geraldina felt she could not bear it if Blanche should not be there. A lump rose in her throat and she felt the tears welling up in her eyes and start flowing down her cheeks. She must be here! She wiped surreptitiously at her cheeks with her handkerchief and began pacing up and down the hall. Everything seemed to be conspiring to push her into confessing. Blanche would not be there! She would have to go to her father and he would guess immediately what had happened. Ernest would divorce her and her name would be mud. Even the glass eyes of the stuffed bear, standing holding a tray for visiting cards, seemed to glare accusingly at her.

There were some swift footsteps and Flora came down the stairs.

'Geraldina!' she cried in astonishment. Geraldina pushed up her veil wearily. Wild conjectures whirled through Flora's head. What was she doing here in the middle of the afternoon without even a maid? Her usually elegant sister-in-law was looking dishevelled and pale. She had not left Ernest, surely? Or, horror of horrors, had Ernest cast her off? Flora had heard from at least three sources of Geraldina's involvement with Captain Grant. She never doubted that the rumours were true.

Geraldina said nothing, only stared at Flora. Her hands inside her muff were trembling. She was afraid to move in case she should betray herself.

Flora was very conscious of Ketton's curious gaze behind her. 'You need a cup of tea, Geraldina,' she said chattily, at last. 'I expect you have been shopping for Mr Milford's birthday. Shopping, especially for fathers, can be so tiring. We have the same problem every year.'

'Yes,' said Geraldina tonelessly, 'that's right.' Then after a moment she pulled herself sufficiently together to add, 'I was trying to find some little things for Charlie and Harry to give him.'

'Well, never mind,' said Flora brightly. 'Come and take a cup of tea with me. I am afraid both Blanche and Daisy are out. Ketton,

Mrs Peat and I will have tea up in my sitting-room, please. Come up, Geraldina. I have moved into Granny's rooms, you know.' Flora hoped she had said enough to satisfy Ketton's curiosity, or at least to ensure his discretion.

As they went upstairs, Flora felt her heart pounding. If Geraldina had been seeing Captain Grant, as she feared, then was not her first duty, in the name of truth, to bring it all out? Yet here she was, taking her in, deceiving the servants and giving her cups of tea. Should she not be casting her off and repudiating her? But even as she thought this, Flora knew very well that she had every intention of continuing to deceive Ernest, the servants and anybody else for that matter. Once she might have held different views, more like Adeline's, but Flora felt she had learnt something in the last few months. She had loved Algy, however unrealistically, and she had lost him. If Geraldina was now unhappy for the same reason, she would not betray her.

She ushered Geraldina into the sitting-room and then said, 'If you would like to tidy up, Geraldina, do use my bedroom in there. Nobody will disturb you and I will call you when tea arrives.'

Geraldina gave Flora a look half of gratitude, half of unease, and walked into the bedroom. She shut the bedroom door carefully and sank down onto the floor, her hand muffling her mouth, and burst into tears. Flora could hear her through the closed door but made no attempt to go in. She only paced up and down the room, frowning slightly and glancing anxiously at the door from time to time.

Geraldina emerged from the bedroom some twenty minutes later in her usual mood of cool unconcern. She had cried for Frank, which was more than she had done for any other man, and now she must put it behind her. She would need all her wits about her if she was to win through. Dust must be thrown in everybody's eyes and impertinent questions parried. She would start with Flora. Flora had allowed her a breathing space which she badly needed, but Geraldina doubted if her staid sister-in-law had any inkling of what she had been up to. What was needed now was to use the situation.

Flora poured out some tea and handed Geraldina the plum cake.

'Is anything the matter, Geraldina?'

'No,' said Geraldina shortly. 'Why do you ask?'

'I thought you might have been seeing Captain Grant,' said Flora calmly, pouring out her own cup of tea and sitting down.

'And what is that to you?' Geraldina noted with pride that her voice was quite steady.

'Pray do not think that I am about to denounce you. Do you wish me to say you have been with me here all afternoon? It might be difficult with Ketton seeing you come in, but perhaps we could think of something?'

'Why ever should you?'

'The family is in enough trouble already,' said Flora evasively, 'what with Blanche and all.'

'What is the matter with Blanche?'

'She has been getting herself into a scrape encouraging too many detrimentals. Had you not heard about Hugh Dunster?'

'Perhaps. I was not attending.' Geraldina's mind was racing. Had she misjudged Flora? It would certainly be an advantage to have an ally – and such an impeccable alibi too. People might guess that Blanche would lie to cover up her sins, but who would think that of Flora? – spinsterish, practically on the shelf. No, Flora would be believed implicitly. Conversely, if Flora chose to denounce her, then that would be believed too. The question was, how far was Flora prepared to go?

'Very well, then,' said Geraldina suddenly. 'I have spent the afternoon in a bed-house with Frank.'

'What's that?'

'Oh, you can guess. One of those discreet meeting places for ladies and gentlemen of the *ton*. It is in Burlington Arcade.'

'But I go shopping there!'

'That is why it is so convenient,' said Geraldina demurely.

'I do not suppose it will ever come in useful for me,' said Flora wistfully.

Geraldina laughed. 'You know, Flora, truly I thought you would play the prude. There is much more to you than meets the eye.'

Geraldina might be unfaithful, promiscuous, the sort of daughter-in-law no respectable family wished to have, thought Flora, but she was also honest. She did not pretend to remorse or guilt she did not feel. Flora felt she could talk to Geraldina without pretence or affectation.

'What are you planning to do about Ernest?' she asked. 'I thought, when you came here, that you must have had some row with him. Are you going to bluff your way through this tangle?'

'I must,' said Geraldina with a sigh. 'If only he was not so prudish and deferential, I could handle him very well. He used not to be like that: the first summer I met him he was quite the heavy swell. I remember thinking him quite an Adonis in his white cricketing trousers and striped blazer.'

'Is he prudish?' exclaimed Flora. 'Somehow I had a very different impression of him. I remember him explaining to me about the horse-breakers in Rotten Row. I thought it was rather modern of him. I mean, it is not the kind of thing men usually mention to their sisters.'

'Did he really? When was this?'

'Oh, before you were married. About five years ago, perhaps. One of the ladies waved to him and I asked him who she was.'

'And he knew?'

'Rather. It was that Bella woman, you know, the one with the ostrich feathers.'

'Bella Wilmington! A bit of all right indeed! How interesting. He has always contrived to give me the impression that his life has been one of spotless purity. I have often wondered at it, for he is rich and not bad-looking.'

Geraldina sat for some minutes in silent contemplation, then she laughed. 'Thank you, dear Flora, for that information. It is precisely what I needed.' She rose and walked over to the mirror above the fireplace and began patting her hair carefully, turning her face slowly from side to side as if to examine her reflection from every angle. What she saw there reassured her. She turned to Flora. 'Well, Flora, what is it to be? My reputation is in your hands?'

'I will do what I can to avoid a family scandal,' said Flora calmly. 'But do not make me your confidante again, Geraldina. I hold no brief for Ernest, but I do not care to see him duped.'

Geraldina looked at Flora with dawning respect. 'Very well,' she said. 'You are honest and I admire that – quite a refreshing change to find in your family, if the truth were told.' She paused to adjust her hat and to draw on her gloves, as if to satisfy herself that the disguise she was putting on was complete.

'What I shall do is this: I shall pretend that I have been shopping for father all afternoon, unsuccessfully, and I did not wish to take Marie because she will dawdle. I stopped to have tea with you, Flora, and I shall contrive to give the impression that I was here for half the afternoon. Of course, if Ernest hears of my little escapade this afternoon he will certainly cast me off. But I do not think he will. In any case, I now have some ammunition. A man with Bella Wilmington in his past cannot be too severe on his wife's peccadilloes.'

'Your muff, Geraldina.'

'Thank you.' She turned and smiled at Flora. 'Allow me to give you one piece of advice, Flora. Do not choose a husband who will play the prude in bed.'

Geraldina observed Flora's flushed cheeks with a certain satisfaction: her sister-in-law might hold her reputation in her hands, but Geraldina was still capable of redressing the balance somewhat.

Geraldina sank back and closed her eyes in the hackney as it rumbled over the cobbles. It was damp and musty but she did not notice. She was exhausted. It felt as if she had left home days before instead of merely hours. So much had happened, so many emotions, so many tears. Frank . . . no . . . no . . . she must not think of Frank. Keep him right away. That way lay disaster.

She turned her mind deliberately to Flora. That was a surprise. Who would have thought Flora, of all people, would be so unstuffy? Previously Geraldina lumped Flora and Adeline together in her mind and dismissed them. Plainly Flora was not the dowdy daughter, the frumpish, churchy old maid, that everybody thought she was. She might yet surprise them all. Certainly Algy Kingsley danced with her at the St Alleyns' and Lady Clevedon's. At the time Geraldina accepted Mrs Peat's explanation that Mr Kingsley was being kind to Flora for Grace's sake. But was it true? Nobody bothered to question it, certainly nobody asked Flora. Mrs Peat was assuming that Flora was at her last prayers and Mr Kingsley, matrimonially speaking, was a lost cause. But Flora's very silence on the matter now seemed suspicious. How would it be if Mrs Peat's so-called dowdiest daughter walked off with the catch of the season?

Mrs Peat would hate it all the more because her precious Blanche had tried and failed. Geraldina dwelt for some time on the pleasure this would give her. She had quietly loathed her mother-in-law for many years. She was to blame for the stuffiness of her son and Geraldina was sure she owed Frank's removal to Mrs Peat's machinations: by himself her father would never have gone to all that trouble bullying his contacts in the War Office unless some powerful influence was behind him.

It was the same with Adeline, Geraldina reflected as the hackney swung round into Piccadilly. Once Mrs Peat fixed her eye on Charles Woodcock, absolutely nothing would stop her from driving the affair to a proper conclusion. Every courtesy must be paid that might possibly promote the desired outcome. Charles and Adeline must be 'accidently' left alone. His parents must be visited and bullied into accepting concert or lecture invitations, which she was sure they did not want. Mrs Peat even tried to push Adeline into learning several old Jacobite songs so that she might warble 'Charlie is my darling' into his heart. Fortunately Adeline's modesty made her refuse point blank.

The hackney drew up at the door and the cabby leapt down, opening the door with alacrity for Geraldina. This high-class dame would not be one to quibble over the fare – ladies were usually amenable to a hint of a threat.

'That'll be two shillings, ma'am,' he said, holding out his hand. He usually asked to be paid before he consented to let down the steps of the cab.

Geraldina looked him slowly up and down as if he were some obnoxious insect that had crawled out that very moment from under the seat.

'I prefer to be paid first,' he said, not moving.

'The fare, as you very well know, is one shilling,' said Geraldina, and before he could answer, one elegant boot kicked him hard on the knee cap. He staggered back and Geraldina jumped down. She tossed him a shilling contemptuously and, sweeping up to her front door she tugged at the bell pull.

Watchet opened the door in time to see the cabby drive away, still cursing volubly over his shoulder.

'Well, do not keep me waiting all day,' snapped Geraldina impatiently.

'I am sorry, Madam. Mr Peat is upstairs in the morning-room, he was asking where you were.'

'Has he ordered tea?'

'He preferred to wait for you, Madam.'

'Have the tea sent up and tell him I shall be with him in a minute.'

Never one for please and thank you, reflected Watchet as he trod his way downstairs. There would be a right carry-on or he did not know the signs. Master looking black as thunder and demanding, 'Where the hell's my wife?' Everyone, right down to the scullery-maid, knew what she was up to. Disgusting, thought Watchet, the way she carries on – though he was not averse to a quick fumble with the second housemaid when she helped him clean the silver in the butler's pantry. She'll come a cropper, sure as eggs is eggs, thought Watchet with satisfaction. He wondered if there was some legitimate business that might keep him busy outside the morning-room: he had a bet with Mr Peat's valet about the outcome of this one, and he wanted to be in at the kill.

Ernest had come back from the office slightly earlier than usual to be greeted by the news that his wife had left the house shortly after lunch. She had not taken her maid and had hired a cab. In spite of Geraldina's wifely submission at the Clevedons' dance, Ernest still had his suspicions. Geraldina's docility aroused several ribald comments from his friends, where before they had preserved a discreet silence. Now, with this latest piece of behaviour, he felt both angry and humiliated. His name was a laughing-stock. She had made a fool of him and he would not forgive her.

'Where have you been?' he demanded coldly, as Geraldina entered the morning-room. 'I have been waiting for you for at least an hour.'

'I am sorry. If I had known you would be home early, I should have come back sooner.' Geraldina picked up the silver tea-pot and poured out two cups of tea.

'Doubtless. Answer my question.'

'There is no need to use that tone of voice with me, if you please. I went shopping for Father's birthday, unsuccessfully, I fear. I stopped on the way back to have tea with Flora.'

'You had tea with Flora?' he repeated incredulously.

'Certainly. Have you any objection?' asked Geraldina, raising her eyebrows.

'I object very much to my wife going out in a common hackney without even a maid to accompany her.'

'Don't be so stuffy. Marie dawdles so. Why should I not go out in a hackney if I wish?'

Ernest had a moment of doubt. Supposing she was telling the truth? Might not a wife, especially a highly strung woman like Geraldina, be justifiably indignant at being cross-questioned thus? No, no, he had done that before, been cozened by her wiles. Delilah! Tommy Clevedon's hints were surely not ill-founded.

'Don't try my patience too far, Mrs Peat. I warned you before, I am not standing for it. Either you toe the line or . . .'

'I never knew, Ernest, that you knew Bella Wilmington,' broke in Geraldina. 'Do you ever see her now, I wonder?'

'Who the devil told you about her?'

'Flora. She said you told her about the anonymas in Hyde Park. Do you know, that surprised me? It really did. You have always given me the impression that you have never even seen such ladies, let alone known such a high-flyer as Bella Wilmington.'

'This is hardly a suitable subject for a lady's drawing-room.'

Geraldina did not reply immediately. She was apparently absorbed in the array of cakes on the cake stand. At last she selected a fairy bun and bit delicately into it. 'I am glad to know you are made of red blood and not milk and water. No doubt her education cost you a pretty penny. What a pity you could not learn anything from it.'

It took Ernest a minute or so to sort out the implications of this speech. 'You actually wanted me to . . . you want. . . . By God, Geraldina, if I had a whip on me now you would soon learn whether I am a man or not!'

'I am not remotely interested in your whip,' replied Geraldina contemptuously. 'That would satisfy you, no doubt. But like everything else about you, it does not satisfy me.'

'I thought I had married a lady. A girl who was pure enough to look up to! To be a guiding light through life!'

'And I thought I had married a man with a root between his legs. Not the contemptible crawler you turned out to be! Take your filthy pedestal back, Ernest. I don't need it and I never have.

I want to be somebody's wife, not their statue.'

Ernest turned white, his lips compressed to a thin, hard line. For a moment he looked quite murderous. He got up. Oh God, thought Geraldina, have I pushed him too far?

'Where are you going?' she asked, impressed in spite of herself by the cold, angry look on his face.

'To pay a visit to a whore,' he said icily, 'since you seem to think that is what I should be doing.' He paused by the door. 'On the other hand, no. I shall go to Belgrave Square and find out if you were telling me the truth about Flora. Then I shall come back to you. I have paid enough for you and you appear to have the same instincts.' The door slammed behind him and Watchet scarcely had time to whisk himself into the drawing-room.

The bitch, the lying, unfaithful, cheating bitch, thought Ernest as he stormed out of the front door and hailed a passing cab. She has the face of an angel and the mind of a whore. If she had betrayed him he would kill her. But before that he would use her for his pleasure. She had asked for it and she would get it: there would be no more gentlemanly restraint. He would . . . Ernest found himself thinking of what he would do and the resulting fantasy was so stimulating that when the cab finally drew up outside the Peats' house in Belgrave Square, it took him a minute or two to remember why he was there.

Chapter Eight

It was nearly Easter before Flora resumed her chaperonage of Daisy to Berkeley Square. Lady Kingsley even came downstairs, leaning heavily on her ebony cane, to express her condolences over old Mrs Peat's death. 'I have written to your Papa, of course,' she said. 'But I imagine it is quite as heavy a grief for you. My grandson told me how close you were.'

Flora coloured up at that. Which grandson, she wondered, for if Sir George had told her, then might he not also have told her of that dreadful quarrel? But before she could collect herself Lady Kingsley asked another question which perturbed Flora even more, although she never considered it until that moment.

'Why are you sitting in the Library, Miss Peat? I seem to remember telling Penton that the Pink Saloon was to be put aside for your use.'

'Well, yes, I usually do,' stammered Flora. 'Indeed, I always used to. Only when I returned after Christmas, Penton showed me in here.'

'Really! I shall have something to say to him.'

'I believe it was Sir George's orders,' Flora was now quite pink. 'I assure you, Lady Kingsley, it was quite as much of a surprise to me. I think he was being kind because he knows I like books.'

Lady Kingsley's hand slowly groped for her lorgnette. She looked Flora very slowly up and down. 'I ... I never thought about it before,' stammered Flora. 'Do you wish me to move to the Pink Saloon? But I like this room,' she finished lamely.

'You are not a minx, are you, Miss Peat? No, I can see that you are not. By all means stay here, my child. I will not have George's arrangements disturbed on any account.' With surprising alacrity

Lady Kingsley returned up the stairs and was soon heard calling for her maid.

Flora did not allow her mind to dwell on this disquieting incident. There was too much else to occupy her thoughts. First of all there was concern over Adeline. She hoped she had done something to help her sister, certainly the reports of her progress seemed to be satisfactory and at least Adeline was seeing people. But from hints she had dropped, marriage plainly had not come up to her hopes. She had said nothing concrete but Flora thought that Adeline had realized that Charles was not interested in relieving distressed humanity, he was concerned only with his own status. Granny was right. Adeline had been wilfully blind and Flora pitied her.

Then there were Geraldina and Ernest. Later on that momentous afternoon Ernest had come round and had spent some considerable time closeted with her father in his study. Flora herself had been summoned down and asked if Geraldina had indeed had tea with her.

'Yes, she did,' said Flora, putting on an air of slight bewilderment. 'Indeed, she spent quite a long time here. We had tea together up in my room. She wished to ask my advice on what Charlie and Harry might give Mr Milford for his birthday.'

'You are sure about that?' demanded Ernest, uneasily.

Flora drew herself up. 'Certainly, Ernest. I am not in the habit of lying. Why do you not question Ketton if you doubt my word. He opened the door.'

'That will not be necessary,' said Mr Peat firmly and Flora was left with the uncomfortable impression that he did not quite believe her. 'Thank you, Flora. You may go.'

Ernest had a curious air of suppressed excitement about him and Flora could see that although he questioned her closely he hardly listened to her replies. His mind was obviously elsewhere. Flora wondered about it on and off for several days.

But there were other things on her mind; Daisy's recital for instance. All Daisy's conversation was about the forthcoming recital. She and Grace were to play piano pieces, recite some poetry, 'Some in French, Flora', and their work for the term was to be on display in the schoolroom. Flora spent the carriage journeys hearing Daisy say her pieces until she was word perfect.

The recital took place on the last Friday of the Easter term. Several comfortable armchairs were arranged in the schoolroom for Lady Kingsley, her maid and Flora. The old refectory table had been moved to the window and Miss Martin had arranged on it specimens of her pupils' work. There was Grace's essay on 'Victoria the Good' and Daisy's on 'The Lady with the Lamp', both copied out in their best copperplate. These were subjects that were both suitable for young ladies and with a bearing on the theme for the term, which was 'Duty'. There were examples of Daisy's Berlin work and Grace's embroidery, some wax and feather flowers, and a shell design of an underwater scene, with pieces of dried seaweed to give verisimilitude.

Flora duly admired everything and praised their industry, their taste, their colours and artistic execution. She was rewarded by a hug and a kiss from Daisy and a shy, 'Do you think Grandmama will be pleased with it, Flora?' from Grace. Flora reassured her and went to sit down.

Daisy and Grace disappeared behind a folding screen. From time to time whispers could be heard, the rustling of papers and then the odd giggle. Miss Martin was hovering by the door, listening anxiously for Lady Kingsley's footsteps. At last there were sounds of doors being opened and then an imperious, 'Benn, where is my cushion?'

'I have it, Madam.'

'Not that one, woman. The one for my ear-trumpet.'

Daisy poked her head out, awed, and looked at Flora. Flora, trying not to giggle herself, motioned her back and composed her features. The tap tap of Lady Kingsley's stick was heard. The footman flung open the door, Flora and Miss Martin rose to their feet, and Lady Kingsley entered, followed in somewhat of an anti-climax by the faithful Benn, carrying the ear-trumpet on a pink silk cushion.

Lady Kingsley sat down and turned to Flora. 'Why is your mother not here, Miss Peat?'

'My brother Tom is expected home from school today, Lady Kingsley.'

'I suppose she does not care to hear a couple of squawking schoolgirls. I cannot say that I blame her.'

Flora made no reply. She saw that Lady Kingsley was taking

pleasure in discomforting her. And yet, it was unkind of her when Grace and Daisy were waiting behind the screen with nerves stretched.

Lady Kingsley grasped her ebony cane and prodded it at Flora's feet. 'Well, Miss Peat. Do you agree, eh?'

'I think that they have both worked very hard and deserve every encouragement.'

'You think I am being rude? Well, perhaps I was. But you are a good girl to stand up for the children. Well, come along Miss Martin. Let us begin.'

Flora had heard '*Le Renard et le Corbeau*' so many times by now that she felt she knew it practically by heart, so she allowed her mind to wander and instead admired the picture the little girls made. They both looked very sweet in their white dresses, she thought. Daisy was all in white with no touch of colour as she was still in mourning, but that only emphasized her dark curls and rosy cheeks. Grace, who was fair and had a delicate, almost colourless skin, wore a pink sash and a single strand of coral beads. Grace was all set to be a beauty one day, Flora decided – one of the ethereal, angelically fair women that were so much in vogue. Her shyness would only serve to make her more attractive.

Daisy was already wearing stays, but nothing would serve to disguise her rampant vitality. Flora found her bounce and cheerfulness some of her most endearing qualities: she hoped that convention would not stifle too much of them. She caught Daisy's eye and smiled. Daisy smiled back and surreptitiously smoothed back her ringlets.

When I'm grown up, thought Daisy, and married with a house of my own, I shall have Flora to live with me. She shan't be bullied any more. And I won't mind at all if she goes out to museums and clever things like that.

Grace was now in the middle of her piece, Chimène's speech from *Le Cid*. Her hands were twisting nervously in her sash, but otherwise she was doing very well, Flora decided. Suddenly there were noises downstairs. Grace's speech faltered and then stopped. Lady Kingsley looked up sharply – she did not appear to need her ear-trumpet now, observed Flora. They could hear steps and then voices. Doors were being flung open.

'Hello, Penton. Everything all right?'

'Welcome home, Sir George. Her ladyship and Miss Lennox are both well. They are up in the schoolroom, I believe.'

'I will go straight up. See to my trunks, will you? Oh, and bring me something to drink.'

They heard footsteps running up the stairs and then the schoolroom door was flung open. Sir George stood framed in the doorway, looking fit and bronzed.

'George, my dear boy! We were not expecting you for another week at least.' Lady Kingsley's lined, old face lit up. George bent to kiss her. She patted his hand gently for a few minutes. Then she resumed her usual tartness. 'Whatever have you done to your hair? You look like some Italian gigolo.'

George laughed.

'Hello, Cousin George.' Grace stood shyly near the piano, her hands behind her back. George kissed her cheek and then Daisy, who had retreated behind the sceen, suddenly came out. 'Hello!' she said, with a beaming smile.

'Why, if it isn't Daisy! Am I allowed to kiss you too?'

'Certainly not,' said Daisy with dignity. 'I am now fourteen.'

'I trust you are not going to offer to kiss Miss Peat, too?' observed Lady Kingsley.

'Really, Grandmama,' said George unperturbed. He came forward and shook Flora's hand and offered his condolences. 'Now what is going on? Have I interrupted something.'

'The girls were giving us an end of term recital,' said Lady Kingsley. 'But I think we may stop now, in the circumstances.' Grace looked relieved and Daisy slightly put out. Everybody was talking at once. Lady Kingsley was demanding George's news, and Grace had so far forgotten her shyness as to tug at his sleeve demanding presents. Flora rose and went over to Miss Martin to take the opportunity of thanking her for all her work. Then she called Daisy over to her.

'I think we should find some opportunity to go, Daisy. They will wish to be left alone.'

Penton came in with drinks. 'Ah, Penton, bring up the small trunk, please. The green leather one. Grandmama, I have brought you some lace and a glass and crystal centrepiece from the Murano works which I think you will like.'

Flora stood quietly by the window and listened to George

talking. He was giving his grandmother news of people he had met, the Prince di something-or-other who sent his compliments, and the old Monsignor in Rome who wished to be remembered to her. Then he turned to the political situation in Italy – what the newspapers thought of Mazzini and of Victor Emmanuel – it seemed to Flora that George brought a larger world back with him, that the schoolroom was filled suddenly with air from the outside, debates and controversies that usually never entered.

The trunk was brought in and George unlocked it.

'Now, Grandmama, yours is at the top.' He unwrapped the base and column of the glass centrepiece and placed them in position. Flora thought the dark blue clear glass with its gold leaf decoration very beautiful. There was a basket of flowers, also in glass, that completed it, fitting into the top of the column, with sprays of twisted glass slotting into holes round the basket and fanning out with delicate crystal drops hanging down. Flora would have liked a closer look at it.

Lady Kingsley surveyed it. 'Very pretty, George. You had better tell Benn to put it in my drawing-room. I shall have it on the rosewood table by the window. Now, George, I must go and have my rest. All this excitement at my age is not good for me.'

George escorted Lady Kingsley to her room and then returned. There were squeals from Grace and Daisy as Grace unwrapped her presents. George stood for a moment by the door smiling as he listened to the ooohs! and aaahs! and watched the eager hands tearing at the tissue paper.

'I think Daisy and I should go,' said Flora, hesitantly.

George turned his head. 'No, do not go just yet, Miss Peat. I have hardly spoken to you. Anyway, it would be unkind to deprive Grace of Daisy's companionship now. I like to see them both enjoying themselves.'

'You will wish to be alone with your family.'

'Miss Peat, will you stop telling me what you think I ought to want and sit down. Daisy and Grace will want their milk and biscuits and you shall have a glass of wine with me. Besides, Penton is busy bringing in my things. Your carriage would only be in the way at the moment, I am afraid.'

Flora laughed and did as she was asked. George poured her a glass of wine and sat down beside her.

'Was your trip successful, Sir George?' Flora asked politely, suddenly feeling pleased that he was back.

'Successful? I saw some friends, visited some places, escaped the English winter and found the statues I wanted. Yes, I suppose it was successful on the whole.'

'What kind of statues?'

'Gods and goddesses.' He saw Flora looking puzzled and added, 'For the garden. They should be arriving in a month or so. They are not particularly valuable but they have to go by sea. They are modern copies of Roman copies of Greek originals, if you follow me. In fact, one of them could be Flora, the Roman goddess of flowers.' Flora looked up, startled. 'Or she could be Proserpina, I am not certain.'

'Do you not prefer something really modern?' Flora said hastily to cover her confusion at hearing her name spoken, even though he was referring to a different Flora entirely, surely? 'Mr Powers, for example. I remember seeing his "Greek Slave" at the Great Exhibition. Mama was very torn between wishing us to see it because it was so popular and not, because it might be considered improper.' She stopped, realizing where her unruly tongue had led her. She should never have mentioned that she had seen a statue of a naked lady – even one which had received the Royal seal of approval.

'I am happy to see that you still say what you think, Miss Peat. Even if you think you ought not to!'

George looked at her complacently. She was looking very well, much improved in fact. Perhaps it was just the dignity of her black silk dress, but it seemed to George that she had more poise. She had arranged her hair in a new way, a shining chignon secured by a jet comb, and with the dangling jet ear-rings and twisted rope of jet and seed pearls around her neck, she was looking most attractive. He had forgotten how amusing she could be. He found he was glad he had returned home now, instead of waiting another week or so.

Flora now recollected herself and shyly thanked George for allowing her to use the library during his absence.

'Not at all,' said George politely. 'I hope you have read all the books on my book list.'

'What book list?' Flora asked quickly.

186

'I think I put it inside *Wuthering Heights*. I thought you were going to read that next and would be sure to find it.'

Flora shook her head, she felt her colour rise and looked away.

She is lying, thought George. Now why?

'Very well, if you have not been reading *Wuthering Heights*, what have you been reading?'

'Carlyle.'

'Carlyle! Good God! Are you turning into a blue-stocking then?'

'You yourself said I was a blue-stocking the first time we met,' observed Flora maliciously. The more so because she knew that George knew that she was lying about the book list.

'If I did then I am sorry,' said George promptly. 'But please do not try to pick a quarrel with me, Miss Peat. I have not yet recovered from the last one!'

'You should not make horrid remarks about blue-stockings then,' said Flora crossly. Then she added, 'Actually, I do not care much for Carlyle. I am only reading him because I think it might be good for me.'

Flora did not know why she was being so provocative and then backing down. She truly did not wish to quarrel with Sir George. She felt the familiar mixture of exasperation and exhilaration, almost as if here was an opponent worthy of her steel. But he was right: it was most impolite to argue with him the moment he stepped through the door.

George held out his hand. 'Come, shake hands with me. Shall we be friends this year?'

'We can try,' said Flora, smiling at him and putting her hand in his. His fingers closed round hers and for a startled moment she saw that her hand was almost entirely enclosed by his.

Mrs Peat sat in her dressing-room thinking over the most encouraging talk that she had had with Mrs Dunster earlier that afternoon. She had feared that Mrs Dunster's obvious reluctance to further a match between Maurice and Flora was not to be overcome. Happily she was mistaken. The two ladies met and exchanged the most flowery compliments which in each case served to disguise the fact that neither of them liked the other. However, in spite of the barbed comments on Mrs Peat having four daughters to dispose of and Mrs Peat's smiling retaliation that she was glad neither of her sons was a gambler, honours were felt to be about even and the negotiations went ahead.

'You must forgive me, my dear Mrs Peat, for seeming a little reluctant to commit myself, but I have always been so close to my first-born that I hesitate to lose him. But now I have had the opportunity to meet Miss Peat, I believe she may well be the very wife for Maurice. Of course, when a girl is still unwed at, what is it,' with a gentle ripple of laughter, 'twenty-eight, one's first question is to ask what is wrong with her?'

'Some girls are a little slow to leave the nest,' replied Mrs Peat with a false, sweet smile. So are some men, she added to herself. Exactly what was Maurice doing at thirty-seven, still tied to his mother's apron strings? She would like to fling that home question at Mary Dunster! But Flora must be taken off her hands at all costs. 'Flora has very serious principles and I have brought her up to know her place. You would not find her asserting her claims before yours. Besides, my husband will be most generous to Flora on her marriage.' That money, she knew, would be very welcome in paying off Hugh's debts.

'I am not a mercenary woman,' replied Mrs Dunster. 'You may therefore believe me when I say I am confident that Miss Peat has exactly what my son needs. But I do not wish to rush the young people. You, of course, will hardly wish for a wedding while you are still in mourning. But perhaps we might consent to an engagement?'

Mrs Peat saw that nothing could be gained by pushing it further. She agreed therefore and the ladies promised themselves that they would seek a better acquaintance between their respective offspring in the coming season.

Mrs Peat could hardly wait to tell her husband about this conversation. No sooner was he arrived back from the office than she pounced on him.

'William! I am beginning to have hopes of getting Flora off our hands at long last.'

'What? Has Mrs Dunster popped the question?'

'I do not find that very diverting, William. There is no harm in mothers mulling over their children's prospects. And Mary Dunster, the dear creature, has been most encouraging.'

'I would find it more encouraging if Maurice was doing his own courting,' remarked Mr Peat dryly.

'Maurice,' said Mrs Peat importantly, 'has been most attentive. Mrs Dunster tells me he is much struck by Flora's intelligence. He danced with her at the Clevedons' dance. In any case, William, what could be more suitable? I am convinced that Flora needs an older man. And he admires her.'

'There is quite a step from admiration, which any young man may have for a pretty girl, to matrimony. I do not say that I am against the match. Maurice will not be very well off, certainly not if Hugh carries on the way he has been doing. However, I could help there. But I will not have Flora bullied, Susan. She has had much to bear this last half year. I do not wish her to feel we are pushing her out of the nest before she is ready to go.'

'Pushing her out! You forget, William, she was twenty-eight in February! She should have been out years ago.'

'I shall have to be convinced that it is what Flora wishes,' said Mr Peat firmly. 'I will not have her pushed.'

'I have never pushed my daughters! A little nudging in the right direction, perhaps, and look how successful I have been with Charles and Adeline!'

Mr Peat saw, with a twinge of his usual exasperation, that his words were going in one ear and out the other. However, he had heard of too many of his wife's prospective matches to place too much credence in this one. It worried him a little all the same. Maurice was too easily influenced by his mother: if she wished him to marry Flora, then Maurice would almost certainly propose. Once that happened, Mr Peat knew that life would be made very difficult for Flora if she refused.

Mr Peat did not want a husband for his favourite daughter who only proposed because his mother told him to. Besides, Maurice was plainly not interested in women; he had never been a heavy swell, never supported a mistress, in fact, on reflection, Mr Peat never remembered seeing him in Society without his mother. Whether he was one of Nature's bachelors, or whether his tastes ran in a different direction, Mr Peat could not say. He had not forgotten the sordid break-up of Mr Ruskin's marriage – there was an object lesson. He would make a few discreet enquiries about Maurice Dunster.

'I shall look into it,' he said at last. 'In any case, it is a relief that Captain Grant has finally sailed. I feared a really fearful scandal that would blast all our daughters' chances of marriage. You know Ernest came to me in quite a state just before Captain Grant sailed? He was sure Geraldina was having an assignation with the fellow!'

'Good gracious!' Mrs Peat lifted her hand to her cheek. 'I hope you calmed him down?'

'Geraldina said that she had been having tea with Flora. Of course, Ernest did not believe that for a minute. However, he demanded to see Flora and she confirmed it.'

'How extraordinary! Whatever did she have to say to Flora, I wonder?'

'My dear, I did not ask! I was only too thankful to be able to pacify Ernest.' Mr Peat had wondered the same thing, but reached a very different conclusion. He was almost certain that Flora was shielding Geraldina, at least to some extent. And for that he was grateful and made it his business to see that Ernest did not cross-examine her. 'Mind you, I think Ernest has been much too soft on Geraldina and I told him so. A man should always feel he is master in his own house.'

In fact, he was extremely cross with his son. 'Well, my lad, you have only yourself to blame! I expect it is your mother who has given you this idiotic notion that women are precious, delicate creatures to be worshipped from afar, when anybody with half an eye can see that Geraldina's nothing like that! If you persist in seeing her as a statue on a pedestal, then you must take the consequences! Women need a good rogering at least twice a week, and if you do not give it to them some other man will come along and do it for you. I have watched you with Geraldina and she looks thoroughly bored! I cannot blame her for behaving outrageously when all she gets from you is "yes, my love", and "no, my love". Put her over your knee next time and wallop her.'

Ernest looked very taken aback. 'No lady . . .' he began.

'You should have started in the mill at seven,' his father cut in. 'I do not think all your fine education has taught you anything. Geraldina's a woman like the rest of them. There is one thing they want and they want it often.' He suddenly wondered if Ernest had problems. 'You do not visit those flagellation houses, do you?'

'Certainly not!'

'Good. Now go home and take my advice. Do not worry about the lady's sensibilities. You have allowed her the reins for far too long. What she needs is your ram-rod.'

After Mr Peat had retired to his study, Mrs Peat remained in the drawing-room thinking over what her husband had said. She saw that he was not entirely happy with the Dunster match. She must work to bring him round to her way of thinking, otherwise he could spoil everything by weakly allowing Flora to decline the only offer she would ever receive.

If only he would allow that she knew what was best for her daughters. Adeline had been a most dutiful girl and now she had her reward – a respectable doctor who was quite devoted to her, a nice house and a baby on the way. Doubtless there was a period of adjustment – from which Mrs Peat's mind delicately shied away – but that would be over now and Adeline had all the security and position of being a respectably married woman.

But Flora, tiresome girl, could be so obstinate. She inherited it from her grandmother, of course, none of the Hebdens was like that, so difficult and wilful.

Mrs Peat decided that she would be very firm. Flora must be made to see that marriage with Maurice Dunster was in her best interests.

It seemed to Flora that at the beginning of April spring had finally arrived. The cold weather had blown itself out and the days were warm and sunny. Almost overnight, the window boxes in Belgrave Square were bright with hyacinths and tulips. The daffodils bloomed in Hyde Park. Most of the trees remained stark and bare, but some of the earlier ones, the hawthorns and willows, had a green haze about them. The birds were already sitting on their eggs.

The Season, too, was beginning. Those families who had retreated to their country estates for the winter now began to return and to plan once more for their daughters. Suddenly the Court and Social columns of *The Times* were full of news of arriving families, like returning swallows. Among these families were the Elkesleys.

Somebody once told Mrs Elkesley that she looked like Queen Victoria and indeed she did, with her short, dumpy figure and somewhat egg-shaped face with slightly popping blue eyes and a receding chin. Like the Queen she doted on anything Scottish and – under protest – dressed her sons in kilts and named her daughters after the heroines of Sir Walter Scott's romantic novels. Mrs Elkesley thoroughly enjoyed the social life and often wondered what she would do when all her daughters were married. She was in no hurry to lose them and was very happy for Jeanie and Effie to remain at home and liven up the place with their billets-doux and beaux.

As soon as she arrived in London she sent out invitations for a small dance. One of these invitations arrived at the Peats' house and, full of zeal, Mrs Peat was determined to escort Flora. Dr and Mrs Woodcock and Mr and Mrs Ernest Peat were also honoured with an invitation.

Blanche was not to go. Mrs Peat, for once, was firm. It was impossible for Blanche to come out properly this season as the Peats could not entertain on the correct scale and nor could Blanche dance. She must just resign herself to staying at home.

Blanche was furious and tried everything from tears and raging to coaxing and wheedling. She must go! She must! Let Alice Banks get her claws more firmly into Hugh and all her hopes would be gone. Somehow she must find a way of meeting him occasionally. At least often enough to ensure that he did not and could not forget her.

'That will do, Blanche,' said Mr Peat finally. 'You have made quite a name for yourself in the last season. No man of any standing is going to offer for a girl who goes with any johnny. Perhaps a season at home will teach you the value of a little more propriety.'

They'll be sorry, thought Blanche, thwarted and resentful. It was her future happiness they were destroying so thoughtlessly.

That evening a quiet cloaked figure, carrying a letter, slipped out of the door. Nobody saw her go and nobody saw her return ten minutes later and silently re-enter the house.

The dinner-party which preceded the Elkesleys' dance was the usual family affair, which everyone acknowledged was obligatory on these occasions but which nobody enjoyed. On this day it was not improved by the fact that everybody except Geraldina was wearing deep mourning. Blanche, who was allowed downstairs for the dinner-party, was wearing white mourning as became her years. Geraldina evidently considered the remoteness of the relationship sufficient for her to wear half mourning. She wore a lilac silk dress, trimmed with black lace, but of so daring a cut that the mourning touch only served to emphasize its allure.

Adeline took one look at Geraldina and resolutely turned her eyes away. Not only was that gown most unsuitable, but Adeline suspected that Geraldina was actually wearing rouge! Unfortunately she seemed to have affected Ernest with her lack of tone. Usually he was quite the gentleman. Perhaps it was permissible for him to wear a small pearl stud at the neck, although jet might have been more suitable, but those heavy side whiskers he was allowing to grow were surely out of place in a mature man and an elder son! Neither did she care for the openly lascivious look he gave Geraldina almost as if he thought his wife was not his wife at all but some lower-class woman.

.Ernest escorted Geraldina into the dining-room and bent over to whisper something to her, Geraldina whispered something back and pinched his fingers lightly. Then, across the table, there was a sly glance at Flora followed by the suspicion of a wink.

Grace was said and the company sat down.

'I hear you are going to Paris soon, Geraldina,' said Charles, looking at her with wet, shiny eyes. 'Open-hearth furnaces, isn't it?' Lucky the man who could get a poke at *her* open-hearth furnace, he thought. God, he envied Ernest having that luscious piece of cherry-pie in his bed. Although, of course, it would not do for a doctor to be suspected of getting up to that sort of thing. 'But you are not interested in the business side, surely?'

'Hardly. But I have promised to bear with it. In return I am to be allowed a shopping spree in Paris.'

'Oh, you are so lucky,' sighed Blanche. 'Paris in the spring! They say that the French fashions are far superior to anything you may find here and Society is much less stuffy.'

'I think that this country is universally acknowledged to have a most superior civilization,' said Adeline firmly. 'The French always strike me as being of most inferior stock.'

'I am afraid that they are ahead of us in steel-making,' said Mr Peat. 'Poor Siemans has failed to arouse interest for his discoveries over here; we must go to France to see what he is doing.'

'I cannot think that Geraldina is complaining,' said Ernest, stroking his new-growing side whiskers. He was feeling extraordinarily pleased with himself. He had decided that he would stand no more nonsense from his wife, she needed to know who was master in the house. Of course, all she wanted was a good rogering twice a week and he, Ernest, was going to see that she got it. He fancied he knew a thing or two about women!

'I am sure most wives would be proud to help their husbands,' said Adeline in a tight, hard voice. It seemed as if life was determined to be unfair, she thought. Here was Geraldina, looking practically like a trollop, able to help Ernest in an important way – talking to clients, entertaining their wives, while she was allowed to do nothing for Charles! Adeline felt that at least she looked and behaved like a lady. Why then did Charles always shut her out from everything? Was not a virtuous woman's price above rubies? She, and not Geraldina, should be the one to be the helpmeet and confidante of her husband.

Poor Adeline, thought Flora, so tense, so striving to do good, and so uncomfortable to be with! But then Geraldina! How had she managed it? In the few moments while the ladies were collecting their wraps Flora sidled up to her sister-in-law and in a whisper asked her if everything was now all right. She felt a surge of the most shameful curiosity. What exactly had happened between Ernest and Geraldina?

'Oysters,' replied Geraldina, at her most bland.

'Oysters?'

'Oysters. And some truly excellent orange brandy.'

It was amazing, reflected Flora in the carriage on the way to the Elkesleys, that a woman's adultery could be wiped out completely by the effects of oysters and brandy on a susceptible young man! She supposed Ernest must have been ready to be won over. He was certainly looking like the cat that had got the cream. In Charles' and Adeline's case it would be different. Flora doubted if the same recipe would have the desired effect on them. Nothing short of a miracle would turn Adeline from what she conceived to be the Path of Righteousness.

Blanche stood in the hall and said good-bye to the departing family. No, she said, with a wistful smile on her face, she did not mind staying at home. She would read the latest instalment of *Wives and Daughters*. 'There's my brave girl,' whispered Mrs Peat. Her unusual docility passed unnoticed in the bustle of ordering carriages and finding coats.

Blanche had no intention whatsoever of staying in with a book. She had, in fact, succeeded in contacting Hugh Dunster and had organized a most spectacular outing, which would forever blast her chances of marriage if it should become known. Hugh was going to take her to Cremorne Pleasure Gardens and they would have a few blissful hours together. She planned to slip out of the mews entrance and be back in bed by the time the rest of the family returned from the Elkesleys.

Cremorne Gardens was situated in Chelsea between the King's Road and the river and consisted of twelve acres of pleasure grounds, offering everything from balloon ascents and fire works to a dancing platform, set under ornamental iron-work in the shape of a pagoda and decorated with hanging lights. Blanche had been there several times as a child to see the equestrian displays or the Stereorama, but she had never been allowed there at night.

Cremorne Gardens were perfectly respectable during the day and even during the early evening. Lads from the East End brought their girls and shared with them penny bags of whelks and pea-nuts or took them to see 'Tony, the learned pig'. There was any number of frolics and larks and a man could end his evening, before the penny steamer took him home, with a kiss and cuddle in the fernery walks.

After ten o'clock the company changed. Then the secluded walks with their temples and arbours became the setting for activities of a very different kind. It was the haunt of the nocturnes, demure immorality in silk and fine linens, and the heavy swells. There was dancing and discreet suppers and assignations to be made among the ferneries, well away from the gaslights. With so much encouragement around, Blanche felt that Hugh could not fail to see that it was Blanche he wanted and Blanche alone.

She had met him, by arrangement, in Mudie's Circulating Library.

'Oh, Hugh, I have missed you so very much,' she whispered, wedging him firmly in a corner of the bookshelves, so that his head nearly knocked the four volumes of Richardson's *Clarissa* off the shelves.

'You are too impetuous, my sweet,' said Hugh breathlessly. Whenever he was with her he always felt as if he had stepped into some emotional hot-house. She was so sure of the importance of her own emotions that Hugh found himself responding in kind. They loved each other, she told him. Of course, she must be right!

But there was something else at the back of Hugh's mind. A growing and desperate need for money. It did not look as if Alice's trustees would allow an engagement, certainly not yet. Hugh felt a moment's pang for Alice. She was sweet and gentle and he was very fond of her. But he dismissed it. Alice was a forgiving girl but he could not help himself: he was sure that she would understand.

'One of the things I most love about you, Blanche,' said Hugh, 'is your ability to know precisely what you want and you are not afraid of getting it. You can stand up for yourself, can't you, Blanche? No shrinking violets for you.'

Blanche smiled. 'I have found it better to say what I want. Then everything is open. But you must decide, Hugh.' And one of the things I want, she thought, is for that insipid Alice Banks to come a cropper.

'I do not wish to hurt Alice,' said Hugh slowly.

'Of course not, Hugh,' Blanche opened her eyes wide. 'I would not dream of taking anything from Alice that was rightfully hers.'

'Come to Cremorne with me,' said Hugh suddenly.

'You are not serious!' Blanche gasped.

'Rather! My stuffy brother has come down with some of the actual, so I'll hire a carriage. If you wear a veil no-one will be a penny the wiser.'

'I want to see everything,' Blanche teased. 'All the things young ladies are not supposed to know about.'

'And so you shall, my love,' said Hugh. So you shall. More perhaps than you bargained for.

Although the house that Mrs Elkesley lived in was unpretentious Georgian, the decoration and furnishings were entirely modern. The walls were covered with pictures of Highland scenes as well as portraits of herself, holding a white rose, naturally, and her family, painted at great expense by Winterhalter. Her sofas were covered in a Hunting Stewart silk and the smaller chairs around the edge of her ballroom had backs made out of antlers.

Flora thought the pictures, with their baying stags and mounds of dead grouse, somewhat out of place in a London house, but dutifully followed her mother's ecstasies as Mrs Elkesley greeted them.

Mrs Peat shepherded Flora resolutely across the floor to where the chaperones were sitting, pausing only to allow Flora to greet Katie Anning. James Anning was there too, but he had long regarded Flora as a jolly older sister and Mrs Peat had no hopes from him.

'I say, Miss Peat. Rather a pity you cannot dance, what?' James' rather beefy face looked sympathetically at Flora. 'You are looking A.1. tonight, isn't she Katie, old thing? Tell you what, Miss Peat, I'll take you in to supper. How will that do? I'll see you get well fed at any rate.'

Flora thanked him and accepted. Mrs Peat frowned and moved on. It would be far more to the point if Flora had waited to see if Maurice would ask her. So much more talk could be exchanged over supper, but Flora, of course, never knew where her own best interests lay. However, it was too late now.

Flora followed her mother across the room, sat down gingerly on one of the antlered chairs and from the vantage point of a large pot of ferns watched the new arrivals.

Mrs Dunster arrived with Maurice but without Hugh. Flora grimaced, but perhaps after the chilly welcome she and Adeline had received she would not be expected to talk to dreary Maurice Dunster. Ellie St Alleyn arrived, talking animatedly to Lord Pateley. What a pretty girl she had grown into, thought Flora. How nice for her, especially as she used to be such a fat little thing.

She was much amused to watch Effie and Jeanie Elkesley

jockeying for position over Lord Pateley. He seemed to be completely taken with the charms of little Effie. Of course, he was one of the important guests and must dance with the daughters of the house. But no matter how much Jeanie fluttered her eyelashes and her fan, Effie was the elder. The younger must give way. Effie triumphantly led the dancing with Lord Pateley.

Mrs Dunster could be seen sitting next to a large dowager countess. She was talking to Maurice, who was hovering in front of her, as if ready to fly off in whatever direction she might ask. Finally, after nodding his head a great many times in agreement at what his mother said, he made a bee-line to where Flora and Mrs Peat were sitting. Flora's heart sank as she watched. He was a very thin young man with lank brown hair and sharp features. Flora turned her head away, she was sure that inside his white evening gloves his hands were clammy.

'My mother sends you her compliments, Mrs Peat and Miss Peat,' he bowed to each, 'she hopes you will join her for supper with her party.'

'We should be delighted . . .' began Mrs Peat, with a now-keep-quiet look at Flora.

'I am afraid that I am already engaged for supper, Mr Dunster,' said Flora quickly.

Maurice looked very put out by this information. 'But my mother said . . .'

'The early bird, Mr Dunster,' said Mrs Peat, wagging her finger roguishly at him. 'You know what they say!'

'I must tell Mama. It will change all her plans.' (And a good thing too, thought Flora, sending a silent prayer of thanks to James Anning across the room.) 'But when I return,' he was addressing Mrs Peat, 'may I ask your daughter if I might have the pleasure of a walk with her? I know she does not dance.'

He bowed politely to Flora. Mrs Peat smiled graciously, the more graciously because she was aware of Flora's indignation beside her.

'I am sure Flora would be delighted.'

'My mother asked me to try to persuade Miss Peat to dance. But I know she will not.'

'Alas, no. We shall be in full mourning until the end of May, you know.'

198

Maurice rose and bowed first to Mrs Peat and then to Flora and left them.

'Really, he is quite absurd,' said Flora, as soon as he was out of ear-shot.

'It is a pleasure to see a man so devoted to his mother,' said Mrs Peat firmly. 'She has so much to bear with from Hugh, if all the tales be true. Nobody but a mother can understand the anguish of having an undutiful child! In any case, Flora, a man with domestic inclinations is not to be sneezed at. He would make any girl a good, steady husband.'

'If he could bring himself to talk to her,' said Flora resentfully. The incredible thought that *she* was now the object of her mother's machinations passed through her mind, but she swiftly rejected it. Mama had, thankfully, given up with her years ago. Surely, it was obvious to anybody's intelligence that Mrs Dunster meant to keep Maurice tied firmly to her apron strings. But Maurice was on his dutiful way back across the room.

Mrs Dunster leaned forward and smiled conspiratorially at Mrs Peat.

Mr Dunster offered Flora his arm and she rose, allowing him to lead her out into the corridor and through the double drawing-room for a short promenade.

'My mother was most gratified by your kind attention in paying her a call, Miss Peat,' he began.

'Was she? I thought otherwise.'

'But she told me how pleased she was.'

That was more than she showed her visitors, thought Flora. She disliked Mrs Dunster, with her hard eyes, and she thoroughly resented the implication that she was 'on the catch'. She can keep her precious son, for I certainly do not want him.

'Your mother showed us round her glasshouse,' said Flora at last, as Maurice seemed unwilling or unable to suggest a new topic of conversation.

'Mama is very proud of her bulbs,' replied Maurice, giving her an approving look. 'My office is so full of them that there is not an inch of window-sill left.'

'Perhaps you should move to a bigger office?'

'I did suggest it, but my father would not hear of it.'

'Why do you not give some away? To your clerks for instance, or the Children's Hospital. I am sure they could do with some cheering up.'

'I would wish them to go to the right sort of people, you know.'

'I am sure your church would suggest suitable recipients.'

'May I offer *you* a plant, Miss Peat?' Maurice looked astonished at his own daring.

'If you wish,' said Flora, feeling that if this inane conversation went on much longer she would scream. 'But I have no green fingers, the plant may die.'

He pondered a moment. 'I shall give you a cactus.'

'That might be more practical,' Flora agreed, 'but I am sure your mother would agree it is hardly gallant.'

'The music has stopped,' said Maurice thankfully. He caught the tone of Flora's words, but it did not occur to him that anybody could seriously doubt the wisdom of his mother. He would tell Mama that Miss Peat had been most kind and encouraging.

At precisely ten o'clock Blanche slipped out of the mews door, and entered the waiting carriage. A circular blue cloak with a voluminous hood covered her dress and hair. There was one awful moment when her crinoline threatened to get stuck as she squeezed out of the garden door and Blanche had visions of herself able to go neither forward nor backward. But she managed to free herself, locked the door behind her and pocketed the key carefully.

Hugh drove to the meeting place with certain misgivings. He had told himself earlier that evening, as he was carefully shaving, that Blanche was more his kind of person. She was unashamedly out for herself, as he was, and he admired that in her and responded to it. He had every intention of making sure of her. He could not risk finding himself with neither Alice nor Blanche. The only reason his creditors were holding off was because of his hopes with the Banks fortune. Somehow, he must have money. Alice was too good a girl to lend herself to such an excursion, but Blanche had come with her eyes open and she must take the consequences.

Hugh had the uneasy feeling that events were moving faster than he could cope with: Blanche's eagerness had accelerated the pace so that he could no longer decide what he wanted but was rushed along willy-nilly by emotions he only half understood and could not control.

When they arrived, Hugh paid off the cab and, taking Blanche's hand, led her into the Gardens. Blanche was amazed and rather alarmed by the crowds that were there. Although it was ten o'clock it was as bright as day, with lights festooned all along the walks and gas-lights all round the pretty iron-work pagoda on the dancing platform. There was an open space in front of the platform with tables and chairs and busy waiters serving drinks. There was a showman, with dogs and monkeys, and gentlemen lounging casually by the bar or bending solicitously over the ladies.

'Come on, Blanche, sit down and I'll get you a drink.'

'We cannot sit here!' exclaimed Blanche.

'Why ever not?'

'It is so crowded! What if I am recognized?'

'You wanted to come here, didn't you? Sit down, there's a good girl or somebody else will snap up our seats,' and Hugh disappeared into the drinks pavilion.

Hugh bought himself a brandy and tossed it back. He promptly felt more in control of the situation. Blanche's kisses in the cab were abandoned enough to satisfy any man, but Hugh preferred to do his own chasing in his own time. He was not going to be a scalp on any woman's belt. Let Blanche rough it for a bit out there, he would see that she came to no real harm and then he would manipulate things his way.

Blanche felt annoyed and not a little frightened. But none of that showed on her face. 'Do not be long then,' she called brightly. She pulled her hood well over her face and trusted that she would not be recognized.

She was sitting in a fairly secluded place and after a minute or so she began to look around her. Opposite was a large table with several gentlemen hovering over two very flashily dressed ladies. Both had bright, golden ringlets, of a shade nature never intended, and they were, to Blanche's incredulity, very pretty. They were also behaving in a very free manner. One of them was relating an anecdote, her face was prim, her eyes expressive of exaggerated virtue, but the shout of ribald laughter that greeted the punch-line told Blanche clearly enough what sort of story she was relating.

The girls were made up far beyond the light touch of rouge Mama occasionally allowed. Their necklines were far lower and more revealing than Blanche ever wore. The men sat down, quite at ease, their legs stuck out, cigars in their mouths, laughing and joking with the girls. So this is what men are like away from home, thought Blanche. They have no respect for ladies at all, which was what she had always suspected. Their polite behaviour, their solicitude for the ladies, was just a façade. That was just the icing on the top, underneath they preferred the easy camaraderie of the anonymas. Doubtless all these men here had respectable wives waiting for them at home – poor stuffy things. Well, Blanche was not going to allow herself to be used like that.

The showman came over to the table opposite Blanche and began to show off his monkeys. The monkeys, dressed as a man and woman, were drinking wine and kissing. And then the male monkey was going round the table kissing the ladies while the female was jumping up and down in a sort of comic fury. Suddenly, the male monkey plunged his hand down the neck of one of the ladies' dresses, making loud kissing noises with his lips. Both girls shrieked and jumped up on their chairs. There was applause and shouts of laughter from the surrounding tables. In spite of herself Blanche was laughing, too, and leaning forward to look.

'Quite a comic sight isn't it?' said a voice behind her. 'They have been trained to do that, you know. May I sit with you?'

Blanche jumped. 'I would rather not, thank you.'

'Oh, come now, don't be so unkind. I can't have a pretty girl like you left all alone.'

'I am not all alone. I am being got a drink.'

'What's wrong with hailing a waiter then? My dear, you are too naïve, you have been given the slip.'

Blanche jumped up and looked frantically around. Where was Hugh? Where on earth was he? Surely he had not gone away and left her? No, no, he would be here any minute and tell this obnoxious man to go away. She should never have come! Only think of the scandal if she did not arrive back home! But of course he would be here soon. She must be polite but firm to this fellow and he would go away.

The stranger observed her alarm with satisfaction and coolly sat himself down and summoned a passing waiter.

'You will take a glass of wine with me, my dear?' he said. 'Some of the good stuff please, not that pap you were trying to serve last week. Now,' he turned to Blanche, 'let's have a look at you, Miss.'

'I have asked you to leave me alone, sir,' said Blanche icily. 'I am waiting for a friend.'

'Well, where is he?'

'That is none of your business.'

'You're here to have a flutter, aren't you? You could make a guinea or two by being nice to a toff like me. I'm in need of a filly, and you look a good fuckable one to me. Besides,' he lowered his voice, 'I guess you haven't been on the job long, and you won't know that you can be picked up by that constable over there for creating a nuisance.'

'Whatever do you mean?'

'Openly soliciting is an offence here, you know. The constable happens to be a friend of mine and I think I can persuade him not to take you in.'

Blanche felt a tickle of fear running down her back. Where was Hugh? Oh God, let him come back quickly. 'If there *is* a constable here,' she said, with a coolness she was far from feeling, 'then I shall tell him who I am and I expect he will take me home.'

The man laughed. 'Don't come the heavy with me, Lady Jane. I like a nice fresh piece like you, and if you're prepared to be nice you won't regret it. Otherwise I can be quite nasty. And I wouldn't want to be nasty to a pretty slice of cherry-pie like you, would I?'

Blanche began to feel sick. Would the policeman believe her? She had taken off all her jewellery to avoid theft. She had not even told Lottie where she was going. Stupid, stupid girl! Why did she ever agree to come out? Panic rose in her throat. She tried to speak, to beg the man to listen to her, but no words came.

She glanced at the man beside her. He was very much the heavy swell, ostentatiously dressed with a large flashy tie-pin. She had heard stories of young ladies being spirited away from their native land to the horrors of some foreign brothel, or being held up to ransom, or taught to pick pockets like poor Oliver Twist, or worse. The man beside her was lounging back now, quite at his ease, his hands in his pockets, a cigar stuck out of the corner of his mouth. No gentleman had ever sat like that in her presence.

'How dare you sit like that in the company of a lady?'

The man slowly took the cigar out of his mouth and deliberately blew the smoke in her face. 'You're no lady,' he said equitably. 'This is no place for ladies. Ladies are at home, tucked up in their neat little beds. You're a piece of cherry-pie like the rest of 'em, though a very stuck-up one.'

Blanche felt her heart pounding with a most unpleasant sensation of fear. The ground was cut from under her feet. There was no point in appealing to this fellow's chivalry. He had plainly misunderstood her quality from the first. She had better try to find a hackney and get home. She rose rather unsteadily. 'I am sorry,' she said, trying to keep the tremor out of her voice, 'but I think I must be getting along now.'

The man pulled her down, 'Oh, no you don't! I've bought you a drink and I expect some return. Sit down and take off your cloak.' Such was the look in his eyes that Blanche did so. She tried to stare haughtily ahead, but his deliberate scrutiny of her figure made her colour rise.

'Now we're getting somewhere,' he said. 'A nice girl like you can afford to flash her charms around a bit. I shall look forward to taking a walk with you down the alley in a little while. You look like a really fresh piece to me.'

He pushed the wine in front of her. Hardly knowing what she was doing, Blanche took a large gulp. How could Hugh have done this to her? How could he? She began not to see anything round her. This was a nightmare from which she would surely wake up. She did not dare to look at the man beside her. What would he do to her? Would he force her to go with him?

The man leant forward and began pawing at her neck with his stubby fingers. The cigar was still in his mouth and a hot piece of ash dropped off and rolled down her cleavage. Blanche shrieked and the man laughed and began fishing it out with his fingers. He stubbed the cigar out and leant forward again to kiss her. His mouth tasted of stale smoke and Blanche squirmed to get away, but as she did so his hand was reaching down her dress, pressing and kneading her breast, and the other hand was squeezing her mouth so tightly that she was forced to open her lips so that he could thrust his tongue in.

Blanche's hands were trying frantically to push him away. Her mouth seemed full of his tongue. Then one of her hands was seized and carried down to the swelling lump under his trousers and held there.

Hugh came out of the drinks pavilion several brandies later and immediately saw Blanche's struggles. He took a purposeful step forward, his fists clenched belligerently. Then he stopped. He had every intention of behaving exactly like the johnny who was trying his luck now, but he wanted no unwilling filly. Properly brought on, Blanche could be a very forward young lady and an extra fillip of gratitude to him for rescuing her was exactly what was needed. The man was struggling to get his hand up her skirts now and the policeman was looking at them. By God, the fellow was going too far! Hugh strode across.

'That's enough, my fine fellow. I'll thank you not to play around with my friend.'

'Hugh!' gasped Blanche thankfully and burst into tears.

'Your friend! She never said! How was I to know?'

'You know now,' said Hugh, shortly. 'She hasn't been with me long. Here, have a tipple on me.'

The man took the half-sovereign, looked at it and dropped it into his pocket. He buttoned up his waistcoat and picked up his cigar.

'Thanks. Good luck with that hard-arsed little cunny,' he said and sauntered off.

'You are a beast!' said Blanche angrily, her face flushed and tearful. 'How could you leave me here like that? You are horrid and I never wish to see you again. I should never have trusted you. Take me home at once. At once, do you hear?'

'All right then, I'm off. Find your own way home,' said Hugh, with an assumption of anger. 'I suppose you think it is all right to accuse me unheard! As a matter of fact I met an old school-friend and somehow I had to stop him coming to meet you.'

'Oh, I'm sorry, I'm sorry!' wept Blanche. 'Please, do not leave me here, Hugh. If you knew what I have been through!'

Hugh allowed himself to be mollified. 'There, there,' he said, sitting down beside Blanche in the vacated seat and putting his arm around her. 'People are beginning to look at us. Come for a walk with me and we can sit somewhere quiet and you can mop your face. Then we'll go home, I promise you.'

Blanche leant gratefully against him. 'I am so sorry,' she whispered. 'Perhaps I should have been able to handle it better. I was just too taken aback to know what to do!'

Hugh turned her more comfortably in his arm and began kissing her and his hand crept slowly down her bodice without raising anything more than a faint sigh of protest.

Blanche slid her arms around his neck. 'Actually,' she whispered, 'I half thought of biting his tongue hard!'

'Well, don't bite mine,' said Hugh. A few minutes later he added, 'God, Blanche, you are a lovely, lovely woman. And your mouth is like a juicy peach. And your skin is warm and soft, and this beautiful nipple I have in my fingers is like a hard, rosy thimble.' And I am going to bull her here and now unless we get somewhere more secluded quickly! He whispered softly in her ear, 'Let us go somewhere a little quieter.'

Dear God, thought Blanche, I want to go with him, but what am I going to do?

Flora sat in her usual position among the wallflowers. She was furious with Sir George Kingsley who had seen her, bowed distantly across the ballroom and made no further attempt to speak to her. He might at least have come over to say hello, thought Flora crossly, instead of dancing attendance on that fluffy, insipid cousin of his, Ellie St Alleyn. Some people may call those china shepherdess looks pretty, she called them affected. She watched George leaning down to hear what Ellie was saying and laughing. I suppose he thinks it is all right for him to talk to a *parvenue* blue-stocking in the privacy of his own home, but he must not be seen conversing with one at a public assembly!

She tried to scold herself into tranquillity. Algy Kingsley had come over to talk to her, he plainly did not think she was beneath him. James Anning had been very kind and taken her in to supper. Admittedly he spent the time throwing pieces of bread roll at his friends, which embarrassed her considerably. James' idea of amusing Flora was to rag young Lord Pateley, which caused Jeanie Elkesley, who was with him, to have a fit of uncontrollable giggles.

Lord Pateley was manfully trying to respond to Jeanie's flirtation. Flora felt quite uncomfortable for him: he was so very awkward. Jeanie put compliment after compliment in his way but he failed to pick them up. She did wish James would leave him alone. But James seemed to enjoy baiting him and roaring with laughter at his confusion. Lord Pateley needed somebody more gentle like Ellie, thought Flora, forgetting for a moment that Ellie was in the role of villainess. Then she scolded herself: whatever was the matter with her? Sir George was perfectly entitled to dance with his cousin. She *liked* Ellie. She must not grow into one of those horrid tabbies always trying to find fault.

Flora was relieved when James eventually escorted her back to the chaperones and she could sit quietly next to Mrs Anning, whose conversation was about nothing more tiring than fashion and her hopes for her girls. At least she was not being cross-examined by her mother on What Did Maurice Say? Especially as the answers were so unsatisfactory. She could see Mama now, sitting next to Mrs Dunster, their heads together.

'This is a sad season for you, Flora,' said Mrs Anning sympathetically. 'But I am happy to see that you are not shutting yourself away entirely. Mourning for parents, of course, is different, but I like to see my girls enjoying themselves. Of course there must be a proper period of seclusion, but after that, well, life goes on.'

Flora responded suitably, then, looking up, she saw Sir George coming towards her. She was wrong! He was not trying to deny their acquaintance. She smiled happily at him.

'Miss Peat, may I persuade you to have a stroll with me?'

'Thank you.' Flora rose and took his offered arm. She could feel the strength and warmth of his arm through his sleeve. She had never taken his arm before and it gave her a curious feeling to realize that he was a good head taller than she was. She had to look up to talk to him.

'I am going to find you a drink,' said George, 'then we can amuse ourselves discussing Mrs Elkesley's taste in pictures.'

'It would be most ill-mannered of me to criticize Mrs Elkesley's taste when she has kindly invited me to her dance,' said Flora primly. 'And I do not need a drink, thank you.'

'So you are critical, then?' said Sir George teasingly. 'Capital.

You will certainly need a drink by the time we have examined all this carnage,' he gestured broadly at the mounds of dead game and deer slung over the backs of deer ponies. He signalled to a passing waiter.

Miss Peat was certainly more his cup of tea, thought George. Ellie was sweet enough, and amusing too, in a naïve way, but with Miss Peat he could say more what he thought and get a straight answer. It did not occur to him that these were the very qualities in her that he had so deprecated the previous autumn.

The waiter returned and Flora obediently took the glass of wine he offered and allowed Sir George to lead her across the room.

'Now this one, Miss Peat. What do you think?' He stopped in front of a large print labelled 'The Drive! Shooting Deer in the Pass. Scene in the Black Mount. Glen Urchy Forest.' In the foreground, behind a wall, crouched two gentlemen with guns. With them were some Highland stalkers. Beyond the wall was a deep gully, down which poured an improbable number of stags – each one with a head clearly destined to adorn some Highland lodge. At any moment, Flora gathered, the sportsmen – if such they could be called – would open fire. As no stag was further away than ten yards, Flora felt that even she might be a good shot in the circumstances.

It must be one of Mr Landseer's efforts, thought Flora, looking critically at the picture. Sir George was plainly prepared to be amused by her observations, Flora knew enough about him now to know that. But could she be quite sure? She had not forgotten the awful episode with the Kingsley family tree. Sir George might be insulted by what she thought of the sportsmanship of these gentry. After all, she reminded herself, a man who in all serious-ness claimed McMurrough, King of Leinster among his ancestors – and she never did find out who he was – was capable of any-thing.

Sir George was looking down at her. 'Come on, Miss Peat, a penny for your thoughts.'

'You may not like them,' said Flora candidly.

George laughed. 'I am not expecting to *like* them. I know you well enough by now, Miss Peat. I am expecting you to say some-thing I thoroughly disagree with!'

'If you want the truth,' said Flora, turning her back on the picture, 'I dislike being brought over here to provide you with amusement. I was thinking that a man who claims descent from McMurrough, King of Leinster, is capable of anything.'

'What the deuce has McMurrough, King of Leinster to say to anything? Who was he anyhow?'

'I do not know,' said Flora angrily. 'He is on your family tree, not mine!'

'Miss Peat, I really do not know what you are talking about. But allow me to reassure you about one thing. I do not regard you as merely providing me with amusement. You do make me laugh, it is true, but I also take you very seriously. I can think of no other woman who is capable of making me change my opinions,' he smiled suddenly, 'even about the late-lamented King of Leinster. Who in all probability did not exist. There, are you satisfied?'

'Thank you,' stammered Flora. She felt both incredibly proud at such a compliment and agonizingly shy.

'You do not have to thank me, you know. Our acquaintance has always been of great benefit to me. I hold your opinions in very high esteem. Your views have made me change my mind about many things I had previously thought immovable. I think I am less self-satisfied, more willing to learn. I hope it is put down somewhere to my credit.'

Flora did not know what to say or do. Part of her felt like bursting into tears, the other part like bursting into song. She felt as if a door inside her was slowly opening. He liked her! He wanted to talk to her. The sounds of talking and dancing around them receded, and all Flora could hear was the thumping of her own heart and all she could feel was George's presence next to her.

'I must thank you too,' said Flora shyly. 'It has been a sort of life-line for me, coming to your house. As if I have been allowed into a wider world somehow.' Yet that was not what she wished to say at all. It was knowing Sir George that had made all the difference, she realized that now.

'Thank you, Miss Peat,' said Sir George, but there was a note of constraint in his voice. He felt a sudden desire to escape from what he had just said, not to look at it too closely. He looked down at Flora, she looked like a washed-out little blackbird in that dress. But even as he thought it he was aware that it was not quite right.

Flora caught the hint of withdrawal and instantly the sounds of the ballroom came flooding back into her ears. She began fidgeting with her bracelet, turning it round and round on her wrist.

'The music has stopped, Sir George. I must get back to Mama.'

She endeavoured to keep the thankfulness out of her voice, but she must get away. She could feel the tears pricking at her eyelids, but she could not explain why they were there. She did not know why, but he made her feel more awkward and uncomfortable than she had ever felt in her life.

Sir George, too, seemed unnaturally silent. His face was uncommunicative, the usually expressive eyes veiled. He offered Flora his arm in silence and although they walked back slowly to where Mrs Peat was sitting, neither of them said a word.

Chapter Nine

HUGH Dunster leant back in his chair and put his feet up on the office desk. What an evening! Blanche was quite an ardent clipper once you got her going. In fact, her sighs and groans of pleasure, although flattering, were also a source of embarrassment in such an exposed place as a laurel arbour in Cremorne Gardens. She had been a virgin too – Hugh had wondered, with her free and easy ways.

He puffed out his chest with a satisfied air. He had for free something for which men would willingly pay fifty golden guineas in the West End bagnios. Yes, it was quite an experience.

Now what? He could have Blanche anytime he wished, so why tie himself down in marriage? On the other hand she was willing to marry him and her dowry was twenty-thousand pounds. The question was, how much of it would Papa Peat insist on tying up in settlements?

Would he expect Hugh to pull his weight in the business? Hugh thought he might be rather good at selling. He knew he had a great deal of personal magnetism and charm and he could see himself on the Continent selling the Peat-Milford name, with a fat expense account and a suite at one of the best hotels as a base. He would have to take one of the Peat underlings with him of course, to brief him on the steel or whatever it was he was supposed to be selling – he could not be expected to know the details.

But what about Alice? He was fond of her, naturally, and always would be. She was a sweet, trusting little thing with those soft, brown curls. Perhaps he should go and see her, tell her about Blanche. He knew he ought to, he could see perfectly well that it was not fair to keep her in ignorance. No, it would hurt her too much and in any case, perhaps things would sort themselves out somehow.

He would leave things alone for a while – Blanche could wait a few weeks – just to see how he felt. There was no hurry.

Algy, in a black quilted smoking-jacket and red velvet smoking-cap with a black tassel, was seated in a deep armchair in his drawing-room in Chelsea. His feet were up on a small footstool and he was smoking a cigar. Beside him was a shell case picked up on the battlefield after Inkermann and Algy was using it as an ash tray. Anny, wearing a simple dress in her favourite rose pink and her fair hair done up in a loose knot with ringlets falling down the back, was sitting on the floor beside him. She was trying to fit together a large jigsaw which was on a tray near her. She had dutifully completed all the pieces around the edge and was now attempting to do the sky. She was looking somewhat helplessly at the jumbled clouds in the picture on the lid and the indeterminate piece of grey in her hand.

Algy was staring into space, frowning slightly, and although he smiled at Anny from time to time, it was plain that his thoughts were elsewhere.

'Oh, drat it,' said Anny at last. 'I do not know why I ever started the horrid thing.' She pushed the tray away from her and sat up. 'When are we thinking of going to France?'

'Mm,' said Algy.

'France, darling. When were we thinking of going?'

'Oh, France. Next month perhaps.' He relapsed into abstraction, twisting the cigar absentmindedly round in his fingers.

Anny got up. 'Algy, what is the matter? I have made at least three remarks to you and you have hardly noticed. Is there anything wrong?'

The familiar sinking came into her heart. She saw herself back in the Glove and Fan Depot, 22 Burlington Arcade. There was a looking-glass in the back room behind the shop where they used to do the accounts and Anny used to check her appearance there. She could see again the pale face with tired black rings under her eyes, the hollow cheek-bones from the diet of bread and cheese and no fresh air, the continual gnawing hunger, the exhaustion, the backache of standing up for twelve hours a day (lunch twenty minutes) and above all, the feeling of hopelessness that she would never get away, that this was what she was condemned to for the rest of her life.

She had always told herself that life with Algy could never last. And she had no wish to emulate Skittles and pass from one man to the next. She had tried to save from the money that Algy gave her, but it was difficult. He was generous, but he liked to see her well-dressed and she liked to dress to please him. There was no more than twenty pounds in the hidden envelope in her jewel box.

Algy put his cigar down and held out his hand. 'Come and sit on my knee.' Anny smiled and did her best to banish her thoughts. 'Were you thinking about that frightful shop?'

'How did you know?'

'You had that wistful look on your face. Never mind, my darling, you will never have to go back there or anywhere else like it.'

'I am sorry to be moping.' Anny turned within his arm and kissed him. 'I cannot remember now what brought it to mind. Do not regard it, it hits me sometimes, but I hope I am not ungrateful for all you have done for me.'

'I am serious, Anny,' said Algy, smiling at her tenderly. 'I think I have been very selfish about you. I love looking after you and providing for you, but it worries you doesn't it, my poor darling? I suppose I am scared that you might wish to go off with somebody else, so I try to keep a hold of you.'

'Algy!' Anny sat up to look at him. 'How could you possibly think that? I cannot imagine wishing to leave you for anybody at all, truly.'

'But there are plenty who would want you to.' Including George he thought. Of course, he did not think that George would poach on his preserves, but if Anny were free . . .?

'I suppose you do not trust me,' said Anny sadly.

'I trust you implicitly. But sometimes I cannot understand what you see in me! But I have put things off for too long. Anny, I am going to give you an annuity. I should have done it years ago, when I knew we were going to stay together, but I shall see my lawyer tomorrow and have it all tied up properly for you. Now, don't cry darling. There, there, I am a selfish brute, but I love you.' He mopped her tears and kissed her. 'That's better. Now tell me what to do about George.'

'What about George? What is the matter with him?'

'I am not sure. Only several things that do not quite fit. He actually went to the Elkesleys' dance – quite unprecedented for him. And when I invited him round here for dinner one evening he declined quite rudely.'

'Did he give you a reason?'

'Our domestic bliss makes him feel uneasy.'

'Whatever is he talking of? It has not worried him before.'

'I have not the foggiest idea. I thought I might seek him out at Brooks's one day. See if I cannot find out.'

It took Algy a week or so to run George to earth. First of all Lady Kingsley told him that his brother had travelled down to Linchmere for a few days to see his bailiff and then that he was gone out of Town to stay with Lord Houghton at Fryston Hall. Lady Kingsley did not say, but Algy strongly suspected that George had picked up some interesting piece of erotica to add to the famous collection tucked away in the Fryston Hall library. House parties at the Houghtons' were certainly far from dull. Algy had heard from Anne Thackeray of a most alarming incident when a youthful Algernon Swinburne read his passionate and sadistic poems to the gathered house guests, including a shocked Archbishop of York. Anne confided that the Archbishop half rose from his seat and looked set to excommunicate the poet when fortunately the situation was saved by the butler, who in the nick of time threw open the door of the drawing-room, 'like an avenging angel', said Anne, and announced, 'Prayers! My Lord!'

A far cry from the inanities of Mrs Elkesley's ballroom.

When Algy eventually found George in Brooks's, George greeted him with only mild surprise. True, he did enquire why Algy was there, but his mind seemed otherwise engaged and he hardly listened to Algy's glib reply that he liked the peace and quiet occasionally.

'Well, come and have a glass with me at any rate,' said George. 'Anny is well, I trust?'

'Beautiful as ever.' George summoned a waiter and ordered

the wine. Algy followed him to a window seat and they sat down. Algy looked out at the bustle of carriages and horses in St James's and wondered how best to start. 'I was not expecting to see you at the Elkesleys',' he began casually, apparently more interested in the progress of two pretty girls down the street than in George's answer.

'Oh, I thought it might be amusing, looking at the latest Scottish monstrosities.'

'Such as Jeanie and Effie Elkesley in tartan,' agreed Algy.

The wine arrived and George poured out two glasses and passed one to his brother.

'I was quite glad to have gone, though,' continued Algy, still looking out of the window. 'I like to keep up with the gossip.'

'I do not think that I heard any,' said George indifferently.

'Oh, it was the usual stuff. Who will be the lucky girl to nail Pateley. Both Effie and Jeanie were having a try, although he seemed more taken with Ellie's charms. And the latest *on dit* that Maurice Dunster is paying particular attention to Miss Peat.'

'What!'

Aha! thought Algy. 'I had supposed myself that Maurice was more interested in the boys. However, it is none of my business and I suppose the Peats will do all that they can to push it through. Anything to get an old maid off the shelf!'

'You cannot be serious!'

'Ask anybody. The Peats want Miss Peat off their hands before they bring that little trollop out. I am not saying anything against Miss Peat, mind, in fact she is rather jolly. But she must be pushing thirty and I daresay she would rather marry Dunster than be a tabby.'

'That milk-sop!' said George contemptuously. 'Always hanging round his mother's skirts. It is disgraceful! I cannot believe that Flora . . . Miss Peat would consider him for a moment!' An angry flush rose to his lean cheeks.

'Oh, she will accept him,' said Algy easily. 'Her mother will go on about gratitude and duty and in the end she will agree. What else is there for her, after all? I do not suppose that she will receive another offer and I daresay she might learn to be fond of Dunster. She is a sensible girl and she'll look the other way at what she cannot mend.'

George stared angrily at Algy as if his fingers itched to throttle him. Algy wondered for a moment if the sacred precincts óf Brooks's would be sufficient to stop George from smashing that clenched fist into his face.

Without speaking, George carefully unclenched his fist, put his half-empty glass down on the window sill and walked out.

'Whew!' said Algy and drained George's half-empty glass in one gulp.

Geraldina celebrated her return from Paris in the middle of May by giving a picnic on Hampstead Heath. She had two aims in mind. To demonstrate to Society in general and Aunt Emma in particular that she was a model wife and mother and to show off an exquisite silk walking-dress made for her in Paris by Worth at staggering expense.

Geraldina was quite content with what her trip to Paris had accomplished. She allowed Ernest to think he had gained the mastery: like most men he preferred to ignore what he did not wish to face. If he chose to think that her relationship with Frank Grant was mere cousinly affection, then she was not going to enlighten him.

As for Frank, he had now sailed out of her life and she would be sensible to face the fact. She was grateful to Paris for that, too, for it gave her something to think about while time passed until she could think of Frank without too much pain. If her host murmured extravagant compliments into her ear and M. Emile Martin, her host's son, gently pinched her fingers during the performance of a Donizetti opera, then that helped as well.

As soon as they returned to England, Geraldina sent prettily worded letters to all those members of her family whom she felt would be most annoyed by the invitation, including Aunt Emma Milford, a terribly religious woman, much given to sacking her servants for reading penny novelettes on the Sabbath. Geraldina remembered spending long holidays with her as a child after her mother had died, with the agonizing boredom of the Sundays, when the only toy she was allowed to play with was the Noah's Ark, because of its religious associations.

She knew that, as far as Aunt Emma was concerned, she was a fallen woman. But Ernest had not repudiated her: she was not huddling for shelter under some railway arch or carrying a baby through the snow. Aunt Emma would jolly well have to accept her and watching her do so would give Geraldina great pleasure. Geraldina knew that Aunt Emma would not actually decline the invitation. Instead she would prefer to accept in a flurry of righteous indignation so that she might deplore her niece's morals.

Geraldina was fortunate. The weather smiled, and finally six coaches made their way up to Hampstead, the last one carrying Watchet, two maids and the picnic hampers. The rugs were arranged on the grass and the guests sat down or wandered about to examine the view. Nanny took Charlie and Harry with the two Rivers children to sail their boats. Isabel's children were very wild after the journey in the carriage and raced through puddles and jumped to startle the ducks. 'Such high spirits,' murmured Isabel fondly.

Geraldina moved round greeting her guests. 'Aunt Emma! How delightful to see you! I should like you to meet my sister-in-law's husband, Dr Charles Woodcock. Charles, Mrs Milford. Charles is writing a treatise on cholera, Aunt Emma. We are all expecting him to do very well.'

Mrs Milford's small eyes were darting from Charles to Geraldina and back again. What the devil did she expect to find, thought Geraldina irritably, her hostess *in flagrante delicto* with her guests? It was hardly her fault if Charles looked at her like a schoolboy after bon-bons.

When her guests were seated or had taken themselves off for a stroll, Geraldina detached Flora from Adeline and suggested that the former might like to accompany her on a short walk. 'Ernest will do the honours for a while,' she said smiling. Flora at once stood up and said that she would love a walk. Geraldina indicated a path up past the ponds and suggested that they might have a closer look at the kite-flyers.

Flora agreed and they set out. They walked on a little in silence, Geraldina swishing at the flowers with her parasol. When they were out of ear-shot Geraldina said, 'I have some information that may interest you, Flora.'

Flora's heart missed a beat.

'How would you like to be Mrs Maurice Dunster?'

'Oh,' said Flora in relief, 'I am aware that it is Mama's latest fancy. I could hardly fail to be since she talks to me of nobody else. But I do not fear for myself – Mrs Dunster is one of the most jealous mothers I know. She, at least, will not agree.'

'Well, you are wrong,' said Geraldina. 'Mrs Dunster has agreed. In fact I chanced to be with your mother during a morning call while Mrs Dunster was there. It has her "highest approbation", I believe that was her term. If she did not describe you as a sunbeam in the home she did everything but! Make no mistake, Flora. If Mrs Dunster wishes Maurice to make you an offer, that is what he will do!'

Flora said nothing, but her parasol began decapitating daisies as they walked.

'What will you do, Flora?' asked Geraldina curiously. 'You cannot wish to stay at home forever, surely? Maurice would be very kind and reliable. Doubtless he would make a good husband. I know what I said about prudes, but will you receive another offer?'

'Probably not,' said Flora shortly. She blinked suddenly and shaded her eyes with her hand. They had been climbing the hill and now London was spread out before them. 'Oh look, Geraldina there is St Paul's!'

Geraldina gave St Paul's a cursory glance and Flora a more searching one.

'Is there anybody else?'

'Whatever do you mean? No, indeed there is not. I have not got another young man in my eye, if that is what you mean. In any event, even if I was stupid enough to allow myself to . . . to have an interest . . . I do not suppose it would be returned. But there is nobody,' she finished quickly, 'so the question does not arise.'

'I see,' said Geraldina, her voice carefully expressionless.

Flora was studying the ground. 'It is getting a little close, do you not think?' she said after some moments' silence. 'I think we ought to be getting back.'

Adeline and Isabel sat on a tree trunk with Blanche sitting near them abstractedly picking daisies. Adeline had a sketch book and some charcoal by her and was drawing a distant view of the ponds with some willow trees and the tiny figures of the children playing. Adeline had felt calmer these last few weeks. The baby was kicking now and her figure was thickened somewhat, in spite of the tight lacing she insisted on. The slight heaviness sat awkwardly on her thin body, but she was enjoying the spring sunshine and was anxious for a chat with Isabel.

'Is it true, my dear Adeline,' whispered Isabel, 'that Ernest took Geraldina back without a word?'

Adeline pursed her mouth. 'It is disgusting. He is infatuated. Only look at him! He is on the town now all right! He used to be sober and dressed like a gentleman: this is her doing.'

'The look she gave him! Did you see it? It quite made me blush!'

'Men know no better,' said Adeline. 'But that she, a lady, should encourage him in his saucy talk! I assure you, Isabel, I blush for my sex!'

'Geraldina's a trollop,' Adeline continued angrily. 'Only look at that bodice, Isabel! Showing all that neck. I am ashamed to say that Charles is not above looking more than he ought.' She had heard Charles whisper to Philip 'My God, look at those!' but she pretended not to hear it, and would not for the world embarrass Isabel by mentioning it.

'Philip, too, my dear,' said Isabel. But men always did like women who flashed their charms, as they said, although of course she would not mention it to Adeline.

Ernest smiled with satisfaction. It was all going very well, by Jove. Even Geraldina's stuffy aunt seemed to be enjoying herself. She was always disapproving of Geraldina, although he was damned if he knew why. He insisted that his wife invited her, she did not want to, but he overruled her and thank God he was master in his own house! Geraldina was looking damned fetching, too. He could see that Charles and Philip were envying him. Well, damn it, they were right! Once he had put a stop to this childish nonsense about that Grant fellow they got along swimmingly. Of course, he knew a thing or two about women; he was taught, most expensively, by Bella Wilmington. And his wife, once he had overcome her reluctance, came up with a few tricks too. But then all women had something of the old Eve in them! They were born with it!

At that moment Geraldina came up to him. 'Dearest,' she said

219

winningly, stroking his sleeve, and allowing her fingers to touch the back of his hand, 'Aunt Emma says that she wishes to talk with you. She has already had me on the carpet for spoiling the children. If you could coax her into a good humour I would be so grateful. She is dear Harry's godmother, remember?'

Ernest drew himself up. 'I shall not allow her to say a word against you, my own. Leave her to me.'

He patted her hand and strode off masterfully to do as he was told.

Blanche sat very silent throughout the picnic. Her family somewhat unkindly put it down to pique at missing her season and left her alone. But Blanche was not thinking of her season, she was thinking of Hugh. Had she given herself for nothing? Did he no longer care about her now he had taken her all? Why had he not even written to her? He might at least have dropped her a note or sent some flowers, something to tell her that he had not forgotten the sweetness of that evening. She had given him her love freely and unconditionally, surely that counted for something?

It had long been the tradition for Lady Kingsley to hold a garden-party to celebrate her birthday. As every year she was convinced that it was to be her last, she derived a great deal of enjoyment from allowing herself to be quite staggeringly rude to anybody who displeased her, on the grounds that by next year she would in all probability be underground. This year would be her seventy-seventh birthday, a good innings by any standard, she could not expect for many more birthdays to be allotted to her.

As always on such occasions, her thoughts turned to her grandchildren, particularly the selfishness of George and Algy in not marrying and having children to ensure the continuation of the family line. It was all very well for George to lead an untrammelled bachelor life, but had he no thought for Grace? What was to become of her? She would be coming out in three or four years and who would do it? Of course, Cousin Jane would jump at the chance, and in any case John would be the next baronet if neither George nor Algy had sons. John was a dear boy, but if Jane was to be chatelaine of Linchmere she did not think that she could bear it!

In her day these things were arranged and at least the grandparents knew where they were. If only George would settle down with some nice girl like Ellie St Alleyn, how suitable it would be in every way. Instead of which he chose to befriend some female of few pretensions to beauty and none at all to birth. In all probability it was one of those intellectual friendships like Dr Johnson and Mrs Thrale, but, of course, you never knew with George. At least Miss Peat was a civil, well-behaved young woman, and she would have twenty thousand pounds. She could not like the idea of such a match, but perhaps she was worrying unnecessarily. Certainly her interference might do more harm than good.

She rang the bell querulously for her maid. 'Benn! Benn! Where are you?'

'You called, Madam?'

'If Sir George is in, tell him to come here will you? I need him to write some invitations for this garden-party.'

'Certainly, Madam.'

'Now, George,' said Lady Kingsley as he came in, 'here is my list. I daresay that this will be my last party, but I still do not wish to see Amelia Elkesley.'

'Of course it will not be your last party, Grandmama,' said George patiently. 'You say that every year.'

'Humph!' But she looked pleased. 'What induced Elkesley to marry Amelia I cannot think. He always did have a streak of obstinancy about him and I have no doubt at all that it was his mama trying to arrange a match between him and that Offord woman that pushed him into it. I told them how it would be and did they listen?'

'No, Grandmama, they did not,' said George. 'So we do not invite the Elkesleys. Do you wish me to ask Cousin Jane?'

'Yes, indeed. Ask Jane and the children and the Colefaxes, of course.'

'I see that you have included Sir Charles and Lady Eastlake. Is Sir Charles well enough?'

'You must write a little note to Elizabeth, George. Assure her that I have this special day-bed for Charles and my screen.'

'Very well.' He looked down the list. 'Why have you asked Ellie St Alleyn and not Timothy?'

'A very nice girl, George, charming, well-behaved, of excellent family. Why should I not invite her, pray?'

'And Timothy St Alleyn is also charming, well-behaved etc., etc. Do not try to fool me, Grandmama, I see precisely what you are hoping for. I shall not be making Ellie an offer. For one thing, she is far too young for me, only just out.'

'You will leave Ellie on the list please,' said Lady Kingsley crossly, 'but you may invite Timothy too, if you wish. What is to become of the family, George, tell me that? It is all very well for you and Algy to pursue your bachelor existence, but what about the name?'

'We have a perfectly good heir in John: he always loves it down at Linchmere. I daresay he will do very well.'

'Have you no thought for Grace, then? I may not be here for her season. Will you trust Cousin Jane to do it properly? Now, if you were married George, or even Algy, although I do not place much hope in him, then your wife could be a chaperone for Grace.'

'I have no intention of marrying merely to provide Grace with a suitable chaperone! And there is nothing at all wrong with Cousin Jane except that when Percy died he was in debt as usual. Jane can bring Grace and Maria out together and I shall provide sufficient funds to do the thing in style.'

'And now look at Algy with that dolly-mop of his,' continued her ladyship, determined not to be mollified. 'I wish sometimes that I had allowed him to marry Sarah Dinsdale. No money, of course, but at least she was a lady.'

'Yes,' said George shortly. 'I had no right to persuade Sarah to break it off. I have felt very badly about it.'

'Nonsense, George. Do not talk such sentimental balderdash. You did your duty as you saw it. She was really quite unsuitable.'

'No, she was not. You said yourself just now that she was a lady. I fear that you and I are to blame, Grandmama, if Algy does not want a wife.' He suddenly remembered Flora's fury as she stood by her affection for her grandmother. She was right, he thought, I should have stood by my brother.

'There is no point in discussing it,' snapped Lady Kingsley. 'Let us get back to the invitations. I have included Miss Peat and Daisy, they will be company for Grace. I suppose Susan Peat will stick the card up in her glass for all to see, but that cannot be helped. I really cannot have Grace behaving as she did last year, hiding in the summer house. What a pity that so many of the women in that family are such sad vulgars, it does spoil Miss Peat's and Daisy's chances of marriage. If it was not for Grace being such friends with Daisy, I would not countenance them coming for a minute.'

'Miss Peat and Daisy will always be welcome in my house,' said George firmly, quite forgetting that six months ago he would have agreed with her entirely. He took the invitation list, asked politely if there was anything else and retreated to his study.

He wrote out the invitations and put them on the hall table for Penton to post. Then he looked over some correspondance from his bailiff in a desultory way for perhaps twenty minutes. He realized he was feeling discontented and restless. Algy's news about Flora had upset him, though, of course, it was none of his business whom she married. He wondered if he could tackle her about it when she came to escort Daisy in the morning, and then decided that he could not. How could such a bright, witty girl be satisfied with such a stick-in-the-mud? She would be bored within weeks! George wondered if it was not his duty, as a friend, to point this out to her.

Still feeling restless he left the house and walked down St James's to visit Swaine, Adeney and Briggs, his gunsmiths. He ordered a new shooting-stick. This purchase was totally unnecessary as he well knew, but he found the masculine smell of gun oil and saddle soap vaguely soothing. He began to think about August. Tommy Clevedon had invited him up to Cumberland to shoot grouse and usually George enjoyed the solid masculine companionship, the undemanding camaraderie, joking with the loaders, the steaming hot baths in the evening after a hard day on the hill and the easy talk that went with the port.

But even the agreeable anticipation of the grouse moor failed to satisfy him. Still feeling restless he wandered down towards Tattersalls, but the sight of horse-flesh proved as unsatisfactory as rifles. What the devil was the matter with him? Perhaps it was all very simple, he needed a woman. There was no need for all this introspection. He would go to his club and have a good meal, and after that he would stroll up to Kate Hamilton's and see if she had a dazzler there he liked the look of.

After dinner George sauntered up Piccadilly and turned towards Leicester Square. During the day the Haymarket and Leicester Square were only half-awake, with most of the shutters up and only a few yawning maids to show that there was any life at all. But they came to life at night when the gaslights flared. Then the pavements were crowded with men and women. The ladies ranged from the well-dressed and highly painted to the wrinkled and diseased, crouching in the corners of the alleyways hoping to sell themselves for a few pennies, enough at least to take them to the gin shop to drown their sorrows.

George touched his hat to a few acquaintances and kept an eye open for pick-pockets. A couple of women were pissing in the gutter, one standing in front of her friend until she finished and then taking her place. The porticos of the theatres were crowded with ladies in their jewels and feathers, either accompanying their protectors or parading up and down the vestibules to attract a client.

George avoided the smiling invitations of the nocturnes and walked on. He did not stop until he was accosted by Tommy Clevedon.

'Hello, George!' Tommy's pleasant, ruddy face greeted him.

'Tommy! How are you?'

'A.1. thank you, old chap. I say, where are you off to?'

'Kate's,' replied George.

'Why, so am I.'

'Let us go together. You can tell me what's new.'

'Several new bits of skirt. Do you remember that clipper with red hair, a regular tigress, the one who lived with Lord Bunwell?'

'Wasn't she the one who emptied the contents of her chamber pot over him one night?'

'That's the one. When he was whacking it up with Fanny Collins. Well, she goes to Kate's. And two other quite pretty girls that I don't know yet.'

The entrance to Kate Hamilton's was in Princess Street, just off Leicester Square. There was a long dark passage with two stalwart guards at the entrance, but these were there to stop an influx of inferior prostitutes from invading Kate's territory rather than to scrutinize the clients. One of them touched his hat to Tommy and nodded to George and the other opened the glass doors for them.

'There was some trouble last month,' remarked Tommy, elbowing his way towards a table.

'Not with the Peelers, surely?'

'I fancy Kate pays them too much for that. No, some vulgar johnnys thought they'd like a night out here. Of course Kate wasn't having that. Spoils the tone of the place. Well, anyway, there was a regular fight. A lot of customers joined in and we got rid of them. I had my hat stove in and a black eye, but it was worth it.'

They sat down near the edge of the room. It was large and brilliantly lit by gaslights. Each lamp, with its hanging lustres, reflected tiny prisms on the walls. Glancing in the ornate looking-glass beside him, George could see the huge figure of Kate Hamilton, sitting on a large throne-like chair on a raised dais. She was a grotesque figure, massive and elephantine, outrageously made up, with large flashing brilliants round her neck and wrists.

It was still only eleven o'clock and the place had not filled up yet, but even so there were plenty of girls parading round, joking with the men and winking saucily at any male acquaintance. Some of them were in full evening dress with lace and low décolletage, and some still had their hats on and carried muffs as if they meant to pick up their quarry and then depart.

The men were lounging casually, hands in pockets, cigars stuck in mouths. Quite often, as Kate knew, they came in for an evening of relaxed feminine companionship, far from the correct inanities of the drawing-room at home. Here they could relax and be themselves. Kate's girls, as well as being good in bed, could cap any man's saucy banter if they wished and no man need think he had to put a bridle on his tongue for fear of shocking his companion. In fact, Kate made most of her handsome profits from the sale of drinks in this room.

'I don't know what it is about Kate,' said Tommy, following George's gaze, 'but she can certainly make things go.'

'Here, Tommy, let me buy you a drink.' George summoned a waiter.

'Champagne or Moselle, sir.'

'Moselle, Tommy? A bottle of Moselle, please. What is it now, eleven shillings a bottle?'

'Twelve, sir,' said the waiter deprecatingly.

'Outrageous! Oh well, bring it, man. No wonder she makes a profit. What are you here for, Tommy? Filly-hunting?'

'If I see anything I like. Mama keeps going on and on at me about settling down, and it was driving me mad so I left the house. Ah, there's one of the new girls, pretty, isn't she?'

'Very,' said George, trying to put some enthusiasm into his voice. But he had not taken a fancy to the girl: her hair was too brassy and her cheeks too rouged. He could see her leaning over a chair and laughing at something somebody said – a high tinkling laugh that irritated him. 'Do you wish to ask her over?' he asked Tommy.

'I'll have a drink first. No point in wasting this stuff on them. Besides, they all want champagne.'

But it was not possible for two, affluent-looking gentlemen to remain alone for long. Kate kept a firm eye on all her girls and if they were not doing business then out they went. A plump, dark girl came up to the table.

'You two lovely gentlemen ought not to be sitting alone,' her look flickered from one to the other and finally rested on Tommy. 'Why not let me and my friend come and keep you company?'

George surveyed her opulent charms with distate. If there was one thing he could not stand it was fleshy women and this one would soon be rivalling Kate Hamilton in girth.

'I haven't seen you before,' Tommy was saying, squeezing her hand. 'What's your name, my dear?'

'Virginia.'

Tommy winked at George. 'Oh well, ask a stupid question . . .'

George drained his glass and got up. 'You look after my friend,' he said, seeing that Tommy seemed satisfied. 'I am going to take a stroll. I shall be seeing you around no doubt, Tommy.'

'Goodbye, old chap.'

George sauntered round. The place seemed to him tawdry and vulgar in spite of the magnificence of the decorations. The girls were not his style; there was not a single one he felt like spending half an hour with, let alone a night. He stood against the wall for a minute or two, surveying the scene. Was he turning into a Puritan? Was he drifting towards a sedate middle age with a fat wife, a dozen hopeful children and too much port after dinner? No! That was not what he wanted, was it?

George took one last look at the throng of swells and anonymas and walked out.

The cool night breezes of Leicester Square were pleasantly invigorating and George began to walk back slowly in the direction of Berkeley Square. As he did so he found he was thinking about Flora. Was she seriously contemplating marriage with Maurice Dunster, as Algy said? She should not have to waste a minute of her time on that little weed, why, it was well known that he could not do anything without his mother's sanction and Flora could not possibly be happy with a man like that. That idiot, Algy, had suggested that she might accept Dunster out of duty towards her parents. They would marry her off to that dreadful prig to get her off their hands. His beautiful, courageous Flora would be the wife of that spineless Maurice Dunster!

George found himself so agitated at the idea, with such a knot of anger against Maurice, that he found himself imagining, with a savage pleasure, an incident where he could knock Maurice senseless into the nearest gutter.

His fantasy took him further – Flora was standing there looking at him with those beautiful grey eyes and with trembling lips. Her hands came out to him. He took them. She was in his arms. He was kissing her and murmuring words of love in her ear.

George jerked his thoughts back into reality. He was in love with Flora? No! Impossible. And yet – the ways she looked and thought and *was*. Had she not become infinitely precious to him? How could he deny that he truly loved her?

All right, all right, he told himself sternly, there is no need to take this threat to your independance too seriously. Love is like influenza: one, it goes away after a while if left to run its course; and two, no sensible man allows it to interfere with his life. His plans would go ahead as usual. He would go to Greece later that summer, perhaps in August, and he would go down to Linchmere with Grace and Lady Kingsley as planned at the end of June.

It was ridiculous to consider himself a marrying man: he liked to feel free to travel, to come and go as he pleased. Besides, Lady Kingsley would never approve. No, by the end of the summer he would be quite happy to see Flora off to Ramsgate, or wherever it was she went.

No, he could not do that! The thought of not seeing Flora for the whole summer was unbearable. Linchmere would be lifeless and meaningless without Flora there to share it with him. Could he not invite her and Daisy down for the summer? He felt a wave of quite extraordinary happiness at the thought. He would be able to show Flora his home, to see her walking in the places he loved. He could take her boating on the lake. Did she ride? He could not remember her mentioning it, but he could teach her and they could visit the local beauty spots.

George turned into Berkeley Square and tried to argue himself back into neutrality. He had been in love before, hadn't he? Why should he waste his thoughts on a girl whose own parents considered her a wallflower? Go back to Kate's, you fool, you will find what you want there. He stopped for a moment, hesitating under the gaslights, but he knew he would not go back.

Flora was beautiful and truthful and different from all the other women he had ever known. She had refused to allow him to turn her into what he thought a lady should be. She remained resolutely and uniquely herself.

For all his experience, George felt curiously uncertain. The very strength of his emotions made him feel resentful, even though he knew he loved Flora. There must be some rational way to deal with this. Perhaps Ovid had some good advice on this sort of thing. Damn Flora, what exactly was it about her that made him feel only half alive when she was not there?

Adeline sat in her morning-room in Upper Cavendish Street awaiting Flora's arrival. She was thinking about Flora as a way of not thinking about Charles. Charles had come in late last night, bright-eyed and a trifle unsteady and smelling of oil of chypre. He said he had been out late with a poor consumptive woman and Adeline had accepted this, but she still did not wish to look at it too closely.

She was worried about Flora, she decided. Once they were close, had no secrets from each other and now they were drifting apart, she did not know why. At Hampstead Flora was friendly but unusually silent and giving nothing away. She went for a walk with Geraldina, too, which was odd. Adeline hoped Flora was not in some scrape with Algy Kingsley or anybody unsuitable like that. If only her sister would confide in her! If it *was* Algy Kingsley then Flora must renounce him and she would realize next time that Adeline was right, he was the sort of libertine no Christian woman could give her heart to.

Adeline wondered if she should drop a hint to Flora on just how humiliating the duties of married life really were. She would spare her sister that if she could. If Flora could be helped into deciding to devote her life to God and His Work then how much better would be her lot! How much happier would she be!

Adeline glanced at the clock. Flora would be here any minute. She quickly took up her catalogues for infant necessities and began going through them with a pencil. Flora would see that she was happy and busy. When Flora arrived Adeline greeted her sister warmly and asked the maid to bring Flora some coffee and herself her hot milk.

'Now, Flora,' she said with a bright smile, patting the sofa beside her, 'come and sit down and tell me how you are. You have been looking a little pale, my dear. I was quite worried about you at Geraldina's picnic. Are you quite well?'

Flora sat up and smiled brightly in her turn. 'I am perfectly well, thank you. If I look a little pale it must be wearing black that does it. It makes me look quite washed out.'

'Flora!' Adeline dropped her voice. 'You have not been having Doubts have you?'

'Doubts?' said Flora, puzzled. 'What do you mean, Doubts?'

'Do not be afraid to confide in me. I can see that something is on your mind. You have not even taken off your coat, or your gloves!'

'Whatever are you talking of, Adeline?' enquired Flora crossly, stripping off her gloves and unbuttoning her coat.

'Something *is* wrong, Flora!' There was a note of hope in her voice.

'Adeline!' Flora was exasperated. 'You are imagining things.' Just keep out, she found herself thinking. I do not wish to be told what God wants me to do! I do not wish you to tell me it is my duty to marry Maurice Dunster! I want to know what *I* want to do with my life.

229

'I see.' Adeline's voice shook. 'You will not confide in me.' She turned her face away. If she lost Flora's confidence what else was there left for her? She was not to be part of Charles' life. That hope was vanished. Sometimes she had the feeling that under the mask of the kind, attentive husband, Charles was quite a different person.

'Adeline,' said Flora unwillingly, 'whatever is the matter with you?'

'I am quite well, thank you,' said Adeline, her voice catching pathetically in her throat. She could feel the tears rushing to her eyes and she blinked hard to stop them running down her cheeks. The maid came in with the tray and hot drinks. Adeline sank back and shut her eyes.

'Thank you,' said Flora, smiling at the maid. 'That is all.' The maid left the room. 'Now Adeline, what is it?'

Adeline made no reply: the tears were running down her cheeks under her closed lids, but she made no attempt to stop them.

'It is Charles, is it not?'

Adeline's tears fell faster. 'Oh, Flora! Flora! He does not seem to care about me. He is always kind and considerate, it is not that. It is just that I feel that I do not matter to him, perhaps I never did, except as a suitable wife for a doctor. I wanted to help him and him to tell me about his work, but he never tells me anything. Nothing of importance, that is. He only shuts me out! And I do not understand why!'

Adeline did not know why she had told Flora this, it was not what she meant to say. It was only as she was saying it that she suddenly realized how true it was. She was going to tell Flora of the oil of chypre and the sick woman, but now this seemed more important. Charles would never be unfaithful to her, she knew, in spite of Isabel's hints.

Flora felt so desperately sorry for her sister's distress that she felt the tears start in her own eyes. She put her arm around Adeline and gently stroked her cheek. However had Adeline allowed herself to marry a man of such brutal insensitivity? There was something nagging at the back of Flora's mind, an incident where Adeline had been terribly hurt. Whatever was it?

'I always imagined something so different,' said Adeline in a whisper, resting her tired head on Flora's shoulder. 'I had such hopes of our life together. I felt I would do anything for Charles, Flora, anything. I never dreamt that he would not even want me. It has all gone now. All my hopes. Only ashes are left.'

Ashes! thought Flora suddenly. How could she have forgotten? 'Jemima,' she said. 'Just like Jemima, Adeline. Do you not remember?'

Adeline held up her hands as if to ward off the blow. Flora put her arms around her and held her tightly. 'Your doll. I remember thinking about her when you were clearing out your toys, but I could not remember what happened. That dreadful nurse we had – what was her name? Betty! Something happened to you then, Adeline, you were so silent and quiet after that. You quite changed. What was it?'

Adeline burst into renewed tears and cried as if her heart would break. She clutched Flora's hand so tightly that her knuckles turned white. She felt her heart contracting with the wildest grief. She had loved Jemima passionately, had whispered all her secrets to her, washed and dressed her every day and slept with her in bed at night. The pain of that sudden loss rose up inside her as if it was only yesterday instead of over twenty years ago. It was the most agonizing, sudden and cruel death she could imagine and somewhere Adeline had never forgotten it.

'She just shot up in flames,' she cried. 'Her lovely lace cap and brown wool hair. It was all so quick, Flora, I suppose she was stuffed with cotton. The last things to go were her feet. I can still see her red shoes turning black in the fire and then just disappearing. It was so quick, Flora, so quick! I was not even allowed to say good-bye. Oh I was so wicked Flora! I wanted to kill Betty, I prayed every night that she would die of something horrible; I would lie there thinking and thinking of the most horrible death I could give her.'

Adeline suddenly had a vision of herself down the long, dark tunnel of the years. She was three years old, passionate and wilful, screaming with rage at the nursery maid who was punishing her for some peccadillo. Adeline felt a thrill of horror as the little creature stamped her foot and shouted. 'I hate you, Betty, I hate you! You are the horridest person in the world, so there!'

'You're the naughtiest little girl I ever did see, Miss. Jesus won't love you if you behave like that. You'll go to hell and burn there for ever and ever. Mark what I say.'

'I do not care!'

'Don't care was made to care!' The maid seized the rag doll and flung it into the flames.

'That's what happens to naughty girls if they don't do what they're told. They burn for ever and ever.'

At length Adeline's sobs grew quieter. She lay for some time with her head on Flora's shoulder, holding her hand. Flora shifted slightly.

'Do not move,' she said, as Adeline stirred. 'My arm is going to sleep. Ah! that is better.'

'I do not think I dared to love anybody again after that,' said Adeline shakily. 'Do you think that is silly, Flora? She was only a doll.'

Flora shook her head. 'You loved her. You were right to hate Betty, she was cruel and ignorant. I loathed her and was happy when she left.'

Adeline sat up and looked around the room with the heavy-embossed wallpaper and the lace curtains across the windows to keep the sunlight from fading the carpets or the furniture, and she sighed. Everything in that room had been chosen by her: the crowded mahogany whatnot, the papiermaché occasional tables, the heavy hanging chandelier. She herself had sewn the valance for the mantelpiece, the frills for the piano legs and the antimacassars for the armchairs. She looked around at it all and had the odd feeling that she was sitting in the room of a person who did not even exist.

Blanche paced up and down her bedroom, her hands clasped behind her back. It was three weeks now! Oh God, where was Hugh? Why did he not come? Surely he had not returned to Alice? Blanche knew how Hugh felt about Alice, she knew there was so much that he could not talk of to her. He did not feel at ease with Alice, free to be himself. Why could he not see that it was she, Blanche, who was the right woman for him? But he would have to realize it for himself, to see that to continue with a betrothal merely out of some misguided feeling of honour would be a violation of his true feelings.

Was there nothing that she could do? She could not call on him. Now her season was postponed she did not even have the opportunity to meet him at parties. She could write though! Yes, why not? Surely they had passed beyond the conventional idea that no unmarried lady wrote to a single gentleman.

Dearest Hugh (she wrote that evening)

Thank you, thank you darling for the beautiful, wonderful hours we passed together. You are a very special and lovely person, do you know that, Hugh? I wonder if anybody has ever quite appreciated just how special you are before? I have been thinking of you all the time, all the time, Hugh. Every moment of the day. You are part of my life now and forever, darling. Oh, darling, darling Hugh, how much I love you, love you, love you.

Why have you not come to see me, Hugh? Please, please do not regret what happened at Cremorne. I have not and never could regret any of it for a single moment! Come on Thursday, darling, to the garden entrance where I met you before, at midnight. I will see that it is unlocked. Go through the garden to the kitchen door. I shall wait for you in Papa's study which is the first door on the right as you come up from the kitchen. Do not fail me, darling, my precious, lovely Hugh. I love you.

Blanche.

She re-read it slowly and carefully half a dozen times, smiling as she did so. She had never taken much notice of the Writing Compositions at Miss Speedwell's Academy, but she was quite satisfied that she could write a very successful love-letter. She sealed it with a heart-shaped wafer and stamped it.

Flora returned to the Kingsleys' after the weekend. Usually, Penton made some pretence of ushering her into the Pink Saloon and Sir George invariably came out of his library and invited her in. They spent most mornings since George's return in a happy companionship of laughter and argument and Flora always looked forward to it very much.

Today, however, George came out of his library and said nothing more than a curt 'Good morning, Miss Peat. Good morning, Miss Daisy'. He scarcely looked at her although he did

smile at Daisy. Daisy, with a concerned look at Flora, ran upstairs, leaving her humiliated sister to follow Penton into the
Pink Saloon. George immediately retreated to his library and
shut the door.

Flora wandered blindly round the Pink Saloon. She felt a lump
in her throat and the tears were stinging her eyelids. Whatever
had she done to deserve such a snub? She thought back over
their last meeting, but it was as warm and friendly as usual.
Of course, she told herself, Sir George has work to do, he
cannot be expected to talk to you all the time, but such explana-
tions did not satisfy her. Then she thought that Lady Kingsley
might have said something against her and Sir George was trying
to keep his distance, but that did not satisfy her either, in fact she
felt even more hurt that he might be influenced so easily into
denying their friendship. Surely it was a real friendship? Had he
not acknowledged as much at the Elkesleys' dance?

On the other side of the hall, George was pacing up and down
his library in an agony of indecision. How could he have behaved
in that way? He could see that she was upset and hurt and yet he
had not been able to stop himself. It had been pure reflex action
to retreat. He tried to dismiss it by telling himself that as he was
not serious it was better that Flora should be let down lightly
now than be humiliated later if she became too fond of him.

He could not get Flora's hurt and bewildered expression out of
his mind. He had not wished to behave like that. Part of him
wanted to tell her of his feelings for her very strongly indeed.
The morning was half over before George had come to any
decision. He kept telling himself that he should leave the house,
go away, visit his club, but the other half of him could not bear
to go and leave Flora looking so hurt. Finally, half against his
will, he found himself crossing the hall and entering the Pink
Saloon.

Flora was standing by the window staring out into the garden
when Sir George came in. He stood there, his hand still on the
handle of the door, as if he could not decide whether to stay or
go. At last Flora turned round and saw him. He was looking
extraordinarily ill-at-ease, Flora saw with astonishment, so much
so that she felt for a moment that she was seeing a stranger. She
had recognized his steps as he crossed the hall and schooled her

face into an expression of polite indifference. She meant to be calm and distant if he should attempt to speak to her.

To her surprise, she found herself coming forward with a reassuring smile and saying gently, 'I wondered if I had offended you in some way, Sir George? But it is not like you to ignore it, if that is so.'

George was feeling so strongly at that moment that he could not believe that Flora did not notice, but there she was, smiling at him with quite unconscious friendliness. He wanted to touch her, to kiss her, to tell her something of what he felt, but the very strength of this feeling made him draw back.

He said harshly, 'Black doesn't suit you, Flora.'

'How dare you!' gasped Flora, the colour coming and going in her cheeks.

'It is true. You look quite washed out.'

'I mean, how dare you call me Flora?' She was by now quite scarlet with a mixture of anger and embarrassment.

'Did I?'

'You know that you did.'

'Then it must have been because I wanted to. I am not going to ask your permission because I know that you would refuse.'

'I . . . I do not think that I would,' stammered Flora.

'Really, Flora?' George left the safety of the door and took a sudden step towards her. 'Would you and Daisy like to come down to Linchmere for the summer? If you would, then my grandmother will write to your mother inviting you.'

Flora stared down at her hands and her fingers began straightening the lace on her cuffs as if they absorbed all her attention. It was a compliment! Surely it was a compliment? He liked her. He wanted her company. No, she could not possibly go. She would feel so awkward, so uncomfortable with him there all the time. She would have to refuse.

'I . . . I must talk to Daisy,' she said, realizing suddenly that her silence had been too long. Whatever was she to say? 'Thank you, Sir George. I think that we would both love to come.'

'I am very glad,' said George, with so much feeling in his voice that Flora looked up startled. Why was he staring at her so? 'I must go,' he said quickly and without another word he left the room.

Adeline sat with some sewing in her garden. She had a wicker day-bed set in the shade of the lime tree and she was busy with some little silk vests for her baby. Beside her Isabel Rivers was sitting primly upright with her feet on a small footstool. In front of her was a tea-tray on a bamboo table and Isabel was pouring some more hot water into the teapot.

'More tea, my dear Adeline?'

'No, thank you. Charles says I may not drink too much tea. Weak ale or milk is all I am allowed.' She moved uneasily and pushed the cushion further up her back. 'I keep having these back pains, Isabel. Your father says I have to be careful not to lift things or bend, but that is impossible. Only think how many times one bends during the day.'

'What does Charles say?' enquired Isabel.

'Dear Charles is so concerned for my welfare. But he finds it a little difficult to talk to me about my condition. I think he is one of those men who are aways a little awkward in their dealings with women.'

'Not women, ladies,' said Isabel, in a sudden spurt of anger.

Adeline's finger slipped. The needle drove into her hand. A small bubble of bright blood appeared. She patted it with her handkerchief, but as swiftly as she wiped it away, more kept coming.

'Whatever do you mean by that, dear Isabel?'

'They like women all right,' said Isabel savagely. 'It is ladies they cannot talk to. When Philip comes in cocky and bright-eyed well after midnight, with the smell of scent and drink on his clothes, he cannot fool me. Of course I have never mentioned a word of it to him; I let him think me as innocent as the day. At least he has the decency to keep his home pure.'

Adeline was silent.

'It is the price we pay as ladies, having a certain delicacy above that of the lower orders,' continued Isabel, angrily twisting the fringe on her dress. 'Of course, I do not care to be treated like a harlot. I have a position to keep up.'

'Charles would not . . .' began Adeline, and faltered. She started again, 'I am sure I have nothing to fear from Charles' behaviour,' she said pathetically.

Isabel looked at her and said hastily. 'Of course, I am not

including Charles in this. I was speaking of men in general. I would not wish to upset you for the world, dearest Adeline. Charles has always spoken of you with the greatest respect, I assure you.'

Isabel felt a pang of compunction for her sister-in-law, though she was perfectly well aware that Charles accompanied Philip on his nocturnal visits. But Adeline was so high-minded, she would not see that men were the coarse brutes they were.

Adeline sat still and silent. Charles could not be behaving in such a way. It was not possible, so soon after their marriage and just when she was not feeling too well with the baby on the way. No man could be so cruel, so unfeeling. Charles may prefer to keep his work entirely separate, but she never doubted that he truly had her welfare at heart. Had he not always said so? She felt sorry for Isabel, having to live with such behaviour from Philip, although Adeline had always thought him a little on the ungentlemanly side.

Adeline argued herself into tranquillity. She refused the support of Isabel's arm in walking back to the house and even insisted on coming to the front door to wave her off. She saw Isabel's carriage disappear down the road with relief and then went upstairs to rest before changing for dinner.

There was no last-minute message from Charles saying that he was going to be late, so the Woodcocks were able to have their dinner without interruption. Charles did not look dissipated, Adeline decided with relief, scanning his face for signs of she hardly knew what. He looked as plump as usual, although somewhat pale. She asked anxiously about his day.

'Quite calm for once,' he replied impatiently: he did wish that she would not pester him with questions. 'I was held up by one of the Clevedon girls breaking an arm.'

'Good gracious! Which one?'

'Griselda. She took a toss while riding in the Park and fell awkwardly. Her horse shied suddenly. She said it was her fault.'

'She would say that, of course. She was always very plucky. There were no problems, I hope?'

'It was a clean break fortunately, though she was badly bruised, poor thing.' And what deliciously soft skin she had, thought Charles, so white and plump where Adeline was skinny.

'I must go and see her as soon as she has recovered a little.'

Later over dinner Adeline tackled another problem that was on her mind.

'Did you visit that poor consumptive woman, dear?' she asked delicately sipping at her Julienne soup.

'No, why?'

'She seems to take up so much of your attention at the moment.'

Charles lifted up a spoonful of soup and examined it critically. 'Oh, that one. I called on her yesterday. There is little that I can do.'

'Are there no medicines she can have?'

Charles frowned down at the soup and rang the bell. 'Excuse me, my dear. This soup has too much pepper in it, Whiley.'

'I'm sorry, Sir, I'm sure. I will mention it to Cook.'

Charles grunted. 'What comes next?'

'Roast fillet of veal, Sir, and boiled leg of lamb with vegetables in season. I think Cook mentioned broccoli, Sir.'

'Good. That's the ticket.'

'Could I not do anything to relieve the poor woman?' asked Adeline when Whiley left the room. 'You know my purse is always open to cases of hardship.'

'Sorry, my dear, what woman is this?'

'Your patient with consumption, dear.'

'Her husband drinks and her daughters have gone to the bad,' said Charles shortly. In fact, she was a total invention, and Charles felt annoyed with Adeline for bringing up the subject. God, all her questions, they made him feel trapped. As a bachelor he always laughed about the chains of matrimony, now he knew what they meant! Nag, nag, that was all women ever did. 'They are not a very edifying family, Adeline. I do not wish to sully your ears.'

'I suppose my ears will survive. I only felt that I should share the burden of your work more than I have been doing.'

'Your place, Adeline, as I have said before, is in the home,' said Charles quickly. 'I may be obliged to see the seamier side of life, but I do not wish my wife to be in any way part of it.' He moved his head uneasily inside a tightened collar. 'Ah,' he said with relief, 'here comes Whiley with the veal. It has forcemeat stuffing, I trust?'

'I ordered it especially,' said Adeline, trying to convince herself that she was gratified by Charles' concern for her sensibilities, when she could feel her emotions strangled in her throat.

'Capital!' said Charles.

The watchman, employed by the residents of Belgrave Square to protect their persons and property from undesirable characters, was, on this quiet May evening, fast asleep in his hut. It was a clear, starlit night and the only sound was the whisper of trees as the night wind gently rustled their leaves. Hugh Dunster had no difficulty in walking straight past the watchman. The dog, who was lying beside his master, raised his head and looked at Hugh, but sunk it back on his paws. He was trained to sniff out a toff and leave him well alone. Only the smell of dirt, old clothes and hunger could rouse the watchman's dog to action.

The watchman's hut was at the top of Wilton Crescent at the entrance to the Knightsbridge Road and Hugh walked briskly along Wilton Crescent and then abruptly turned down the mews running behind the Peats' house. Curious eyes might see him if he walked openly down the square, the mews was sheltered from all but the servants and Hugh felt safer there.

He reached the garden door and opened it: the handle turned smoothly in his hand. Hugh had been in the Peats' garden only a few times before and did not immediately recognize it. It looked a pale blue in the wash of moonlight and the stucco on the house was a ghostly white. To his right was the shrubbery with its convenient cover of laurel and lilac. To his left stretched a side lawn with a fountain in the middle and a prim border of flowers surrounding it.

He found his heart thudding with excitement and anticipation: the fact that if Peat found out what he was up to he would undoubtedly take a horsewhip to him, if nothing worse, only added to the thrill. Hugh remembered the stories he read as a child, where the hero succeeded in carrying off the treasure from right under the noses of the villains. He wondered what Blanche had to say to him. Was she pregnant? Well, he held all the cards: she was so very much in love with him that she would play it his way. She had told him that what he wanted was more important to her than anything else in the world, his happiness was what counted.

He need not move a step until he felt that he wanted to.

He trod carefully across the grass and entered the basement of the house. All was quiet. The servants were gone to bed long ago. There was only the dim glow of the damped-down fire in the kitchen range. In its light Hugh could see the coal scuttles filled for the morning, the blacking put to soak for the housemaids to clean the grates and the huge black kettle on the hob.

Blanche was standing by the window as Hugh entered the study. The clock on the mantelpiece said ten minutes past midnight. She was wearing her prettiest night-dress and wore a pink cashmere shawl over her shoulders. Her hair was loose, falling over her shoulders and down her back in a shower of gold. There was a paraffin lamp behind her and Hugh could see the shape of her body with the curve of her breasts as a dark shadow under her night-dress.

Blanche spun round as Hugh came in and flung herself into his arms. 'Oh, God, Hugh, wherever have you been? I have been so worried! Have you any idea what I have been through waiting here? You are ten minutes late!' Then she stopped and laughed. 'If I did not love you so much I would be very angry.' She pulled his head down to kiss him. It was a hard, eager, demanding kiss and Hugh felt the thoughts he had come with slip away. It was as if she contrived to move them both back to the excitements of the night at Cremorne and hold them there.

At last she released him and stepped away. 'You see, Hugh, it is useless. We love each other far too much to allow ourselves to pretend that the feelings we have are not very, very special! You cannot deny it!'

Hugh undid a button or two of his jacket and sat down gingerly on one of Mr Peat's mahogany chairs.

'Brandy, darling?' Blanche indicated a decanter and glasses.

Hugh accepted a glass. He had a slightly uneasy idea that things were not going to plan, but he could not put his finger on it. He did love her, didn't he? She was the most exciting woman he had ever met and she loved him. What more did he want?

'Are you shocked by my forwardness, Hugh,' asked Blanche playfully. 'I do not believe in playing games with men, I prefer to be open and honest about what I want.' She sat for a minute and sipped her brandy and then added quietly, 'Why did you leave me without a word for so long? Could you not even have written me a little note? Hugh, did you think that I was angry with you for what happened at Cremorne? It was inevitable, it just had to happen sooner or later. I love you Hugh, do you not understand? If I seem to be upset it is because I am waiting for you to make a decision. I am not using my love as a trap, Hugh, please believe that. It is a free gift, I do not wish you to feel that I am influencing you in any way. You must be free to decide for yourself. I know how difficult it is for you: you feel tied to Alice, even though you did not understand what you were doing when you became engaged and I respect that. But it is your choice, Hugh.'

'You do not understand,' began Hugh, hardly understanding himself. He saw Alice's gentle brown eyes for a moment. Alice trusted him to wait until time softened the hearts of her trustees. He felt a pang of something lost, but pushed it away. He had never truly wanted to get involved with Alice, he told himself, he only did it because she looked so vulnerable. He did not wish to hurt her and yet he must. Blanche was the first woman he had chosen for himself, she was right there. It was completely spontaneous, how could he deny something of such importance to him? Was his feeling for her not one of the strongest things in his life?

Every precept of selfishness and self-interest by which Hugh had largely governed his life shrieked at him to secure this golden gift from the gods, but he found himself saying something quite different.

'Blanche, let me be honest. I have to marry somebody with money – you will hear the gossip anyway and that part at least is true. Sometimes, I do not know if I really am the good-for-nothing everybody says I am, or if somewhere there is something worthwhile inside me. I have this feeling that I do not truly know who I am. Blanche, are you sure? About me, I mean?'

'Darling, darling Hugh! I believe in you, implicitly. I *know* you are a very talented and special person. *I* do not need convincing! Listen to me, Hugh. Too many people in your life have wanted you to prove something before they will trust you: your parents, for example, and Maurice. Even Alice – though I do not wish you to think that I am saying anything against her for one minute

– even Alice expects you to satisfy her trustees before she will marry you. I am not like that, Hugh, I only want you to be yourself and I am not interested in having you prove *anything*. Just be yourself with me, that is all that matters.'

Hugh rose and walked to the window and, parting the curtains for a moment, looked out into the moonlit garden. Was not this what he had always longed for? Somebody to believe in him without question? And yet, who was this person Blanche believed in so fervently? Did he really exist? She seemed so sure of her judgement; how could he, with all his doubts, presume to question it?

All the fantasies started to evaporate in the chill wind of his doubts. The idea that he would be supported as befitted a gentleman by his father-in-law, his hopes of being able to put down a decent stake at Crockford's for a change, his dreams of scoring over Maurice, they all vanished before this awful chasm of self-doubt that now opened at his feet. The only thing that seemed stable was Blanche's love: she assured him that it was a free gift, there were no ties or obligations.

'I shall go and talk to your father in the morning, Blanche,' he said, turning back into the room and letting the curtain fall back. He felt curiously flat and weary.

Blanche came towards him, tears shining in her eyes. 'Oh, my darling! Just now it seems very, very hard, I know. I really do understand, Hugh. But do not go tomorrow, give me time to have a word with Papa first and persuade him. It is not right that you should do all the work.'

'Very well. Thank you.' Hugh buttoned up his jacket once more. 'I shall write to Alice. Blanche, I may not be very good company for a while.'

Blanche went to him and put her hands up to his face and held it, looking into his eyes with her own very blue ones. 'Dearest, I have told you, I love you and I *don't mind*. It is right that we should be together, I *know* that. When all this horrible business is over, which I loathe as much as you do, then you will see that it is right. Sometimes, one has to fight for happiness, Hugh, it does not come easily. Nothing does that is worth while.' She kissed him gently and pressed herself close to him. 'Hugh, I want to say something, too. I know people say things about me, they say that I am a frivolous little bitch, I know that. But it is not true. I can be upset, worried and insecure, just as you are darling. I, too, question myself a great deal and wonder if what I am doing is right. I am a sensitive person, Hugh, I too can be hurt.'

Oh God, thought Hugh, I need this love, I need it, I can never let her go. His arms went round her. 'Darling, don't cry. Sweetheart, it is all right. I love you, Blanche. You are a very warm, loving person. You need not convince me, I can see it and that is why I love you. Though God knows what I have done to deserve it! I am fond of Alice, I respect her, but I never pretended to her that I loved her. And I never, never felt for her half of what I feel for you, and that is true.'

The familiar tides of passion carried him away, heightened explosively by the secrecy of their meeting, the lateness of the hour and Blanche's warm, responsive body. Hugh sat down again and pulled Blanche onto his knee, pressing her to him and shutting out the world outside. He found his old, familiar voice.

'Darling, how can I sample your exquisite charms, if I cannot undo these buttons. What is this you are wearing, anyway?'

'My Alexandra night-dress.'

'No wonder the Prince of Wales tries his luck elsewhere if this is what he has to put up with. Take it off, sweetheart.'

Chapter Ten

Mrs Peat so discounted Flora, as being of no interest to anybody, that she gave no particular significance to Lady Kingsley's invitation for Daisy and Flora to spend the summer at Linchmere. She supposed that Flora was invited to save Lady Kingsley the task of onerously chaperoning Grace and Daisy everywhere and said very little about it.

It was Mr Peat who enquired one evening whether Algy Kingsley was going down to Linchmere for the summer, or Sir George. Flora had time only to discover how much she wished to keep from her family, when Daisy answered for her.

'No, I do not think so, Papa. I heard Grace say that she was sorry that Cousin Algy was not coming and I believe Sir George will be going to Greece. Is that not so, Flora?'

'I believe so,' said Flora, although she knew perfectly well that George was not going to Greece until the end of August.

'Are you well-acquainted with Sir George, Flora?' pursued Mr Peat. 'Or has he not come in your way much?'

'Sir George never comes near his guests,' said Blanche waspishly. 'They are stuck in the Pink Saloon while he keeps himself to himself next door in the library.'

'He is away much of the time,' said Flora unwillingly. 'He has just come back from three months in Italy.'

True, thought Mr Peat, but you still have not answered my question. Flora turned back to her book, although Mr Peat could not but notice that her mind seemed far away and that the pages remained unturned. She was offering no clues as to how she felt. Mr Peat found this so unusual that he could not resist a further probe one afternoon tea-time when only Flora and Mrs Peat were with him.

'You are looking blooming these days, Flora,' he began. 'I hope there is some lucky fellow in your eye.'

'I am very pleased with Flora,' said Mrs Peat graciously. 'She has improved beyond all recognition. Mrs Dunster was saying so, only the other day.' She reached out to tilt the shade of the paraffin lamp to cast slightly more light on her embroidery. 'It is exactly as you say, William, a girl begins to bloom when a young man takes some notice of her. And dear Flora has been attracting quite a lot of attention recently!'

She smiled with coy intent at Flora and continued to sew the bright red petals on the chrysanthemum she was embroidering, her sharp needle darting in and out, creating scarlet petals like drops of blood on the white linen. 'Every girl must wish to be married,' she went on, deftly snipping off the loose ends with a pair of sharp embroidery scissors. 'I am delighted that somebody so suitable as Maurice Dunster has expressed a wish to know Flora better.'

Damn Susan for interfering, thought Mr Peat irritably, why could she not see that it was unlikely to be Maurice Dunster who was putting the light in Flora's eyes?

'I am absolutely delighted,' went on Mrs Peat. 'A match between Maurice and Flora will give pleasure to both families. Mrs Dunster tells me she has always longed for a daughter and I am sure nobody could be kinder or more considerate than Mary Dunster. Really, Flora is very lucky to be accepted by a family where she will be so welcomed.'

For once Flora felt relieved at her mother's obsession with Maurice Dunster. Her feelings about Sir George were in so confused a tangle – a heady mixture of alarm and excitement – that she did not wish to look at them too carefully and certainly did not want her father's inquisitive remarks. At least she knew precisely where she was with Maurice: he was not the one who was making her feel this delicious insecurity.

'I met Maurice Dunster today in Mudie's,' she said at last. 'And I told him not to propose, for I could not accept.'

Mrs Peat dropped her sewing and clutched at her heart. 'You did *what*?' she said faintly.

'Oh, I did not mention it directly, of course, but I think he understood me all the same.'

'What is this, pray?' cried Mrs Peat angrily, finding her voice. 'You are twenty-eight, Flora, and have not received even one offer! And now, when you are absolutely at your last prayers an eligible connection is offered to you and Miss decides that she will not have it! Do you think that you will ever receive another? One offer in the nine years you have been out will not get you off the shelf!'

'Now, Susan, that is enough,' said Mr Peat. 'I should be most seriously displeased if I thought that Flora was being coerced by you and Mrs Dunster into accepting an offer she did not want. I do not care for Maurice myself. I would prefer a son-in-law who paid his addresses to Flora rather than hiding behind his mother's skirts.'

'If Flora is so obstinate,' said Mrs Peat crossly, twisting her needle into her embroidery and pulling the thread with little sharp tugs, 'you will never have another son-in-law.'

'Nonsense, my dear. Certainly Maurice has been paying Flora some attention, but so, from what you tell me, have Algy Kingsley and James Anning.'

'We need not waste a moment's thought on Algy Kingsley,' snapped his wife. 'We all know *his* situation and James, I am sure, looks on Flora as a sister, nothing more. You are an ungrateful and obstinate hussy, Flora. Do not imagine that there will be another offer because I can tell you there will not! I spent a lot of time and trouble, which I could ill afford, pushing Mary Dunster into accepting the idea. From now on you must be content to be the chaperone. You have made a fine start with Daisy! The only invitations you will receive from now on are ones like Lady Kingsley's where your only use is to chaperone Daisy and Grace!'

It is not like that at all! thought Flora. But she said nothing. Mrs Peat was resentful at what she felt was Flora's attempt to be irritatingly superior.

'Oh, I wash my hands of you, Flora,' cried Mrs Peat, folding her sewing up angrily and shutting it in her embroidery bag with a snap. 'Do not come whining to me when you are a soured old maid, for I shall not help.'

Family prayers were a serious affair, held every evening at ten o'clock in the hall, except on the evenings the family were entertaining. There was a row of chairs for the family facing the ornate reproduction in a glass case of 'Una and the Lion' and behind them stood the servants. The upper servants, that is the house-keeper, Cook, Ketton and Briggs, stood directly behind the family chairs, with the housemaids and kitchen maids, bored and resentful, standing against the wall.

Blanche determined that tonight after prayers she would speak to Papa. She muttered her way through the Lord's Prayer and the Collect for the week with only the haziest idea of what she was saying. Papa must agree, she thought frantically, he just must. Suppose he decided to cut her off without a penny. Could he do that? *Would* he do it? Of course, if it was for herself, Blanche would not care, but Hugh, she knew, needed money. That had been the only moment when she allowed herself any doubts, when he seemed suddenly so lost and stumbling. He needed money and she had it. All these problems would be resolved when they were married, she was sure of that.

Finally it was over and Mr Peat pronounced the blessing. The servants, in an orderly procession headed by Ketton, retreated back to their basement and the family, with the exception of Mr Peat, retired upstairs to bed. Mr Peat went into his study and after waiting a few moments in the dark of the hall, Blanche followed him.

She knocked on the polished mahogany door and entered. The study looked dark and sombre with its rich red Turkey carpet and dark wood desk. Mr Peat's presence somehow gave the room a solid masculine atmosphere and the pile of correspondence on the desk, the heavy cut-glass ink-wells and the array of pens and blotters and pen-knives made it seem a place of weighty res-ponsibility, the hub, in fact, of the wealth of Peat-Milford.

It seemed a completely different room from the exciting, mysterious place where Blanche had met Hugh not twenty-four hours before. But the chair they sat in was still there, as was the tray with the decanter and glasses.

'Well, Blanche, what is it?'

'I came to see you, Papa,' said Blanche, suddenly so nervous that her legs gave way and she had to clutch at the desk for support.

Mr Peat looked up, frowning. 'What is it,' he said again. 'Is anything the matter?'

Blanche sat down and tried to steady her nerves. 'Papa,' she began, but her voice trembled so much that she had to stop. Mr Peat had put down his pen and was looking at her with an uncomfortably searching gaze.

'Well?'

'This may come to you as something of a surprise,' said Blanche at last, hoping she sounded cheerful, but to her annoyance she found she could not continue. She burst into tears.

Mr Peat got up so quickly that he knocked his papers on the floor.

'Oh no!' he said. 'Oh no! I see exactly how it is! I might have guessed! You stupid little fool, have you no sense? The way you have been carrying on, I am not surprised. I only wonder that it has not happened before.'

Blanche sat up with a jerk and looked at him angrily through her tears. 'It was not like that at all, not as you imagine. I love him and I know he loves me!'

'Oh God!' Mr Peat came towards her. 'And I suppose that makes everything all right, eh? The world well lost for love, is that it? Well, at least you have the sense to come to me and not your mother. Who is it, then?'

'Hugh Dunster, and we want to get married.'

'You cannot be serious! Hugh Dunster? That Dunster plucked your rose, I can well believe; that he wants to get his hands on your money, that, too, I can believe, but that you love him? No! You must be mad! That man has never done a day's work in his life. He was sent down from Oxford. If he has done more than draw his salary from Dunster's I shall be very surprised!'

'Don't you understand anything about love?' shouted Blanche. 'I love him and he loves me. I believe in him! I do not wish to be talked out of it because of what is prudent or what people think. Nobody has ever cared, I mean truly cared, about Hugh before. It is that milk-sop Maurice who gets everything: he is the blue-eyed boy. Nobody thinks that Hugh can do anything!'

'I would like to beat some sense into you,' said Mr Peat savagely. 'I have never heard such nauseous twaddle in my life. I suppose it has not occurred to you that if your precious Hugh had shown any ability to get off his arse and work, then he would be welcomed in any business with open arms? If he had any talents at all, he would not *have* to be stuck in Dunster's! And another thing. I thought he was engaged to the Banks girl?'

'He does not love her! It is me he loves!'

'And you saw to it that it was broken up!' He felt a surge of sympathy towards the hapless Hugh, trapped by this predatory woman.

'I knew how it would be!' shouted Blanche, 'I knew you would put all the blame onto me! Hugh is a grown man, you know, he is perfectly free to make his own choice. I did not influence him at all, in fact, I was very, very careful to let that be entirely his decision. If Hugh, of his own free will, decides that I am the right person for him, then why may he not break off an engagement, which is not an engagement at all, with a woman he no longer loves? Why am I having to take all the blame for this? If Hugh and Alice really loved each other, then I could not have come between them as you are suggesting!'

Mr Peat took a turn or two about the room. He could see all too clearly how it came about. Susan had exactly the same ability to see things only her way, to manipulate people to her own ends with no consideration for any other human being; if they did not like it then they should have looked out for themselves, was her motto. Blanche, doubtless, felt the same. He suddenly felt tired. Blanche had made her bed – and slept on it too, by all accounts – very well then, let her have him. When mutual disillusionment set in, as it would, then doubtless it would be all Dunster's fault. Blanche would be blameless.

He felt old and rather tired. He had failed both as a father and as a husband. Why had he allowed Susan to bring up her daughter with no regard for anything save her own convenience? Ernest's marriage was saved only by a certain amount of deceit and double-dealing, he was sure. At least Ernest was dotingly fond of Geraldina. Adeline was allowed to enter marriage as if she was entering Holy Orders, and was discovering unhappily that Charles was not cut out to be a saint. What lies was Blanche telling herself about her lazy and dissolute choice?

'Very well, then,' he said curtly at last. 'Marry the fellow. I have nothing more to say. But I will not allow him to batten on your money. I will tie it all up in a trust for you and any children you may have. You will have the income, that is all. I have no mind to support a son-in-law in the gambling dens. It has taken me thirty years to earn my brass and I have no intention of allowing Hugh Dunster to spend it for me.'

'I am sorry that you have chosen to allow yourself to be upset,' said Blanche coolly, getting up to go. 'Hugh is coming to see you tomorrow at the office. I hope you will not allow yourself to be prejudiced against him.'

'I will treat him entirely on his merits,' said Mr Peat grimly.

Hugh felt extraordinarily unwilling to sit down and write to Alice. He could not face going to see her, and he knew that he ought to write, but he kept postponing it. He took a walk in the Park, he found several pieces of business which cried out for his immediate attention, but at last he found himself, pen in hand, sitting staring at a blank sheet of paper.

He told himself that it was his own free choice. Blanche had not pushed him. Alice would be the more unhappy if she found herself married to a man whose heart was elsewhere. But the thought of her soft, brown eyes swimming in tears quite unmanned him and for several minutes he could not write. Then he resolutely pushed the thought away. If he had given her no hint, it was purely to spare her feelings: he had hoped it would all work itself out somehow. It crossed his mind fleetingly that by not allowing Alice to know how he felt he had stopped any chance of her participating: it was a three-cornered fight, but one of the combatants was not informed that the battle was on. However, she was too shy and vulnerable, it would only have hurt her unbearably. He picked up his pen.

My dear Alice,

This is a very difficult letter for me to write. I have tried several times to tell you but I simply could not face it. Alice, I am very fond of you and I honour you, but I have fallen in love with another woman. It happened some months ago, but I did not tell you before because I knew it would hurt you. It has been very painful for me these last few weeks, I wish you to know that. I hate hurting you but I must ask you to release me from our engagement. Forgive me.

Hugh

Hugh told himself that he was doing the right thing: Blanche was the right woman for him. She allowed him to be himself, he did not have to pretend that he had some high motives when all he really wanted was money and security from his debts. Of course, he was prepared to work, if something congenial was offered. And then Blanche was no prude, she granted him access to her lovely body with no conditions attached. The most Alice allowed him was a kiss on the cheek. Admittedly, he never asked for any more, but he was sure she would have been prim about it if he had done.

He sealed the letter, stamped it and went straight down to the post box at the corner of the road to post it. It slipped into the tunnel of the letter box and was lost. Hugh returned to the office feeling as if he had posted notice for his own execution.

It was past eleven o'clock at night in the Peat household, but all the lights were still on and there was a surprising number of people in the kitchen downstairs. Mr Peat had seen Hugh that afternoon and, not one to shirk an unpleasant job, he chose that very evening to announce to his family that Blanche and Hugh had obtained his consent to be married. The resulting drama, sparked off mainly by Mrs Peat's hysterics, was reflected in the excitement at the news among the servants. By the time the housekeeper had tenderly waved burnt feathers and sal volatile under Mrs Peat's nose and Ketton had fortified Mr Peat with brandy, there was no secret that they had not guessed relating to the marriage.

True, the housekeeper had packed off the housemaids to bed, but Ketton was there and Cook. Lottie, Blanche's maid, was seated on a broken chair by the sink talking animatedly to Briggs, Mrs Peat's abigail. There was a ham and some cold beef on the table, together with pickles and bread and several bottles of Mr Peat's best port.

'Nothing would surprise me about that little madam,' the housekeeper was saying. 'Lady Muck, that's my opinion of her, always was and always will be.'

'It's her Ma's fault,' replied Cook. 'She spoiled her something dreadful. I often thought that what Miss needed was her backside tanning. If she'd been my girl I'd have tanned it for her good and proper. Right cheeky she can be, too, always answers back, has a pert reply for everything. Still, I pity Mrs P., though she was always one for making the worst of everything, with Miss Blanche throwing herself away like that.'

'She's no better than she should be,' said Ketton austerely. 'I have reason to believe she's been meeting him secretly at night . . . and in this house too! Brandy glasses dirty,' he added cryptically. '*I* know. I think Mr Peat is lucky to get the young man to marry her at all, the way she's been carrying on.'

'He's after the money, it's plain as the nose on your face.'

'I think it's ever so romantic,' put in Lottie, evidently feeling that some of the glory reflected on her. That nice Mr Dunster had slipped her half a crown and she wasn't going to tell on Miss Blanche, wild horses wouldn't drag anything from her.

Up in the drawing-room Mrs Peat was recovering. With the aid of cushions, a small footstool and some sal volatile, held by Flora, and several cups of China tea offered by a resentful Blanche, she was at last able to sit up and lament the lost opportunities. These ranged over a wide area: the splendour of the dance she had planned for Blanche, the subsequent invitations she would have received and the brilliant match she might have made.

Then she turned on Flora. If Flora had not been so selfish as to throw away her chances with Maurice Dunster, this would never have happened. If old Mrs Peat had not so selfishly died when she did then Blanche might have had her season *this* year and she would have met somebody far more eligible and not thrown herself away on that, she could hardly bear to say his name, that good-for-nothing Hugh Dunster.

Flora put down the sal volatile and retreated to the window seat. She did not wish to become involved. She had very little sympathy for Blanche and Hugh and did not see how they could possibly be happy together. Blanche, as she knew well from nursery days, would stop at nothing to get what she wanted and Flora did not suppose that Hugh stood much of a chance once Blanche had dug her talons in.

'All my hopes cut up!' Mrs Peat stared resentfully first at Blanche and then at Flora. 'All the dearest wishes of my heart, gone! How I am ever to face Mrs Dunster, I do not know.'

'All Mrs Dunster ever wanted was to keep her precious Maurice intact,' said Flora, feeling profoundly irritated by her mother's assumption of the part of the woman who is always badly done by. 'The only reason she wished Maurice to marry me was my dowry. This way, she gets her money and keeps her hands on her blue-eyed boy.' Flora spoke with bitterness, for she felt that it was her mother who had promoted the entire business with Maurice Dunster and now left her to shoulder all the blame when it went wrong.

'Flora! Such indelicacy! Mary Dunster should think herself honoured that Blanche should ally herself with her family. What do they have after all? A small-time business and a very limited amount of capital behind them. And Hugh Dunster ... Oh, it does not bear thinking of.'

Blanche looked from one to the other impatiently. 'We are supposed to be discussing my marriage, not your fantasy might-have-beens,' she said pettishly.

'I hope you do not expect me to give you a large wedding, Blanche,' said Mrs Peat crossly. 'What with the expense of Adeline's wedding and our being in mourning, I really cannot see why we cannot wait until we are out of deep mourning at least. It is only another three months after all. People will think it so peculiar that everything is so rushed. They will think, indeed, I am sure I cannot blame them ... and to rush things in such a way. Well, I do not know what they will think!'

'I don't give a fig for what people think,' snapped Blanche. 'My happiness should come first.'

'That at least is very true,' returned Mrs Peat, dabbing angrily at her eyes. 'You certainly do not care how I am made to look. With all your advantages, to be throwing yourself away on a nobody. One, moreover, who has wasted any money he may have had. I am out of all patience with you! And I cannot understand why you, William, do not do something to stop it.'

'You do not listen, Susan,' said Mr Peat wearily. 'Blanche has been fool enough to anticipate the wedding. Unless you wish to see Blanche going up the aisle carrying her belly before her, we must have the wedding soon and as quietly and decently as possible. Luckily, we are in mourning; that, at least, provides the excuse for a quiet wedding. Blanche and Dunster will get married a fortnight from today and I want the entire family to put on a brave face. People may wonder, but if they see that we are satisfied then they will soon cease to gossip.'

'Whatever does it matter if people gossip?' said Blanche. 'Nobody seems to be thinking about what I feel, I notice! I love Hugh and I see no reason to be ashamed of it.'

'None at all,' said Mr Peat dryly, 'if you had not broken his engagement to that poor Banks child.'

'I did not break up his engagement to that simpering little prude,' cried Blanche angrily. 'In any event, if she cannot keep her man, it serves her right! And you can stop looking so superior, Flora! You could not catch a man even if served to you by his mother on a plate! You are a frump, Flora, and dear churchy Adeline is not much better, and you are all jealous because I have the pluck to go out and get what I want!'

'I think that you have said enough, Blanche,' said Mr Peat firmly. 'There is no need to insult your sisters. You have made your choice and I have given my consent. Let that be all.'

'I consider *your* behaviour to be quite as selfish, Flora,' said Mrs Peat, looking at Flora with dislike. 'Dear Blanche acts just as her feelings tell her. I understand that, for I am very sensitive myself. You do not possess that fastidiousness, Flora, and yet you selfishly refuse to accept a match your parents think best for you.'

'Women have so few privileges, Mama,' said Flora wryly. 'Let me at least exercise my prerogative of refusal.'

The day of Lady Kingsley's garden-party dawned sunny and bright. The gardeners had been out since dawn, setting up croquet for those guests who were feeling energetic, taking out the trestle tables and putting up the red and white striped awning that covered them in readiness for the food and drink.

The Kingsleys' garden was surprisingly large and as well as a lawn for croquet there was a sunken rose-garden and a small shrubbery. At the end of the lawn, right at the back of the garden, were several chestnut trees. The gardeners had repaired the swing that hung from one of the branches and the tree house, with its rope ladder, that had once been used by George and Algy. In front of the trees and hidden from the house by a beech hedge was a sand-pit and this, too, had been repaired and filled with clean sand.

In front of the beech hedge and finishing the formal expanse of lawn were five marble plinths supporting the statues of gods and goddesses George had brought back from Italy.

The benches in the shrubbery and rose-garden had been newly painted for those who wished to sit and admire the flowers, or merely laze and gossip.

Lady Kingsley liked her garden-parties to be informal, and children were instructed to wear clothes that were suitable for tree climbing or digging in the sand-pit: she had no use for the type of child in starched white pinafore or neat sailor suit who attempted to join in the adult conversation. Children should be children, she said, and told them firmly to go away and play.

Lady Kingsley sat out on the verandah, protected carefully against the wind by a rug, a screen and a parasol, and watched over her guests. The ever faithful Benn hovered in the background, ready to summon any guests her ladyship might wish to talk to, or to fetch her tea and cakes. Maids in starched aprons and print dresses were standing by the tables or dashing to and from the kitchens with trays full of food.

Daisy and Flora had been bidden to come early to take charge of Grace, who was showing signs of being overcome with shyness. Daisy was wearing a white cotton frock with a white sunbonnet and had been given strict instructions by Mama not to dirty it and return home looking like a ragamuffin. 'But that is stupid,' Daisy said scornfully. 'How can I play with Grace in the tree house if I am not allowed to get dirty?'

Flora was now in half-mourning and wore a new grey silk dress, exactly the colour of her eyes, although she had not noticed it until she looked at herself in the glass. The dress was bordered with black silk floss and she carried a parasol in black and white zig-zags, for the weather promised to be very sunny. Her glass told her that she was looking her best. Even Briggs, who did her hair for the occasion, said that she looked better out of black, which made her look whey-faced. She felt very nervous, why she could not say, for the Kingsleys were always most kind to her and she would know most of the guests.

Her hands were sweating under her new French silk gloves, but she managed to shepherd herself and Daisy to pay their respects to Lady Kingsley and then they walked across the lawn towards the sand-pit to find Grace. Sir George was nowhere to be seen, Flora noticed with a certain relief, and she found herself hoping that he would come while she was with Grace and Daisy, for she now felt a certain awkwardness in his company.

They found Grace standing unhappily by the trees peering anxiously at the open French windows leading from the house to see if the first guests were arriving. She looked poised for flight.

'Poor Grace,' said Flora smiling and forgetting her own worries for a moment. 'How many other children are coming?'

'John and Maria and the Colefax children,' said Grace gloomily. She looked imploringly at Daisy, who was standing, legs apart, surveying the food on the table with satisfaction. Poor Grace was already shaking with nerves and her hands were twisting her sash and reducing it to a mass of creases. 'And I shall have to talk to the grown-ups,' she continued tearfully, 'and everybody will ask me how I am and I shall not know what to say!'

'Don't worry, Grace,' said Daisy stoutly. 'I shall be here. In any case, we can keep out of their way most of the time.'

'But they will come over and be *kind*,' said Grace despairingly.

'I think you should both see what you can find in the way of buckets and spades,' said Flora, thinking that what Grace needed was something to do, 'and a ball or hoop if you have them.'

'Come along, Grace,' cried Daisy, tugging at her sash. The little girls ran off.

Flora watched them go, black-booted feet flashing and Daisy's black curls bobbing wildly beneath her sunbonnet. She turned back towards the house and unfurled her parasol to protect her eyes from the sun. Sir George was coming across the lawn towards her. Flora felt her heart thudding from nerves and the colour fade from her cheeks. She tried to scold herself back to normality: how can you be so silly, she told herself, he is a friend and he has been extremely kind to you.

George came up, smiling. He raised his hat to her and then offered her his arm.

'Good afternoon, Flora. Come and look at your namesake. I do not believe that you have seen my statues yet, have you?'

They turned back towards the trees, Flora extremely and quite tinglingly conscious of her hand on his arm.

'I have never been in your garden at all before,' replied Flora, noticing with embarrassment that her voice sounded different somehow and hoping that he did not notice it, 'although I have seen your statues at a distance from the windows in the Pink Saloon.'

George had a number of good resolutions for his own preservation, among them the absolute necessity of treating Flora as a friend only; to be affectionate, yes, but cool. He even went so far as to give himself an agenda of topics that he might discuss safely and the statues were the first on the list. Flora stopped dutifully in front of them. All the gods and goddesses were draped extremely scantily, Apollo boasting only a fig leaf and even Flora appeared to be wearing nothing more than a wreath of flowers and carrying a cornucopia for decency.

The statues looked back at them, frozen in their marble attitudes, but every one of them displaying a kind of knowledge and self-awareness that George and Flora were trying to hide so unsuccessfully.

Flora looked at her namesake whose hand was held out as if in welcome. She never knew what wild impulse of dalliance prompted her, for she had never done such a thing before, but she found herself mimicking the statue's gesture and saying, with beckoning eyes and a saucy smile, 'Come, Sir George, choose between us.'

George's reaction was swift and without premeditation. He took hold of her and kissed her.

But I love him, thought Flora in surprise, as discovery succeeded shock. All the confusion and turmoil of the last few weeks had been leading simply to this. She loved George. How odd she had not realized it before!

'George,' she whispered, hardly aware that she was speaking.

George smiled and reached out to stroke her cheek with his finger. 'I have been longing to do that for quite some time.'

'I had no idea.'

'That I wished to kiss you?'

'That I felt this way about you. I have just been feeling very confused.'

'And I was wondering why I felt positively murderous when Algy told me about Maurice Dunster!'

'I think your brother might have known me well enough to guess that I would not be encouraging Maurice Dunster,' said Flora indignantly.

'Oh, he probably did,' said George a trifle ruefully. 'I can see now that he was doing some probing. As I nearly punched him in the middle of Brooks's I daresay he understood very well how things were with me.'

Flora laughed happily, but there was no time for any more, for Lady Kingsley was heard calling across the lawn and Flora turned to see a small group of guests wending their way towards them.

'Damn them,' said George. 'Come back with me, Flora.'

Flora shook her head, she did not think that she could face the prying eyes of the guests and the scrutiny of Lady Kingsley. She needed a period of quiet reflection. 'I must go and see how Daisy and Grace are doing.'

Lady Kingsley was calling again, more impatiently this time.

'Very well. I shall see you later then.' He stroked her cheek once more and left her. How soft and warm her lips were, he thought, and how happy she looked after he kissed her, with her face more relaxed somehow, and younger, and how tenderly those beautiful grey eyes of hers looked at him.

It was not until he was half way across the lawn that the doubts began to creep back. Was he committed too far this time? All he had done was give her a quick kiss. Anybody might do that to a pretty girl, surely? He had not told her that he loved her and he certainly never mentioned marriage, so there was still time to think again.

Flora wandered down towards the trees lost in a happy dream. She had never been kissed before and it was lovely. She remembered that startled moment of delicious anticipation as he bent towards her and she realized that he was going to kiss her. It was what she wanted, although she had not known it until that moment. The warmth of his mouth, the strength of his arms as he held her to him and the lovely caressing touch of his fingers on her cheek. She never guessed it would be like that.

It did not seem possible that George was the same person as the brusque, aloof man who had so alarmed her all those months ago. Had he changed or had she? She was so absorbed in her feelings and reflections that she failed to notice that Daisy and Grace were quite near until there was a stifled giggle above her head.

She looked up, startled, wondering how long they had been there and oh, God, had they seen her and George by the statues? They were sitting in the tree house some fifteen feet up and two pairs of legs with frilly drawers and white stockings (now generously smirched with green) were hanging over the edge of the tree house platform.

'Daisy! Grace! Come down this minute! You bad children, if you have dirtied your frocks Miss Martin will be very cross.'

'We have not, honestly, Flora,' said Grace, beginning to descend the rope ladder.

'We took them off!' cried Daisy in triumph. The two girls descended, clad, to Flora's horror, in nothing but bodices and drawers. The guests were beginning to arrive, too. Flora could catch a glimpse of swaying dresses through the trees. Any minute they could be upon them, and whatever would they say to find Daisy and Grace half-undressed? But Flora could not find it in her heart to scold, she felt too warm and loving towards the whole world and they really did look rather sweet in their liberty bodices and frilled pantalettes.

'What on earth have you done with your petticoats and frocks? And your crinolines?'

'Oh, they are quite safe,' said Daisy. 'We were very careful, Flora. They are behind those bushes.' She pointed.

'For Heaven's sake go and put them on. All the guests are arriving. Whatever would they think?'

'What have you done now?' said Algy, suddenly appearing round a corner. He took one look at them and burst out laughing.

'See, Cousin Algy does not mind,' cried Grace, pirouetting round on one foot.

'If you do not get dressed at once, and go and wash your hands, which are filthy,' said Algy sternly, 'I shall put you both over my knee and spank your bottoms!'

The girls gave a shriek and fled giggling into the bushes.

'I suppose I ought to have kept a better eye on them,' said Flora smiling. 'It never occurred to me that they would do such a thing!'

'Never mind about them. Miss Martin will be coming here in a minute. George said I was to look after you. I hope you have not been quarrelling with him again. George looked a little distrait to me.'

He noticed with amusement the colour flying to her cheeks. She was looking extremely pretty this afternoon and her blushes only gave her a lovely touch of colour. Perhaps George was come to his senses at last. He might do much worse, Algy thought reflectively. If only Grandmama could be persuaded to give it her blessing.

'Your brother has been most kind,' murmured Flora, giving Algy a quick mischievous glance.

Algy laughed. 'About time too. But I shall not tease you, Miss Peat. Come and be introduced to somebody. Let me see whom I can find.'

The lawn was now filling up with little knots of people. Flora recognized Ellie St Alleyn and her brother choosing mallets on the croquet lawn, and there were Sir Thomas and Lady Colefax talking to Lady Kingsley.

'There is Ida Clevedon,' said Flora, smiling as Ida raised her hand to her across the lawn. 'I must enquire after Griselda. She broke an arm, did you know?'

'Yes. She is in the country convalescing at the moment. If you wish to talk to Ida, Miss Peat, you may have the pleasure of being introduced to Millais who is with her.'

'Do you mean the painter?' asked Flora, looking at the fair-haired young man beside Ida with interest. 'He is very handsome!'

'I see you are a connoisseur of masculine beauty, Miss Peat.' Only a woman in love could allow herself to make such an observation without embarrassment, he thought. George must have been more oncoming than he had given him credit for.

'No, no,' cried Flora, flushing and recollecting herself. 'I meant that he looks like Apollo, or one of the Greek gods.'

'I do not know about that, but he is a nice chap. Tolerable shot, too,' replied Algy, and led her across the lawn.

The garden-party was now in full swing. George was with a lively group playing croquet. He was partnering his little cousin Ellie St Alleyn and flirting outrageously, shocking Cousin Jane who was partnering Timothy. George tilted his boater rakishly over one eye. He could flirt with whom he liked, could he not? Ellie was a peach and she knew that he was not serious. George had been a catch ever since he came down from Oxford thirteen years ago and he thoroughly enjoyed being a bachelor. He was in no hurry whatsoever to lose that privileged status. A scandalized shriek of laughter from Ellie caused Lady Kingsley and Lady Eastlake to exchange significant looks at the other end of the lawn.

'I fear not, Elizabeth,' said Lady Kingsley sighing. 'George seems to have set his face against it. But perhaps he will yet change his mind. Ellie is such a pretty, lively girl.'

'I do hope so.' Lady Eastlake shaded her eyes with her hand and looked at the croquet players. 'It would be so suitable and such a comfort to you, dear Catherine. A nice little thing, Ellie.'

'Algy, of course, is a hopeless case,' said Lady Kingsley. 'I live in dread of hearing that he has allowed himself to be beguiled into some shocking mésalliance.'

'I am sure that Algy would never forget what he owed his family,' said Lady Eastlake comfortably.

At the other end of the garden the croquet game was finished. The players drifted up to the tea tables to refresh themselves with sandwiches and tea or fruit cup. George took Ellie's arm and led her to a bench near the tea urn and brought her some tea and a large bowl of strawberries which he popped into her mouth one by one with his fingers.

'You have turned into a very pretty girl, Ellie,' he said with satisfaction. 'You look like a delicious strawberry yourself in that pink dress.'

Ellie would make any man a suitable wife. She was sweet and pretty and quite malleable. She was quite prepared to take an interest in George's concerns, for instance, and not push her own ideas – which must necessarily be immature and unformed – at him. How restful it was to sit here with a pretty girl whose view of life was so uncomplicated.

Men had serious challenges in the world outside: they must make the decisions, support their families and carry out a host of arduous duties of which the weaker sex was totally ignorant. A man did not need a challenge at home as well. He wanted peace and calm, a gentle hand to soothe his brow and make his tea. A girl like Ellie, good and pretty, would make his home a restful haven for him. The alternative, in the shape of a clever, argumentative, badly bred female, seemed like wilful self-destruction.

Perhaps Grandmama was right.

'Come, Ellie,' he said, getting to his feet, 'let me show you the rose-garden.'

Flora chatted happily to a number of people introduced to her by Algy. Lady Colefax was most kind and remembered meeting her at Christmas, to Flora's gratification. Tommy Clevedon took her for a walk in the shrubbery and regaled her with stories of his life as a subaltern in the Crimea. He seemed to spend all his time chasing up non-existent supplies through a sea of mud, but he told it all in his usual droll fashion and Flora found that she could make him laugh with her own pithy remarks.

Eventually the desire to see George again overcame all else and Flora managed to sip away without Algy finding her and introducing her to somebody else. She went first to the sand-pit and tree house: George was nowhere to be seen among the guests, so perhaps he was come down here, hoping that she would miss him and come too. But only Daisy and Grace were there, now stripped of shoes and stockings and playing with little Rose Colefax in the sand. The Colefax boys were up in the tree house.

'Miss Martin has been a brick,' Robert shouted down hopefully when he saw Flora. 'She brought us masses of ices and blancmanges. Only we did not have very many of the strawberries because those girls have been making pigs of themselves down there.'

'You should have come down, then,' shouted back Daisy. 'Really, boys are stupid!'

Flora promised to see that some more strawberries reached them in due course. Wherever was George then? She half-expected to see him by the statues but he was not there. She had last seen him across the lawn talking to Ellie St Alleyn. It was stupid of her to be so jealous. She knew from Algy that they were both fond of Ellie and why not? She had always liked Ellie, had she not?

She tried to summon back that moment by the statues, but it was grown dim. It now seemed like something she had imagined, the fading image of a dream. But it was real, perhaps the most real thing that had ever happened to her. If only she could find George.

She had not yet been to the rose-garden which was hidden away out of sight of the main lawn, down a few steps into a sunken area. It was designed like a Dutch garden with formal shapes and little paths between. Around the edge was a wooden colonnade with a mass of climbing roses supported by a trellis. The roses were all out now and the white, pink and red blooms scented the entire garden and hid all those who entered the rose-garden from outside eyes.

Flora hoped that George might take her for an assignation among the roses. Perhaps he was already there?

He was – with Ellie.

They were sitting on a wrought iron bench under an arbour of sweet briar and Flora reached the outer colonnade in time to see George put his arm around Ellie and Ellie rest her head on his chest. He was looking down at her tenderly and stroking her fair curls. Such a pang of pain compounded with murderous rage shot through Flora that the world turned red before her eyes. How could he? How *could* he? When not an hour ago he was kissing her? How could he be so unfeeling, so cruel as to allow her to believe that he loved *her* and then sneak off with that insipid little cousin of his and start canoodling in some secluded place?

There was more whispered talk. Ellie's hand was now resting in George's and he bent and kissed her cheek. Flora could see Ellie's blushing protest and George giving some teasing reply.

Flora remembered being told by her brother Tom – it was one of his gruesome stories from Marlborough – that when you were stabbed it felt like a dull hammer blow. She felt the same. There was a dull, thudding pain in her heart which numbed all her senses. She felt tired and heavy from so many unshed tears, so much painful realization. Of course, she recalled, he never actually said that he loved her! She supposed he had carefully refrained from doing so, but somehow that made it worse, not better. She felt completely humiliated. She had been deliberately duped – not in so many words, of course, that would be un-gentlemanly! She had been so open, so unguarded! Oh God, he must be laughing at her naïvety now.

George and Ellie were talking earnestly now, George patting Ellie's hand and Ellie looking up at him. Flora could see them through the gaps in the trellised roses quite clearly. Finally, they walked out of the garden, Ellie on George's arm, back towards the other guests.

Flora sank down on the nearest bench and burst into tears. My heart, my heart is breaking, she thought wildly. It was so painful a wound that she felt that there was one huge bruise across her chest. At last she could cry no more. She sat up and mopped her eyes carefully. Her face looked blotchy and red and swollen and she had to wait, sitting on that bench, until the ugly and tell-tale colour faded. Then she walked back to the guests.

'So that is the eldest Miss Peat,' whispered Lady Eastlake to her hostess. 'What a washed-out little mouse she looks.'

Flora seized a bowl of strawberries and made her way back to the tree house. She caught a glimpse of George across the lawn. He had left Ellie now and was talking to Tommy Clevedon. Flora slipped away through the shrubbery. The children greeted the strawberries with shrieks of joy and Flora stayed there, quietly helping the girls with their sand-castle until she saw that it was time to go home.

She was invited to help Grace, she told herself sternly and she would find her best solace in doing exactly that. Daisy and Grace enjoyed her company and she must try to be satisfied with that. But oh! to go home. All she wanted was to sit in the dark of the carriage and weep. Daisy and Grace exchanged a concerned look but Flora did not notice. Did he not think her good enough, then? Were all his protestations of respect and admiration so much wind? She would like to kill him! Oh George! She wished she had never been born.

Sir Thomas and Lady Colefax came to the sand-pit to collect their children and Flora shepherded Daisy and Grace to wash their hands and tidy themselves up. The guests were beginning to leave now and the carriages were being announced. Flora and Daisy, now properly dressed with shoes and stockings on, went to make their farewells to Lady Kingsley. George and Algy were standing behind her chair, but Flora could not look at George. She had the feeling that if she so much as glanced at him she would disgrace herself by bursting into tears. Pride strengthened her knees and steadied her voice. She thought she had herself well under control, but all three Kingsleys noticed her distress. Algy, in his kind-hearted way, attempted to relieve Flora by addressing some joking remarks to Daisy. Lady Kingsley scrutinized her very sharply and said she hoped that the fresh air down at Linchmere would put some colour back into her cheeks. George said nothing, only stared frowningly at Flora, but he excused himself to his grandmother and escorted Flora and Daisy to their carriage.

'You are looking very pale, Flora,' he said, fighting down a most uncomfortable feeling of guilt. He opened the carriage door for her and let down the steps. 'Are you all right?'

'Quite, thank you,' said Flora coldly. 'Get in, Daisy, pet.'

Daisy climbed in and sat looking at them with bright, inquisitive eyes. George took hold of Flora's hand and held it firmly, stroking the back of it with his thumb. 'What is it?' he asked unwillingly.

'Oh for God's sake, George,' cried Flora, her voice thick with swallowed tears. 'Do you think that I am made of stone? I am not a toy to amuse your leisure hours until you find some newer and prettier girl to trifle with!' Her tears overcame her and pulling her hand from his grasp she jumped into the carriage and slammed the door.

Lady Kingsley turned to Algy.

'Well, my grandson, whatever is that you are wearing?'

'It is the latest thing, Grandmama. My Prince of Wales peajacket. Do you not like it?'

'Now Algy, it is high time that you settled down. I am seventy-seven now, you know. I cannot be expected to last much longer.'

Algy's face hardened. 'I have settled down,' he said shortly, 'with Anny.'

'A shop girl! I mean marriage, Algernon. Not an illegal union with a woman, for lady I cannot call her, who cannot be introduced to your family.'

'When I wished to marry,' Algy reminded her, 'you would have nothing to do with it. I do not want to quarrel with you, Grand-mama, so please leave my affairs alone.'

There was a short pause. Lady Kingsley had no wish to alienate her grandson, so she allowed his shortcomings to drop. 'And now we have George,' she went on pettishly, 'and do not waste your time telling me that you had not noticed that he is infatuated with the Peat girl, for I should not believe you. She practically lives here and now he has insisted I invite her down to Linchmere for the summer! It is not what I hoped for at all! If it was not for George saying that he was still going to Greece in August as planned, I would fear that this time he was serious. However, at least he has the sense to pay some attention to Ellie, so perhaps he will see that she is really far more suitable before it is too late.'

'Do not look to me to meddle in it,' said Algy shortly. 'God knows I have suffered enough from interference from my family.'

Mrs Peat was in no mood to enquire after the Kingsleys' garden-party. It was extremely odd, to say the least, that Lady Kingsley had not invited her and Mr Peat. Flora might be on the shelf but she still needed her Mama as chaperone. She never begrudged her daughter anything, but she did think it quite selfish of Flora to consider only her own pleasure when a little prompting might have reminded Lady Kingsley that her mother would enjoy seeing the place where dear Daisy was doing so well.

Flora was thankful for the lack of interest. She could not have borne a minute enquiry into the afternoon. As it was, she was able to get away with the vaguest replies. If only she need not go back on Monday, for how could she face Sir George again?

Fortunately there was a cast-iron excuse ready to hand: she was needed at home to help with all the preparations for Blanche's wedding.

'There are a thousand and one things to be done,' said Mrs Peat at the breakfast-table the following morning, 'and if the whole thing is to take place in such a hurry, then I cannot see that everything will be ready without some help from you, Flora. Blanche is far too busy at the moment answering letters of con-gratulations [for the notice of the engagement had appeared in *The Times* the day before] and writing thank you letters. In any case, I can send one of the maids with Daisy. I am sure that Lady Kingsley will think it perfectly suitable when she knows the circumstances.'

'Indeed, I am happy to stay at home,' said Flora quickly. 'I must write to Lady Kingsley to thank her for the garden-party, so I shall explain the situation then.'

'You had better write it straight away after you have finished your breakfast. And then come to my dressing-room, please, Flora, and I shall give you a list of what I wish to be done.'

When Lady Kingsley received the letter the following morning she read it out loud to George at the breakfast-table.

'So we shall not be seeing Miss Peat again until the summer holidays,' she ended. 'I cannot say that I am sorry. A pleasant enough young woman, but not one I wish to see becoming too intimate. I wish you had not seen fit to invite her and Daisy to Linchmere, George, but I daresay that there is no harm done.'

George said nothing, only stared frowningly at his plate. The kidneys and crispy bacon which seemed so appetizing a few moments before now seemed to make him feel quite revoltingly carnivorous. He pushed away his plate and after a few moments of toying with his coffee, pushed that away too.

Perhaps Miss Peat has realized that any match with George would be sternly resisted by his family, thought Lady Kingsley with satisfaction. She is staying away as a warning to George. Certainly, he looked quite downcast and silent, even for such a reserved man. Looking at him covertly across the table Lady Kingsley caught a glimpse of something she had never seen on George's face before, a mixture of guilt and misery. Whatever had been going on? Heaven forbid that he was thinking seriously of marrying the girl!

Chapter Eleven

HUGH received only one communication from Alice Banks and that was a short letter some two days after the announcement of his engagement in *The Times*. In it she merely said that she had received his letter, that she never wished to hold him against his inclination and that she and Mama wished him and Blanche every happiness. There was a small parcel with it containing Hugh's letters to her, a lock of his hair and a number of trinkets. Hugh spread them out slowly on his desk. Everything was there that he had ever given her, she had kept nothing back. There was a small locked deed-box at the back of Hugh's desk and he took it out and unlocked it with a silver key hanging from his fob watch. He took out a packet of letters, one of Alice's brown curls, which twined itself round his fingers as he lifted it out, and a little oval miniature of her in a gold frame. He had had it painted shortly after the Royal Academy Exhibition last year, he remembered, and it was done by an aspiring A.R.A. It was not a very good likeness, but it caught something of the sitter's sweetness in the softness of the brown eyes and curve of the lips. Hugh sat silently for a moment, looking at the little array of objects on his desk, some of his and some of hers. Then he put them all back carefully in the deed-box and locked it once more.

That evening found him in Belgrave Square, this time openly, bearing a posy in a silver holder for Mrs Peat and a sapphire and diamond ring for Blanche. The diamonds and sapphires were very small, chips merely. Blanche said, with a laugh, that left to herself she would make do with paste, but all her friends were asking her where was her ring and she did not feel properly engaged without one!

Fortunately Mr Dunster gave Hugh some money and Hugh

had a decent stake at Crockford's for once and came out three hundred pounds richer, so he was able to pay for the ring without too much embarrassment and choose a present for Mrs Peat as well. The rest of the money he would keep quiet about, he decided: there might well be times when he wanted to go out for a quick fling or put a tenner on some horse at the races.

'Well, Mr Dunster,' said Mrs Peat coldly, as Ketton showed him into the drawing-room. Blanche was not there, only Flora and Daisy were sitting side by side on the sofa, looking through a book together.

'I have come to see you, Ma'am,' said Hugh, bowing and giving his future mother-in-law the benefit of his boyish grin. 'I have brought you this little trifle, with my deepest respects.'

'Hugh, my dear boy! You really shouldn't have!' Mrs Peat dabbed at her eyes. It was a long time since any young man had brought her flowers and she was not immune to Hugh's rakish charm.

'I have no doubt at all where Blanche obtained her looks,' continued Hugh. He barely glanced at Flora and Daisy, who had stopped reading at his entrance and were listening in awed fascination. 'Although I suspect that you were even prettier!'

'Ah, you are a flatterer,' said Mrs Peat, smiling and thinking how pleasant this sort of nonsense was. 'But you and Blanche have been very imprudent, you know, and I must scold you for it.'

'But I am so very much in love,' pleaded Hugh, spreading out his arms as if it was Mrs Peat and not Blanche who was the object of his devotions. 'But you will make allowances for a lover, won't you? I am sure that you know what it is to feel so strongly.'

'Of course,' Mrs Peat simpered, 'Blanche is very like me in many respects – we are both very sensitive people. When I first met William, my husband, I was so desperately in love that my sisters quite thought I was going into a decline. I even went so far as to find an excuse for not going to Church so that we might have a stolen meeting! As my dear father was the Vicar, you may imagine that it needed some planning!'

This one was easy game all right, thought Hugh. He wondered if he could persuade her that he needed at least some of Blanche's capital. God, the vanity of woman! Of course, once upon a time she must have been very pretty, but she was now only a vain, selfish, middle-aged woman. He wondered where Blanche was and how soon he could get away.

Suddenly Flora could bear it no longer: there was too much unfairness in Hugh's easy conquest compared with her own loss. With a hasty excuse she left the room. She had to be alone otherwise she would burst into tears. She wanted to curl up in Granny's chair, with Granny's old shawl round her and shut everybody out.

She ran up to her bedroom and closed the door. She could not bear it! How was she going to live with this awful sense of desolation and betrayal? She sat there with lips trembling and tears rolling down her cheeks. Her heart ached and she found she was hugging herself in a desperate attempt to assuage the sense of loss or at least to hold herself together. She felt totally bereft. Her feelings about George were now such a mixture of grief and bitterness that she could only long for annihilation, anything to end the agony in her heart, to blot it out forever. Oh God, she wished she could hate him for what he had done to her!

Had she just imagined it all then, that tender and lovely moment by the statues? In that moment her whole heart went out to meet him. She felt then that he loved her. She knew that it was true. Did a man kiss a woman so tenderly and warmly and hold her to him and mean *nothing* by it? Was he not even concerned with how she might feel, toyed with and then abandoned? Had she deceived herself so much? The tears fell down her cheeks, faster and faster, until the garden outside was only a misty blur. Flora put her hands over her face and wept bitterly.

Gradually, the sad thoughts settled and the tears dried. She mopped at her eyes and blew her nose. She was crying more during the last few days than she had in the previous twenty years, since she was quite a little girl, in fact. Flora wondered if in some obscure way crying was good for you. She sat up. It was over, she must face that. She found herself thinking of Adeline with a sudden sympathy. Adeline, too, had put her trust in somebody and was let down badly: she would understand how Flora felt. Adeline's tears and anxieties now seemed tragic and sad instead of merely irritating, for she had the added burden of living with her mistake.

Flora decided she would visit her sister in the morning.

Adeline knew that something had happened to Flora the moment that her sister walked into the room. She had been too unhappy herself over the past few months not to recognize it in Flora's dark-ringed, sad eyes and taut, unhappy mouth. She looked thinner and there was something in the tension of the neck and shoulders that tightened her face as if the muscles were forcibly holding her together. She looked pale and washed-out too, so that the grey of her dress, instead of setting off her luminous grey eyes and the wild-rose flush on her cheeks, only served to emphasize a uniform drabness.

Adeline felt a surge of joy and instantly tried to push it down, for how could she feel happy when her sister was obviously so miserable? But it sat there and sang triumphantly. God was answering her prayers! He was rescuing her from the barren, spiritual void and sending her somebody He wished her to help and comfort. Adeline had felt for many dreary weeks that all her prayers for service had gone unanswered. God did not find her worthy to help Him in His work. He had withdrawn His comfort from her and left her only bitterness. But she was wrong! God was only testing her faith and surely Flora was sent by Him for spiritual nourishment?

Adeline rang the bell for coffee and allowed Flora the usual enquiries about her health and how was Charles and what a pretty baby's jacket she was knitting. Flora talked feverishly, her hands picking at the flounces on her dress. Every now and then she glanced warily at Adeline and hesitated in her flow of small talk as if wondering how to begin.

'You have come about something, have you not, Flora?' said Adeline at last. Flora stopped abruptly. 'Please trust me, dearest. I can see that you are unhappy and you know that I will do everything I can to help.' Adeline imagined that perhaps Maurice Dunster had proposed again and Flora needed help in seeing where her duty lay.

Flora saw that in some way Adeline was keyed up for these revelations and she hoped that she was not going to be treated to one of Adeline's homilies on Duty and Forbearance.

Hesitantly at first, and then more easily, she told her sister everything. How she had met George, the quarrels, the reconciliations and then the kiss in the garden and her jealousy and pain on finding him with Ellie St Alleyn.

Adeline looked at her with a curious expression on her face: a mixture of resentment and envy, as if she was both fascinated and repelled by what Flora was telling her. Flora was sitting with her head bowed, her hands covering her face. Everything was flooding back into her mind so acutely that she could see nothing but a series of painful moments re-enacted inside her head.

Adeline rose abruptly and walked to the window. She did not know what she had expected but it certainly was not so shameless a display of emotion.

'I . . . I do not know what to say, Flora!'

'Have I upset you?'

'No! No! Yes, you have! Flora, how could you!' Adeline spun round, her face flushed. 'How could you allow yourself to be so . . . so animal? Have you no idea of moderation? Of good taste? You have allowed yourself to be swamped by this disgusting emotion to the extent of forgetting all your womanliness and letting him kiss and fondle you as if you were a kept woman! How could you allow yourself to do it, Flora?'

'But I love him!'

'Love!' echoed Adeline scornfully. 'All you are talking about is brute lust, Flora. Love is about service and denial and unselfishness. All you want is to satisfy your own desires. You say that he respects you; well, I beg to differ! How can he when you allow him to talk to you in a most ungentleman-like manner. Sir George insults you in the grossest way and you seem proud of it! I call it disgusting. Your own behaviour has brought you to this sorry pass, Flora, and it serves you right. Sir George naturally finds Ellie more of a lady.'

'You must be jealous to be so cruel,' cried Flora.

Adeline gasped as if a bucket of cold water had been thrown over her. 'How dare you!'

'Oh yes, you are. You are jealous because you have never allowed yourself to feel. If you had, you would never have chosen such a self-opinionated brute as Charles Woodcock! You have denied all your feelings and where has it got you? Charles is not allowed to kiss and fondle you and he never argues with you, does he? And how do you feel about that! You hate it! You feel that he has no real affection for you and is only satisfying his brute lust, as you have it. He is always so distant and polite, you complain. You are never allowed anywhere near his real life! He shuts you out. At least my pain is the pain of living, yours is the pain of being half-dead. You are the one it serves right, Adeline, not me!'

Adeline stood by the window, her eyes stony. Her fists were clenched by her sides and Flora could see a vein ticking in her neck.

'I think you must leave the house, Flora. If you are suggesting that I should indulge in the cheap feeling that you relish, then you are mistaken. Tragically, I think. Because up to this moment I always believed that we had something in common, a sort of sensitive gentility that is given to few ladies. But I am sadly wrong. You have been corrupted, Flora, and in your present state I cannot help you. I can only pray for you. And that I shall do, that you may be shown the true path.'

'I wish I had never come,' Flora burst out. 'I thought, Adeline will understand, she is unhappy too. You are cruel and selfish. Yes, selfish! You see things only from your own point of view, the view of a little tin god you have set up in your heart. You have to be right! If you were ever wrong your whole world would collapse. And it would be no bad thing! But I am sorry if I have upset you . . .'

'You have not upset me,' interrupted Adeline coldly, 'except that I feel that you have betrayed our deepest ideals.'

'I do not share your ideals and perhaps I never did,' said Flora.

Adeline turned away and there was nothing more to be said. Flora picked up her gloves and put on her bonnet and then quietly and thankfully she left the house.

At last the wedding day dawned and Blanche woke up to a cloudless sky. There were a few grey wisps of cloud on the horizon but nothing that could possibly mar the weather, at least until after the wedding. This was her Wedding Day! At last she was to marry Hugh! So dreams come true, after all, Blanche reflected, provided that you wanted them enough. And she did want Hugh, more than she had ever wanted anything before.

Soon he would be hers and her real life would begin.

She looked at herself critically in the pier-glass as Lottie slipped the skirts of her wedding dress over her head and smoothed it out over the crinoline and lace petticoats. She tied the ribbons round the waist and Blanche held out her arms for the bodice. The white book-muslin trimmed with tiny puffs and divided by insertions of lace gave the whole dress a delicate, airy look, as if Blanche was floating along in a light cloud. There was a wreath of orange blossom made like a crown, so that Blanche's profusion of yellow curls might riot artlessly unimpeded, and a veil of Valenciennes lace.

There would be eyes for nobody else, thought Blanche, twisting and turning in front of the glass. Yes, Lottie was very clever with her hair, she must admit. All the same, she was glad she was hiring a new French maid now that she was to be married. How poor, simple Lottie cried and begged to be allowed to stay with her! But Blanche felt that she preferred a French maid. Lottie could stay with Flora. She would give her half a guinea to console her.

As the wedding would be very quiet neither Flora nor Daisy were to be bridesmaids. Blanche alone walked up the aisle on her father's arm. There were several most satisfactory tributes to her beauty. Charles' eyes nearly started from their sockets, she noted, she saw him gulping hard as she passed. Mrs Dunster was standing to attention clenching her hands. Just as Blanche reached her three buttons popped off her gloves and fell to the floor.

Blanche smiled beatifically at Mrs Dunster's set face and went to stand beside Hugh. She gave his arm a light pinch. Hugh looked down at her.

'I am trying to purify my thoughts, darling,' Blanche whispered, lacing her fingers in his and squeezing his hand.

'Are you succeeding?'

'No.'

Hugh gave a short laugh which caused his scandalized mother to exchange speaking glances with her elder son and the vicar to frown warningly. He cleared his throat. 'Dearly Beloved,' he intoned, 'we are gathered together . . .'

Adeline sat next to Charles and stared resentfully at the vicar. Her own wedding in this very church seemed a lifetime ago. With what hopes had she herself walked up that very aisle and given her hand and her life to Charles? Blanche regrettably was treating the whole thing like some cheap vaudeville act, with herself in the principal role. She was making a mockery of such a sacred sacrament, thought Adeline angrily, watching Blanche reach out to give Hugh's hand a little squeeze.

Charles had come in late again last night, smelling of that cheap scent and his eyes bright as boot buttons. She glanced at him out of the corner of her eye, standing next to her in a black morning-coat and top hat, wearing the character of a respectable well-to-do doctor. How like a whited sepulchre underneath! Why did God not hurl a thunderbolt down and strike him dead upon the spot? A man who did not uphold the sanctity of the marriage tie was worse than a Brute.

'. . . in the Holy Estate of Matrimony?' said the vicar with awful emphasis. 'Wilt thou love her, comfort her, honour and keep her in sickness and in health; and forsaking all other, keep thee only unto her, so long as ye both shall live?'

Perhaps I wrong him, thought poor Adeline, fixing her eyes earnestly on the vicar. Charles could not treat such a sacrament so lightly, could he? Where have I gone wrong, she pleaded to a God who seemed deaf to her prayers and cries for help. I offer Charles and Flora my service and my help and they spurn me and go after worldly gods. She looked across at Flora, standing next to Daisy, and felt bitterly betrayed. Love must be earned, and what had Flora done with her indulgent wallowings to deserve Love? Adeline denied herself for Charles' sake, never said a word to him about his callous behaviour, nor upbraided him, and all she received in return was rejection.

'With this ring I thee wed, with my body I thee worship, and with all my worldly goods I thee endow,' said Hugh enthusiastically.

God meant a spiritual worship, of course, thought Adeline.

Flora turned her head slightly and smiled at Daisy who was sitting next to her. What a dear Daisy was! She guessed, of course, about George when Flora cried all the way home after the garden-party, but she kept quiet about it.

'I may be only fourteen but I know better than to tell Mama,' Daisy said indignantly. 'I think Sir George is a beast, Flora! He knows it too, otherwise why was he looking so uncomfortable?'

Flora's thoughts fell slowly and sadly into their usual pattern. She loved George, she had lost him. He had, over the months, come to mean more to her than she had ever anticipated. Love had grown quite naturally out of their somewhat stormy relationship, or at least that was how it seemed to her. But she was mistaken about George's feelings and she must bear her loss and not allow it to sour her life. Dear Granny would have advised her thus, she was sure.

But how could she when every morning she awoke to the same sense of loss? And every day at the breakfast-table she had the agony of waiting for her mother's inevitable comments on the engagements announced in the Court and Social columns of *The Times*. So far the blow had not fallen, but it was simply a matter of time. Flora could only await that final blow and hope that she had the courage to meet it.

Her thoughts were interrupted by a sudden rustling in the congregation. The vicar was pronouncing the blessing and the service was over. The organist began to peal out 'Love divine all loves excelling' and the congregation rose to its feet.

By Jove, what a stunner, thought Charles, watching appreciatively as Hugh kissed his bride. I should have chosen Blanche and gained myself a ripe little peach instead of this cold fish. Adeline was nothing but bones and flannel night-gown. She was determined to be a martyr. In bed she would never even look at him. In fact, several times he noticed that her lips were moving and he wondered incredulously if she was praying. Good God, did she really wish to pray during a bit of nooky? If only she would relax occasionally, then he might enjoy himself more. He might even stop his visits to Madame Cora's, he thought virtuously.

Blanche and Hugh now collected their parents and made their way to the vestry. Charles glanced round the church and caught Geraldina's eye. He bowed. She acknowledged his greeting and smiled slightly.

There was a bustle over collecting prayer books and pushing hassocks under the seat as Hugh and Blanche stepped out of the vestry, followed by Mr and Mrs Peat and Mr and Mrs Dunster. The organ began to peal out Mendelssohn's Wedding March. Everybody collected their prayer books and gloves and the ladies straightened their bonnets and began to leave the church.

Only close family were invited to the actual wedding, so the number of guests at the wedding breakfast was necessarily small, augmented only by a few other relations and close friends. Dr and Mrs Woodcock were invited, as were Philip and Isabel Rivers. There were a few Dunster relations and an old aunt or two, and of course, Gerald Milford.

'God, what a boring lot,' whispered Blanche to Hugh, as she stood with him at the head of the stairs to receive their congratulations and good wishes.

'I do not know which are worse, yours or mine,' replied Hugh.

Mrs Peat saw to it that there was a sumptuous cold collation on the dining-table: the wedding might be a hole-in-the-corner affair, but Mary Dunster need not think that they could get away with treating Blanche in the shabby way that they treated dear Hugh. Down the centre of the table were plates piled high with collared eel, mayonnaise of trout and several boiled fowls with béchamel sauce. There was lobster salad and pigeon pie and around the edge of the table was a profusion of blancmanges, in cunning turrets of white and pink, jellies, compôtes of fruit and scattered dishes of summer fruits. The centrepiece was a huge épergne in silver-gilt, the base being of vaguely classical design with three cupids and a nymph supporting the central column. On the top was a basket of flowers which in its turn supported three more nymphs who were holding aloft a small pedestal on which Bellerophon, mounted on the winged horse, was conquering the Chimera. Mrs Peat was very proud of the piece, she was sure that Mrs Dunster did not possess anything half so fine.

Blanche and Hugh greeted the guests and Flora and Daisy busied themselves finding seats for Cousin Helen and the Dunster aunts and directing maids towards them with plates and offers of food. It was amazing, thought Flora, to see how much aunts always ate. Cousin Helen, whose bulk loomed large and who had difficulty in sitting on one chair only, only pecked at her food. Hugh's aunts Mary and Cecily, both of them thin as rakes, consumed vast helpings of pigeon pie and went on to despatch several portions of fruit tart and blancmange.

Adeline had not spoken very much to anyone. She exchanged

a few words with Isabel and then sat down on a chair by the window. She was half hidden by a large pot of ferns and she sank back feeling heavy and dull, putting her hand gratefully on the cold glass of the window. In the alcove next to her Ernest and Philip Rivers were talking. Adeline thought of calling out and joining in the conversation, but then felt too heavy to bother. Nobody would mind that she sat quietly and drank her orange cup. Everybody was aware of her delicate condition and she was not expected to bear any very strenuous part in entertaining the guests. Daisy, prompted by Flora, stopped to ask her if she needed anything and would she like a cushion for her back? 'No, thank you, dear, I am quite all right,' replied Adeline, thinking that there was only Daisy left of her family who showed any true concern for others. After that she was left alone.

From the next alcove Philip was asking Ernest, 'How was Paris? I was thinking of taking Isabel there one year, but somehow we never found the time.'

Ernest assumed the face of a man of the world. 'My dear Rivers, never go to Paris with your wife! It is fatal believe me! Geraldina ordered four hundred pounds' worth of clothes from Worth and I had the devil of a job to fetch her home! No, no, you must go as a bachelor.'

'Oho! Did Mrs Peat not allow you to sample any of the wares?' laughed Philip, taking a large gulp of the wine in his glass.

'The men were after Geraldina like bees round jam!' said Ernest, 'I can tell you that there was no more beautiful article, even La Païva, than my wife. The French women are elegant, but nothing can beat a good English filly, I say.'

'Quite, quite,' said Philip, intoxicated by this talk of the glitter of the Second Empire. He dropped his voice. 'Have you ever been to Madame's in High Holborn? Every girl there is a stunner: knock your Cora Pearls into a cocked hat any day!'

'Is that where you and Charles [Adeline froze] used to go in your bachelor days? Near the Casino de Venise?'

'That's it. Only we still go occasionally.' Here Philip's eye dropped in an exaggerated wink. 'Well, you know how the ladies are, Peat, they lie as stiff as a corpse, in, out and that is your lot. So Charles and I go for a bit of nooky every week or so.'

'I hope your wives do not know,' said Ernest, slightly alarmed.

'Mrs Woodcock does not of course and Charles would not hurt her feelings for the world. Isabel may suspect, I daresay, but she is happier relieved of my attentions, so she doesn't enquire too closely.'

Ernest looked across to where Geraldina was talking to her father, and his thoughts were entirely self-satisfied, but he clapped Philip on the shoulder in a conspiratorial sort of way and gave him a man to man nod and then the conversation turned to other matters.

No! No! No! No No! No! Adeline threw herself back in her chair and dug her nails into the palms of her hands to stop herself from screaming. But the scream went on and on inside her head. Charles had . . . he had . . . she could hardly bring herself to say his name, even to herself. Well, she knew now how Charles had treated their marriage! God's most Holy tie! Forsaking all other indeed! He could not wait even six months after their marriage before he was off to some whore house trying his disgusting intimacies on some low woman.

She had kept herself pure for him! She had been what he wanted, had she not? He told her that he wanted a lady, modest and refined to look up to. When did it start? Who was she? What was it like, him and her together? Oh God, no! No! No! She must not think of that!

Adeline found that her hand was fiddling with the finial on the top of a small cake-stand near her. She hastily removed it. My God, the place was filled with it! The chair legs, with their bulbous decoration, looked suddenly obscene. The thick tassels on the dining-room curtains, the moulded edifices of pink blanc-mange on the table. She looked at Hugh talking to Blanche, he was leaning forward, smiling slightly, his eyes running lazily over her. Ernest was standing with one hand on Geraldina's shoulder, caressing it: Gerald Milford was sitting chatting to her mother, and every now and then she rapped the back of his knuckles coyly with her fan, 'Oh, Gerald, you flatterer!' Adeline could hear her saying. It was disgusting and horrible! Every man and woman in the place were indulging their baser natures!

Never had she said one word of reproach to Charles for being such a boor. She served him and thought only of his interests. He had not even cared! Had probably not even thought twice before going off with some filthy slut to satisfy his revolting, animal pleasures. The thoughts rose red and angry inside her head. She felt as if she contained a volcano, which might explode at any moment.

She held her arms across her swelling belly and stood up. Her one thought was to reach the peace and quiet of the den. Somewhere, anywhere out of sight, where she could be alone before she shouted and screamed the whole obscene, disgusting thing out. She barely reached the door when Charles, coming in from the hall, caught sight of her.

'Ah, hello, my love,' he said jocularly. 'Feeling a little bit tired, then? Shall I get Isabel to come up to you?'

Adeline turned and looked at him, her face quite screwed up with emotion. 'Go and tickle your whores,' she said in a low, vehement voice. 'That is all you are good for, you filthy swine!'

'I say . . .' began Charles.

Adeline turned and spat full in his face.

Flora saw her sister's agitated exit and rose at once. With a hasty excuse to Cousin Helen she followed Adeline, nearly colliding with Charles who was just come in and was wiping his face with a handkerchief. He was looking pale and shaken but Flora had no time to think of that. She brushed past him and caught hold of her sister half way up the stairs. Adeline was sobbing and choking and stared at Flora wildly as if she did not really see her.

'Come in here,' said Flora, pulling her sister into her bedroom. 'Sit down, my dear Adeline. You look terrible. Whatever is it?'

Adeline could not sit down. She strode up and down the room as if she had to have some physical release. Then she began to cry, huge, angry sobs that seemed to turn into a sort of growl in her throat. She clawed at her handkerchief with angry nails until it was shredded in her hands. 'The filthy beast! I hate him! I hate him!' she kept saying. 'I spat in his face, Flora. Is that the correct behaviour for a true lady in the circumstances?' She laughed, harshly and bitterly.

Flora had never seen Adeline like this before, her face so contorted with rage, her eyes so hard and angry. Now Adeline's hands were pulling at the mound on her stomach, as if to tear it from her, to rip it out and trample on it.

'That boor!' Adeline spat out. 'The filthy hog! I shall never, never go near him again! Never, do you hear, Flora? It is all over! Finished!' She turned and looked at Flora, her hurt and angry eyes looking straight into Flora's grey ones, so that Flora had the distinct impression that she had never seen her sister properly before. 'Do you know what he does, Flora,' went on the harsh, tight voice, 'and Philip too? They visit a whore house once a week! Barely six months married and he goes to one of those places to tail some disgusting slut! And his wife! His wife is expected to take him afterwards. Do you understand me, Flora? He comes home from those places and has intimacy with me! He grunts, Flora! Grunts! Exactly like some pig! And never, not even the first time, when I was so frightened and hurt, and, oh God, so willing to be taught, to do the right thing, never has he said a single word to me!'

Then she was able to weep. She sank down on the sofa and cried and cried as if she would never stop. Flora said nothing, but sat down beside her and with a grateful sigh Adeline turned to her and wept on her shoulder.

'I hate him,' sobbed Adeline. 'I hate him for destroying my faith and trust in him. I hate him for pretending that he wanted a pure and ladylike wife to look up to, when all he really wanted was to use me to make himself look respectable. I do not believe that I ever meant anything to him and if you make your vows to a nobody then it does not matter if you break them, does it? Oh Flora, I feel so bitterly hurt and betrayed and so lied to and deceived, like some horrible gilded sepulchre and underneath there is rottenness and worms.'

'Oh Adeline, Adeline!' Flora stroked her hair sadly. 'I feared it might be so, but how could I say, when I had no proof? I had no right to come between a husband and wife.'

'You were right though and I was wrong,' said Adeline more quietly now, 'about feelings, I mean. I always hated him touching me, even when we were engaged, but I would never allow myself to see it. I prided myself stupidly on my refinement – whatever that may be. I thought that it was my mission to serve God through Charles and that little things like finding him repulsive were not important. I think I knew, really, that I could not talk to him. I did try once or twice, but he never liked it.'

281

'There was never a moment when you felt it might be right?'

'Never,' Adeline shook her head. 'I never even thought of my own feelings in the matter. And of course they are important. But it is all too late now. The damage is done.'

'Not quite,' said Flora gently. 'You still have that.' She patted Adeline's stomach gently.

'I would like to kill it,' said Adeline. Flora looked up startled. 'Yes, I know I am wicked and it is a new life and all that, but it was conceived in pain and disgust. The thought that I am carrying a horrible, squirming, piggish baby that belongs to Charles is unbearable.'

'You should not speak so! Your baby at least is innocent.'

'Why not,' retorted Adeline, the hysteria coming back into her voice. 'Do you think I was not praying and praying all those months for a chance to do some good, to help and support that brute downstairs? All I wished for was to be a true wife to him, Flora, you would think God would grant that, surely? This is what I receive. A lying, unfaithful, cheating boor! What God would send another soul into the world of such a union? I do not want this baby, Flora! I feel sick and disgusted even to think of it!'

Her hands were clutching at her stomach again and her back arching in spasms of hysteria. Flora looked in mounting apprehension and then rang the bell agitatedly. It was some time before a maid came.

'Fetch Dr Woodcock at once, please. Mrs Woodcock is ill. Not Dr Charles, Betty, get Dr Thomas. Try not to alarm any of the guests. Hurry now!'

Blanche sank back in her seat in the first-class railway carriage and kicked off her shoes. The train was taking them to Brighton for their honeymoon. After that, at Blanche's persuasion, they were going to Paris. There they would work on a freelance basis for both Mr Dunster and Mr Peat, selling to the Continent and hopefully building up a network of useful contacts for both companies.

'Of course Hugh can sell,' said Blanche indignantly, when she had first approached her father with the idea. 'I have absolute confidence in him.'

Mr Peat could not see much to justify this, but he let it pass. If Blanche and Hugh had been prematurely indulging themselves, making feet for children's shoes, as they said, then it was imperative that Dunster be found a job abroad for a year or so. He cared for Blanche the least of all his daughters, but he would not allow her to become the subject of speculation and scandal.

Blanche loved Brighton: she liked the cosmopolitan, slightly raffish atmosphere of the place. Officers were often on leave there, men brought their mistresses down for secret weekends, and there was always an air of illicit pleasure about the place, elusive and vague, but echoed in the elegant shops with exactly the kind of sophisticated trifles to tempt a lady who was not too straight-laced. Blanche liked to feel that even if she was respectably married, the gentlemen on the promenades would think that she was not. She liked their slight bows if she chanced to glance in their direction, the interest in their faces as they strolled by, idly twirling their canes.

They would reach Brighton in under two hours. The smoke was going past the window in puffs and the wheels were beginning their pleasing clackety-clack. She turned her head to look at Hugh. He had tossed his hat up onto the rack and was lying back in his seat watching her from under his lashes. It was a calm, steady look. Blanche found it slightly unnerving and at once crossed over to sit next to him and, taking his face in her hands, turned it round to kiss him.

'Dearest, at last. Hugh, do not look so solemn, you remind me of that horrid old vicar! The way he said, "let no man put asunder" and gave me such a look! I do not know what he thought that I was going to do.'

'Run off with Maurice at the church door,' said Hugh lightly, but his eyes were still watchful.

'Darling, do not joke about it,' said Blanche reproachfully. 'You know that you are the only man for me. Ever since I first saw you at the Royal Academy exhibition last year, I said to myself this is the man for me. And you see!'

'It was there?' said Hugh frowning.

'That was where I first noticed you, yes. You seemed so different from all the others somehow. More alive and awake. I liked the way that you could not be bothered to look at all the paintings praised by the critics. You knew what you wanted to see and then you went home. I admired that in you, Hugh: the ability to know your own mind. I felt, here is a man who knows what he wants and is direct enough to go straight out and take it. I watched you for a long time, Hugh. My observation period, I called it. I hope you are flattered!' Blanche laughed and tilted her head at him coquettishly.

Hugh felt extraordinarily uneasy. He had the feeling that, far from being a free agent, he was little more than a puppet, manipulated by jigging strings and made to dance to Blanche's tune. Of course, it was all nonsense, he told himself firmly. Blanche allowed the choice to be entirely his, hadn't she? There was no pressure, no blackmail. But still the notion that he had been watched, nurtured until he was ripe enough to fall tumbling into her lap, stuck unpleasantly in his mind.

He looked at her. Could those limpid blue eyes ever be calculating, those golden curls hide a wantonly malicious brain? For who had been with him that day last summer at the exhibition, but Alice?

That night Adeline lost her baby. She went into premature labour almost as soon as Dr Woodcock came hurrying up the stairs. There was no time to summon help and none of the guests laughing and chatting downstairs noticed either Adeline's or Dr Woodcock's absence.

Adeline remembered very little of what followed. She heard Charles' voice in the distance at one point saying, 'I think I have a right to see my wife!' But he did not come in. Perhaps Flora or Dr Woodcock turned him away, she did not know.

The baby, a boy, was born dead late that night. Charles was not there. He had taken himself off in a mood of sullen resentment and spent the rest of the night drinking brandy in the Argyll Rooms.

Nobody expected him to be a saint, did they? Surely he was allowed some fun sometimes? It was Adeline who was unbalanced and hysterical, he had always thought so. Now she had lost his son and he would never forgive her for that, never. If she had shown a proper concern for him she would have taken more care and not allowed it to happen. She meant to hurt him by losing the baby. Well, she would not have the satisfaction of seeing that he cared twopence. If that was the way she wanted it, she could have a marriage of convenience. He had been a most indulgent and fond husband: his conscience at least was clear.

Flora was up with Adeline for several nights. Adeline was suffering from dreadful nightmares and pangs of remorse at losing her baby. Nobody else in the family showed anything but the most superficial sympathy. Adeline blamed herself dreadfully and talked endlessly to Flora about Charles and her marriage: all the sordid, humiliating details, the way Charles had neglected her while pretending concern, it all poured out. Underneath she felt the bitterness of realizing that she had been completely wrong about so many things.

'Not the least, unjust to you, dearest Flora,' said Adeline tearfully on more than one occasion.

'Charles is giving some ultimatum about your going back,' said Flora. 'But Papa has told you that this is your home if you wish it, Adeline.'

'Yes, I know. I shall have to see Charles of course. He thinks that it is all my fault.'

'He knows very well it is not, however.'

'I shall not be going back to him,' said Adeline firmly. 'As Papa has offered me a home, I shall stay here and, who knows, I may one day be happy. At least I can try to understand myself better.'

'We shall grow old together,' said Flora, smiling bravely.

Flora left her sister and went downstairs for a belated breakfast.

'Ah, there you are, Flora,' said Mrs Peat. 'How is Adeline this morning? Have you seen that Ellie St Alleyn is engaged to be married? It is in *The Times* this morning.'

'No,' said Flora dully. She was instantly aware that she was feeling nothing and at the same time concealing a deep and spreading pain. She did not know what to do or think. She realized that she had had the assumption, the conviction even, that somehow George would be part of her life. The realization that their relationship must sink back into mere company acquaintance instantly, from this very moment, was so painful a reversal of all her hopes and wishes that she simply could not take it in.

But her mother was waiting for her comment.

'How . . . how nice for Ellie,' she said at last.

'Yes, and she is only eighteen. What a triumph for her mother! Of course, he is not much older. I wonder what her parents think of it?'

'Not . . . not much older?' stammered Flora, her mind spinning.

'Yes, Alfred Pateley. I do not suppose that he can be more than twenty himself.'

Daisy had already left for her lessons at the Kingsleys by the time Flora learnt the news of Ellie's astonishing engagement. Daisy ran upstairs to Grace at once and pulled her friend to the window seat and drew the curtains around them. They had seen George and Flora together at the garden-party, watched them by the statues from their vantage point up in the tree house, and Grace had been very excited at the prospect of having Flora as a cousin. 'He will have to marry her now, you know,' she had told Daisy.

'Oh Grace! I have so much to tell you and it is all horrid!' cried Daisy in a burst as they settled down together on the window seat. 'I think I have learnt a lot about Life from Flora,' she ended, looking at Grace's downcast face. 'I do not care if he is your cousin, Grace, but he has been a cad!'

'I thought it was all going to be so nice,' said Grace sadly. 'You would have been a sort of cousin too, Daisy.'

'I never wish to talk to him again,' declared Daisy, full of indignation for her sister.

At the end of the morning, when Daisy came downstairs, she found Sir George waiting for her in the hall.

'It is all right, Penton,' he said, as Penton opened the front door for Daisy. 'I shall see Miss Daisy to the carriage.'

Daisy looked at him from under frowning dark brows. He was looking very stern, she thought. She and Grace had vowed to let him know how much they disapproved, if the occasion arose. Now that it had she did not feel at all confident. The carriage door was already open and inside, on the seat, was a huge bunch of flowers. The reds and pinks and whites of the roses, with lacy asparagus leaves, glowed in the darkness of the carriage and Daisy could smell the strong, heady scent even before she stepped inside.

'They are for Flora,' said George shortly. 'I take it that she is not coming back?'

Daisy climbed into the carriage and sat down. She leaned forward, her eyes shining with indignation, and took a deep breath.

'You have made Flora very unhappy,' she said with resolution, sitting up stiffly on the carriage seat. 'If this bouquet is a sop to your conscience you can take the horrid thing back!'

George glared at her.

'I know I am being very rude to talk to you like this. But I love Flora and if you do not care for her at all then I wish you would leave her alone. Because your sending her flowers, which is an easy thing to do, will only make her feel worse!'

George took a letter out of his pocket and handed it to her.

'Give this to Flora,' he said curtly, 'and do not dare talk to me in that fashion again.'

'I know I should not have spoken so,' said Daisy with satisfaction.

'Mind your skirts. I am going to shut the door.'

George stood back and signalled to the coachman and the carriage moved off down the street. Daisy, torn between curiosity and dread, turned the letter over and over in her hands.

The carriage slowly drew up outside the Peats' house in Belgrave Square. Daisy, in a state of suppressed excitement, jumped down almost before it stopped and rushed past Ketton, who had opened the door, and ran up the stairs. She found Flora in the morning-room.

'Flora! Flora! Come up to the den, I have something for you.'

With a wild lurch, the world suddenly stopped spinning for Flora. She felt an agitation so intense that she wondered if she might be going to faint.

'Yes, and there are some flowers for you from Sir George and Ketton is putting them in water and you can decide what to do with them later and oh, Flora, come on!'

'Quiet, Daisy,' said Flora. 'Do you wish the whole house to know?'

She followed Daisy up to the den. Daisy took George's letter, now slightly crumpled, out of her pocket. 'Sir George said I was to give you this,' she said.

Flora took it, looking at the heavy, black characters spelling 'Miss Peat' on the front. She turned it over slowly and said nothing for a few moments.

'Are you not going to open it?' asked Daisy curiously. She had somehow imagined that Flora would tear it from her grasp and rip it open there and then. How could she wait, not knowing?

'I . . . I dare not just now,' said Flora shakily. 'Leave me alone for a while, Daisy. You shall know about it later.'

As soon as Daisy had gone Flora sat down by the window and broke the seal.

My dearest Flora,

I have been thinking of you ever since you left and I find I cannot bear that you should think ill of me – even though I know I deserve it. You were right to be angry because I think I was very selfish that afternoon. I should have come to you much, much sooner – I wanted to, but somehow I found myself flirting stupidly with Ellie, trying to convince myself that I was still heart-free.

But it was not true. That moment by the statues was very precious to me: the softness and sweetness of your lips, those beautiful grey eyes, what you said, how you looked, everything. I did not realize how selfish I was being in not wanting to acknowledge how much I felt for you, until you made me see that I had hurt and distressed you.

Let me make it plain now: I love you and I no longer wish to hide it either from myself or from you.

It was Ellie you were referring to, was it not? You might have seen us in the rose-garden. She was confiding in me that she is in love with Alfred Pateley, and begging me to try what family influence I possess to persuade her mother in his favour.

Our families have been trying to arrange a match between Ellie and myself for several years. Ellie wished me to make it very clear to her mama that Pateley, and not myself, was the very man for her. I have always been fond of Ellie and I think she is fond of me, but neither of us have ever wanted anything closer.

Dearest Flora, I believed, by the statues, that you might care for me too and I cannot bear to think that I might have jeopardized my own future happiness by my behaviour.

I want to put it right between us, but it takes two, you know. So please come back.

Yours always, my lovely Flora,

George Kingsley

Flora looked up from her letter trembling and crying with happiness. She read and re-read it before she finally allowed herself to believe what was written there. George loved her! He had behaved badly, but that which hurt most – his behaviour with Ellie – would bear another explanation. And the news of Ellie's engagement confirmed it.

He truly loved her. She had not imagined it all by the statues. He had said on that occasion that he had wished to kiss her for some time and indeed, she had felt that desire in him, at the Elkesleys' dance, for instance. And it was true! She had spent so many unhappy nights wondering where and how she had deluded herself when it all felt so real. It was not the same as that day-dream love for Algy and yet George's behaviour had seemed to indicate that she was similarly deceiving herself.

Now she could acknowledge everything she felt for him. She loved him and she wanted to marry him. Nothing else could give her the degree of intimacy she longed for.

She ran downstairs to her bedroom and on a sudden impulse rang the bell.

A flushed and hurried Lottie came in. 'You called, Miss Flora?'

'Yes, Lottie. I did not have the time to do my hair properly this morning. I wish you to do it now, please.'

'But, Miss Flora, the gong will be going for luncheon in twenty minutes.'

'I fear that cannot be helped,' said Flora with decision, smiling at Lottie's puzzled face behind her in the glass. She began taking the pins out of her hair.

When Flora finally entered the dining-room half an hour later, Mrs Peat's first words were explosive. 'Upon my word, Flora, you are nearly twenty minutes late.'

'Ten minutes,' said Flora.

'You have done your hair,' said Daisy happily. 'You do look lovely, Flora.'

Mrs Peat had by now actually looked at Flora. What on earth was come over the girl? Her skin looked soft and glowing, her eyes were sparkling. Flora has no business to look like that, she thought confusedly.

'Flora, do you not think that you are a little old now to wear such a mass of ringlets?'

'No,' said Flora. 'Daisy, pass me the salad, please. Thank you, my love.'

'And why are you late?' went on Mrs Peat, feeling obscurely cheated. 'You went upstairs fully half an hour before the gong went. I heard you myself on the stairs. That should have given you ample time.'

'I am afraid not. I wished Lottie to do my hair again.'

'Well . . .' said Mrs Peat, baffled. 'Well.'

The following morning George paced anxiously up and down his library looking at the clock on the mantelpiece from time to time. In another ten minutes Daisy would be here, but would Flora? She might not come at all and only reply to his letter through Daisy. Or perhaps she would never forgive him. How would he feel if there was just a blank, a silence?

Why had he not realized earlier how much he wanted Flora? Now there was this awful possibility that he had discovered it too late. How much was his vaunted bachelor freedom truly worth? Far from having a life of limitless satisfaction, being able to go where he wanted when he wanted, his life had been totally circumscribed by the necessity to keep his emotional distance. Had he not once gone to Afghanistan to escape some threatened entanglement? What he had mistakenly called freedom could more properly be termed solitary confinement.

There was a noise outside on the cobbles. A carriage was drawing up. He could hear the coachman jumping down with a clatter and Penton going to the front door. George felt a sudden rush of nervous anxiety. He found that he could not move from his place by the desk. He wanted to rush to the door, fling it open, know everything at once, but he remained rooted to the spot, listening painfully. He heard Daisy running up the stairs and Penton shutting the front door. Then there was silence.

George turned his face to the window and stood looking out

but seeing nothing. The flowers were blooming outside and the grass was full of jigsaw patches of sunlight where the sun shone down between the trees, but he hardly noticed. Flora did not want him. She was not coming back. She had not even replied to his letter.

'George,' said Flora gently.

George swung round. 'Flora! Is it you?' He seemed dazed. 'I thought you meant not to come. I didn't hear you come in. Why are you here, Flora?'

'To see you.'

George looked at her uncertainly. 'You received my letter?'

Flora nodded.

George did not seem to know how to continue. 'Flora, perhaps you may not want this, but it is what I want. I mean, I do not wish to force you into anything, which is why I have not spoken to your father. I have been so blind where you are concerned and so selfish too, that I am afraid of asking you. Dearest Flora, don't say no at once. Oh, God, I do not seem to be able to say what it is I want! Not in any way that I think you might be inclined to accept.'

'I want *you*!' said Flora simply.

George looked up abruptly and met her eyes with a kind of shock. The impact was so strong, although neither of them moved an inch, that he found himself trembling.

'Marry me, then!' George's world suddenly righted itself. He moved swiftly round the desk and pulled her into his arms.

'Yes, yes!' cried Flora.

'Kiss me.'

Flora's kiss was ardent, passionate and almost totally inexperienced, and George had to coax her mouth open by running his tongue gently along her lips until they parted. He then held her very close and kissed her very thoroughly. He felt as if a miracle was happening. Flora was saying his name over and over again in between kisses.

'George! George! I love you.'

'Dearest Flora. Your mouth is as soft and warm as I remembered. I love you, Flora.' He took her face in his hands so that he could look at her more closely. 'I do not wish for anything more than to be with you. I tried to tell myself after the garden-party that I did not want to marry and settle down, that I preferred a life of travelling when I wanted and being accountable only to myself. I wanted to be free. But I am happy to give it up to stay at home, if you are there.'

'But I do not want to settle down and stay at home!' cried Flora, pulling herself free.

'You don't?'

'Oh please, please do not say that that is what you truly wish. I am longing to travel and do things. I don't think that I could bear to settle down. I have been doing nothing else for twenty-eight years! Do you realize that I have never even been outside England! I want to meet different people, eat strange foods, look at places I have never seen. I do not know what the world is like, George. I know only my small, very small, corner of it.'

'You don't feel that I ought to stay at home and look after you?'

'I do not!'

'You may not like climbing mountains with me, or exploring old ruins. It can be very hot and uncomfortable, you know, not at all romantic. And you may not care for some of the riff-raff I associate with.'

'May I not decide that for myself?'

'Flora, are you sure? I always assumed that I would have to give up these things if I married. I am perfectly happy to give them up to be with you. I wouldn't lament my lost freedom.'

'You don't sound perfectly happy,' observed Flora.

George looked ruefully down at her and laughed. His voice lightened. 'I want to be with you more than I want my freedom.'

'I want both,' said Flora firmly, smiling in her turn.

George took her back into his arms. 'Right, you're on! Now kiss me, my precious girl, and tell me that you love me, because I love you. Now, where would you like to go for our honeymoon? Choose. The world is yours. But you will have to buy some proper climbing boots, I warn you.'

Some time later George rang the bell and Penton appeared.

'Yes, Sir?' he said impassively, but his eye had taken in every detail of their happy faces and dishevelled appearance.

'Miss Peat is going to marry me, Penton, and we are going upstairs to see my grandmother. Bring some champagne up, please. Oh yes, and you had better bring up the brandy as well. I do not know how she will take the news.'

'I wish you both very happy, Sir and Miss,' said Penton, giving George a fatherly smile. 'I was here before you were born, Sir George, so I hope you will not think me impertinent if I say that the opinion below stairs is that Lady Kingsley will not be too displeased to see you and Miss Peat. I do not anticipate that you will need the brandy.'

'I hope you are right,' said George with feeling. 'However, bring it up all the same. I do not wish her to think that we are taking her approval for granted!' He smiled down at Flora and took hold of her hand. 'Come upstairs, Flora.'

Flora sat in the drawing-room that evening in a state of happy nervousness. Her mother must be told. But how? What would she say? And George was coming to see Papa in ten minutes! She must say *something*.

Adeline was sitting on the sofa with a shawl over her legs. She had discarded her black mourning and wore a new dress in a soft violet silk with a prettily pleated skirt. Daisy was sitting beside her with some shells in her lap and Adeline was helping her to decide which ones would varnish best and look prettiest on a birchwood box she was decorating.

Mrs Peat was looking cross. All she had to show for an entire year of unremitting work was to see her favourite daughter married to a charming wastrel. Adeline was back on her hands – seemingly for ever. Still, at least she had discarded that endless sewing for the poor and the books of sermons. If only Charles would conveniently die of apoplexy! He was drinking far too much, if Isabel was to be believed, and spending the nights in Heaven knew what low houses. Dr Woodcock had warned him of the dangers. Well, it would serve him right if he did die, she thought righteously, for he had kept every penny of poor Adeline's dowry. She would pray that he got what he deserved.

Then there was Flora, looking quite irritatingly happy, when all she had done was turn down a most suitable offer. Her head was turned by her association with the Kingsleys and now she thought herself above her company. Not that they would do her any good. She was merely a suitable chaperone for Daisy, but doubtless she was imagining herself to be on terms of greater intimacy than her true position warranted.

'Mama,' said Flora, taking the plunge.

The front door bell rang suddenly.

'Good Gracious!' cried Mrs Peat. 'Whoever can that be? We are not expecting any visitors this evening. Unless, Adeline, it could not be Charles, could it?'

Adeline looked up alarmed.

'Mama,' said Flora desperately, 'you must listen to me.'

'Ring for Ketton, please, Daisy,' said Mrs Peat, 'and we shall soon find out.'

Daisy rose obediently.

'Mama!' said Flora again. 'Don't ring, Daisy. I know who it is.' All three faces turned towards her. 'It is . . . it is Sir George Kingsley. He has . . . he is coming to talk to Papa. About me.'

'Nonsense, Flora,' said Mrs Peat sharply. Sir George want to marry Flora? The very idea was ridiculous. And how like Flora to indulge in such childish fantasies.

'But it is true, Mama,' said Flora. 'He loves me and this morning he asked me to marry him and I said "Yes".'

'And how long has this been going on for, pray?' cried Mrs Peat angrily. It might have been Blanche, she thought, if only she had played her cards right. Flora was to stay with her parents, to perform all those little services for which an unmarried daughter could be so useful. 'I hope you have not trapped him into it, Flora. Such marriages never work, you know.'

'But Mama,' cried Adeline. 'Aren't you happy for Flora? It is a brilliant match for her and she deserves her happiness.'

'Of course I am happy for her,' snapped Mrs Peat. 'I just never expected Flora to . . . but, naturally, as a mother, I am delighted.' She schooled her features accordingly.

'Just think what you may write to Mrs Dunster, Mama,' observed Daisy.

Mrs Peat's mind wavered for a moment longer between resentment at Flora's undutiful behaviour in being so matrimonially successful, and satisfaction in the letter she would now be able to write to Mrs Dunster. Satisfaction won.

'Mary Dunster had no business to think so poorly of Flora being unmarried at twenty-eight,' she said, smiling happily as she mentally composed the opening lines. 'Flora was waiting for the right man to come along. She is very like me in that. I knew William was the only man for me the moment I clapped eyes on him.'

The door opened and Mr Peat entered.

'There is a certain gentleman waiting for you in my study, Flora,' he said smiling. 'I would hurry if I were you. He seems very impatient to see you.'